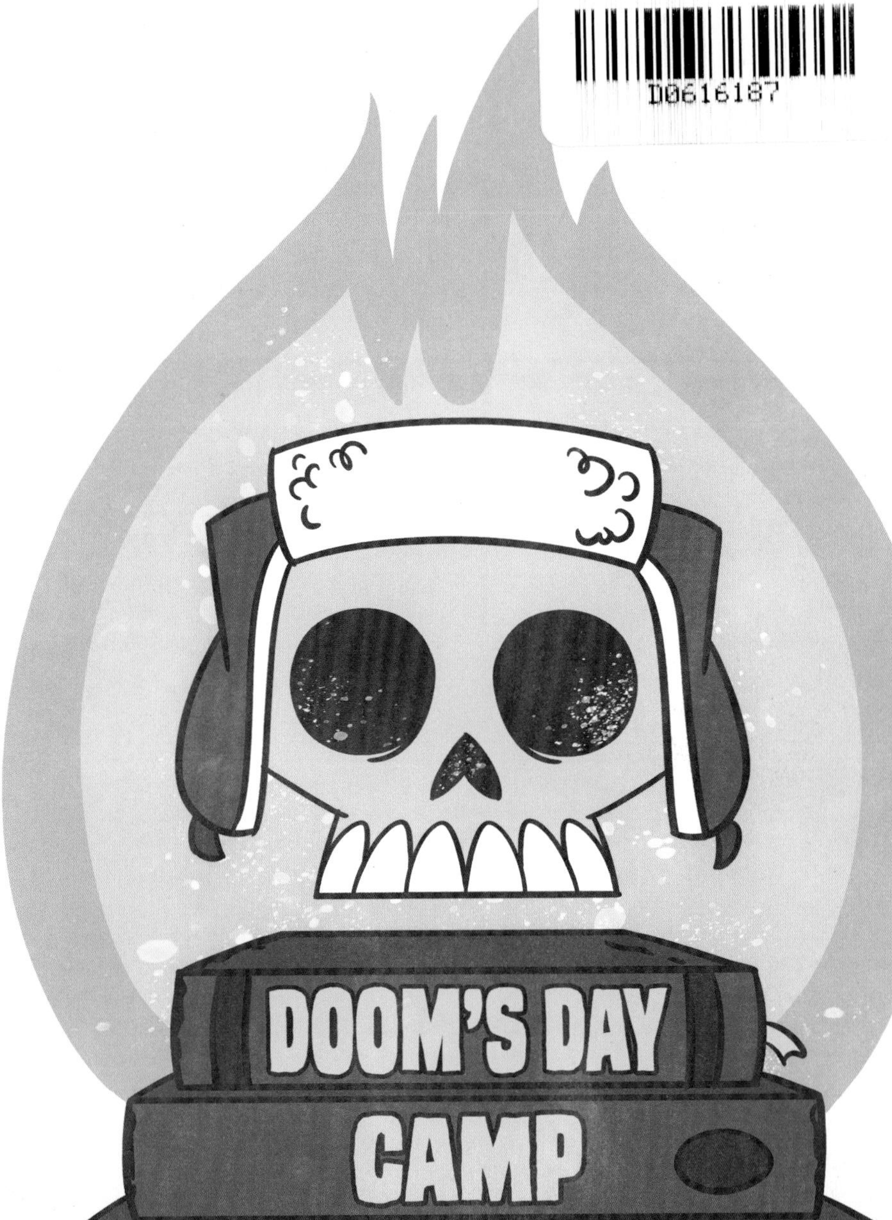
DOOM'S DAY
CAMP
JOSHUA HAUKE

RAZORBILL

FOR MY GIRLS

THE END TIMES WOULDN'T BE NEARLY
AS MUCH FUN WITHOUT YOU.

RAZORBILL

An imprint of Penguin Random House LLC, New York

First published in the United States of America by Razorbill,
an imprint of Penguin Random House LLC, 2022

Copyright © 2022 by Joshua Hauke

Library of Congress Cataloging-in-Publication Data
Names: Hauke, Joshua, author, artist.
Title: Doom's day camp / Joshua Hauke.
Description: New York : Razorbill, 2022. | Audience: Ages 8-12 years | Summary: In a postapocalyptic world where everyone has unusual abilities, Doom Thorax, whose only power is reading, gets left in charge and is responsible for the survival of all the other kids at camp.
Identifiers: LCCN 2021036210 | ISBN 9780593205389 (hardcover) | ISBN 9780593205419 (trade paperback) | ISBN 9780593205396 (ebook) | ISBN 9780593205945 (ebook) | ISBN 9780593205938 (ebook)
Subjects: CYAC: Graphic novels. | Ability—Fiction. | Camp—Fiction. | Survival—Fiction. | Humorous stories. | LCGFT: Apocalyptic comics. | Humorous comics. | Graphic novels.
Classification: LCC PZ7.7.H389 Do 2022 | DDC 741.5/973—dc23
LC record available at https://lccn.loc.gov/2021036210

Manufactured in Canada

3 5 7 9 10 8 6 4 2

TC

Color flats by David Scott Smith
Edited by Christopher Hernandez

Text set in SmackAttack BB

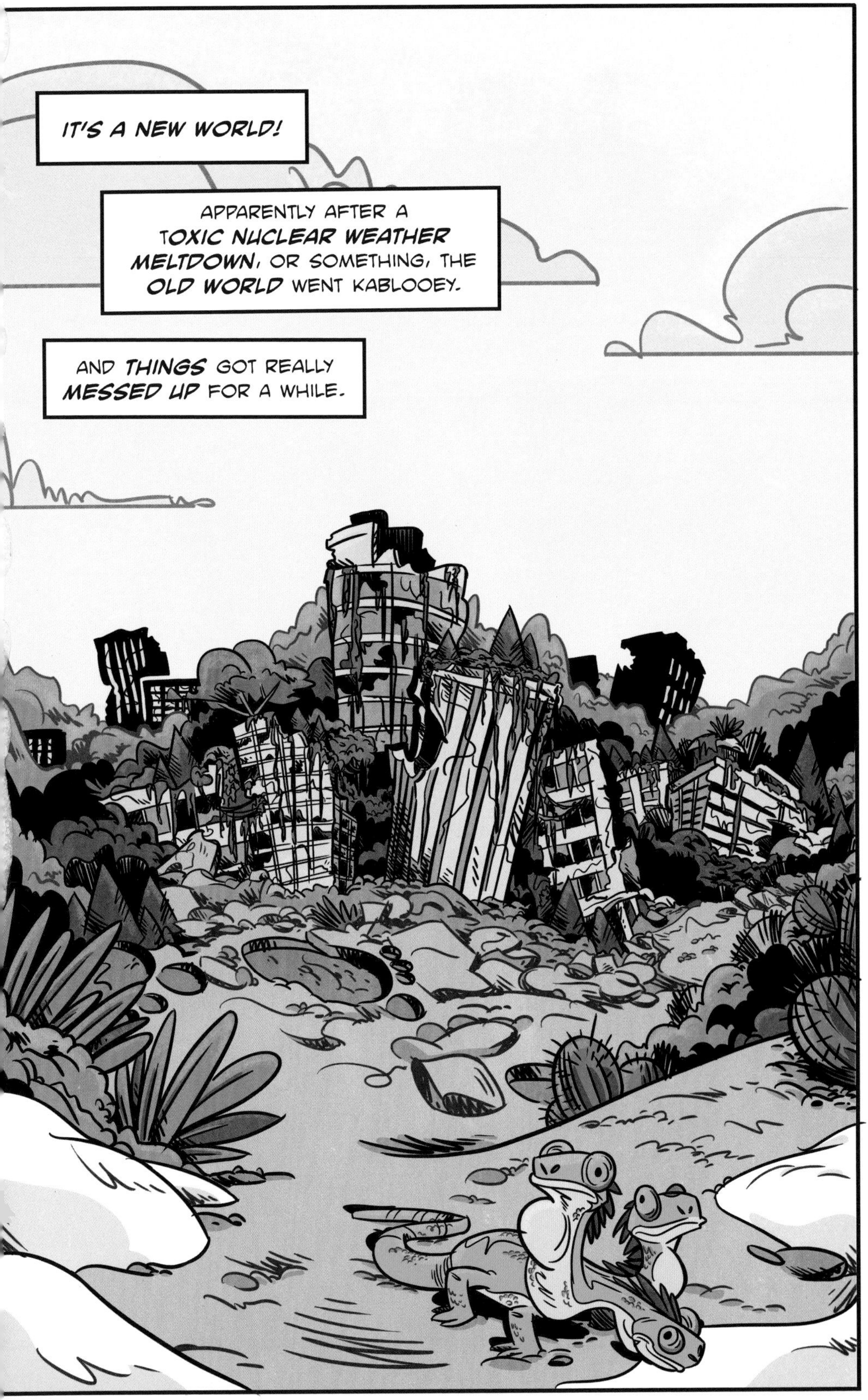
IT'S A NEW WORLD!
APPARENTLY AFTER A TOXIC NUCLEAR WEATHER MELTDOWN, OR SOMETHING, THE OLD WORLD WENT KABLOOEY.
AND THINGS GOT REALLY MESSED UP FOR A WHILE.

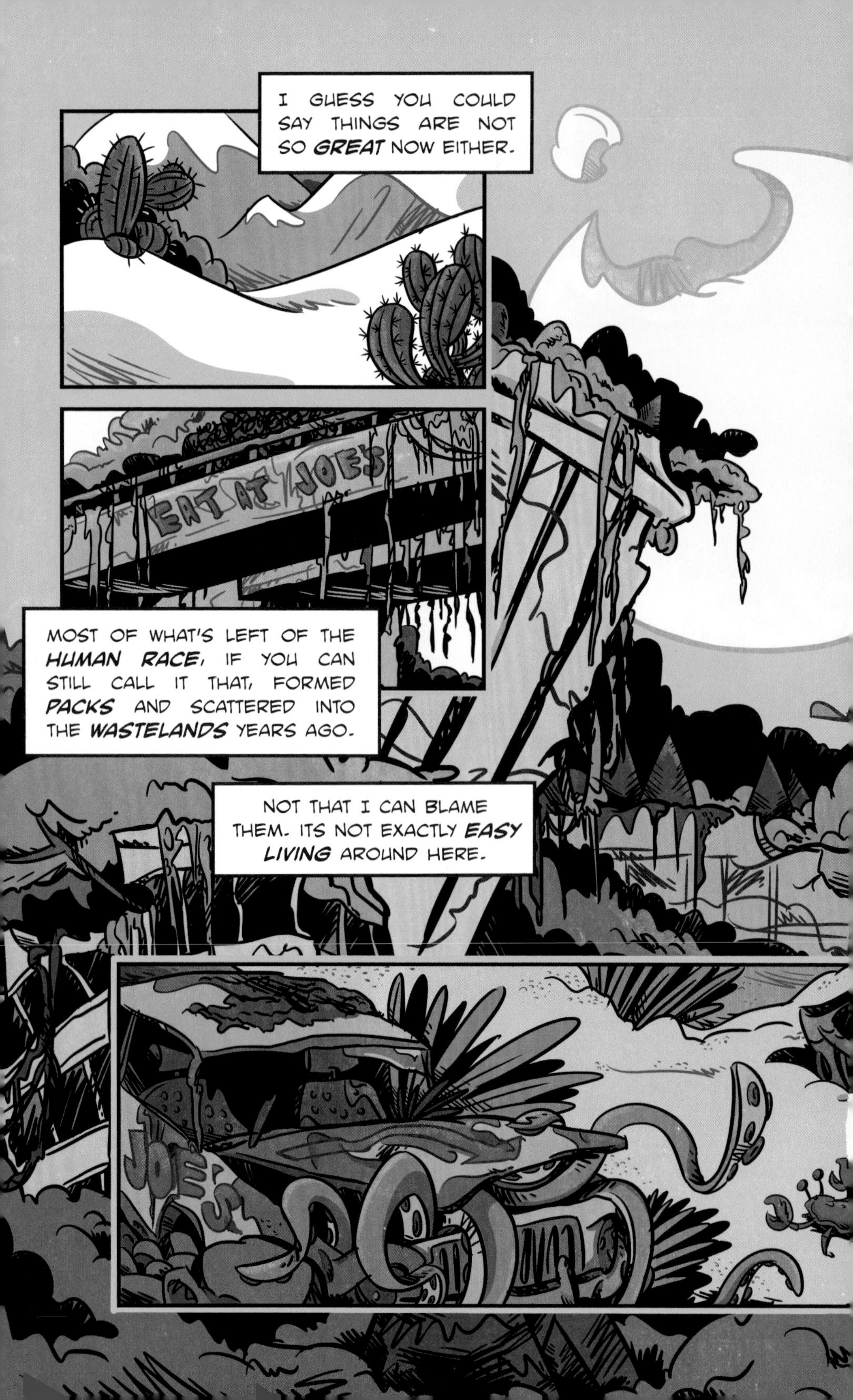
I GUESS YOU COULD SAY THINGS ARE NOT SO GREAT NOW EITHER.
EAT AT JOE'S
MOST OF WHAT'S LEFT OF THE HUMAN RACE, IF YOU CAN STILL CALL IT THAT, FORMED PACKS AND SCATTERED INTO THE WASTELANDS YEARS AGO.
NOT THAT I CAN BLAME THEM. ITS NOT EXACTLY EASY LIVING AROUND HERE.
JOE'S

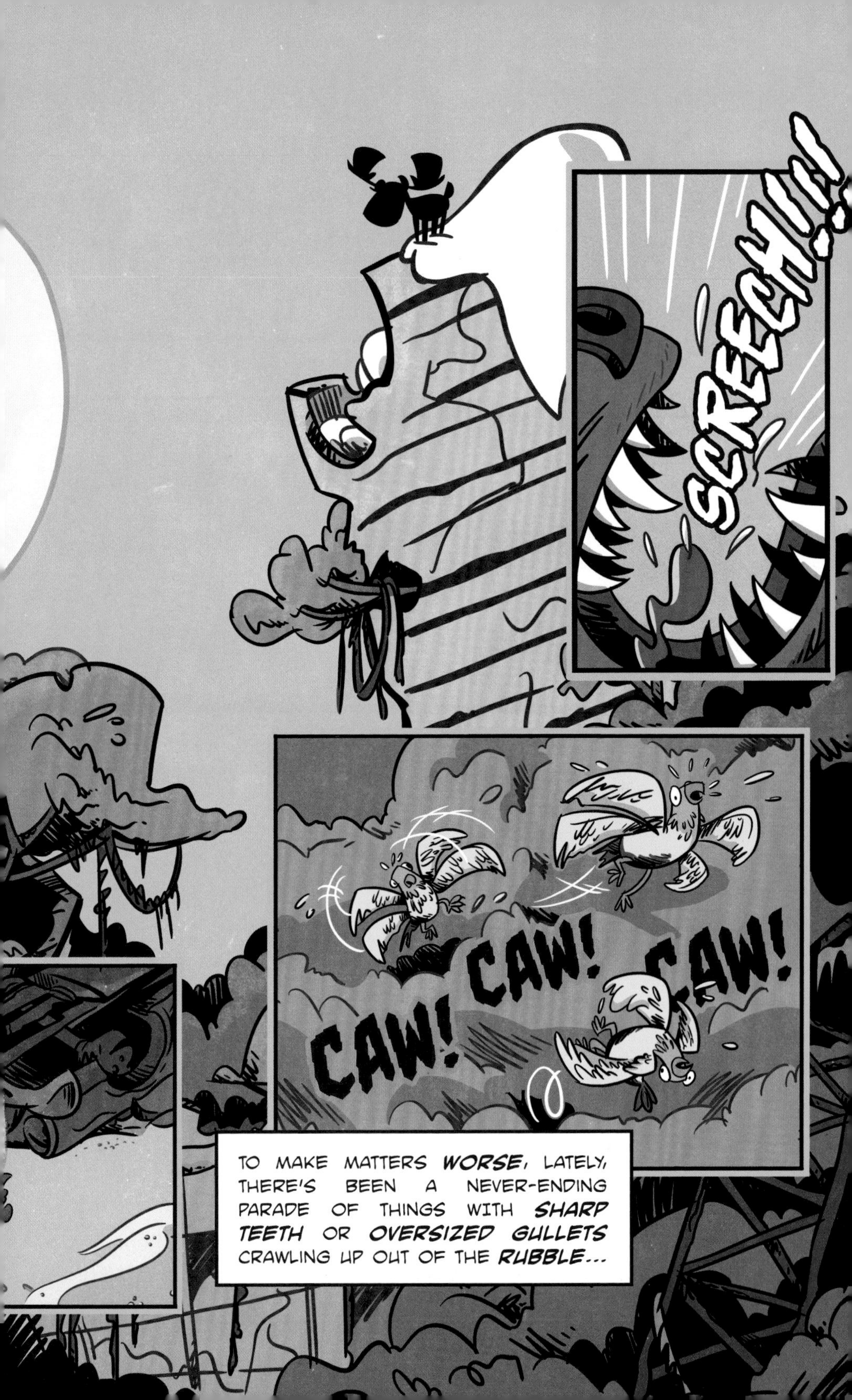
SCREECH!!!!!
CAW! CAW! CAW!
TO MAKE MATTERS WORSE, LATELY, THERE'S BEEN A NEVER-ENDING PARADE OF THINGS WITH SHARP TEETH OR OVERSIZED GULLETS CRAWLING UP OUT OF THE RUBBLE...

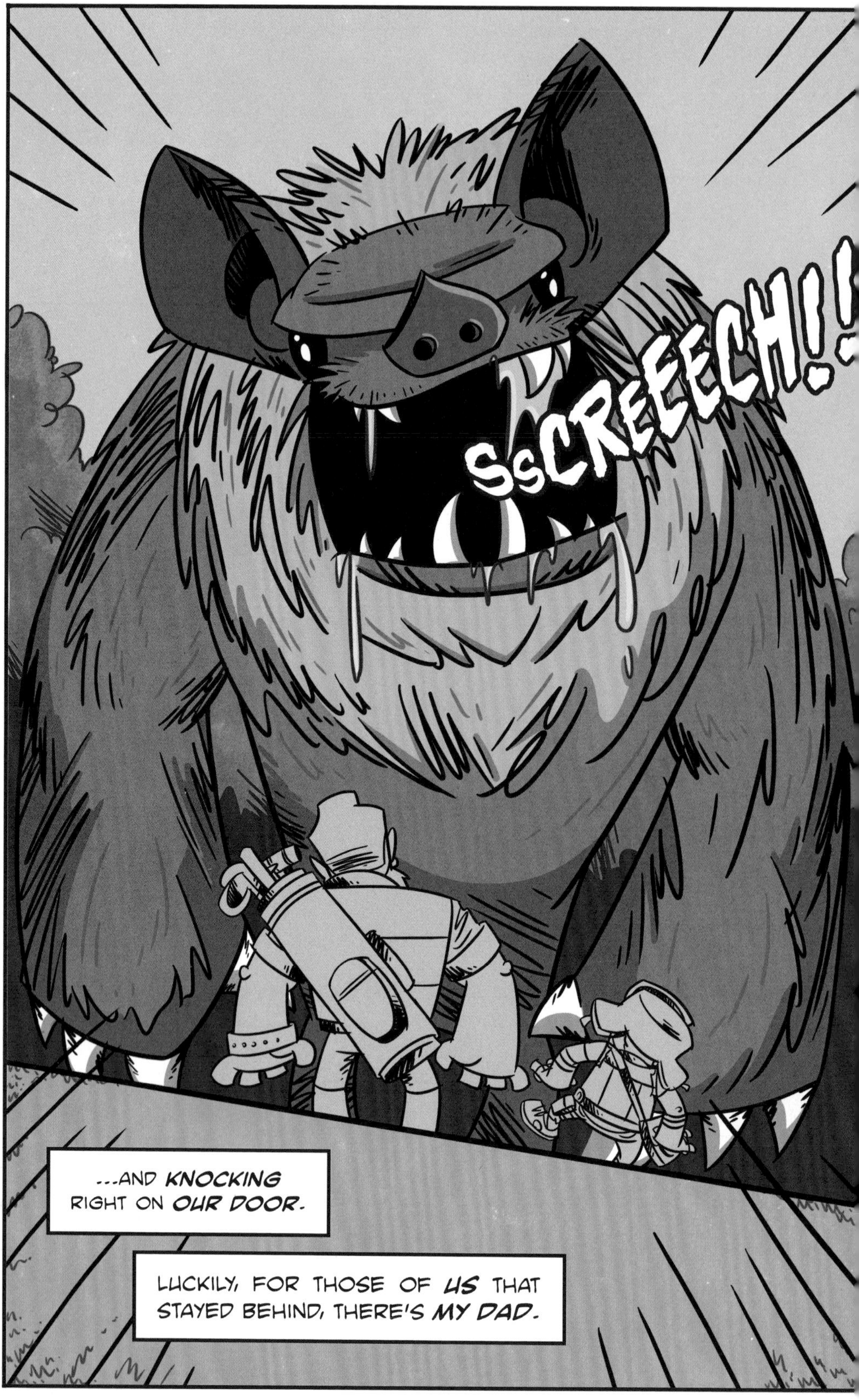
SSCREEECH!!!
...AND KNOCKING RIGHT ON OUR DOOR.
LUCKILY, FOR THOSE OF US THAT STAYED BEHIND, THERE'S MY DAD.

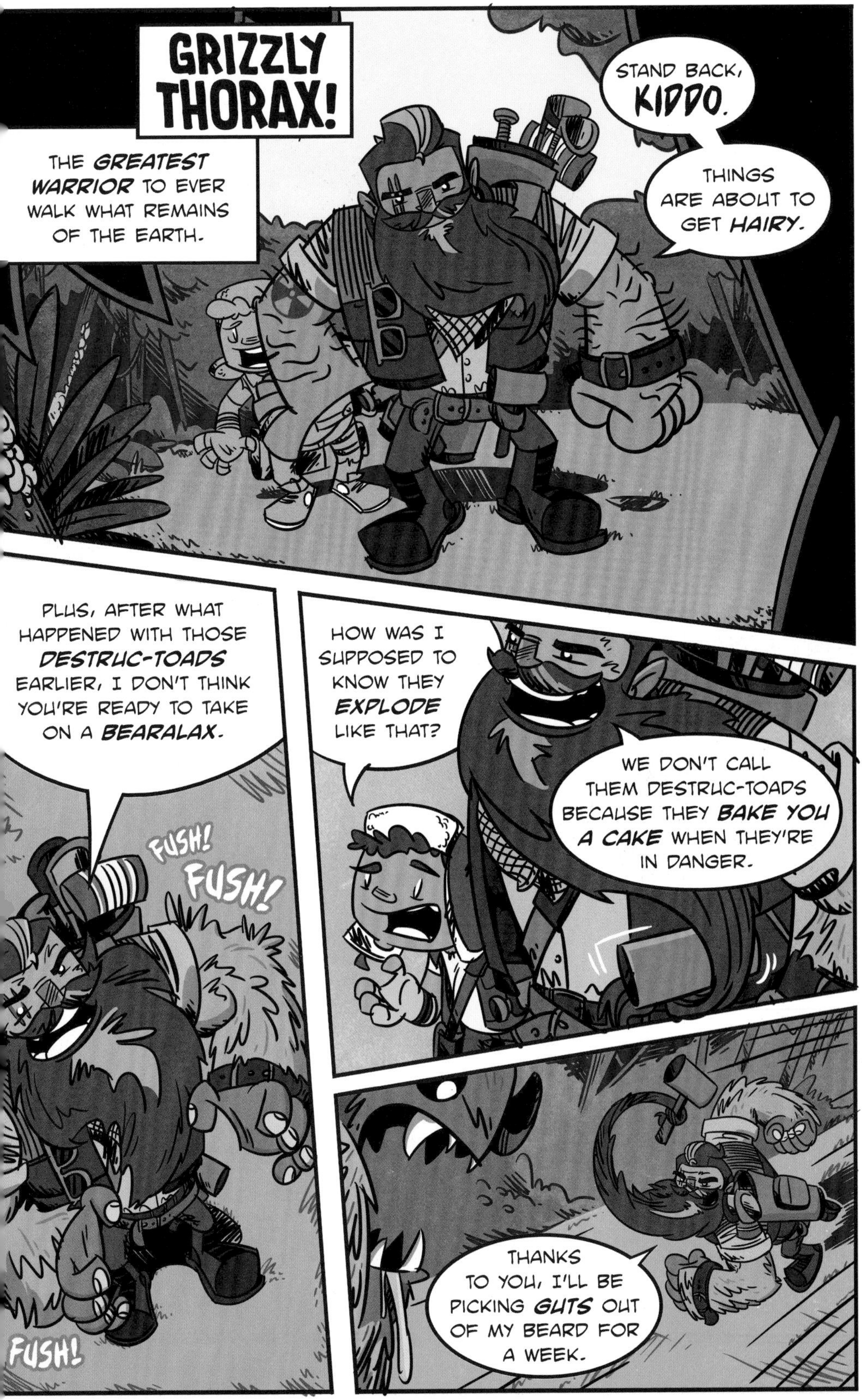
GRIZZLY THORAX!
THE GREATEST WARRIOR TO EVER WALK WHAT REMAINS OF THE EARTH.
STAND BACK, KIDDO.
THINGS ARE ABOUT TO GET HAIRY.
PLUS, AFTER WHAT HAPPENED WITH THOSE DESTRUC-TOADS EARLIER, I DON'T THINK YOU'RE READY TO TAKE ON A BEARALAX.
FUSH!
FUSH!
FUSH!
HOW WAS I SUPPOSED TO KNOW THEY EXPLODE LIKE THAT?
WE DON'T CALL THEM DESTRUC-TOADS BECAUSE THEY BAKE YOU A CAKE WHEN THEY'RE IN DANGER.
THANKS TO YOU, I'LL BE PICKING GUTS OUT OF MY BEARD FOR A WEEK.

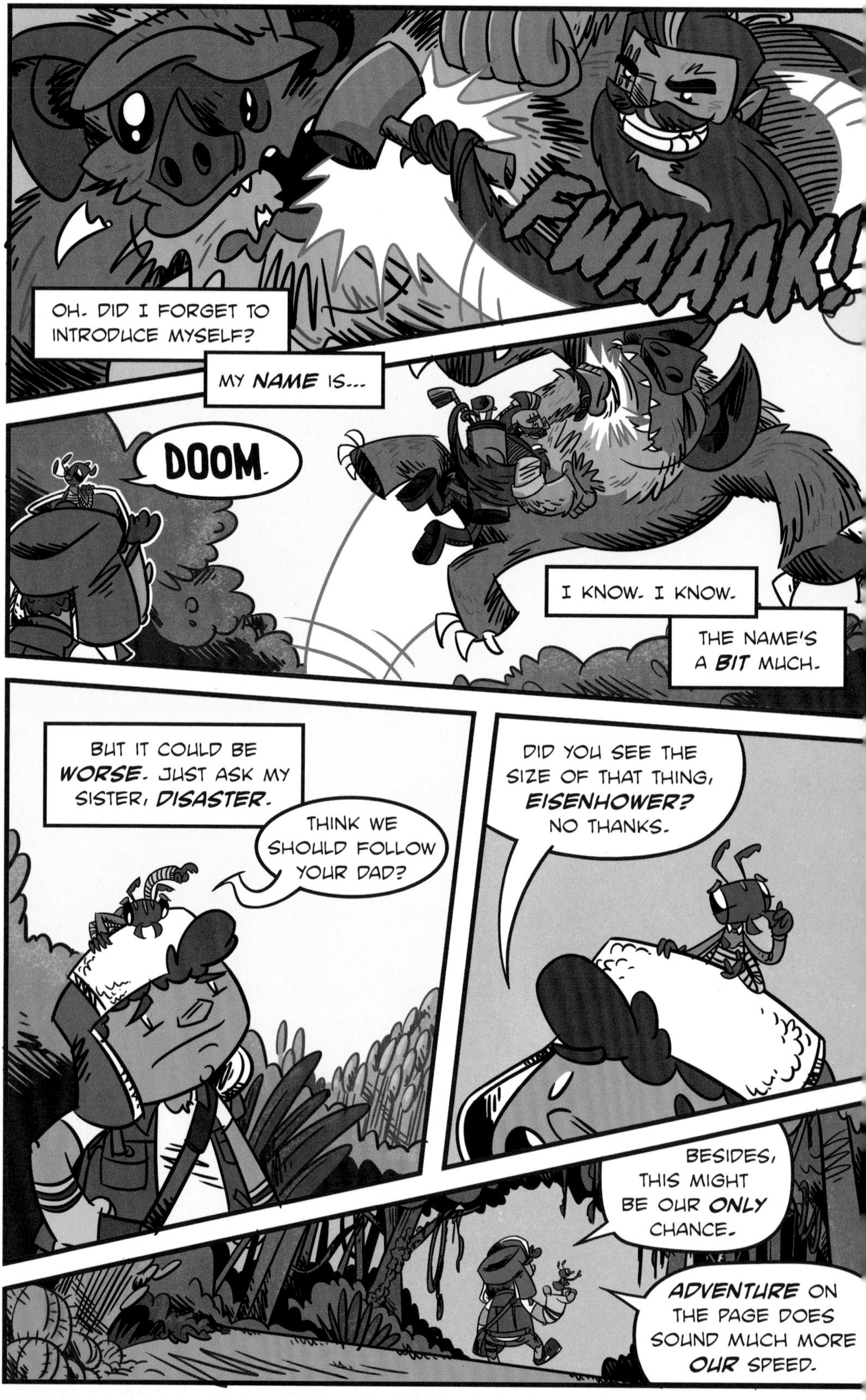
FWAAAK!
OH. DID I FORGET TO INTRODUCE MYSELF?
MY NAME IS...
DOOM.
I KNOW. I KNOW.
THE NAME'S A BIT MUCH.
BUT IT COULD BE WORSE. JUST ASK MY SISTER, DISASTER.
THINK WE SHOULD FOLLOW YOUR DAD?
DID YOU SEE THE SIZE OF THAT THING, EISENHOWER? NO THANKS.
BESIDES, THIS MIGHT BE OUR ONLY CHANCE.
ADVENTURE ON THE PAGE DOES SOUND MUCH MORE OUR SPEED.

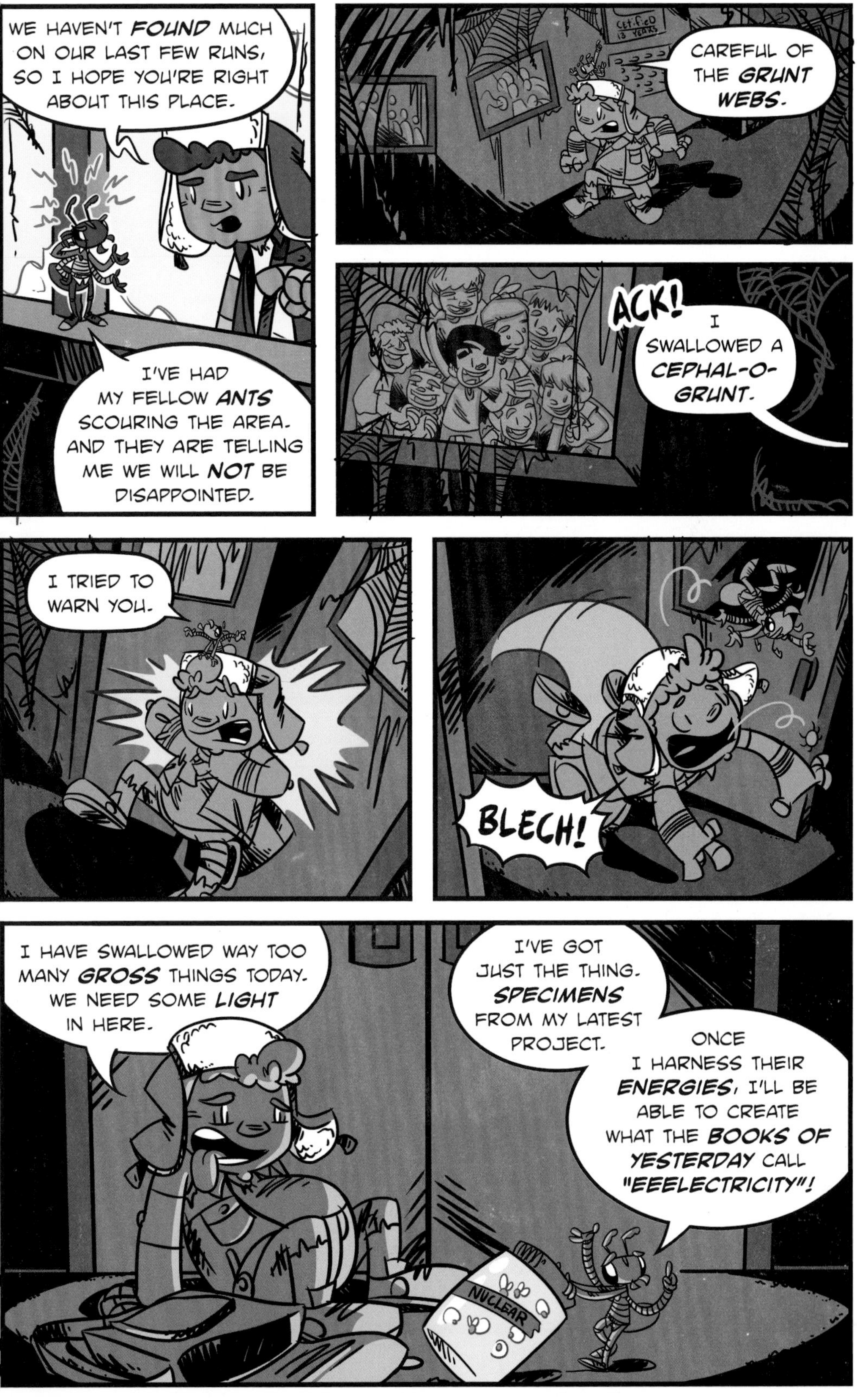
WE HAVEN'T FOUND MUCH ON OUR LAST FEW RUNS, SO I HOPE YOU'RE RIGHT ABOUT THIS PLACE.
I'VE HAD MY FELLOW ANTS SCOURING THE AREA. AND THEY ARE TELLING ME WE WILL NOT BE DISAPPOINTED.
CAREFUL OF THE GRUNT WEBS.
ACK!
I SWALLOWED A CEPHAL-O-GRUNT.
I TRIED TO WARN YOU.
BLECH!
I HAVE SWALLOWED WAY TOO MANY GROSS THINGS TODAY. WE NEED SOME LIGHT IN HERE.
I'VE GOT JUST THE THING. SPECIMENS FROM MY LATEST PROJECT.
ONCE I HARNESS THEIR ENERGIES, I'LL BE ABLE TO CREATE WHAT THE BOOKS OF YESTERDAY CALL "EEELECTRICITY"!
NUCLEAR

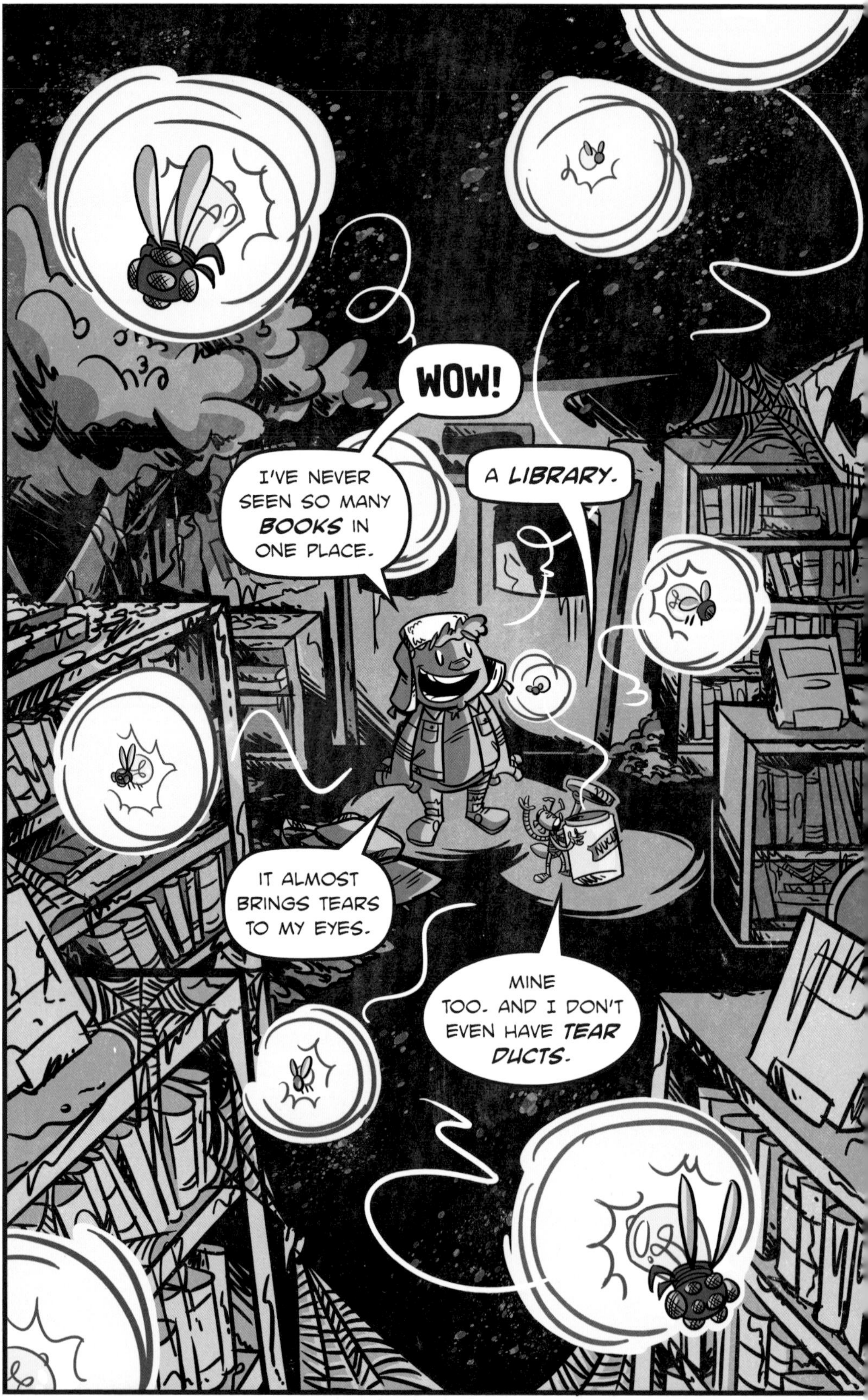
WOW!
I'VE NEVER SEEN SO MANY BOOKS IN ONE PLACE.
A LIBRARY.
IT ALMOST BRINGS TEARS TO MY EYES.
MINE TOO. AND I DON'T EVEN HAVE TEAR DUCTS.

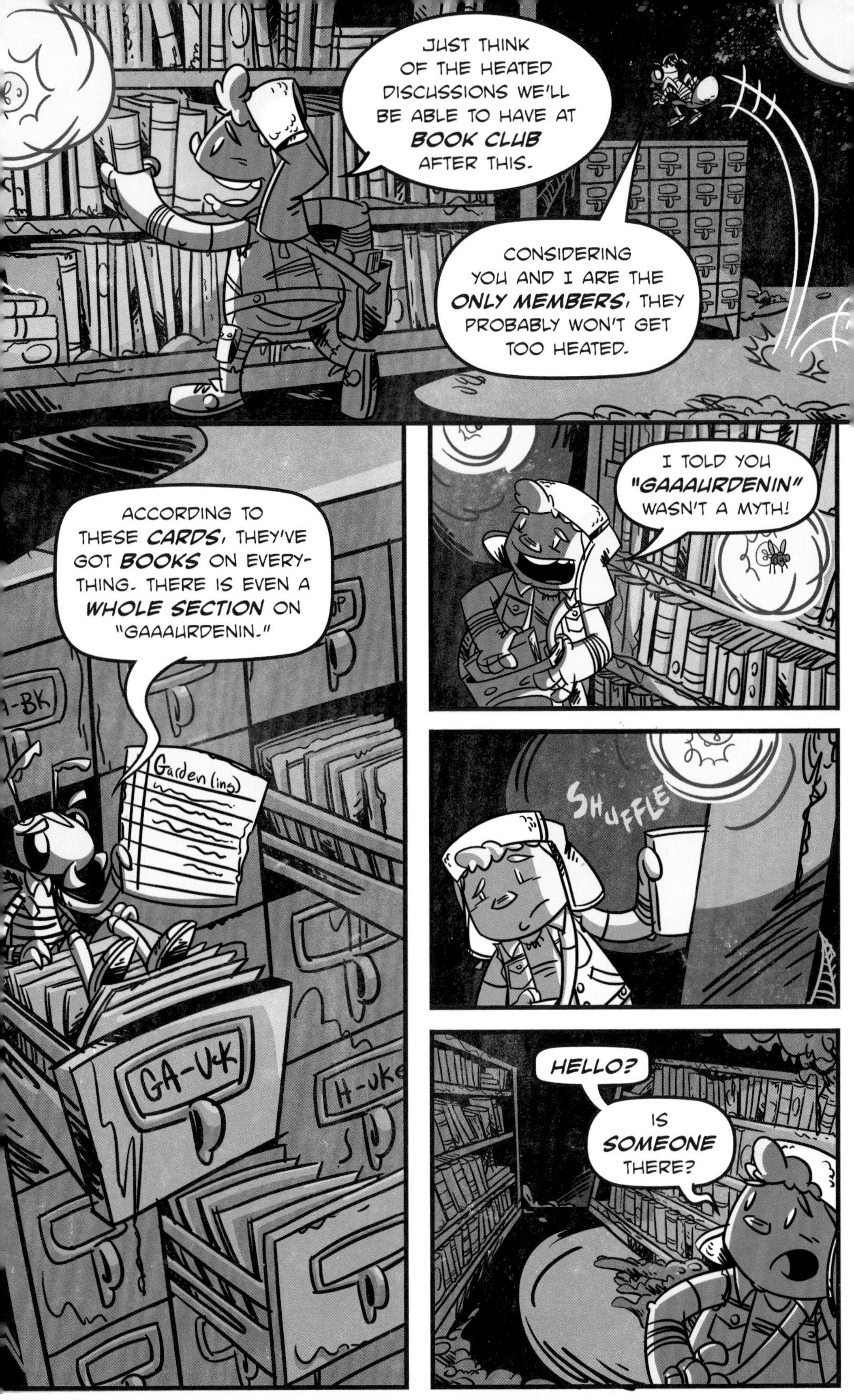
JUST THINK OF THE HEATED DISCUSSIONS WE'LL BE ABLE TO HAVE AT **BOOK CLUB** AFTER THIS.
CONSIDERING YOU AND I ARE THE **ONLY MEMBERS**, THEY PROBABLY WON'T GET TOO HEATED.
ACCORDING TO THESE **CARDS**, THEY'VE GOT **BOOKS** ON EVERYTHING. THERE IS EVEN A **WHOLE SECTION** ON "GAAAURDENIN."
Garden(ing)
GA-UK
H-UK
I TOLD YOU **"GAAAURDENIN"** WASN'T A MYTH!
SHUFFLE
HELLO?
IS **SOMEONE** THERE?

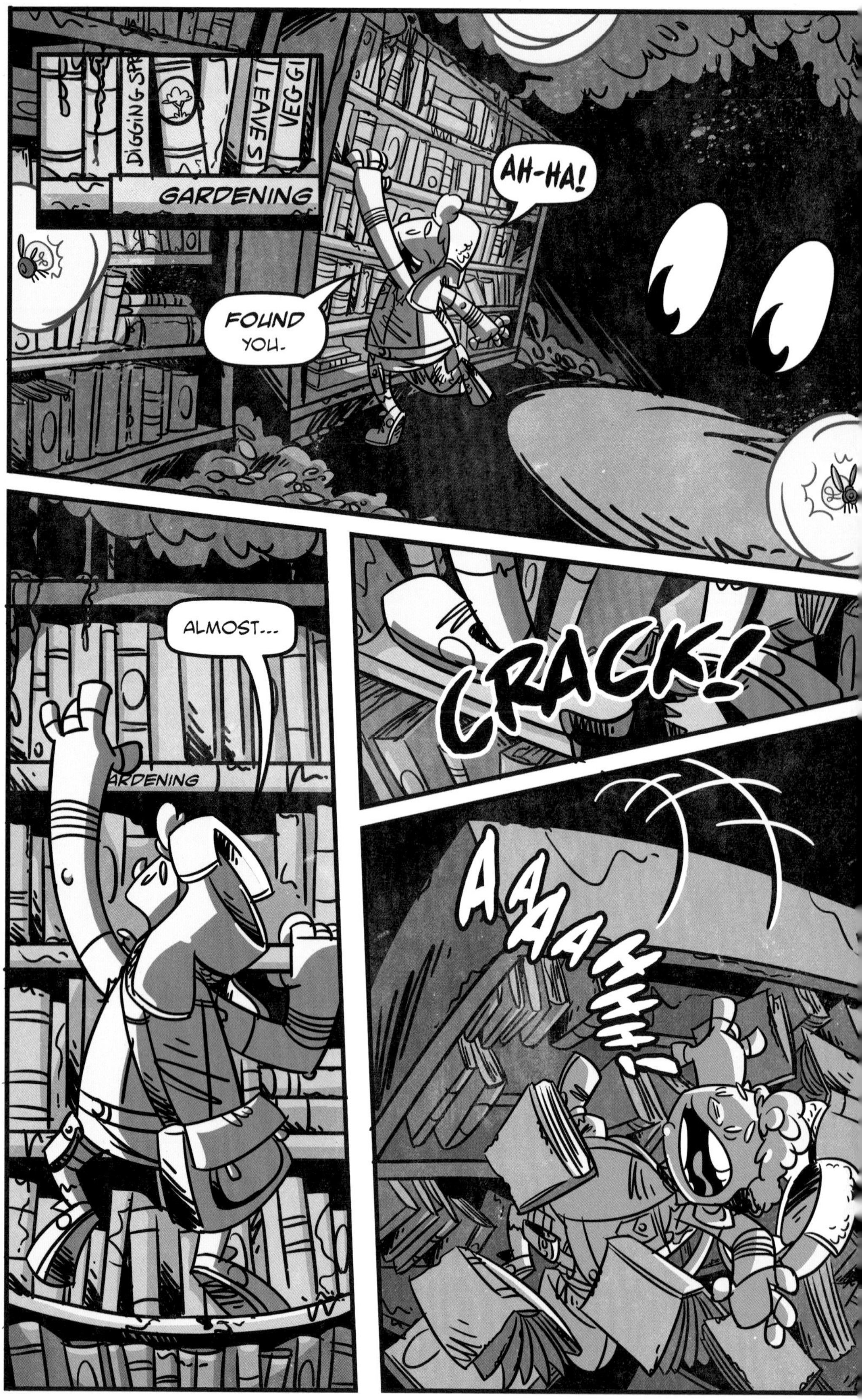
DIGGING SP
LEAVES
VEGGI
GARDENING
AH-HA!
FOUND YOU.
ALMOST...
ARDENING
CRACK!
AAAAHHH!

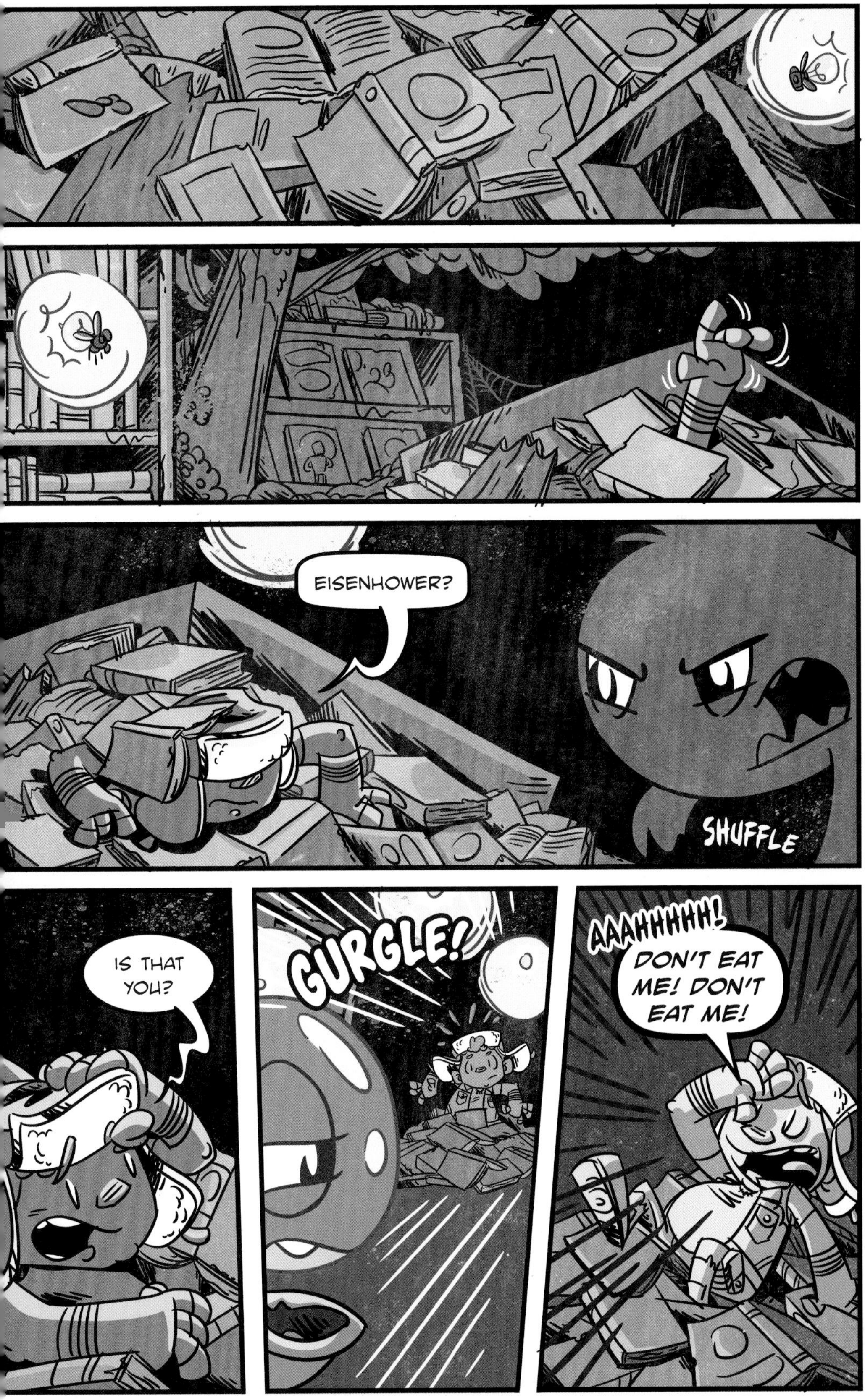
EISENHOWER?
SHUFFLE
IS THAT YOU?
GURGLE!
AAAHHHHH!
DON'T EAT ME! DON'T EAT ME!

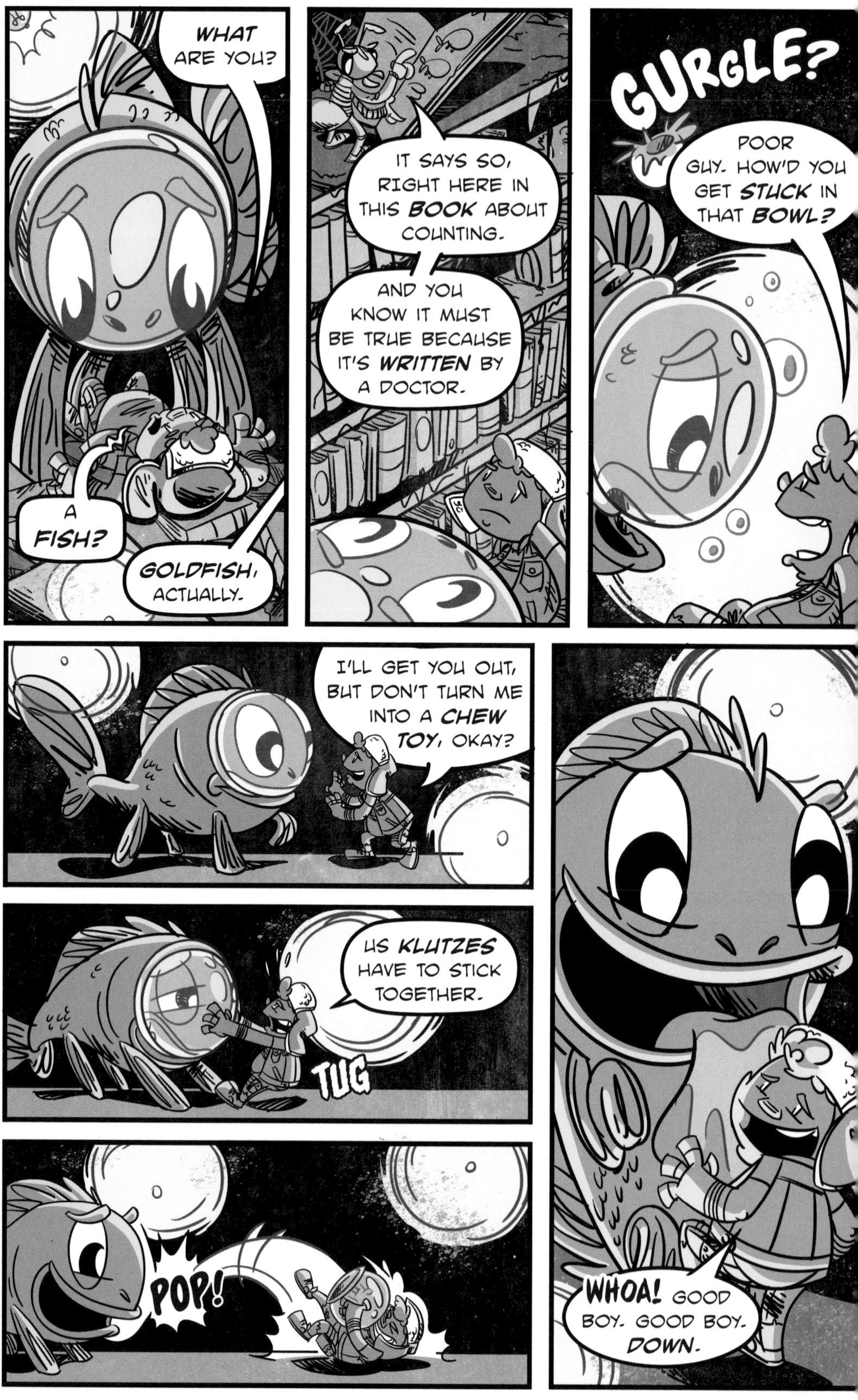
WHAT ARE YOU?
A FISH?
GOLDFISH, ACTUALLY.
IT SAYS SO, RIGHT HERE IN THIS BOOK ABOUT COUNTING.
AND YOU KNOW IT MUST BE TRUE BECAUSE IT'S WRITTEN BY A DOCTOR.
GURGLE?
POOR GUY. HOW'D YOU GET STUCK IN THAT BOWL?
I'LL GET YOU OUT, BUT DON'T TURN ME INTO A CHEW TOY, OKAY?
US KLUTZES HAVE TO STICK TOGETHER.
TUG
POP!
WHOA! GOOD BOY. GOOD BOY. DOWN.

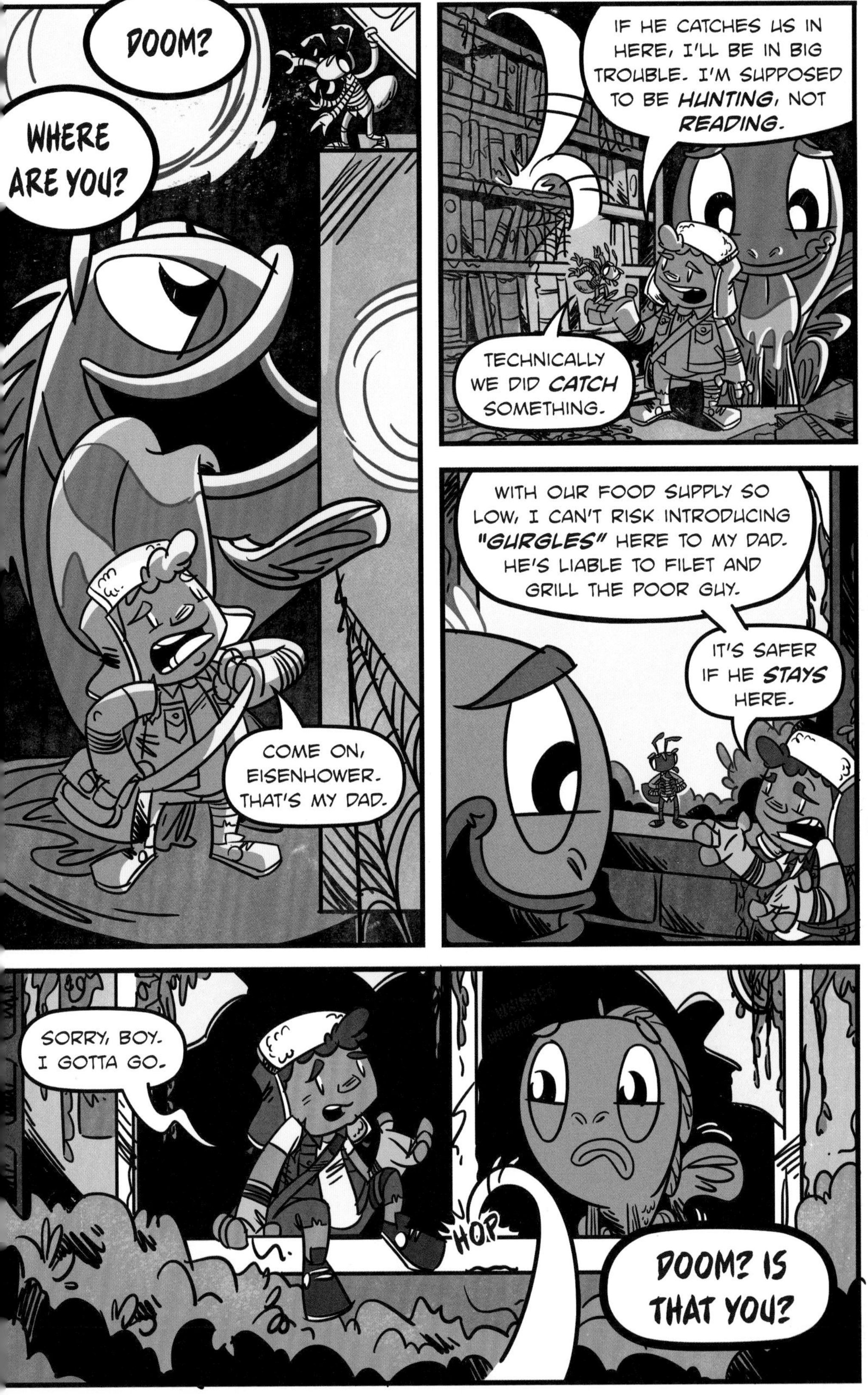
DOOM?
WHERE ARE YOU?
COME ON, EISENHOWER. THAT'S MY DAD.
IF HE CATCHES US IN HERE, I'LL BE IN BIG TROUBLE. I'M SUPPOSED TO BE HUNTING, NOT READING.
TECHNICALLY WE DID CATCH SOMETHING.
WITH OUR FOOD SUPPLY SO LOW, I CAN'T RISK INTRODUCING "GURGLES" HERE TO MY DAD. HE'S LIABLE TO FILET AND GRILL THE POOR GUY.
IT'S SAFER IF HE STAYS HERE.
SORRY, BOY. I GOTTA GO.
HOP
DOOM? IS THAT YOU?

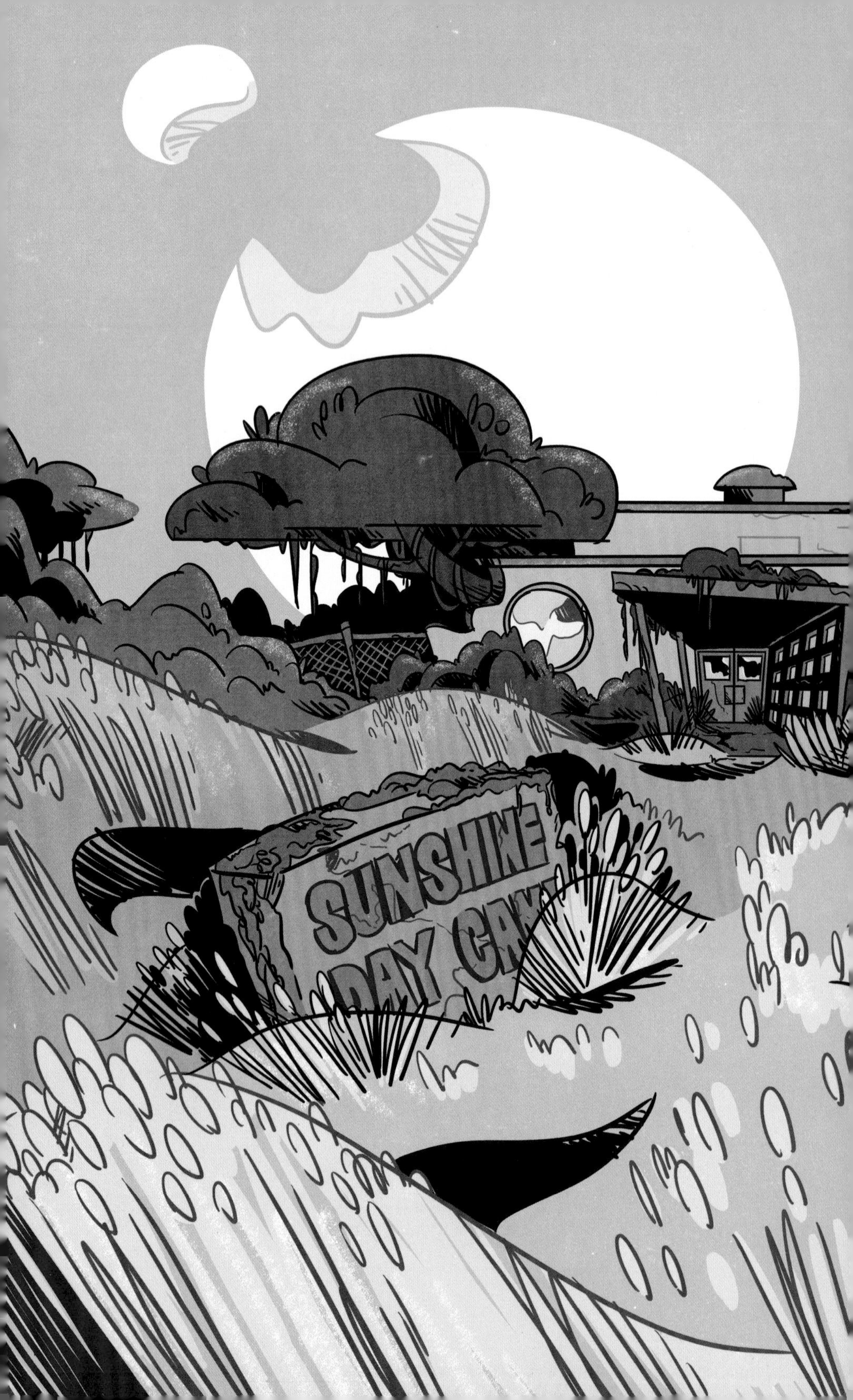
SUNSHINE
DAY CA

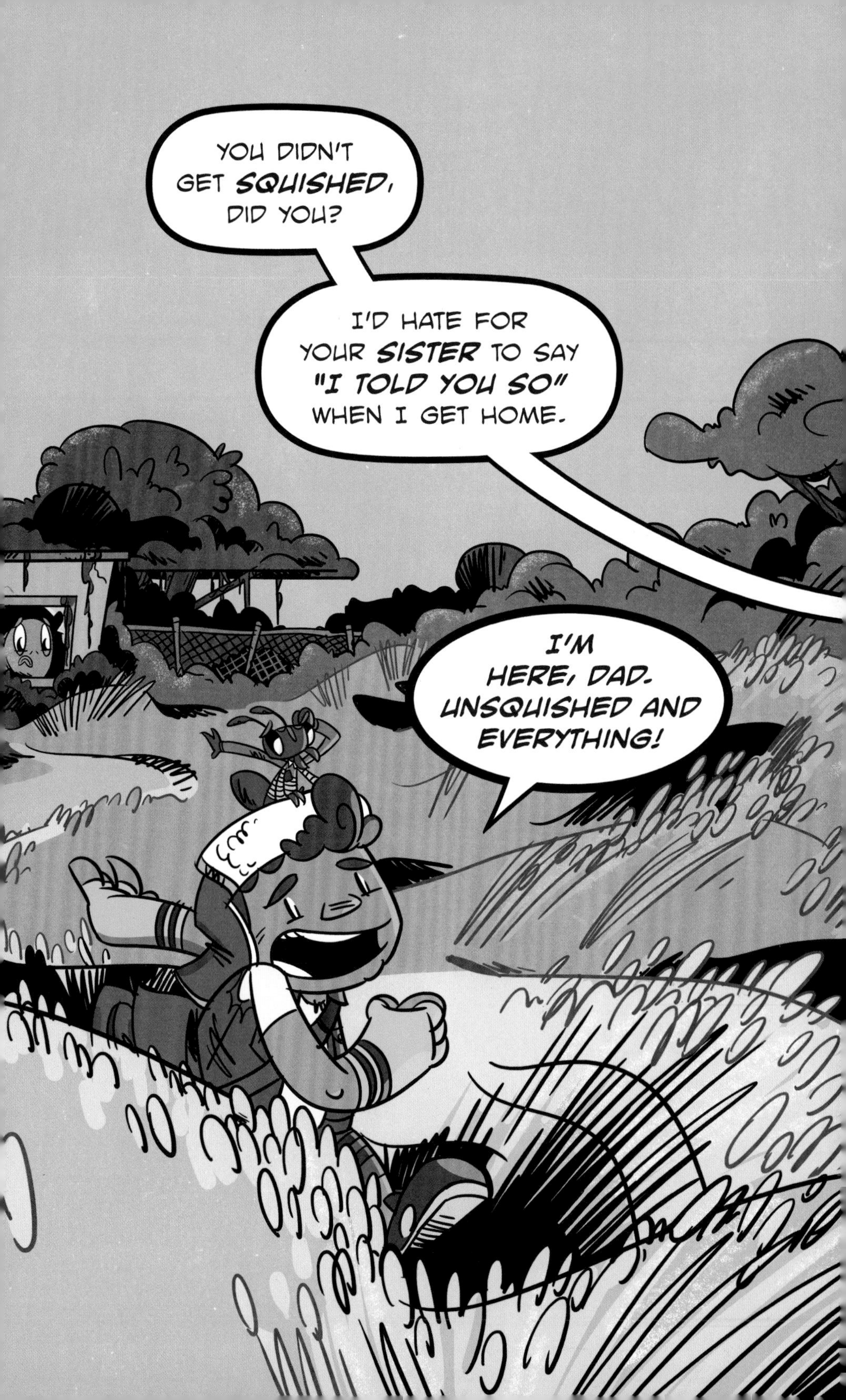
YOU DIDN'T GET SQUISHED, DID YOU?
I'D HATE FOR YOUR SISTER TO SAY "I TOLD YOU SO" WHEN I GET HOME.
I'M HERE, DAD. UNSQUISHED AND EVERYTHING!

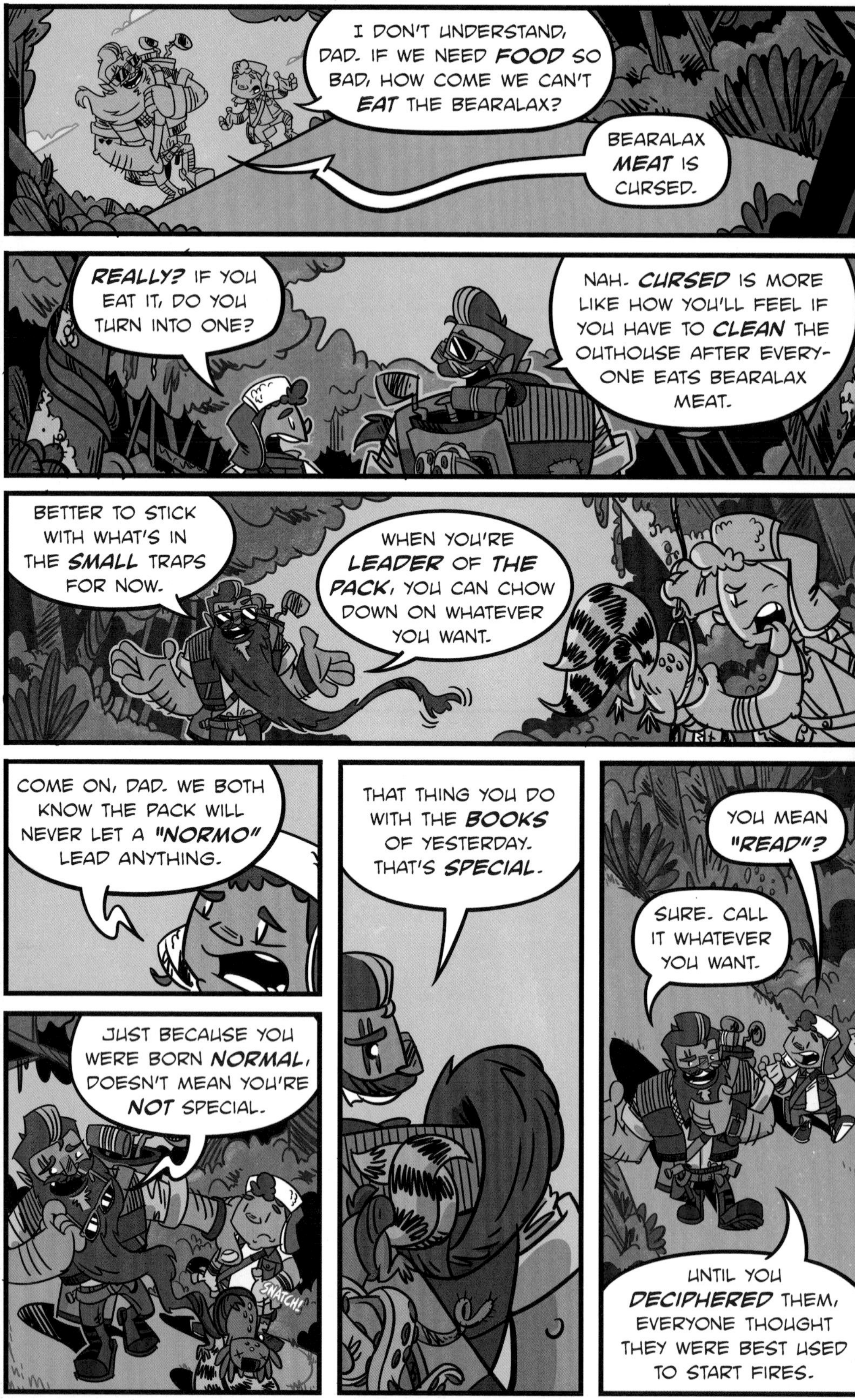
I DON'T UNDERSTAND, DAD. IF WE NEED FOOD SO BAD, HOW COME WE CAN'T EAT THE BEARALAX?
BEARALAX MEAT IS CURSED.
REALLY? IF YOU EAT IT, DO YOU TURN INTO ONE?
NAH. CURSED IS MORE LIKE HOW YOU'LL FEEL IF YOU HAVE TO CLEAN THE OUTHOUSE AFTER EVERY-ONE EATS BEARALAX MEAT.
BETTER TO STICK WITH WHAT'S IN THE SMALL TRAPS FOR NOW.
WHEN YOU'RE LEADER OF THE PACK, YOU CAN CHOW DOWN ON WHATEVER YOU WANT.
COME ON, DAD. WE BOTH KNOW THE PACK WILL NEVER LET A "NORMO" LEAD ANYTHING.
JUST BECAUSE YOU WERE BORN NORMAL, DOESN'T MEAN YOU'RE NOT SPECIAL.
SNATCH!
THAT THING YOU DO WITH THE BOOKS OF YESTERDAY. THAT'S SPECIAL.
YOU MEAN "READ"?
SURE. CALL IT WHATEVER YOU WANT.
UNTIL YOU DECIPHERED THEM, EVERYONE THOUGHT THEY WERE BEST USED TO START FIRES.

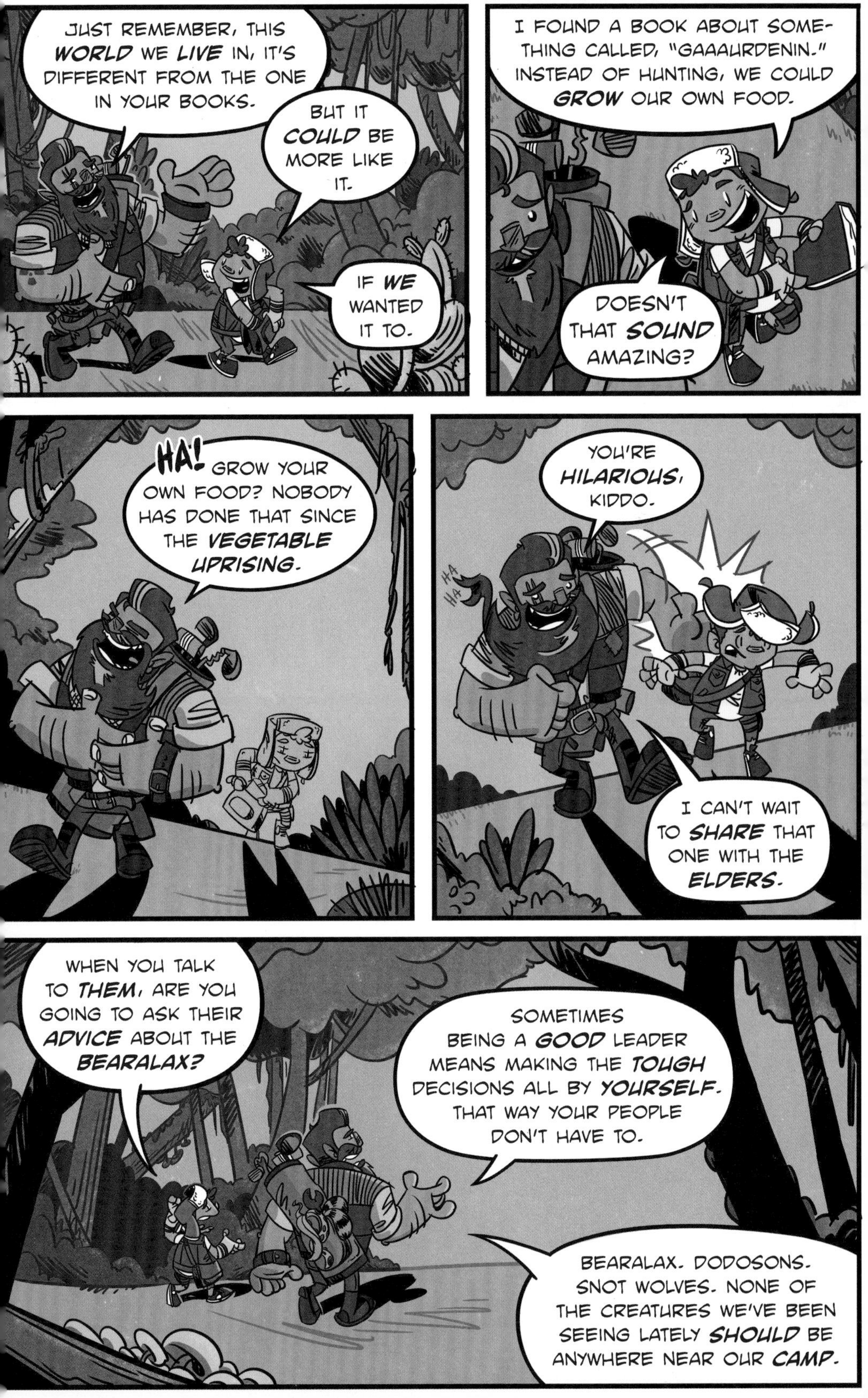
JUST REMEMBER, THIS WORLD WE LIVE IN, IT'S DIFFERENT FROM THE ONE IN YOUR BOOKS.
BUT IT COULD BE MORE LIKE IT.
IF WE WANTED IT TO.
I FOUND A BOOK ABOUT SOMETHING CALLED, "GAAAURDENIN." INSTEAD OF HUNTING, WE COULD GROW OUR OWN FOOD.
DOESN'T THAT SOUND AMAZING?
HA! GROW YOUR OWN FOOD? NOBODY HAS DONE THAT SINCE THE VEGETABLE UPRISING.
YOU'RE HILARIOUS, KIDDO.
HA HA
I CAN'T WAIT TO SHARE THAT ONE WITH THE ELDERS.
WHEN YOU TALK TO THEM, ARE YOU GOING TO ASK THEIR ADVICE ABOUT THE BEARALAX?
SOMETIMES BEING A GOOD LEADER MEANS MAKING THE TOUGH DECISIONS ALL BY YOURSELF. THAT WAY YOUR PEOPLE DON'T HAVE TO.
BEARALAX. DODOSONS. SNOT WOLVES. NONE OF THE CREATURES WE'VE BEEN SEEING LATELY SHOULD BE ANYWHERE NEAR OUR CAMP.

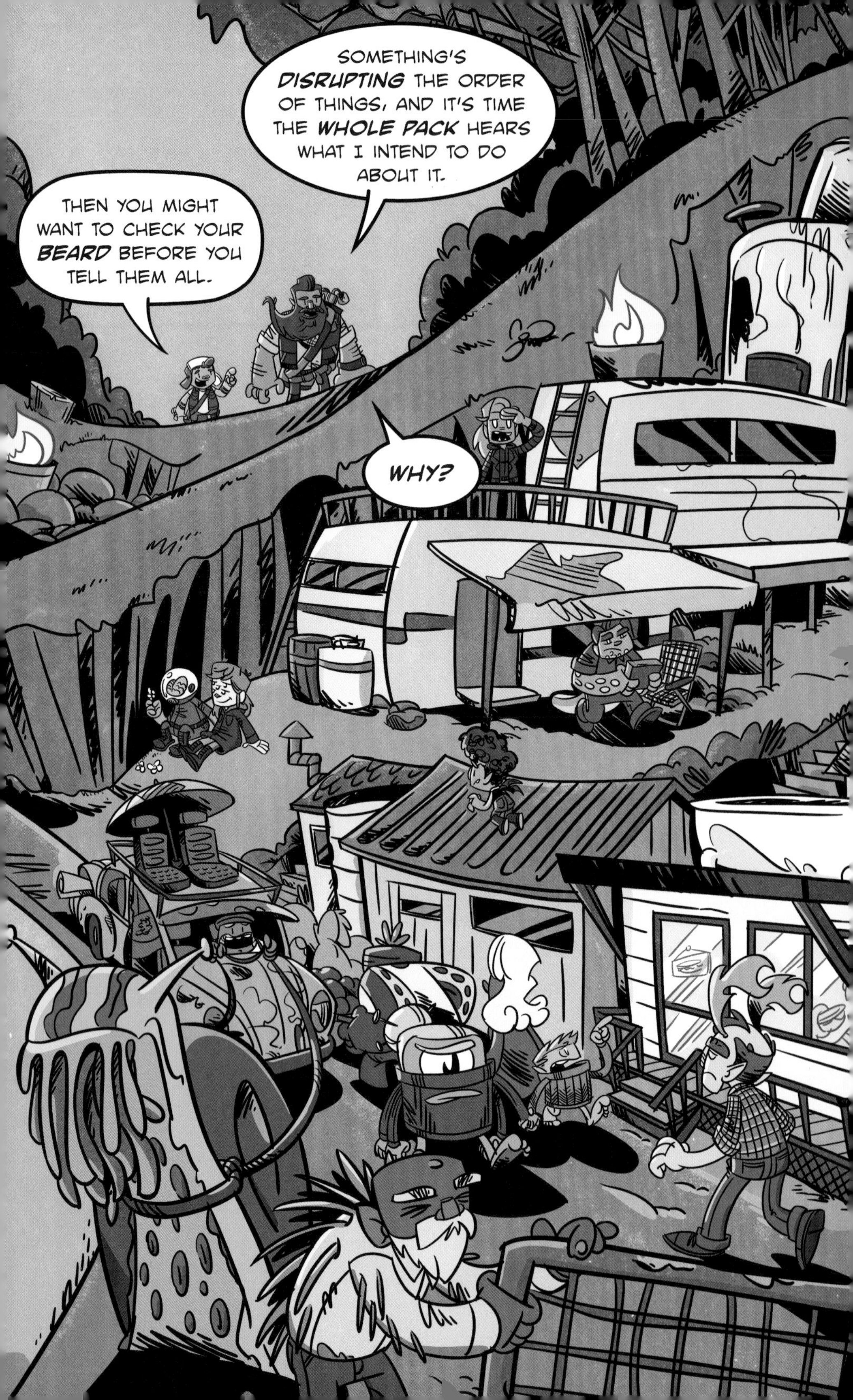
SOMETHING'S DISRUPTING THE ORDER OF THINGS, AND IT'S TIME THE WHOLE PACK HEARS WHAT I INTEND TO DO ABOUT IT.
THEN YOU MIGHT WANT TO CHECK YOUR BEARD BEFORE YOU TELL THEM ALL.
WHY?

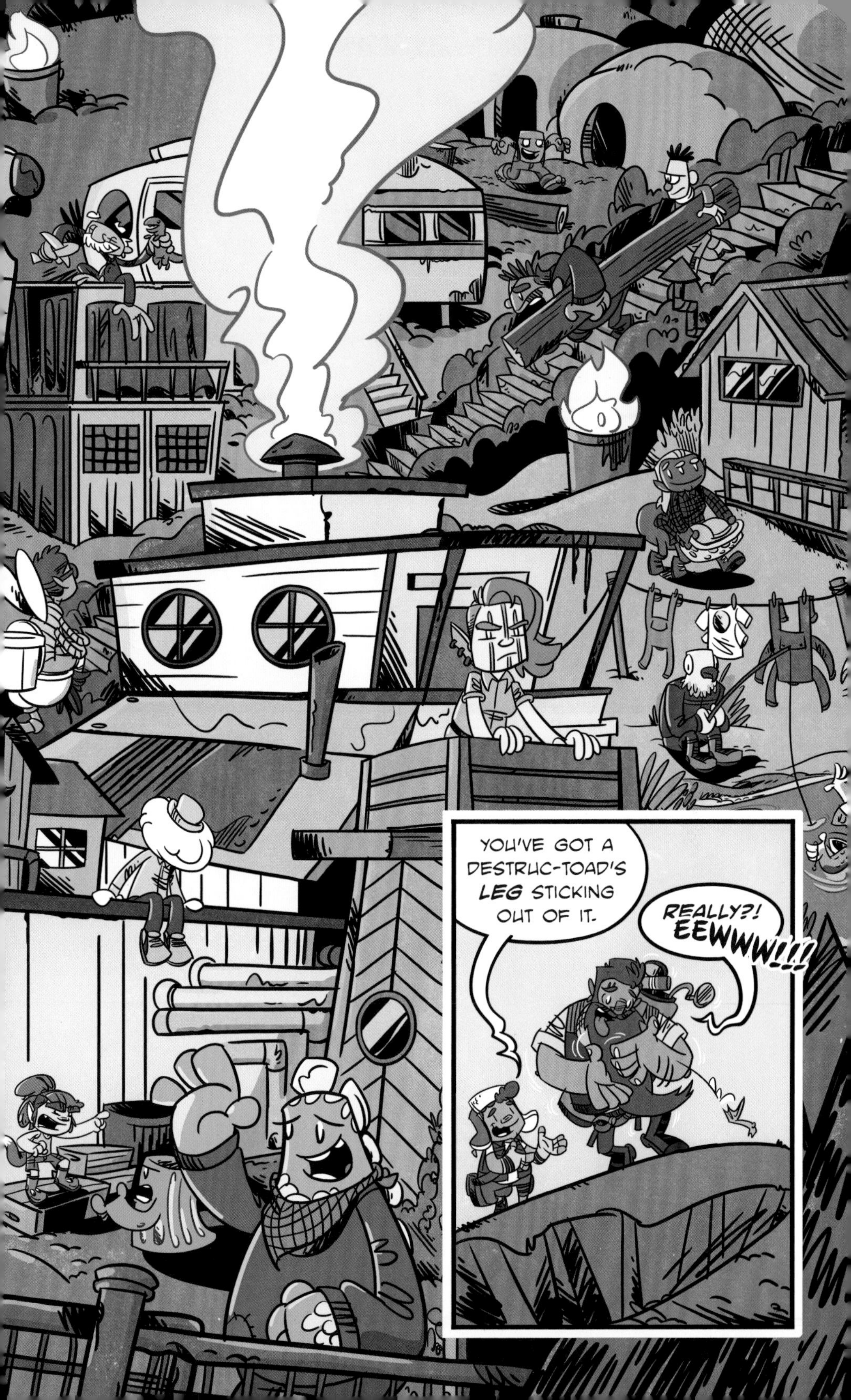
YOU'VE GOT A DESTRUC-TOAD'S **LEG** STICKING OUT OF IT.
REALLY?! EEWWW!!!

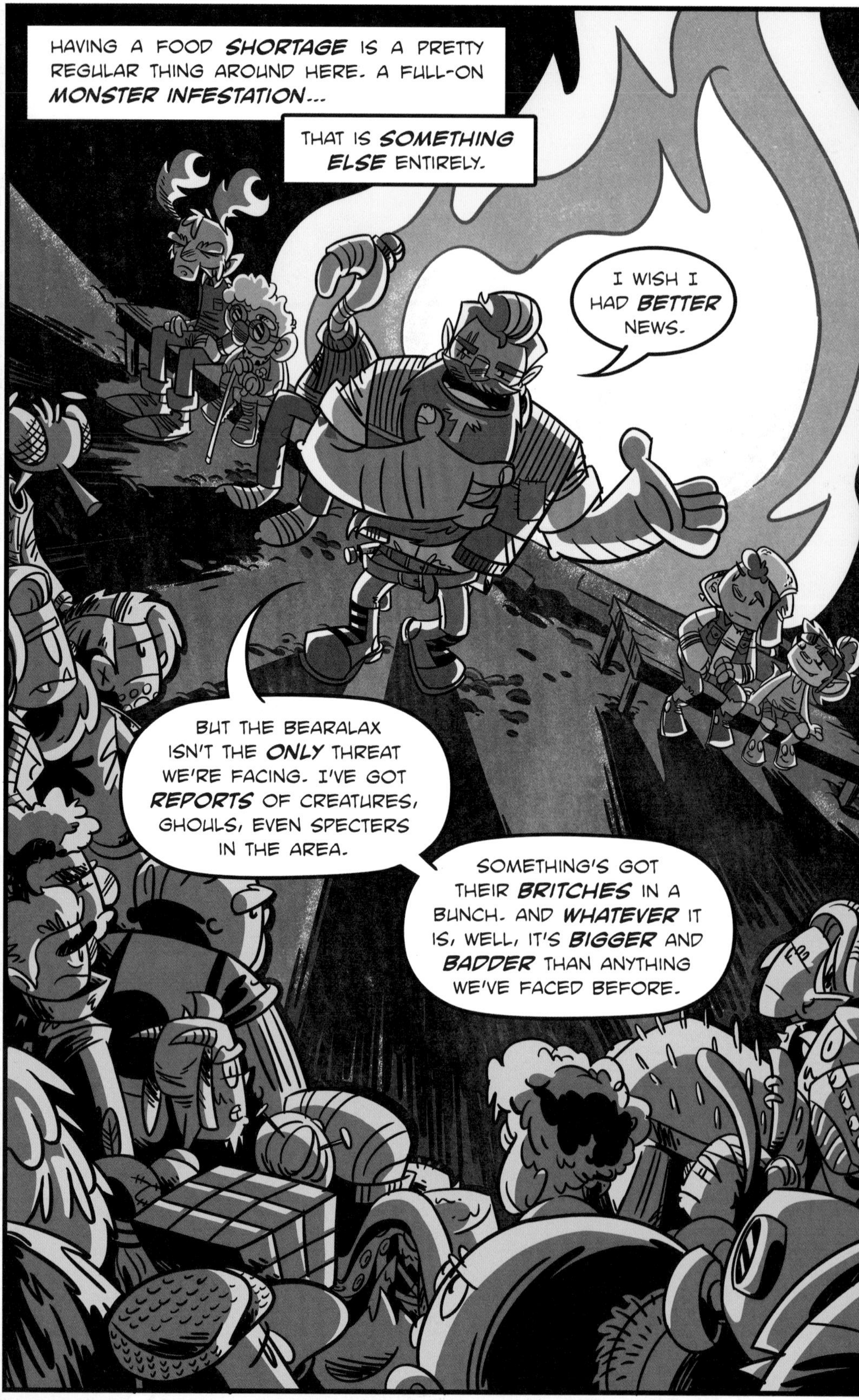
HAVING A FOOD SHORTAGE IS A PRETTY REGULAR THING AROUND HERE. A FULL-ON MONSTER INFESTATION...
THAT IS SOMETHING ELSE ENTIRELY.
I WISH I HAD BETTER NEWS.
BUT THE BEARALAX ISN'T THE ONLY THREAT WE'RE FACING. I'VE GOT REPORTS OF CREATURES, GHOULS, EVEN SPECTERS IN THE AREA.
SOMETHING'S GOT THEIR BRITCHES IN A BUNCH. AND WHATEVER IT IS, WELL, IT'S BIGGER AND BADDER THAN ANYTHING WE'VE FACED BEFORE.

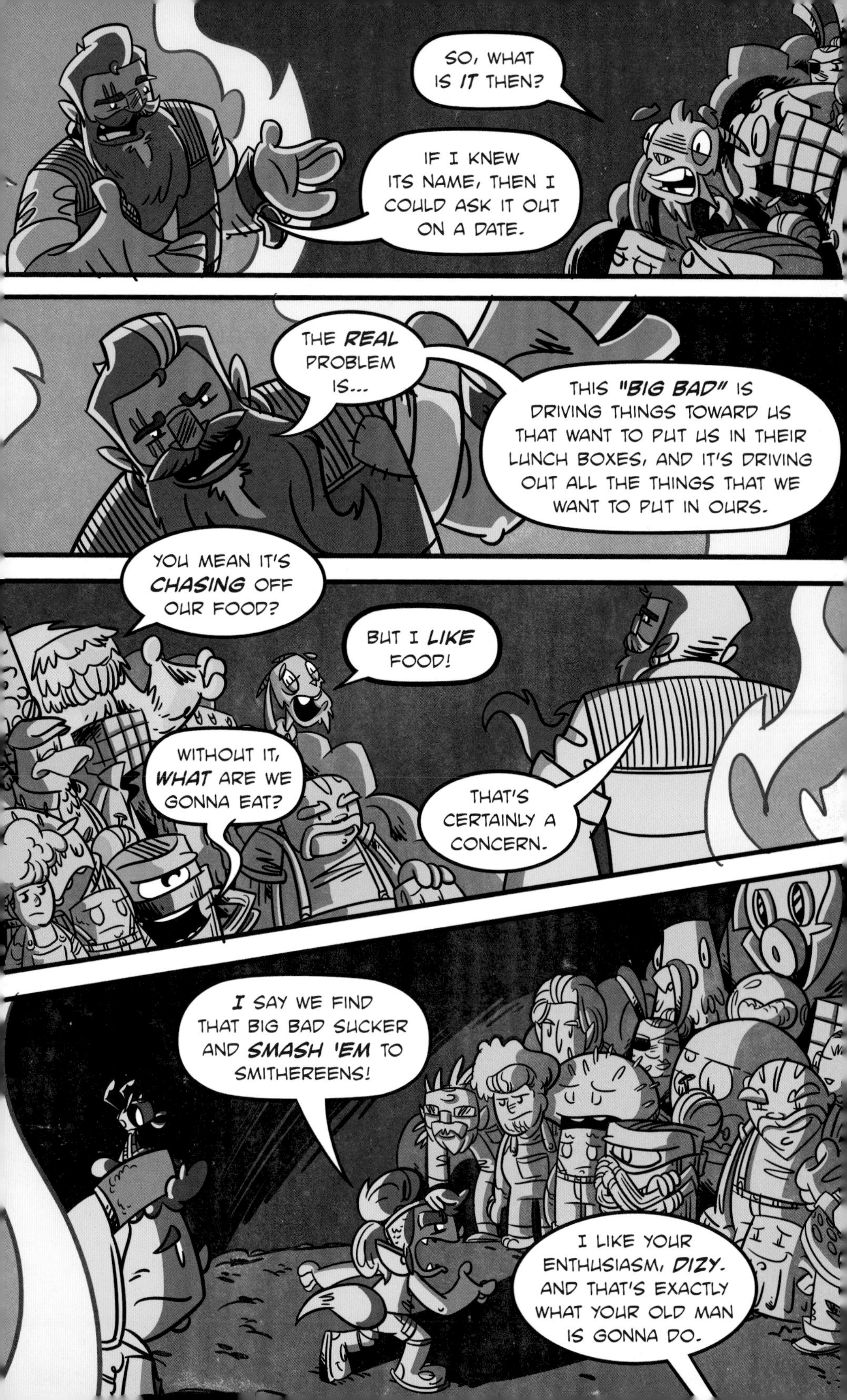
SO, WHAT IS IT THEN?
IF I KNEW ITS NAME, THEN I COULD ASK IT OUT ON A DATE.
THE REAL PROBLEM IS...
THIS "BIG BAD" IS DRIVING THINGS TOWARD US THAT WANT TO PUT US IN THEIR LUNCH BOXES, AND IT'S DRIVING OUT ALL THE THINGS THAT WE WANT TO PUT IN OURS.
YOU MEAN IT'S CHASING OFF OUR FOOD?
BUT I LIKE FOOD!
WITHOUT IT, WHAT ARE WE GONNA EAT?
THAT'S CERTAINLY A CONCERN.
I SAY WE FIND THAT BIG BAD SUCKER AND SMASH 'EM TO SMITHEREENS!
I LIKE YOUR ENTHUSIASM, DIZY. AND THAT'S EXACTLY WHAT YOUR OLD MAN IS GONNA DO.

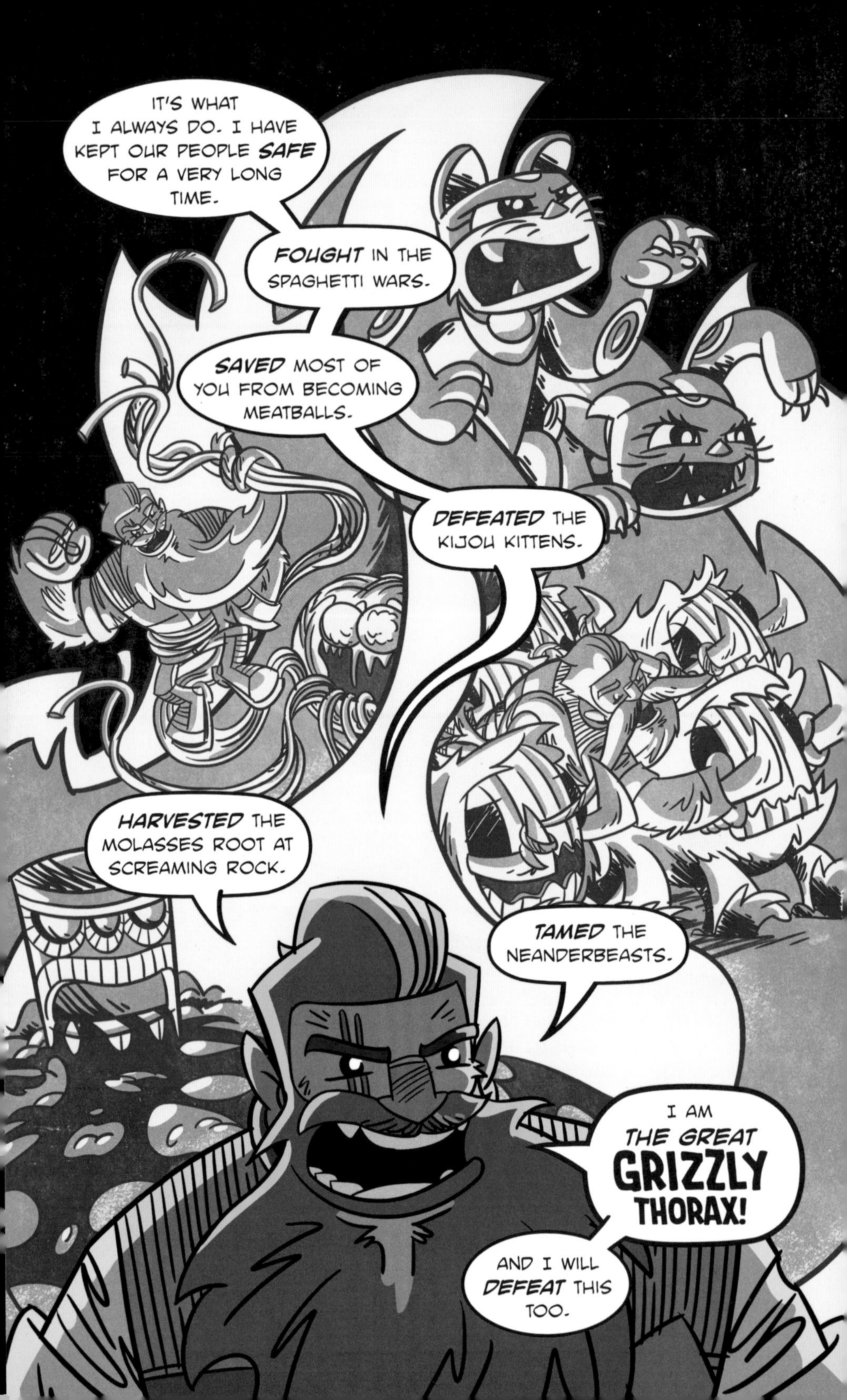
IT'S WHAT I ALWAYS DO. I HAVE KEPT OUR PEOPLE SAFE FOR A VERY LONG TIME.
FOUGHT IN THE SPAGHETTI WARS.
SAVED MOST OF YOU FROM BECOMING MEATBALLS.
DEFEATED THE KIJOU KITTENS.
HARVESTED THE MOLASSES ROOT AT SCREAMING ROCK.
TAMED THE NEANDERBEASTS.
I AM THE GREAT GRIZZLY THORAX!
AND I WILL DEFEAT THIS TOO.

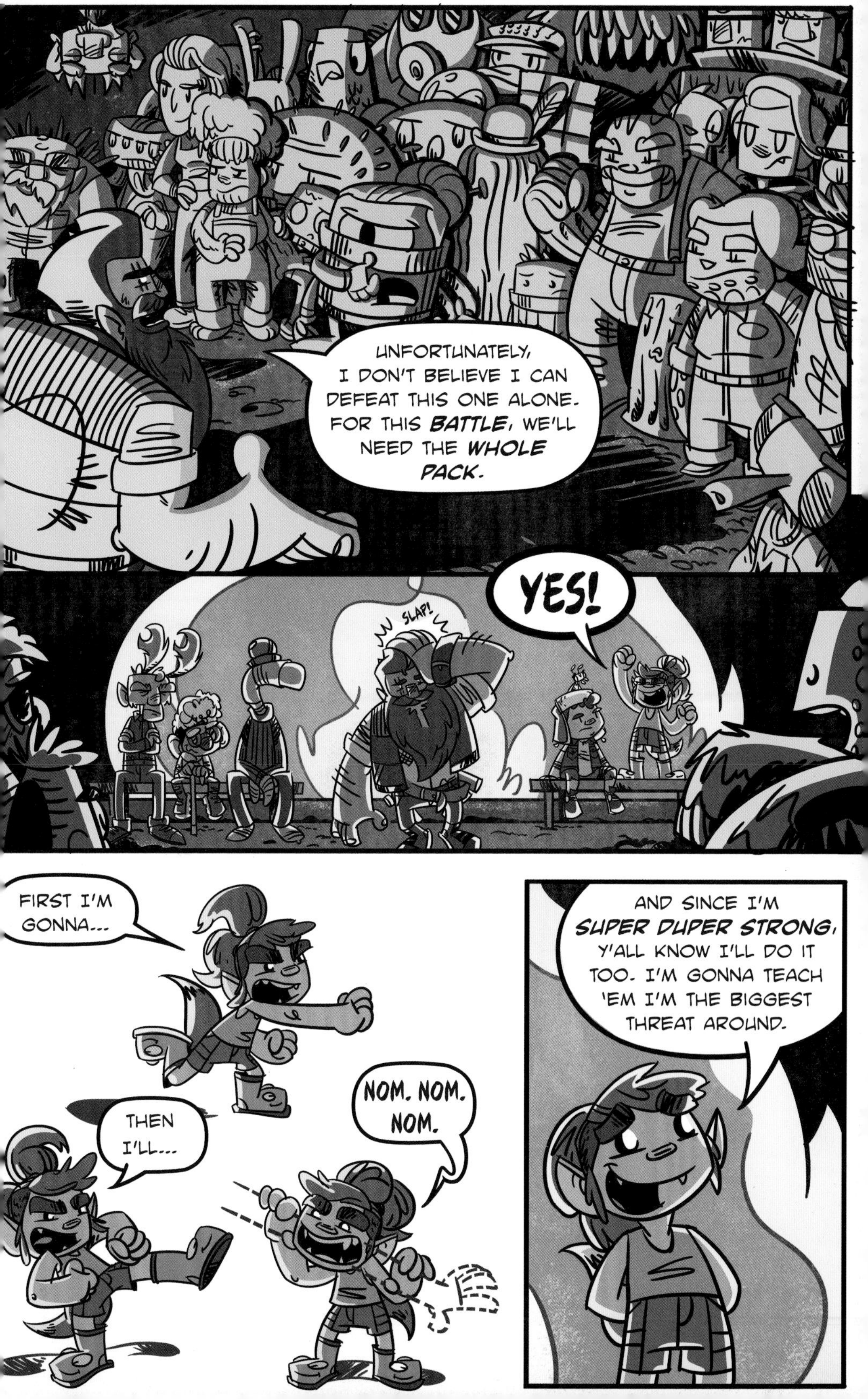
UNFORTUNATELY, I DON'T BELIEVE I CAN DEFEAT THIS ONE ALONE. FOR THIS BATTLE, WE'LL NEED THE WHOLE PACK.
SLAP!
YES!
FIRST I'M GONNA...
THEN I'LL...
NOM. NOM. NOM.
AND SINCE I'M SUPER DUPER STRONG, Y'ALL KNOW I'LL DO IT TOO. I'M GONNA TEACH 'EM I'M THE BIGGEST THREAT AROUND.

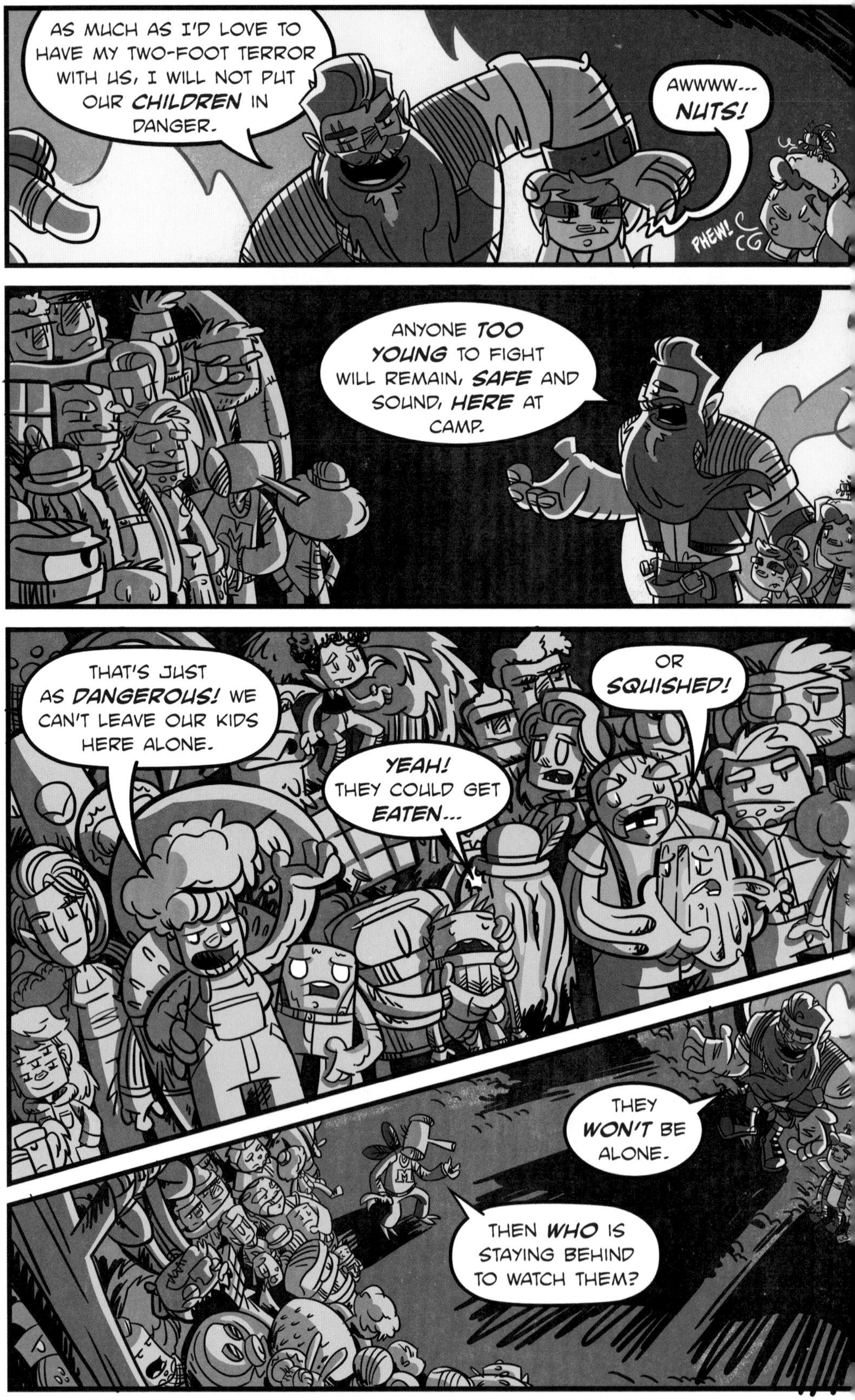
AS MUCH AS I'D LOVE TO HAVE MY TWO-FOOT TERROR WITH US, I WILL NOT PUT OUR CHILDREN IN DANGER.
AWWWW... NUTS!
PHEW!
ANYONE TOO YOUNG TO FIGHT WILL REMAIN, SAFE AND SOUND, HERE AT CAMP.
THAT'S JUST AS DANGEROUS! WE CAN'T LEAVE OUR KIDS HERE ALONE.
YEAH! THEY COULD GET EATEN...
OR SQUISHED!
THEY WON'T BE ALONE.
THEN WHO IS STAYING BEHIND TO WATCH THEM?

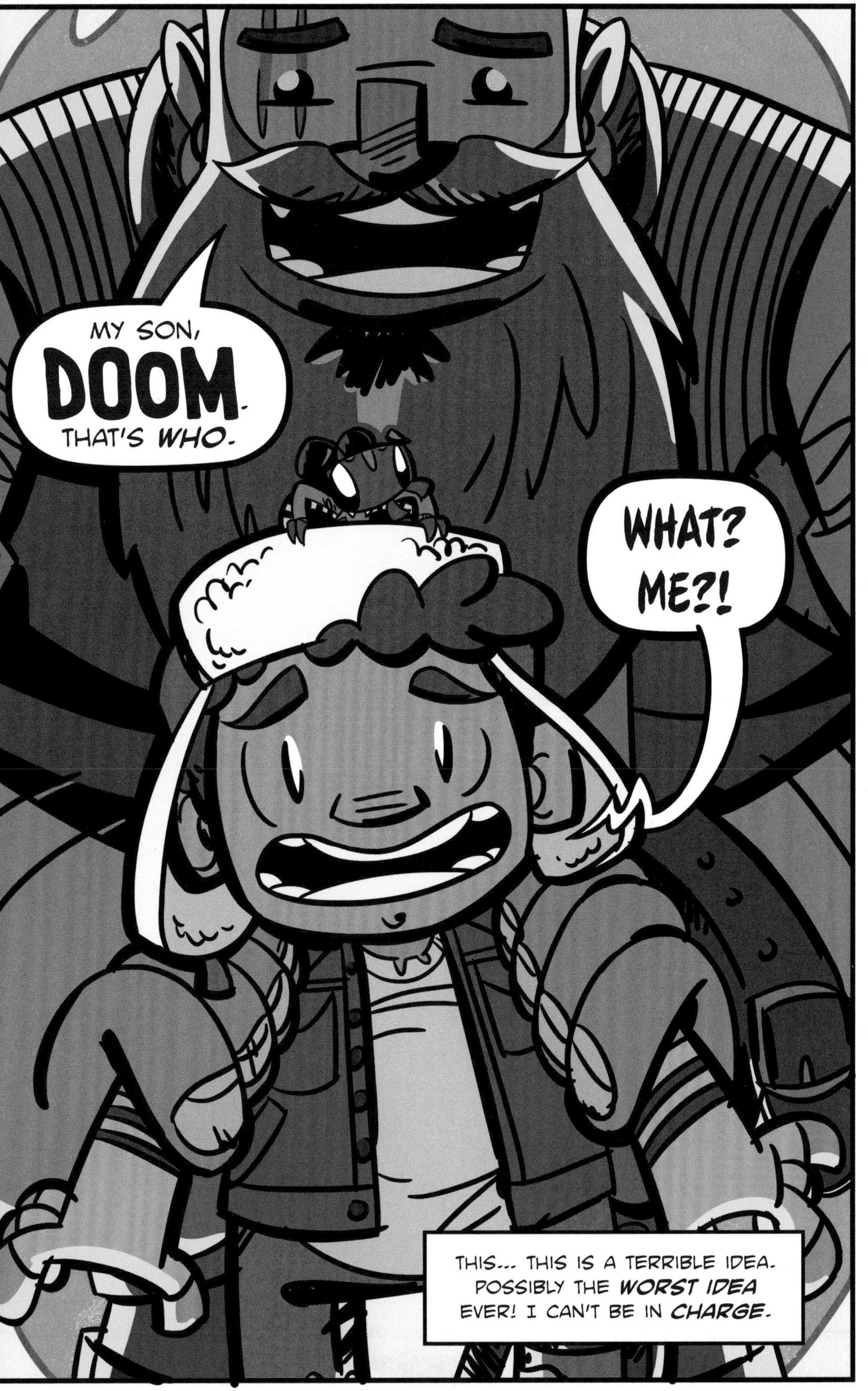
MY SON, DOOM. THAT'S WHO.
WHAT? ME?!
THIS... THIS IS A TERRIBLE IDEA. POSSIBLY THE WORST IDEA EVER! I CAN'T BE IN CHARGE.

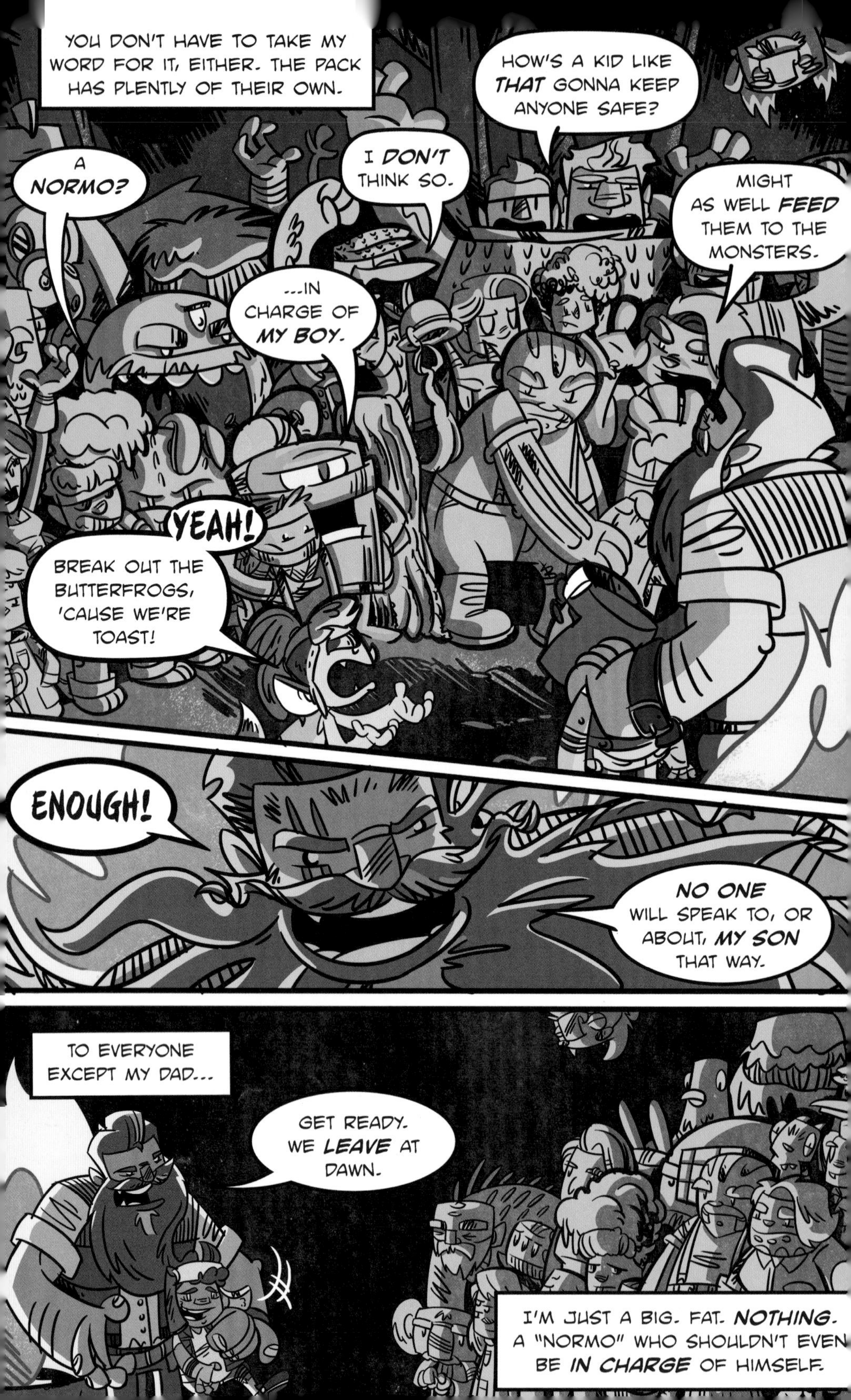
YOU DON'T HAVE TO TAKE MY WORD FOR IT, EITHER. THE PACK HAS PLENTLY OF THEIR OWN.
HOW'S A KID LIKE THAT GONNA KEEP ANYONE SAFE?
A NORMO?
I DON'T THINK SO.
MIGHT AS WELL FEED THEM TO THE MONSTERS.
...IN CHARGE OF MY BOY.
YEAH!
BREAK OUT THE BUTTERFROGS, 'CAUSE WE'RE TOAST!
ENOUGH!
NO ONE WILL SPEAK TO, OR ABOUT, MY SON THAT WAY.
TO EVERYONE EXCEPT MY DAD...
GET READY. WE LEAVE AT DAWN.
I'M JUST A BIG. FAT. NOTHING. A "NORMO" WHO SHOULDN'T EVEN BE IN CHARGE OF HIMSELF.

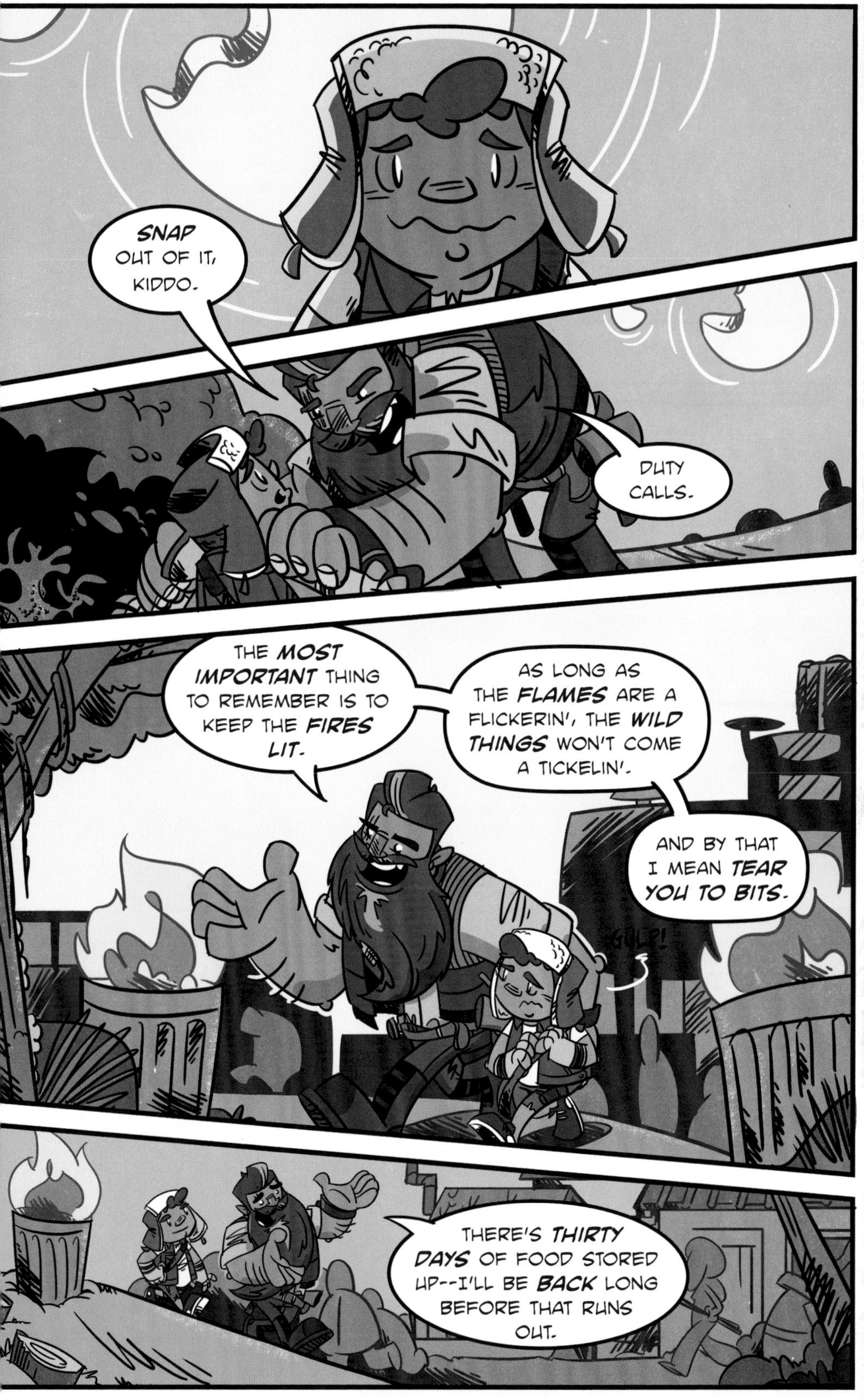
SNAP OUT OF IT, KIDDO.
DUTY CALLS.
THE MOST IMPORTANT THING TO REMEMBER IS TO KEEP THE FIRES LIT.
AS LONG AS THE FLAMES ARE A FLICKERIN', THE WILD THINGS WON'T COME A TICKELIN'.
AND BY THAT I MEAN TEAR YOU TO BITS.
GULP!
THERE'S THIRTY DAYS OF FOOD STORED UP--I'LL BE BACK LONG BEFORE THAT RUNS OUT.

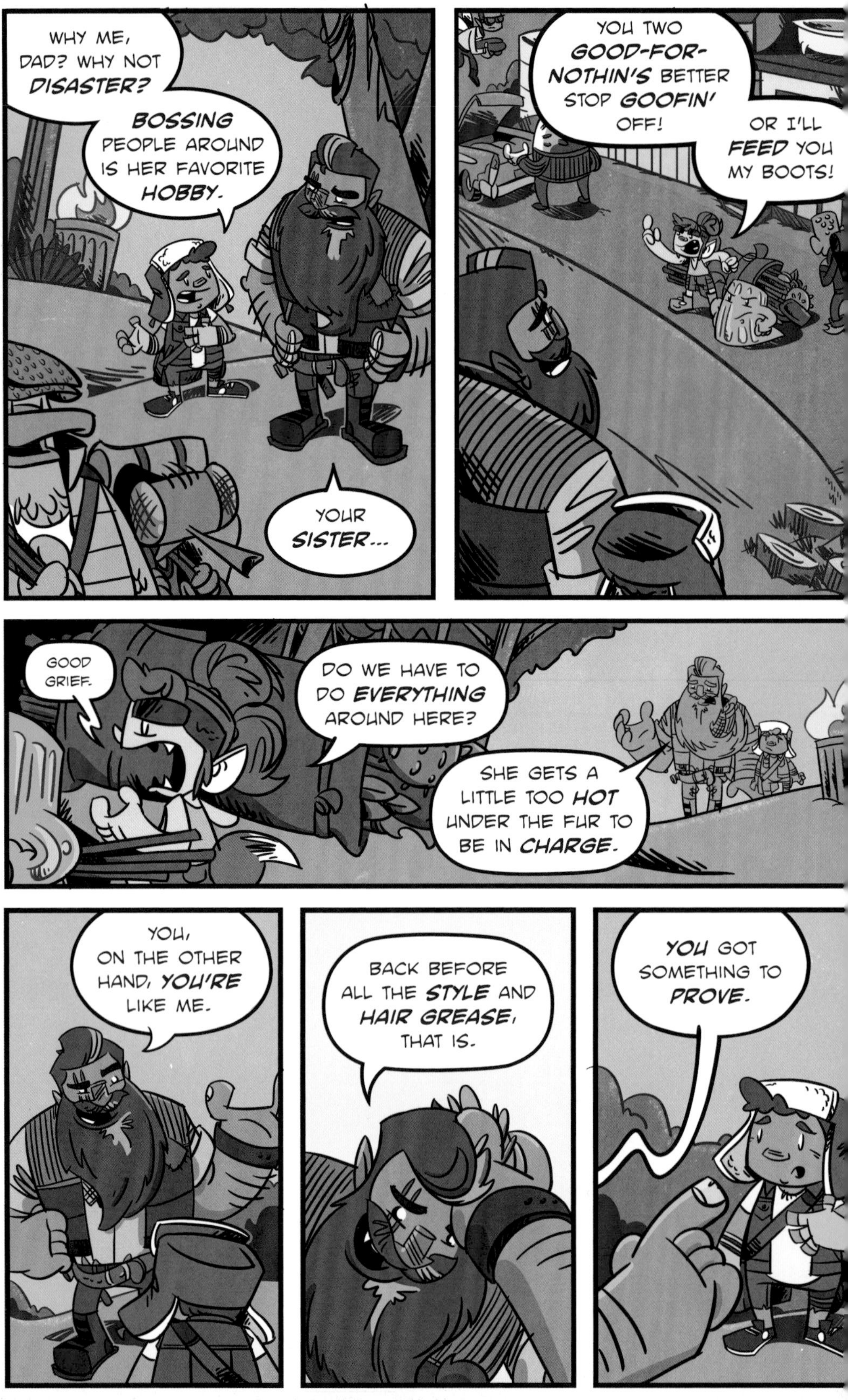
WHY ME, DAD? WHY NOT DISASTER?
BOSSING PEOPLE AROUND IS HER FAVORITE HOBBY.
YOUR SISTER...
YOU TWO GOOD-FOR-NOTHIN'S BETTER STOP GOOFIN' OFF!
OR I'LL FEED YOU MY BOOTS!
GOOD GRIEF.
DO WE HAVE TO DO EVERYTHING AROUND HERE?
SHE GETS A LITTLE TOO HOT UNDER THE FUR TO BE IN CHARGE.
YOU, ON THE OTHER HAND, YOU'RE LIKE ME.
BACK BEFORE ALL THE STYLE AND HAIR GREASE, THAT IS.
YOU GOT SOMETHING TO PROVE.

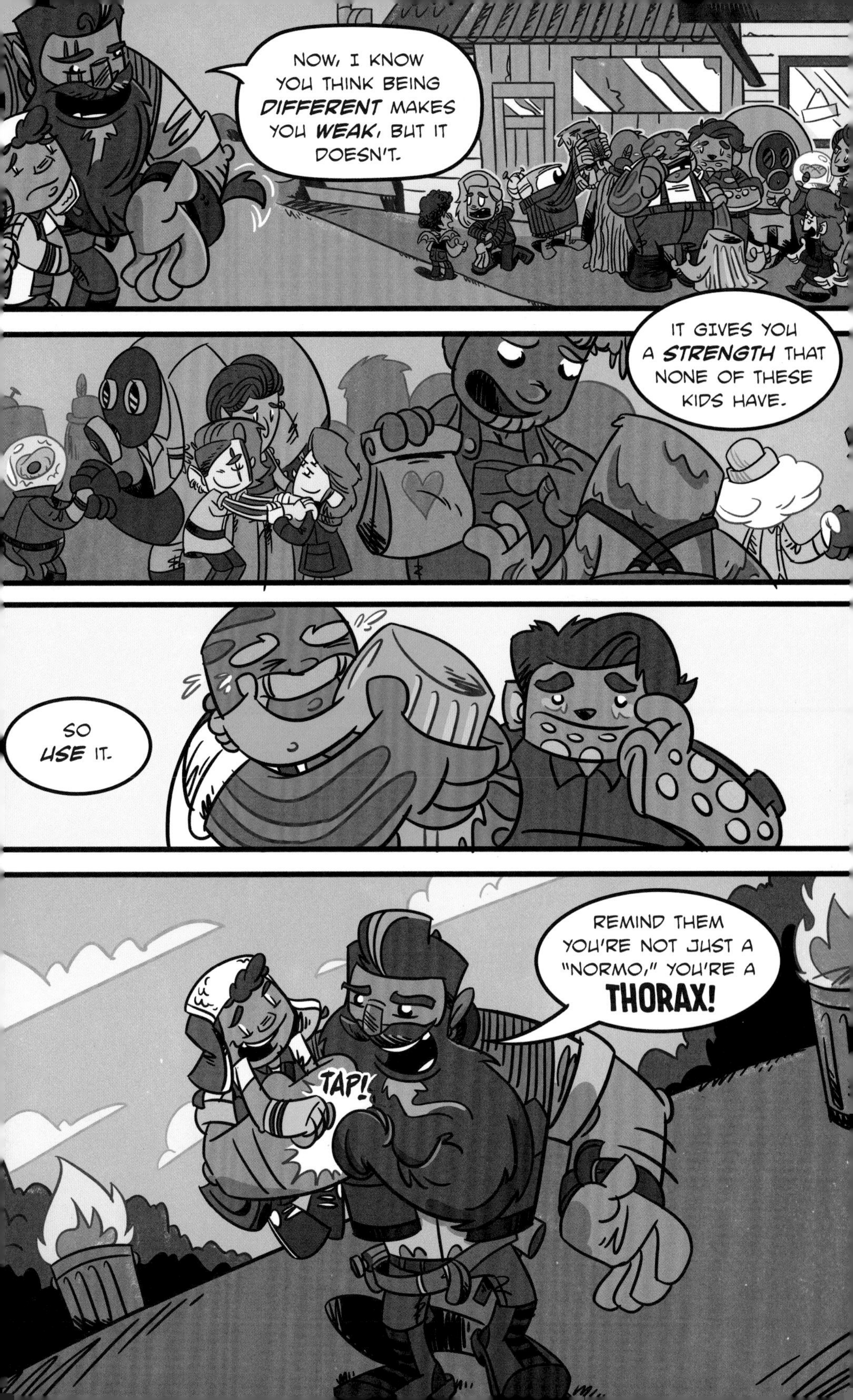
NOW, I KNOW YOU THINK BEING DIFFERENT MAKES YOU WEAK, BUT IT DOESN'T.
IT GIVES YOU A STRENGTH THAT NONE OF THESE KIDS HAVE.
SO USE IT.
REMIND THEM YOU'RE NOT JUST A "NORMO," YOU'RE A THORAX!
TAP!

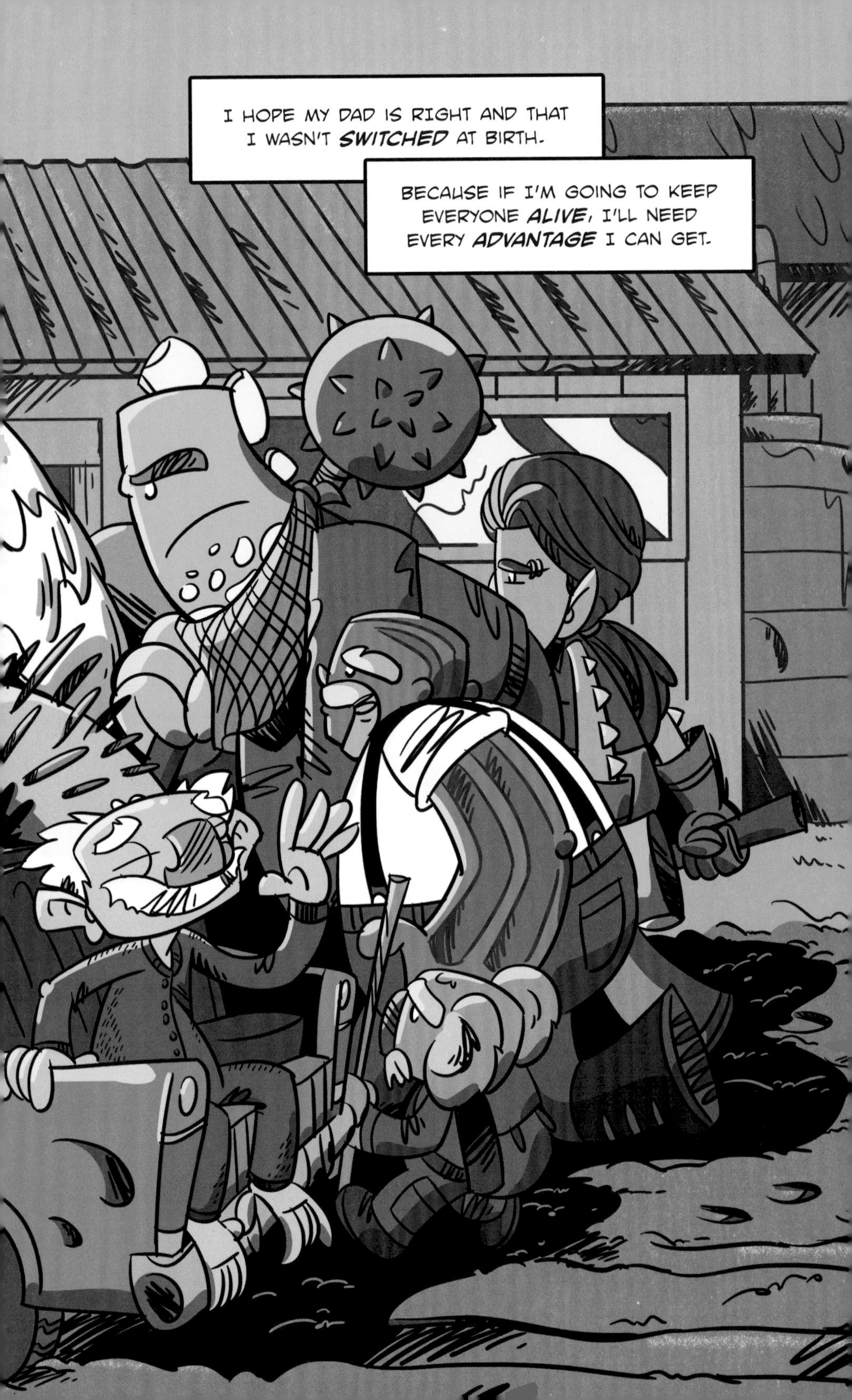
I HOPE MY DAD IS RIGHT AND THAT I WASN'T SWITCHED AT BIRTH.
BECAUSE IF I'M GOING TO KEEP EVERYONE ALIVE, I'LL NEED EVERY ADVANTAGE I CAN GET.

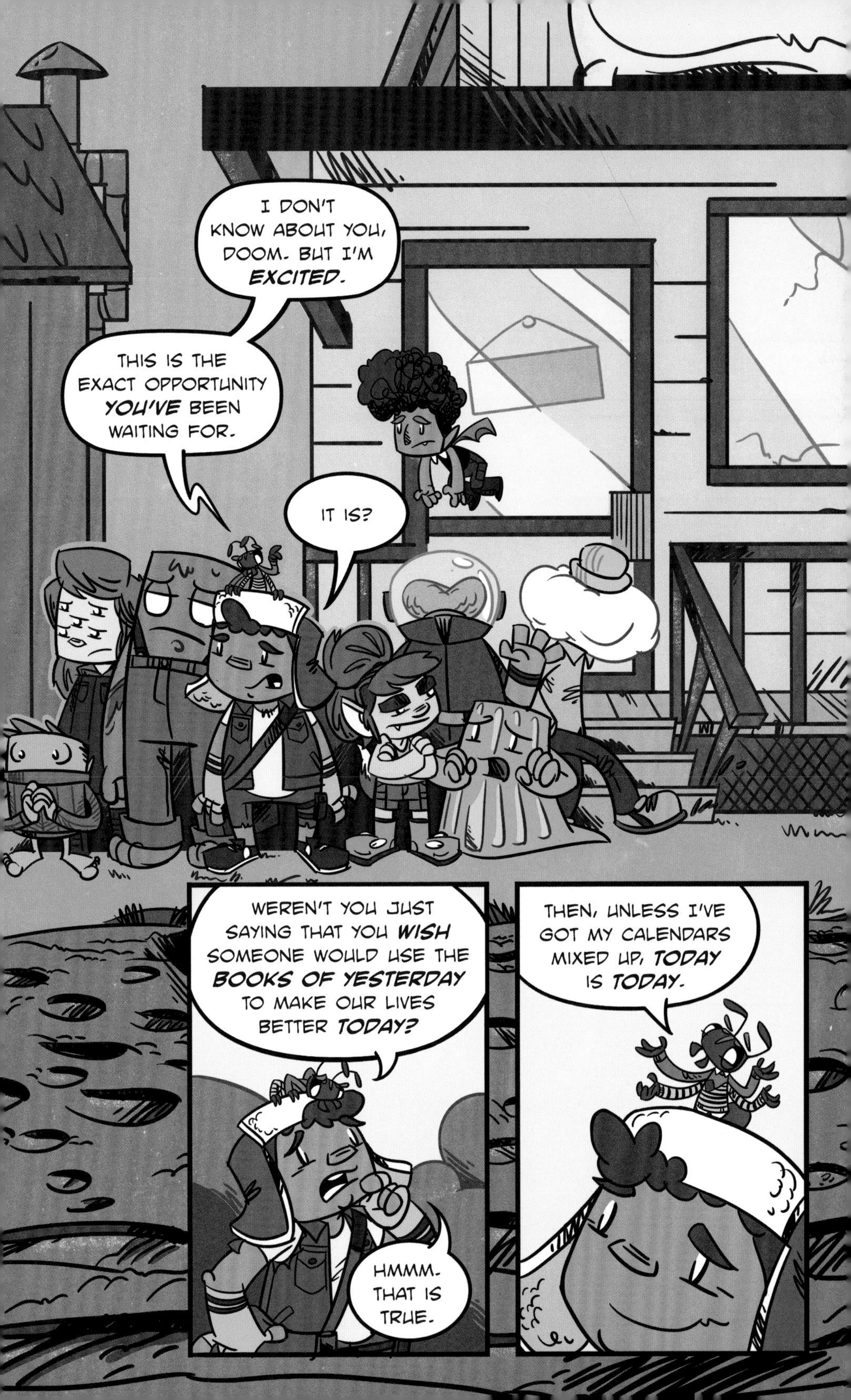
I DON'T KNOW ABOUT YOU, DOOM. BUT I'M *EXCITED*.
THIS IS THE EXACT OPPORTUNITY *YOU'VE* BEEN WAITING FOR.
IT IS?
WEREN'T YOU JUST SAYING THAT YOU *WISH* SOMEONE WOULD USE THE *BOOKS OF YESTERDAY* TO MAKE OUR LIVES BETTER *TODAY*?
HMMM. THAT IS TRUE.
THEN, UNLESS I'VE GOT MY CALENDARS MIXED UP, *TODAY* IS *TODAY*.

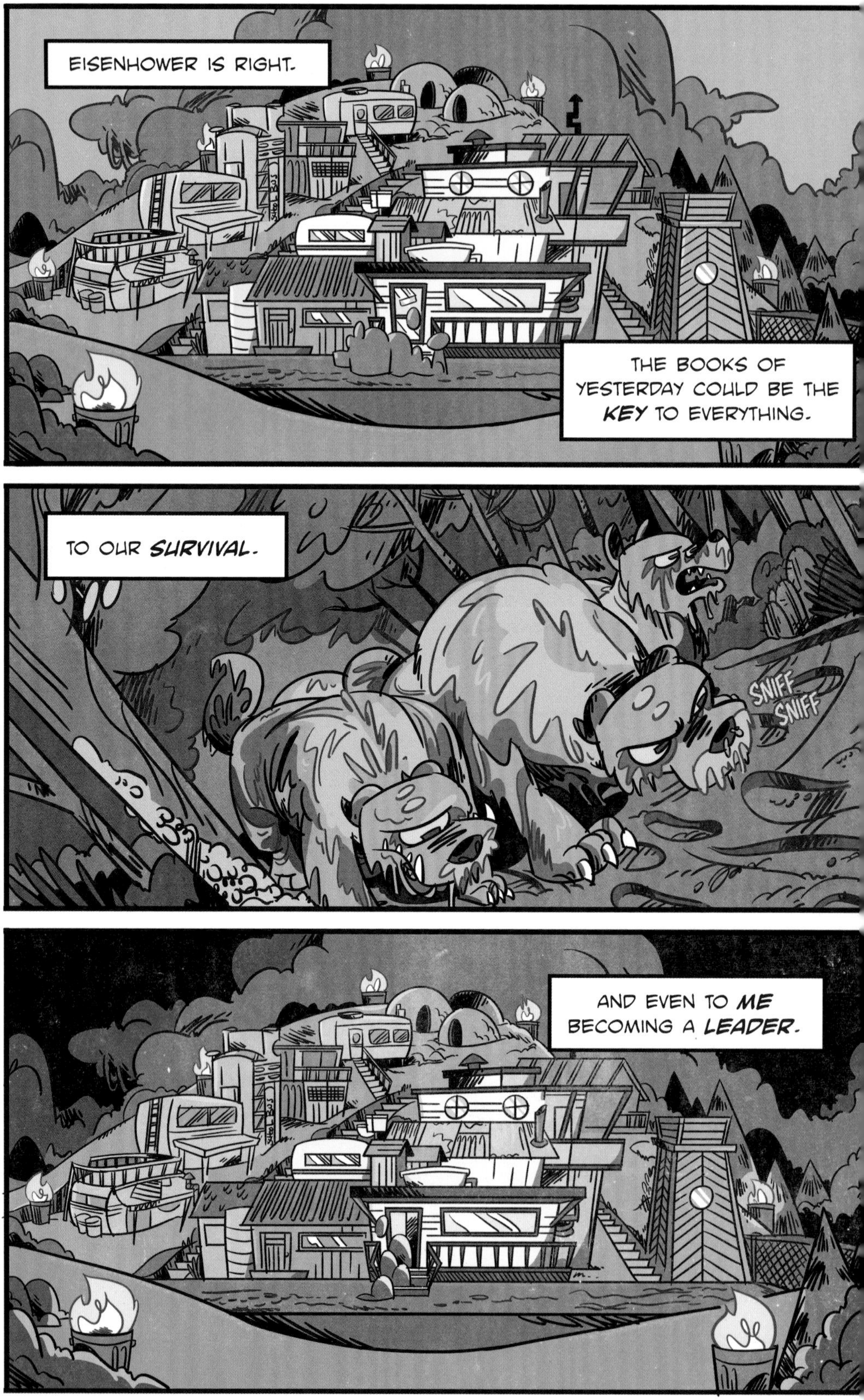
EISENHOWER IS RIGHT.
THE BOOKS OF YESTERDAY COULD BE THE *KEY* TO EVERYTHING.
TO OUR *SURVIVAL*.
SNIFF SNIFF
AND EVEN TO *ME* BECOMING A *LEADER*.

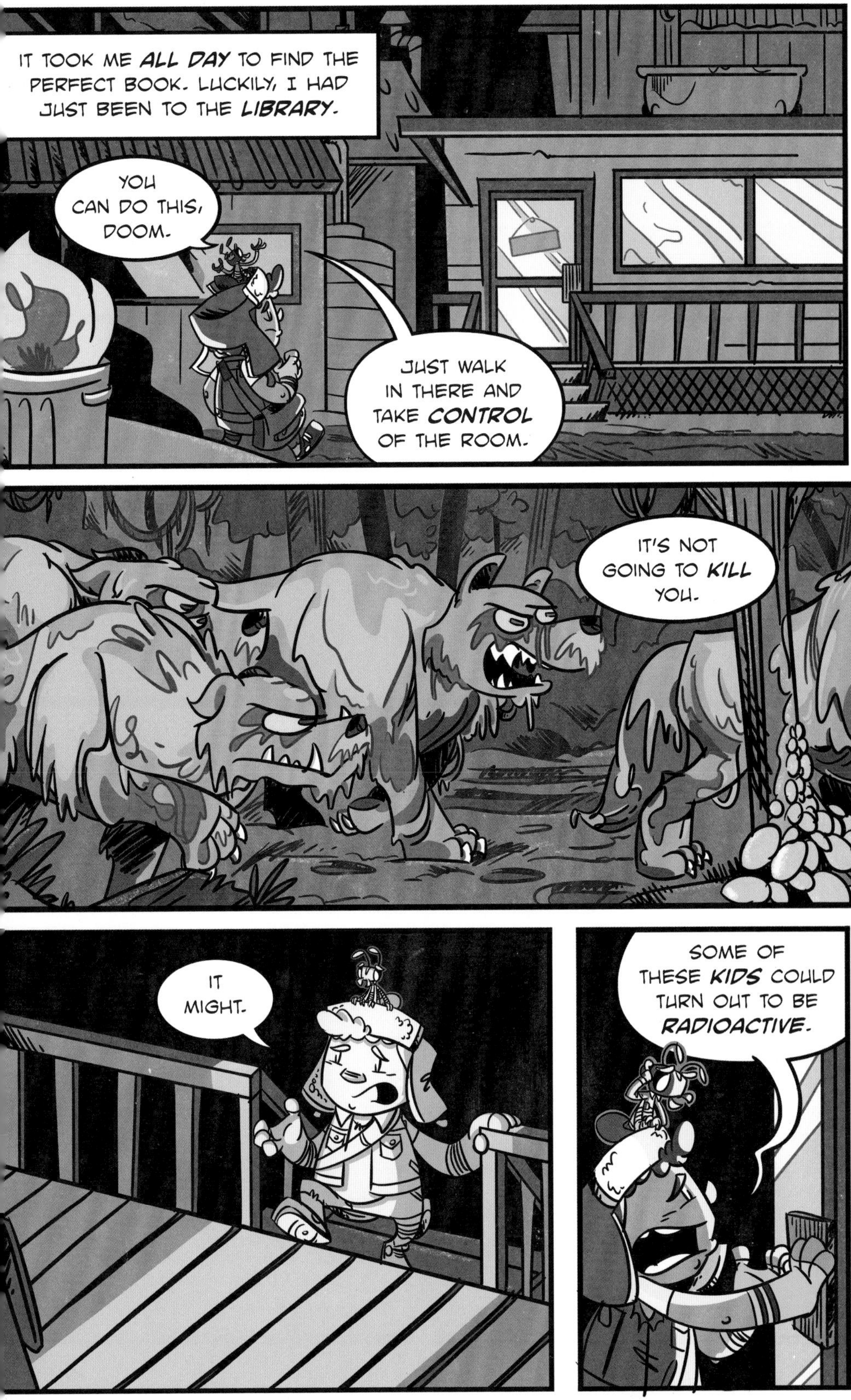

IT TOOK ME ALL DAY TO FIND THE PERFECT BOOK. LUCKILY, I HAD JUST BEEN TO THE LIBRARY.
YOU CAN DO THIS, DOOM.
JUST WALK IN THERE AND TAKE CONTROL OF THE ROOM.
IT'S NOT GOING TO KILL YOU.
IT MIGHT.
SOME OF THESE KIDS COULD TURN OUT TO BE RADIOACTIVE.

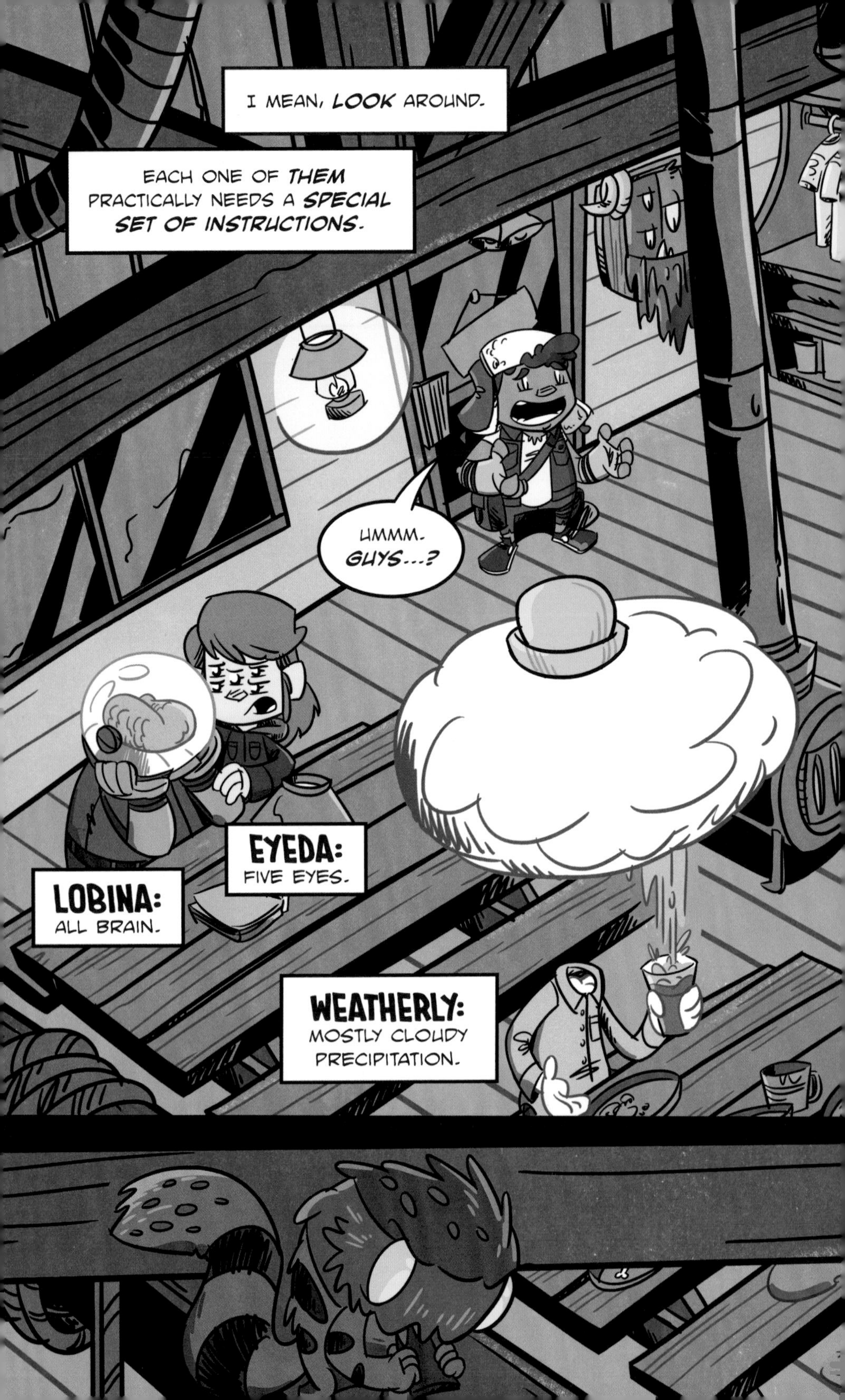
I MEAN, LOOK AROUND.
EACH ONE OF THEM PRACTICALLY NEEDS A SPECIAL SET OF INSTRUCTIONS.
UMMM. GUYS...?
EYEDA: FIVE EYES.
LOBINA: ALL BRAIN.
WEATHERLY: MOSTLY CLOUDY PRECIPITATION.

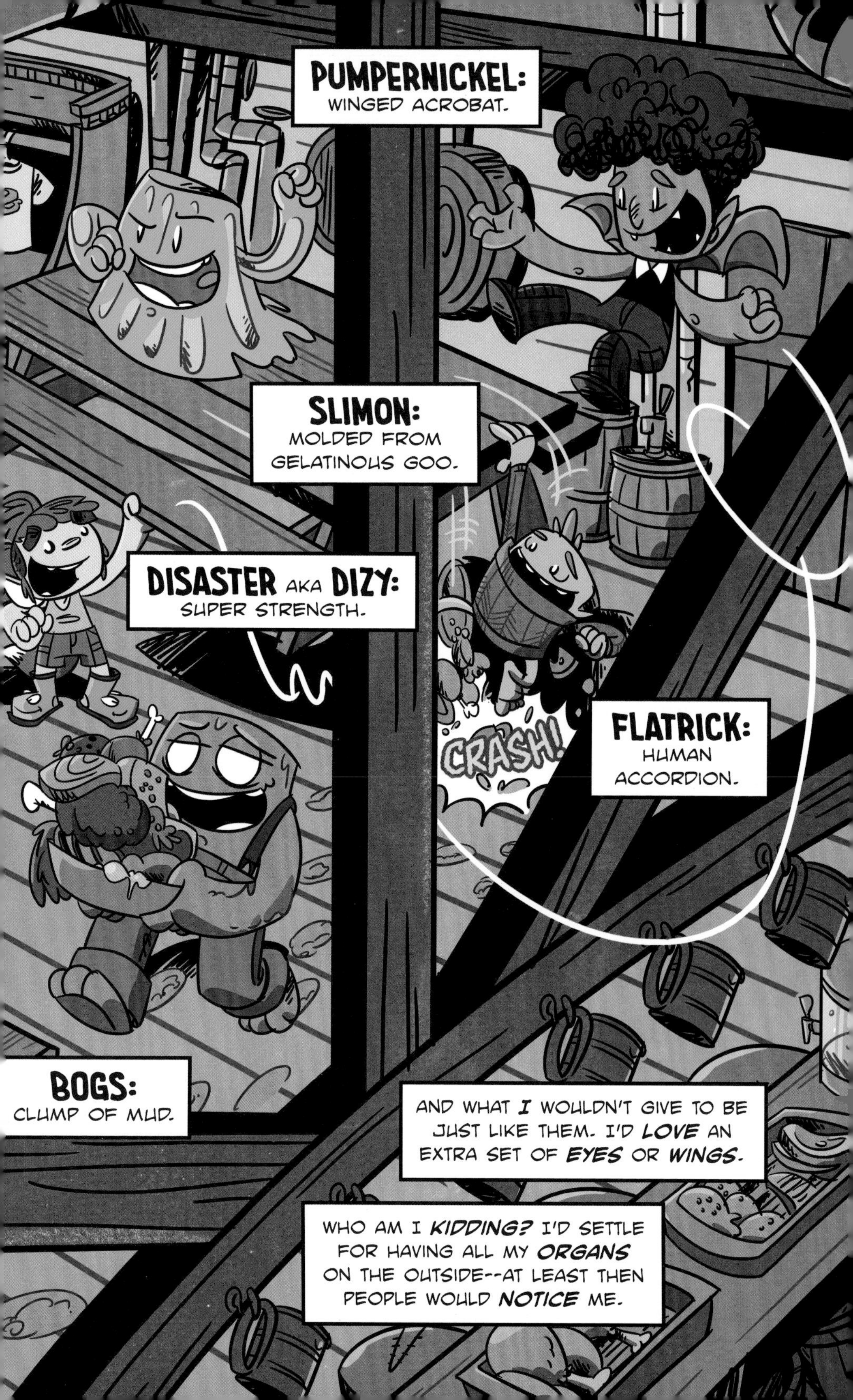
PUMPERNICKEL:
WINGED ACROBAT.
SLIMON:
MOLDED FROM GELATINOUS GOO.
DISASTER AKA DIZY:
SUPER STRENGTH.
CRASH!
FLATRICK:
HUMAN ACCORDION.
BOGS:
CLUMP OF MUD.
AND WHAT *I* WOULDN'T GIVE TO BE JUST LIKE THEM. I'D *LOVE* AN EXTRA SET OF *EYES* OR *WINGS*.
WHO AM I *KIDDING?* I'D SETTLE FOR HAVING ALL MY *ORGANS* ON THE OUTSIDE--AT LEAST THEN PEOPLE WOULD *NOTICE* ME.

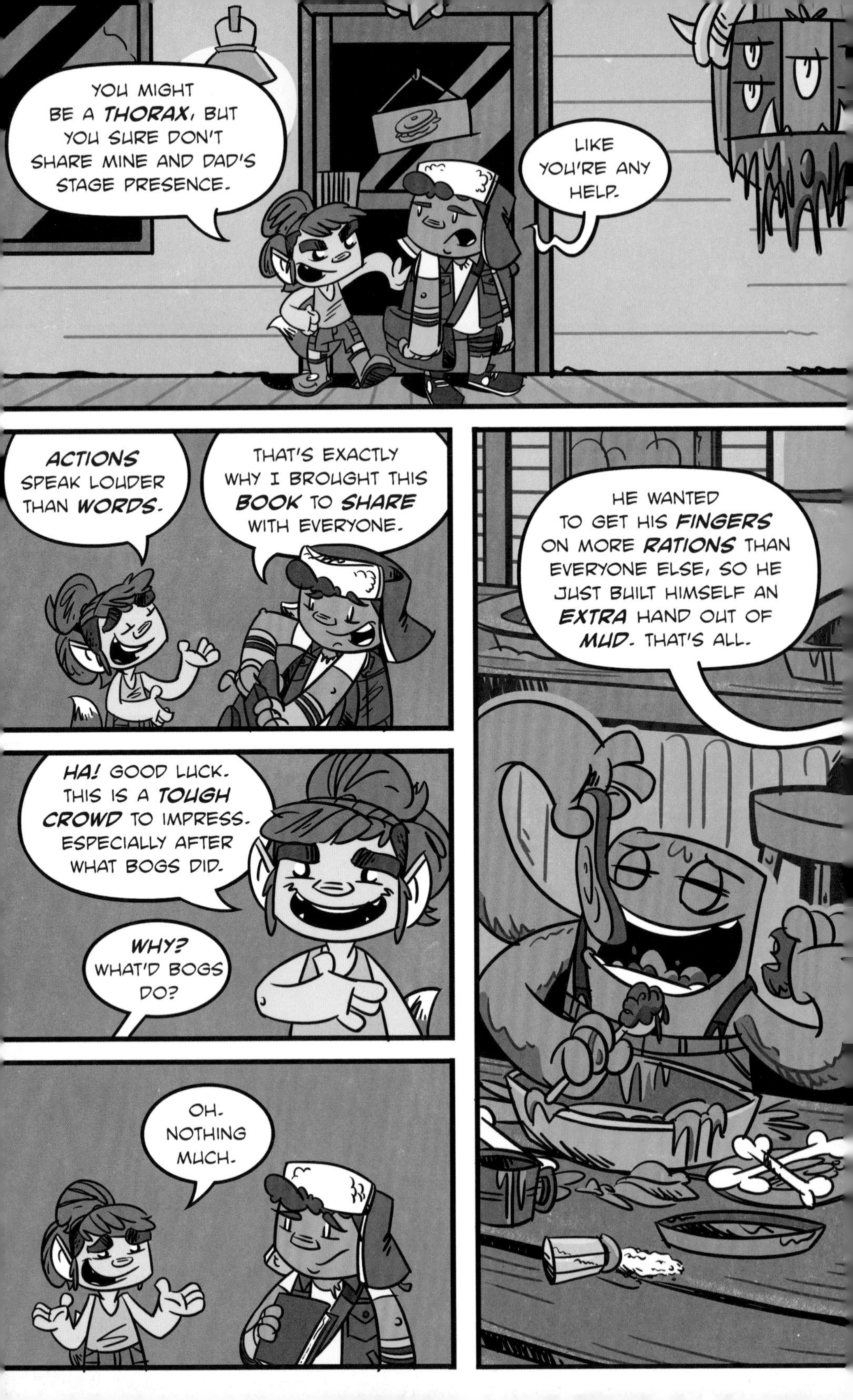
YOU MIGHT BE A THORAX, BUT YOU SURE DON'T SHARE MINE AND DAD'S STAGE PRESENCE.
LIKE YOU'RE ANY HELP.
ACTIONS SPEAK LOUDER THAN WORDS.
THAT'S EXACTLY WHY I BROUGHT THIS BOOK TO SHARE WITH EVERYONE.
HA! GOOD LUCK. THIS IS A TOUGH CROWD TO IMPRESS. ESPECIALLY AFTER WHAT BOGS DID.
WHY? WHAT'D BOGS DO?
OH. NOTHING MUCH.
HE WANTED TO GET HIS FINGERS ON MORE RATIONS THAN EVERYONE ELSE, SO HE JUST BUILT HIMSELF AN EXTRA HAND OUT OF MUD. THAT'S ALL.

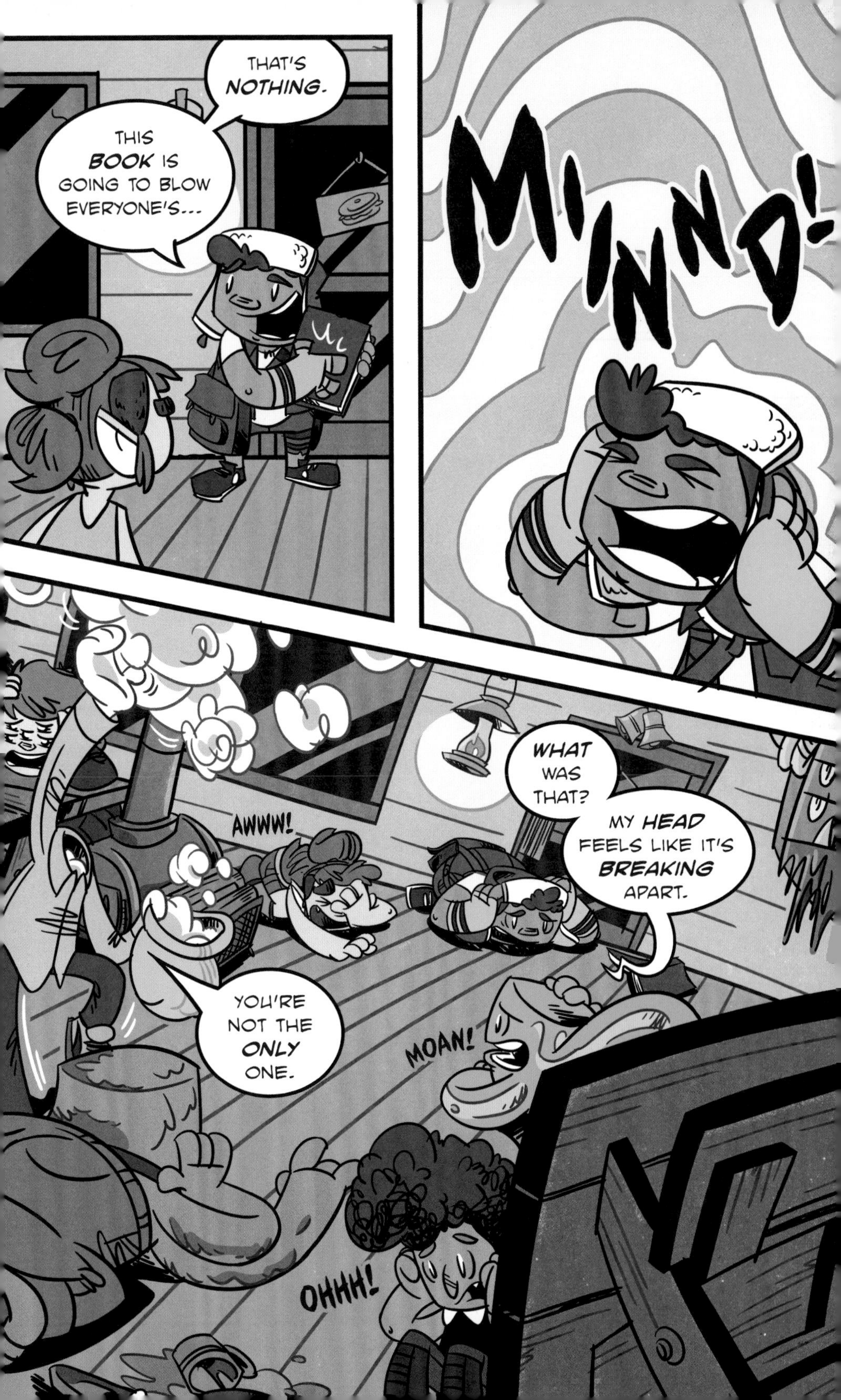

THIS BOOK IS GOING TO BLOW EVERYONE'S...
THAT'S NOTHING.
MIINND!
WHAT WAS THAT?
MY HEAD FEELS LIKE IT'S BREAKING APART.
AWWW!
YOU'RE NOT THE ONLY ONE.
MOAN!
OHHH!

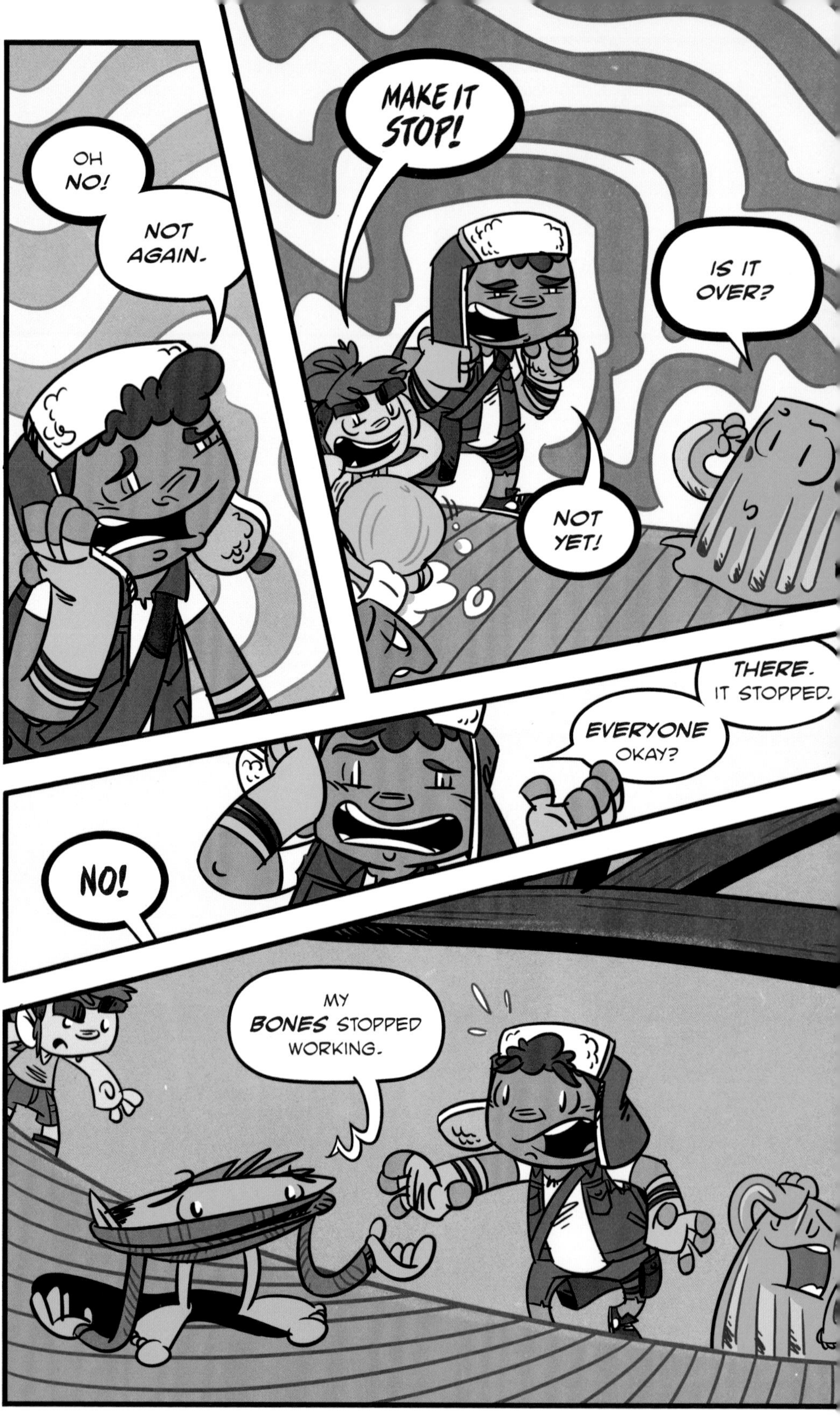

OH NO!
NOT AGAIN.
MAKE IT STOP!
IS IT OVER?
NOT YET!
THERE. IT STOPPED.
EVERYONE OKAY?
NO!
MY BONES STOPPED WORKING.

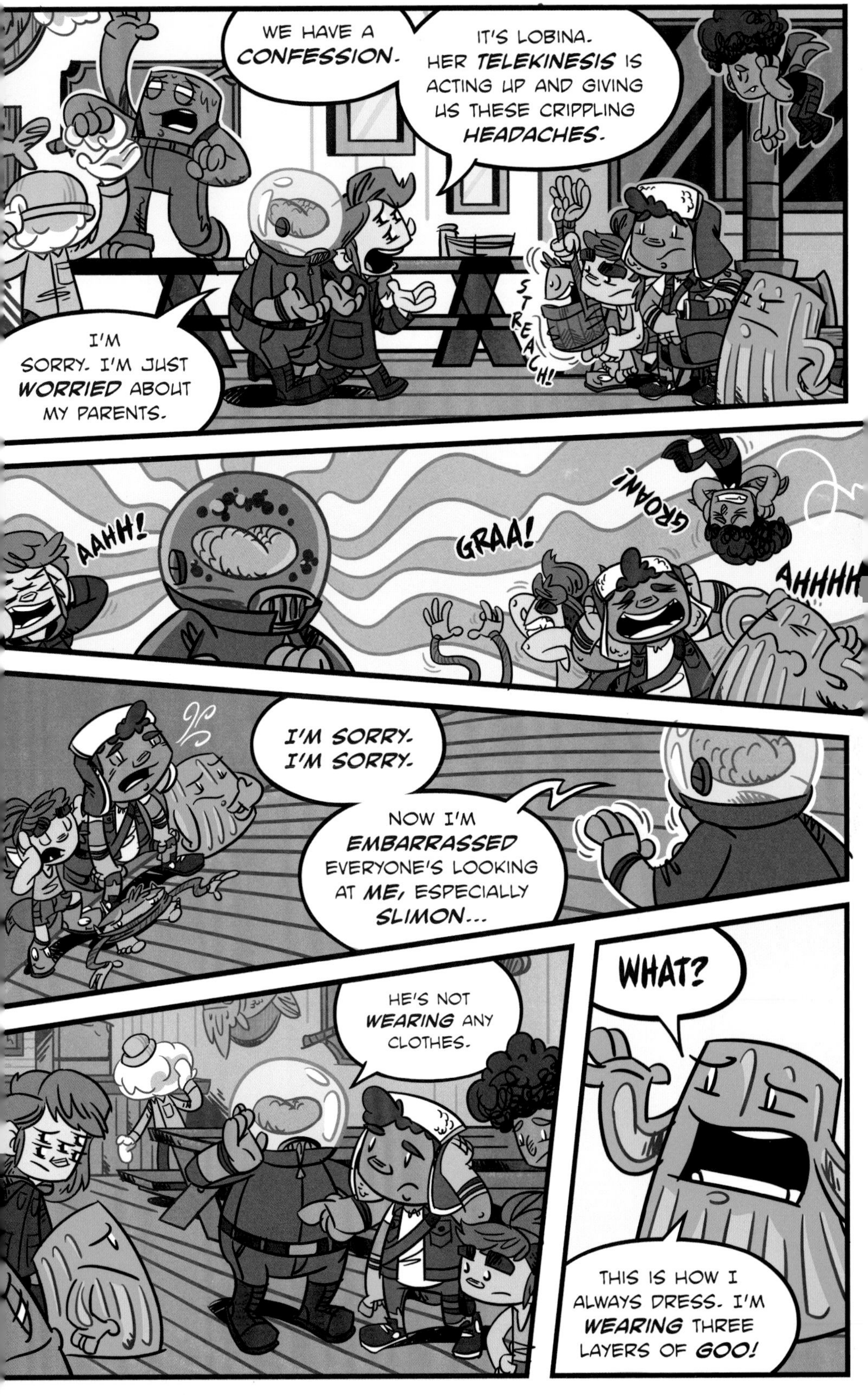
WE HAVE A CONFESSION.
IT'S LOBINA. HER TELEKINESIS IS ACTING UP AND GIVING US THESE CRIPPLING HEADACHES.
STREACH!
I'M SORRY. I'M JUST WORRIED ABOUT MY PARENTS.
AAHH!
GRAA!
GROAN!
AHHHH
I'M SORRY. I'M SORRY.
NOW I'M EMBARRASSED EVERYONE'S LOOKING AT ME, ESPECIALLY SLIMON...
HE'S NOT WEARING ANY CLOTHES.
WHAT?
THIS IS HOW I ALWAYS DRESS. I'M WEARING THREE LAYERS OF GOO!

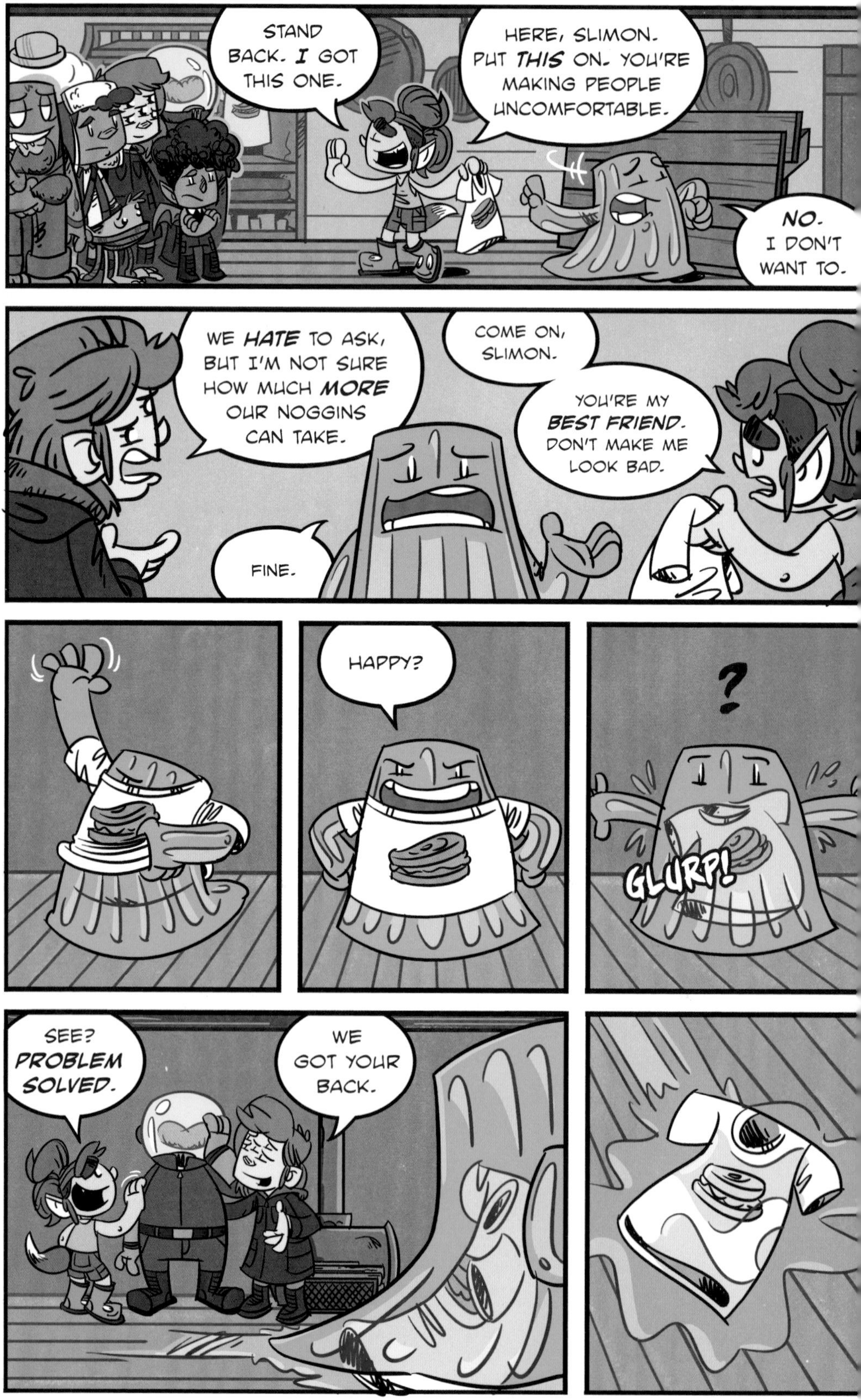
STAND BACK. I GOT THIS ONE.
HERE, SLIMON. PUT THIS ON. YOU'RE MAKING PEOPLE UNCOMFORTABLE.
NO. I DON'T WANT TO.
WE HATE TO ASK, BUT I'M NOT SURE HOW MUCH MORE OUR NOGGINS CAN TAKE.
COME ON, SLIMON.
YOU'RE MY BEST FRIEND. DON'T MAKE ME LOOK BAD.
FINE.
HAPPY?
?
GLURP!
SEE? PROBLEM SOLVED.
WE GOT YOUR BACK.

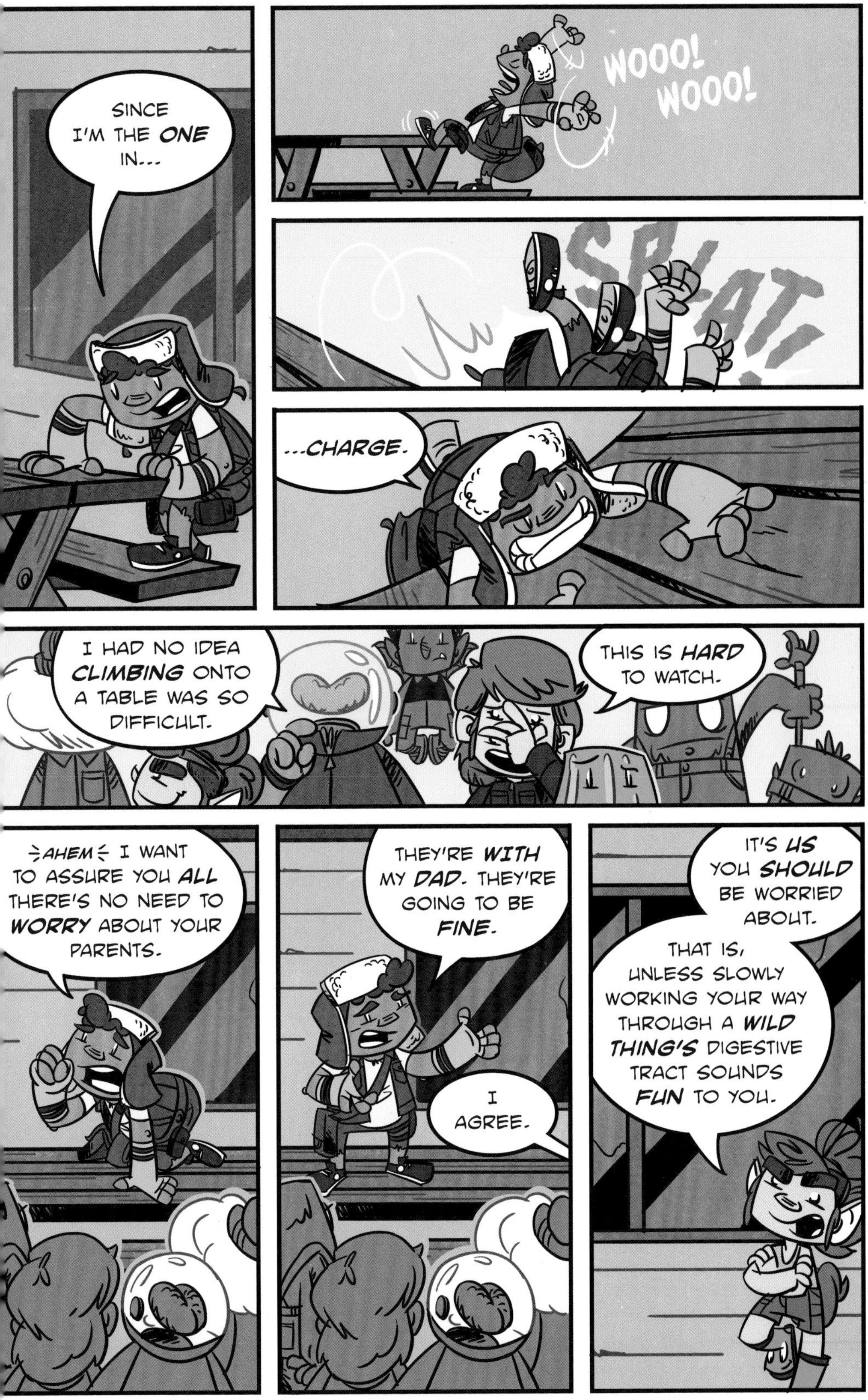
SINCE I'M THE ONE IN...
WOOO! WOOO!
SPLAT!
...CHARGE.
I HAD NO IDEA CLIMBING ONTO A TABLE WAS SO DIFFICULT.
THIS IS HARD TO WATCH.
AHEM I WANT TO ASSURE YOU ALL THERE'S NO NEED TO WORRY ABOUT YOUR PARENTS.
THEY'RE WITH MY DAD. THEY'RE GOING TO BE FINE.
I AGREE.
IT'S US YOU SHOULD BE WORRIED ABOUT.
THAT IS, UNLESS SLOWLY WORKING YOUR WAY THROUGH A WILD THING'S DIGESTIVE TRACT SOUNDS FUN TO YOU.

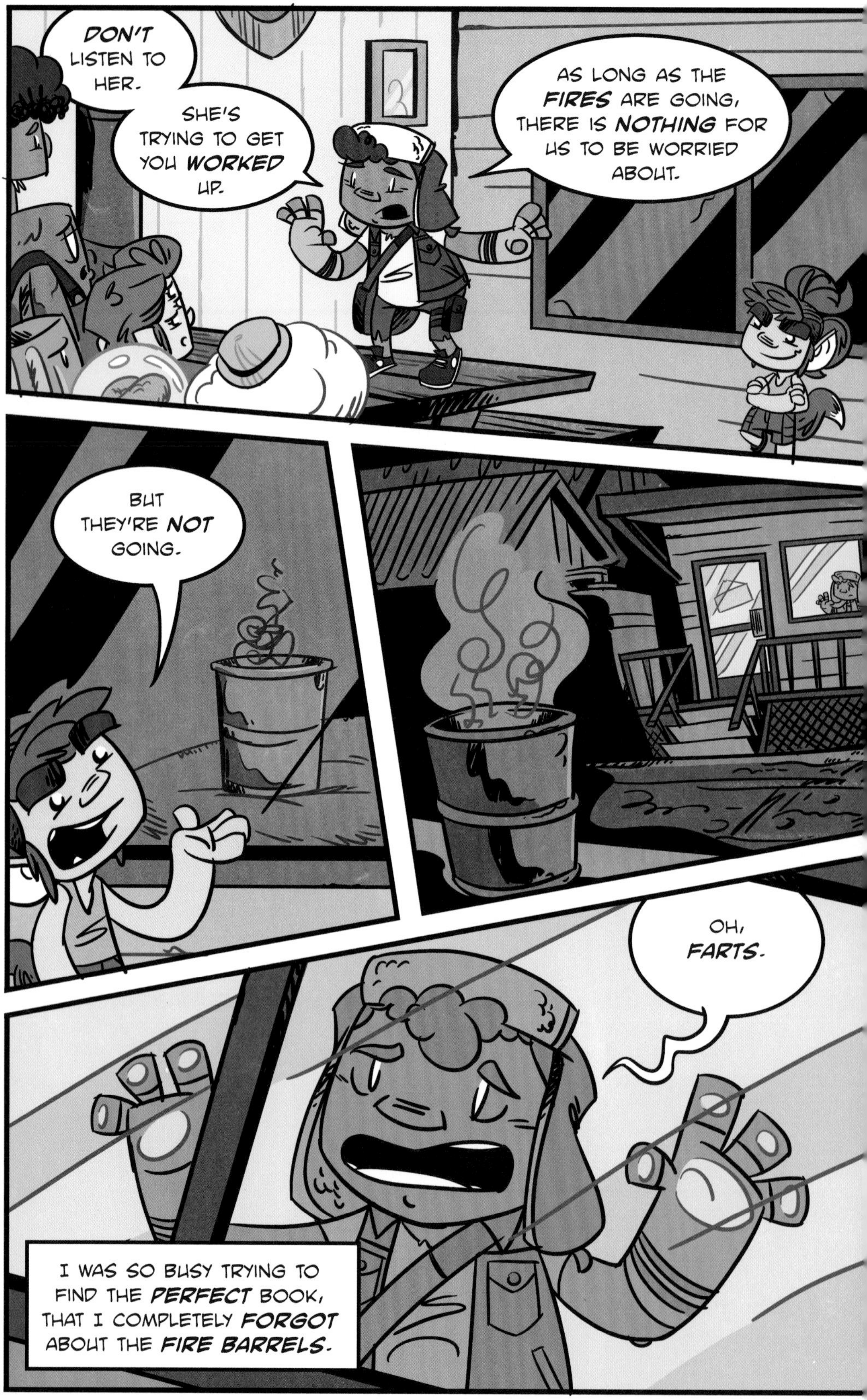
DON'T LISTEN TO HER.
SHE'S TRYING TO GET YOU WORKED UP.
AS LONG AS THE FIRES ARE GOING, THERE IS NOTHING FOR US TO BE WORRIED ABOUT.
BUT THEY'RE NOT GOING.
OH, FARTS.
I WAS SO BUSY TRYING TO FIND THE PERFECT BOOK, THAT I COMPLETELY FORGOT ABOUT THE FIRE BARRELS.

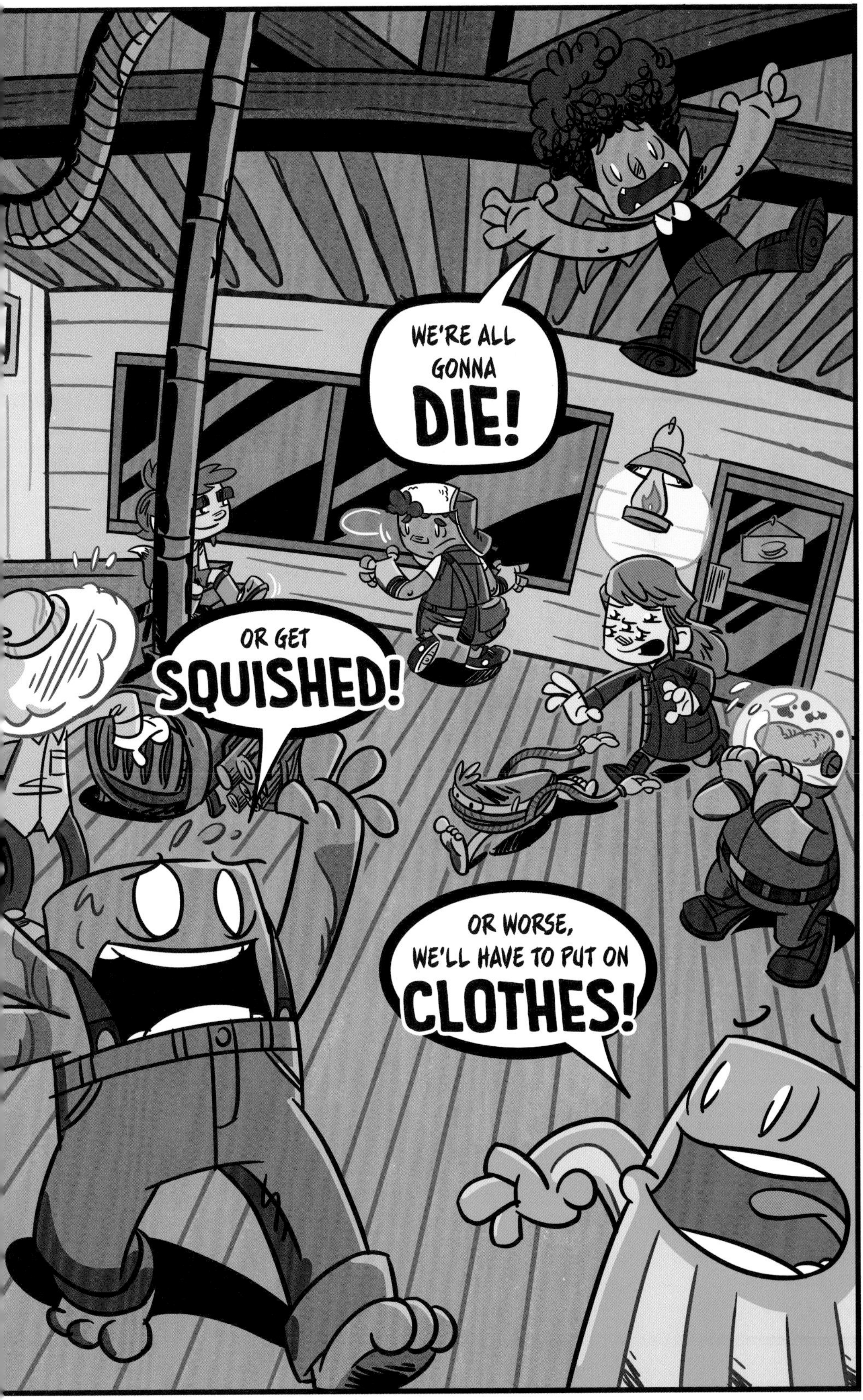
WE'RE ALL GONNA DIE!
OR GET SQUISHED!
OR WORSE, WE'LL HAVE TO PUT ON CLOTHES!

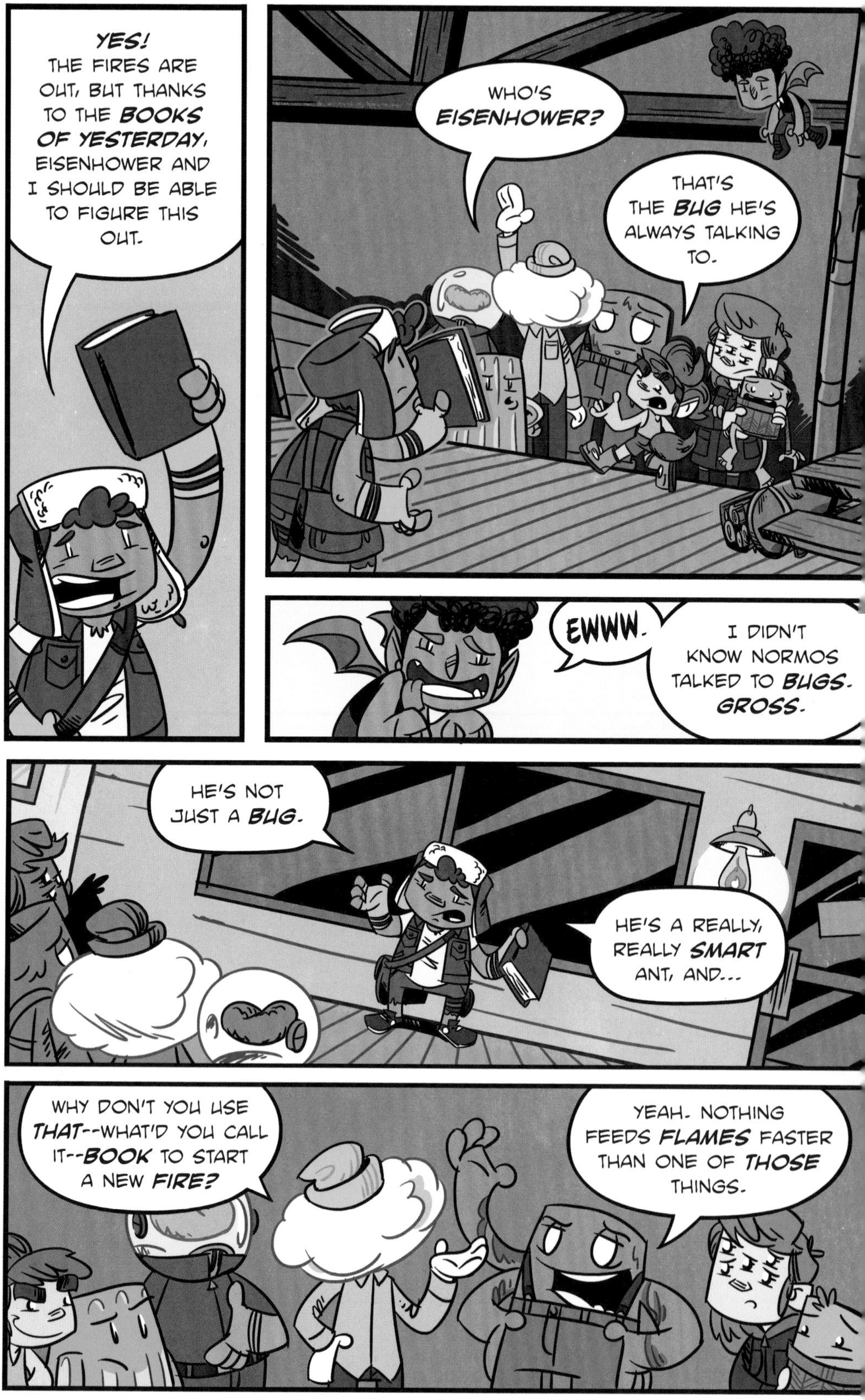
YES! THE FIRES ARE OUT, BUT THANKS TO THE BOOKS OF YESTERDAY, EISENHOWER AND I SHOULD BE ABLE TO FIGURE THIS OUT.
WHO'S EISENHOWER?
THAT'S THE BUG HE'S ALWAYS TALKING TO.
EWWW.
I DIDN'T KNOW NORMOS TALKED TO BUGS. GROSS.
HE'S NOT JUST A BUG.
HE'S A REALLY, REALLY SMART ANT, AND...
WHY DON'T YOU USE THAT--WHAT'D YOU CALL IT--BOOK TO START A NEW FIRE?
YEAH. NOTHING FEEDS FLAMES FASTER THAN ONE OF THOSE THINGS.

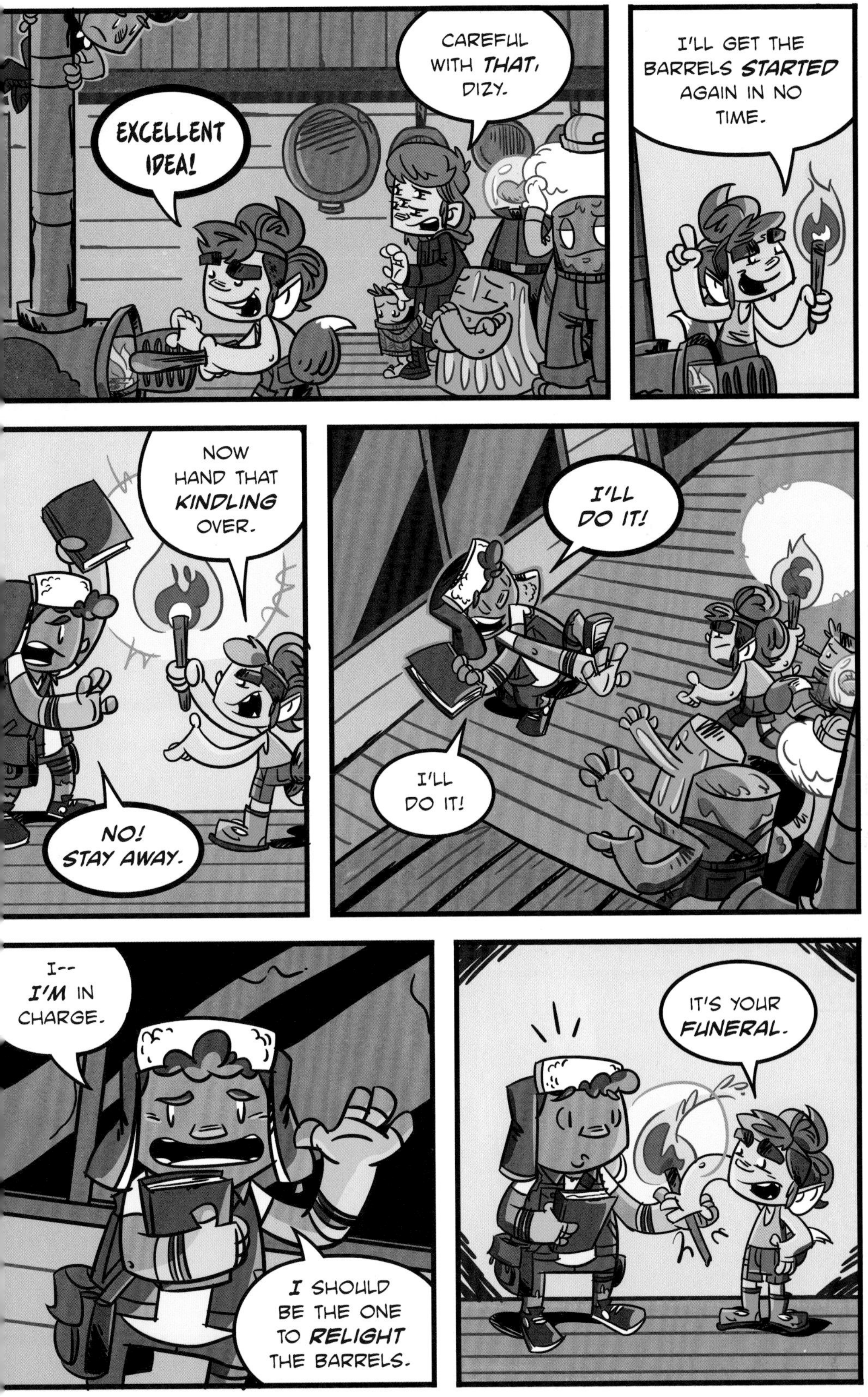
EXCELLENT IDEA!
CAREFUL WITH THAT, DIZY.
I'LL GET THE BARRELS STARTED AGAIN IN NO TIME.
NOW HAND THAT KINDLING OVER.
NO! STAY AWAY.
I'LL DO IT!
I'LL DO IT!
I-- I'M IN CHARGE.
I SHOULD BE THE ONE TO RELIGHT THE BARRELS.
IT'S YOUR FUNERAL.

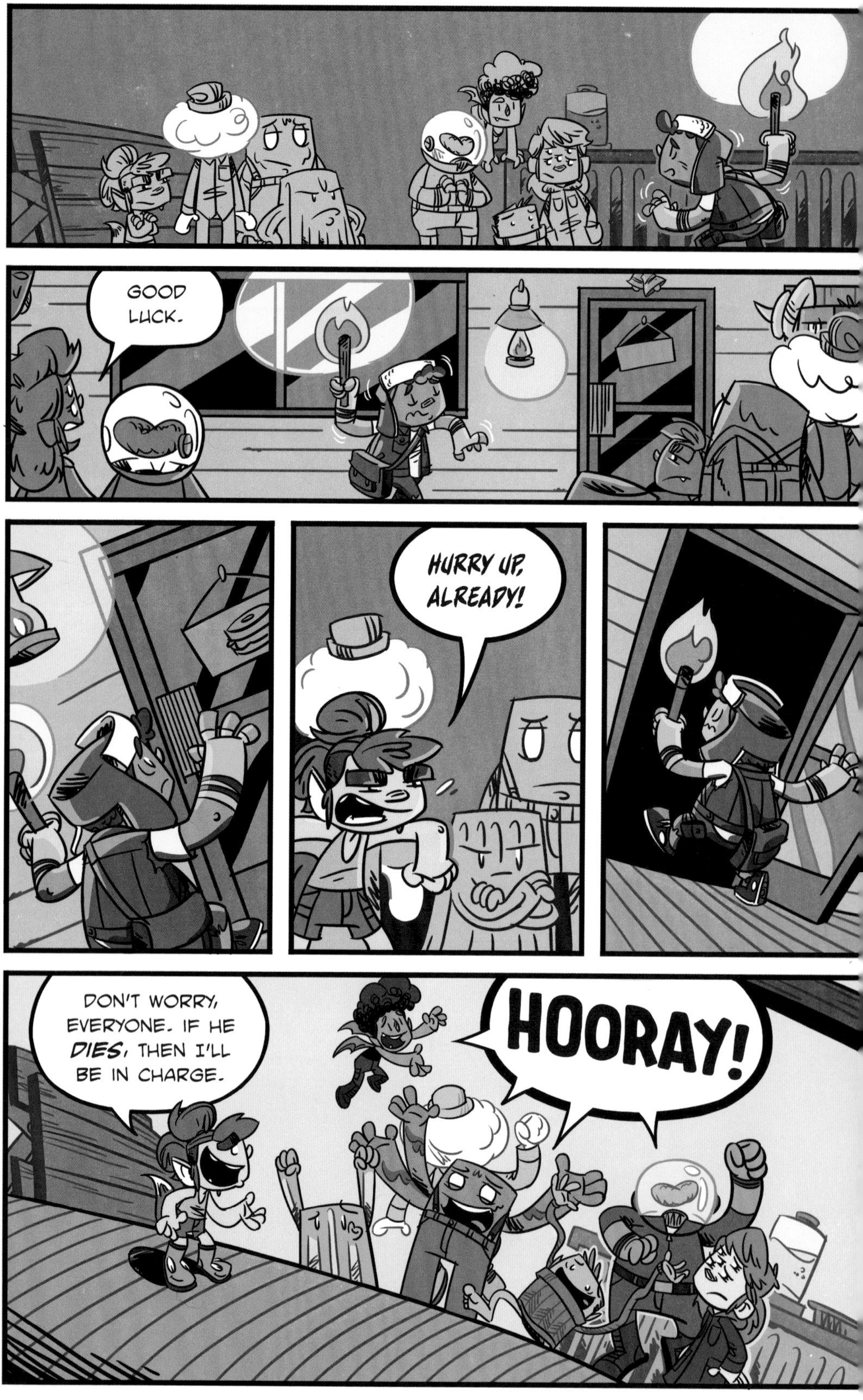
GOOD LUCK.
HURRY UP, ALREADY!
DON'T WORRY, EVERYONE. IF HE DIES, THEN I'LL BE IN CHARGE.
HOORAY!

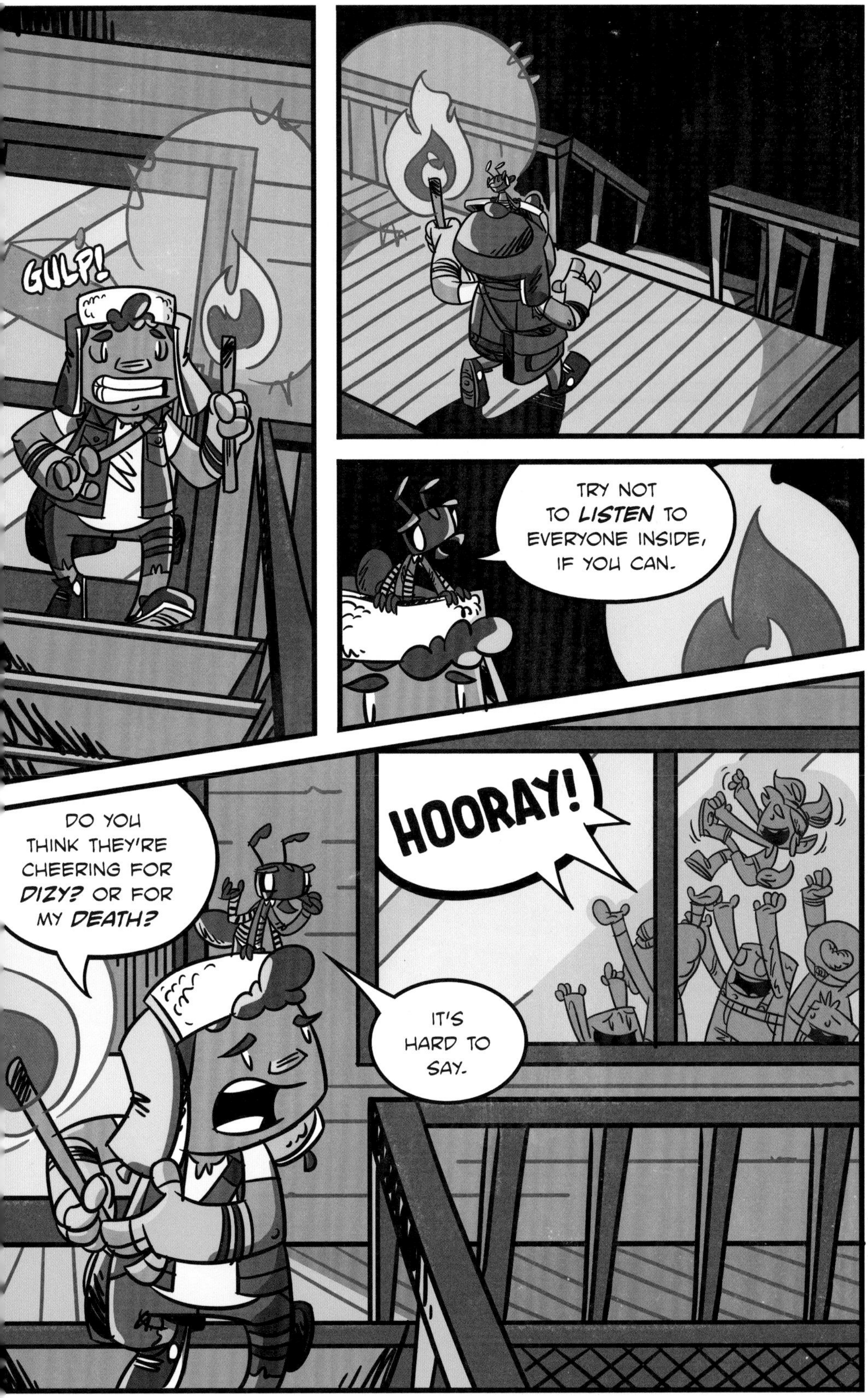
GULP!
TRY NOT TO LISTEN TO EVERYONE INSIDE, IF YOU CAN.
DO YOU THINK THEY'RE CHEERING FOR DIZY? OR FOR MY DEATH?
HOORAY!
IT'S HARD TO SAY.

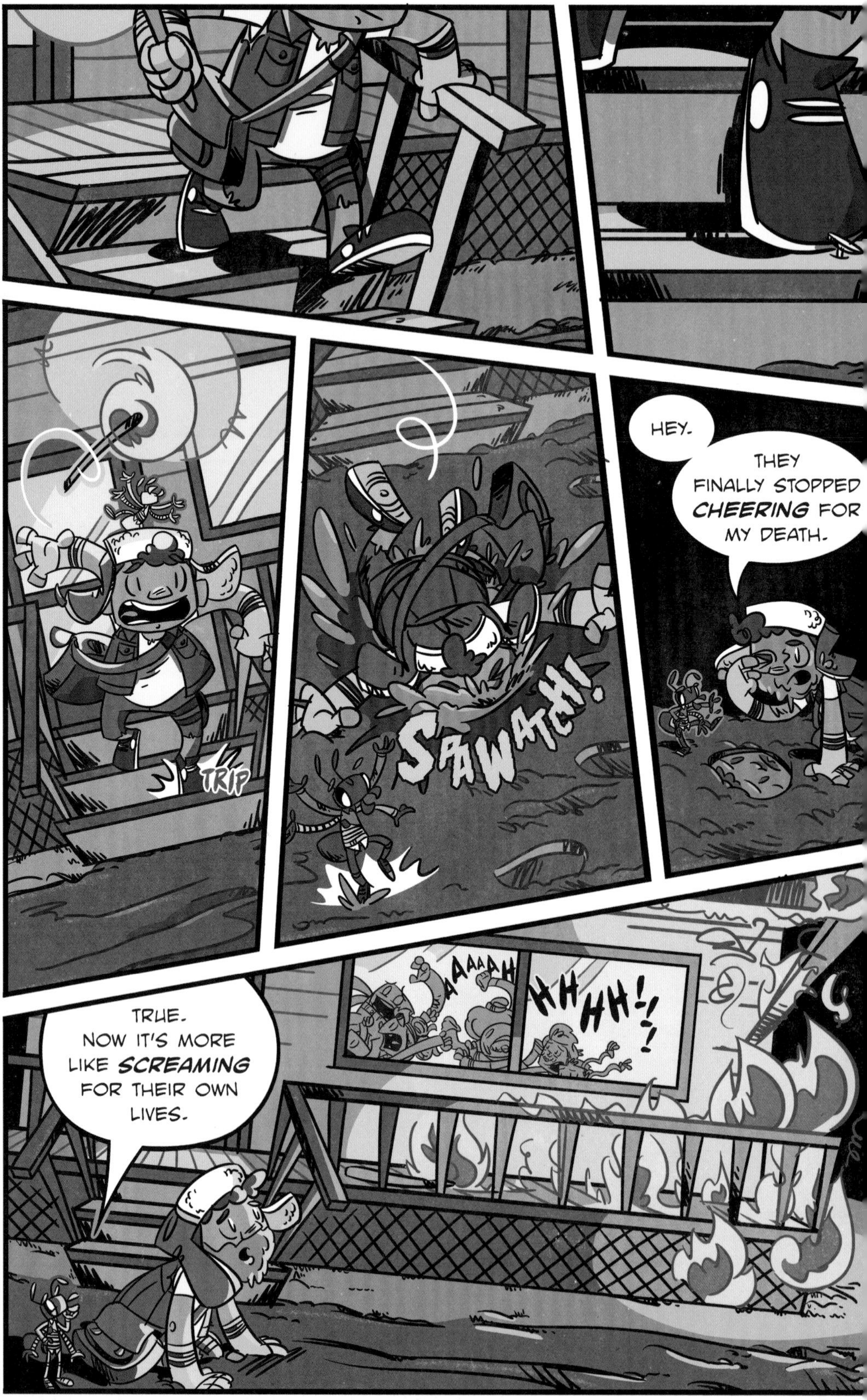
TRIP
SPAWATCH!
HEY.
THEY FINALLY STOPPED CHEERING FOR MY DEATH.
TRUE. NOW IT'S MORE LIKE SCREAMING FOR THEIR OWN LIVES.
AAAAAHHHHH!!!

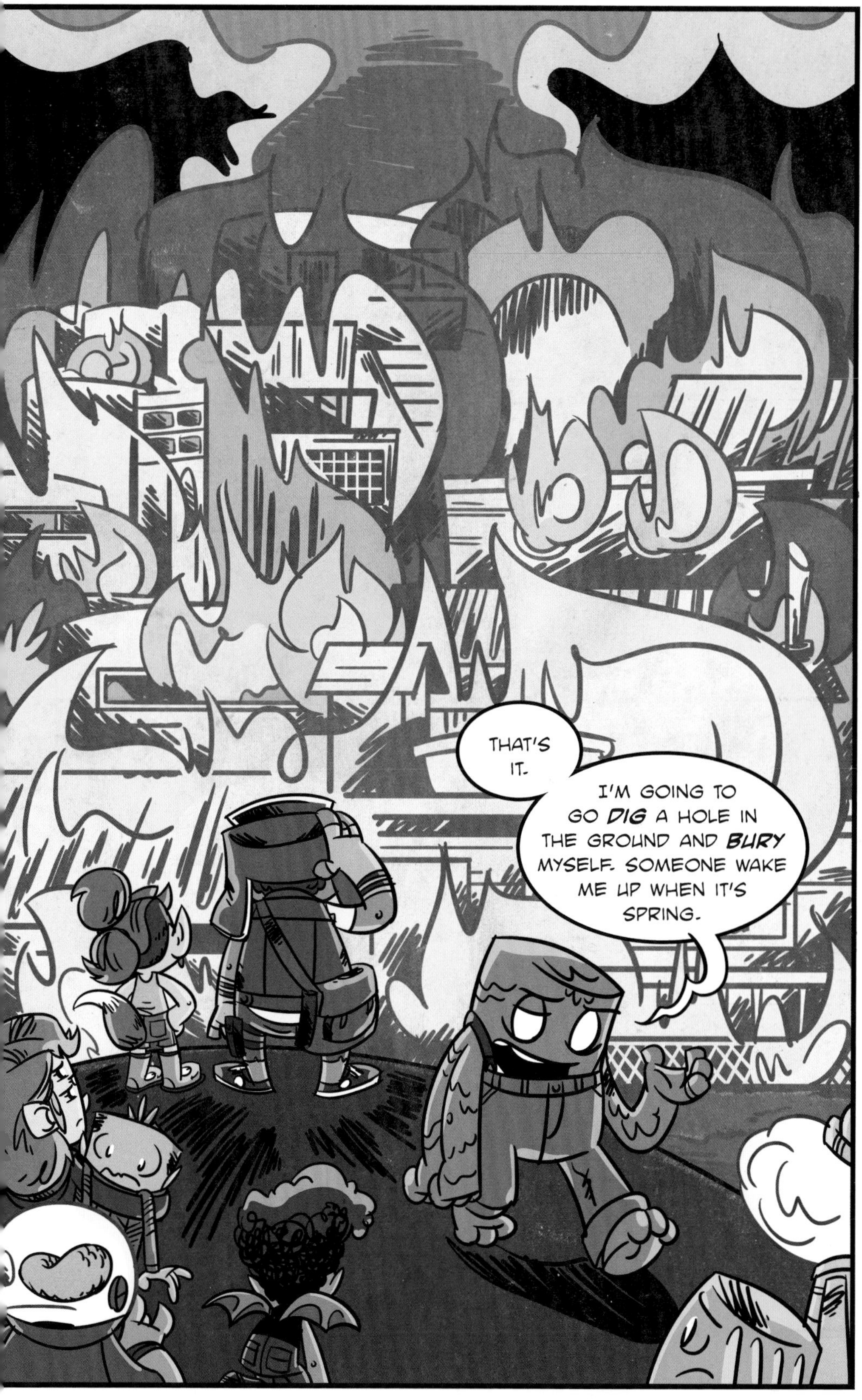
THAT'S IT.
I'M GOING TO GO DIG A HOLE IN THE GROUND AND BURY MYSELF. SOMEONE WAKE ME UP WHEN IT'S SPRING.

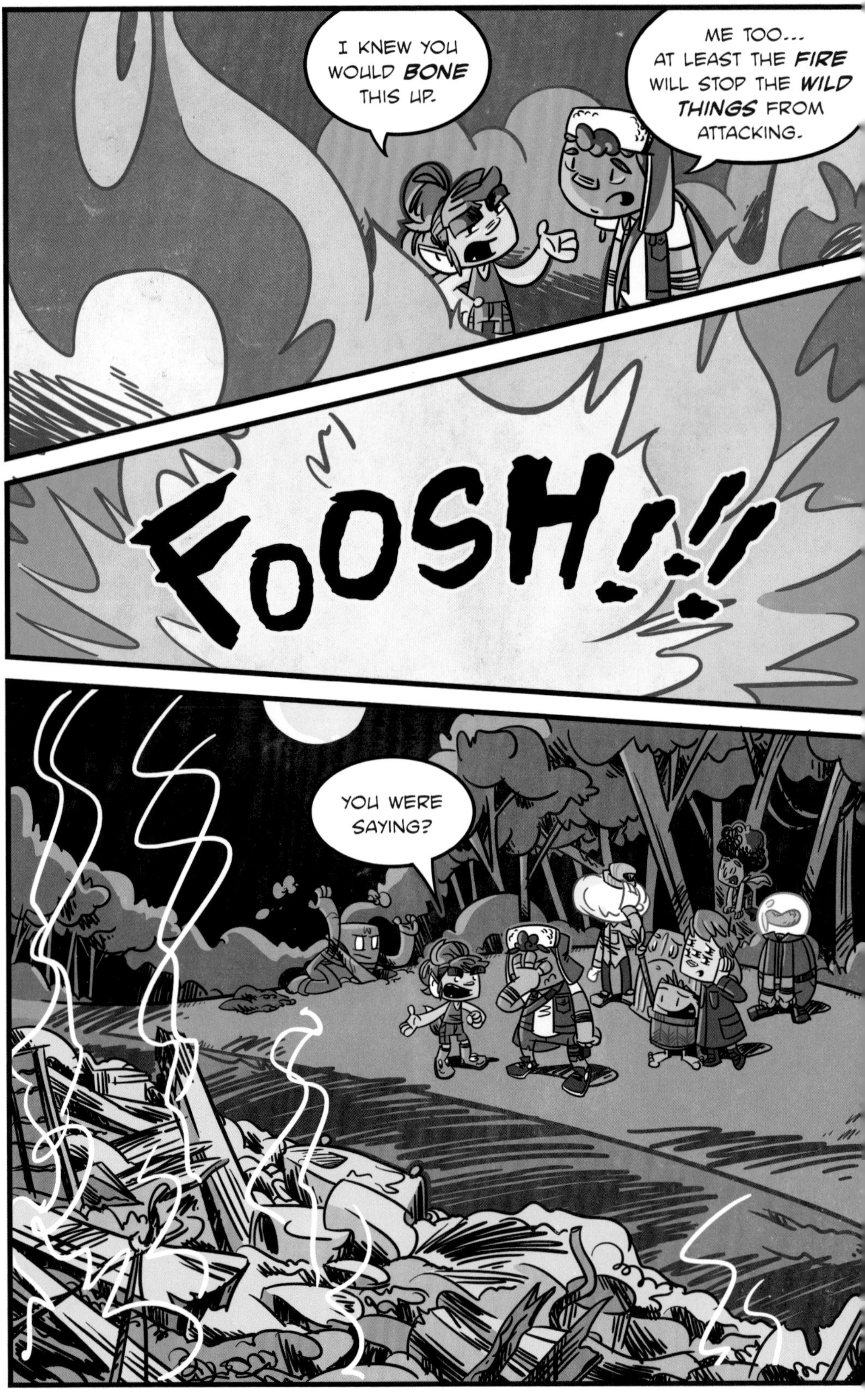
I KNEW YOU WOULD **BONE** THIS UP.
ME TOO... AT LEAST THE **FIRE** WILL STOP THE **WILD THINGS** FROM ATTACKING.
FOOSH!!!
YOU WERE SAYING?

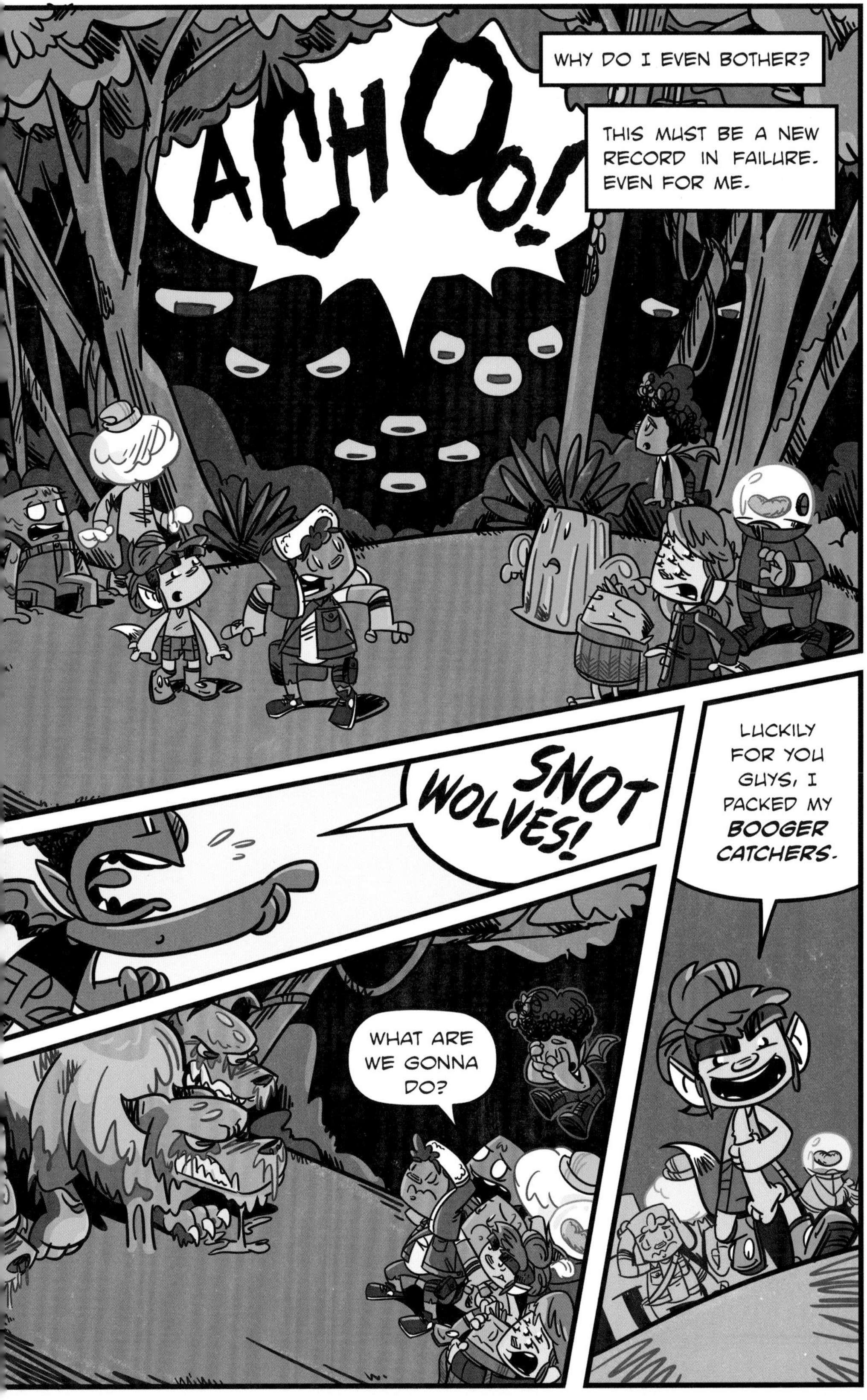

ACHOO!
WHY DO I EVEN BOTHER?
THIS MUST BE A NEW RECORD IN FAILURE. EVEN FOR ME.
SNOT WOLVES!
WHAT ARE WE GONNA DO?
LUCKILY FOR YOU GUYS, I PACKED MY BOOGER CATCHERS.

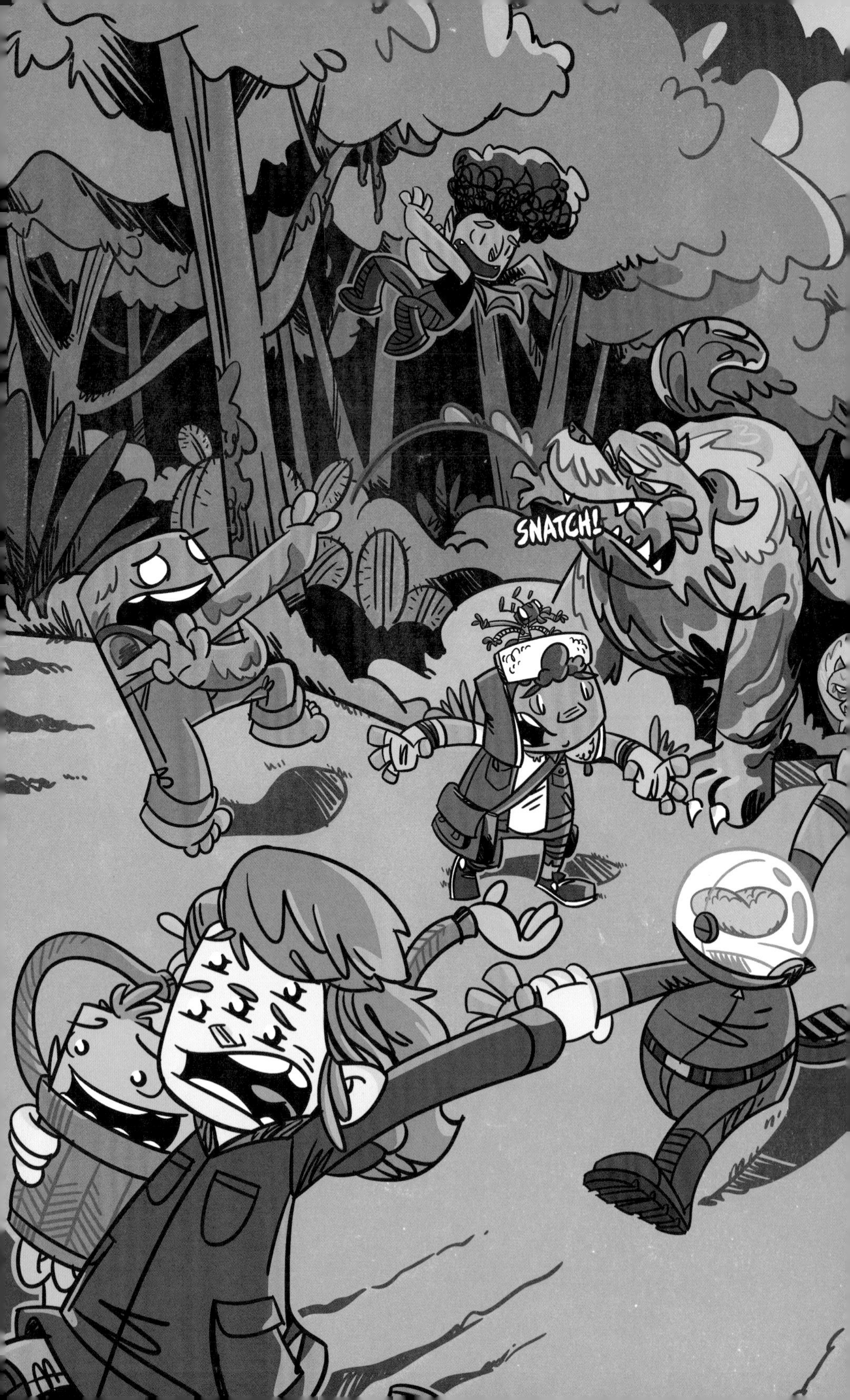
SNATCH!

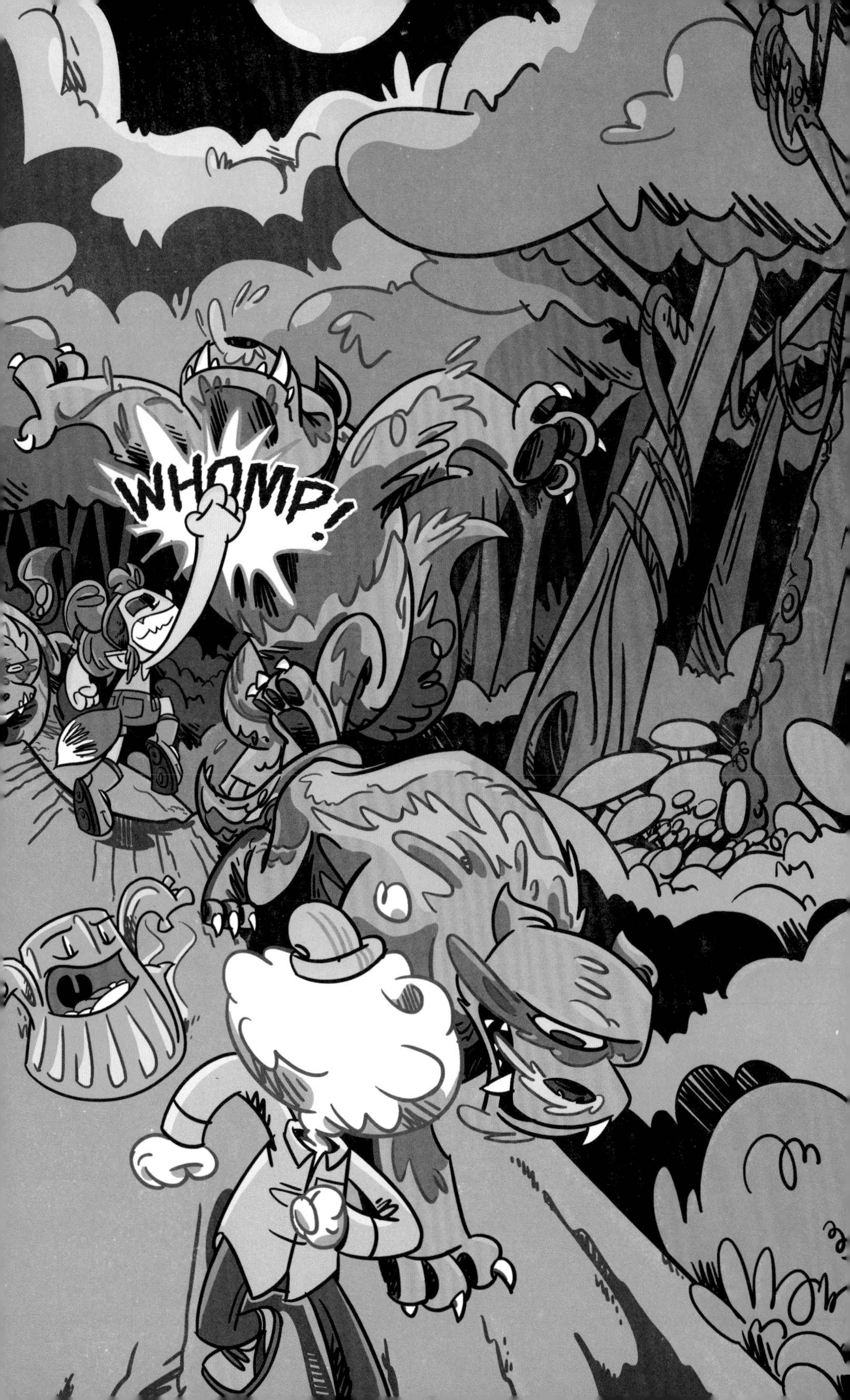
WHOMP!

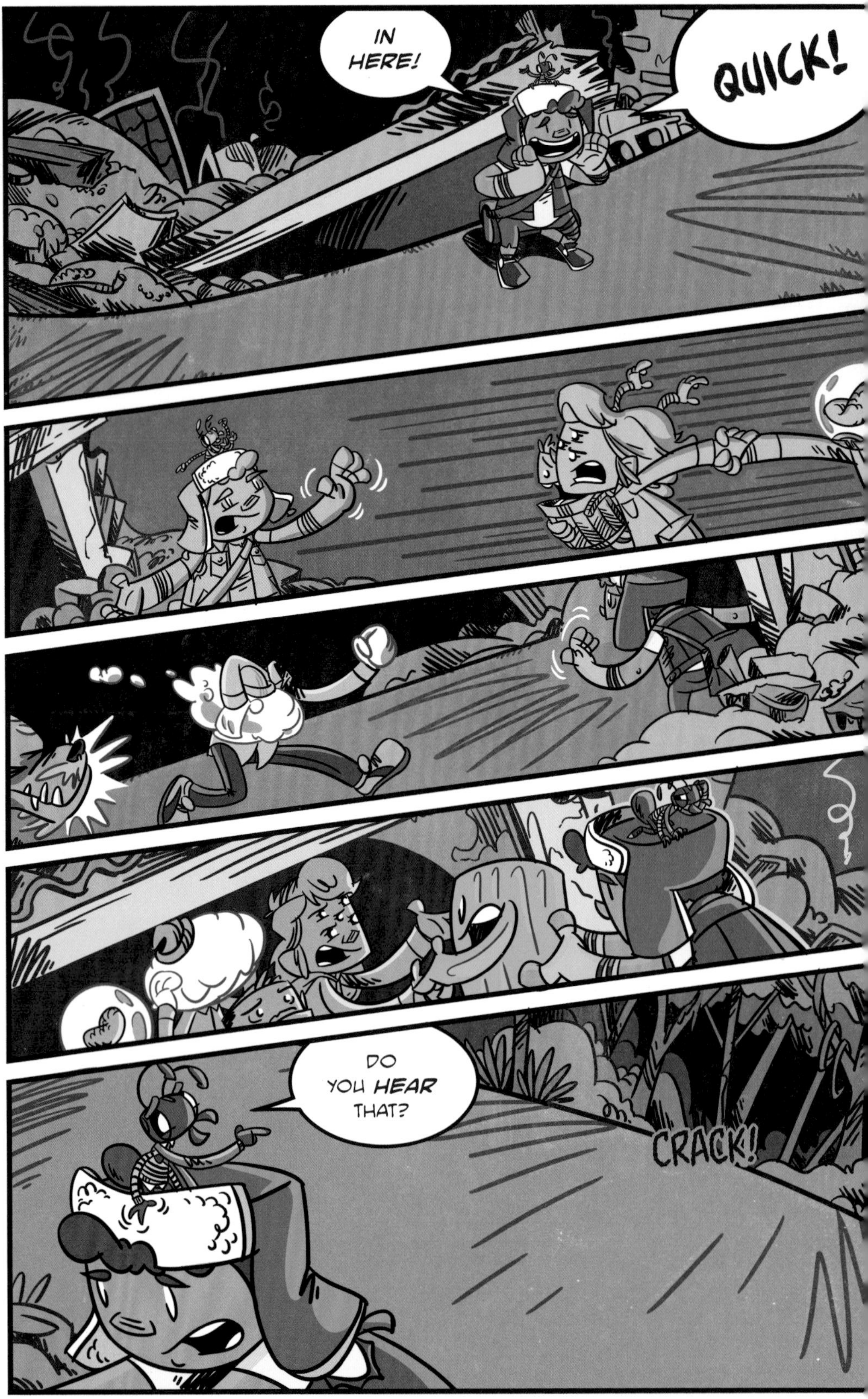
IN HERE!
QUICK!
DO YOU HEAR THAT?
CRACK!

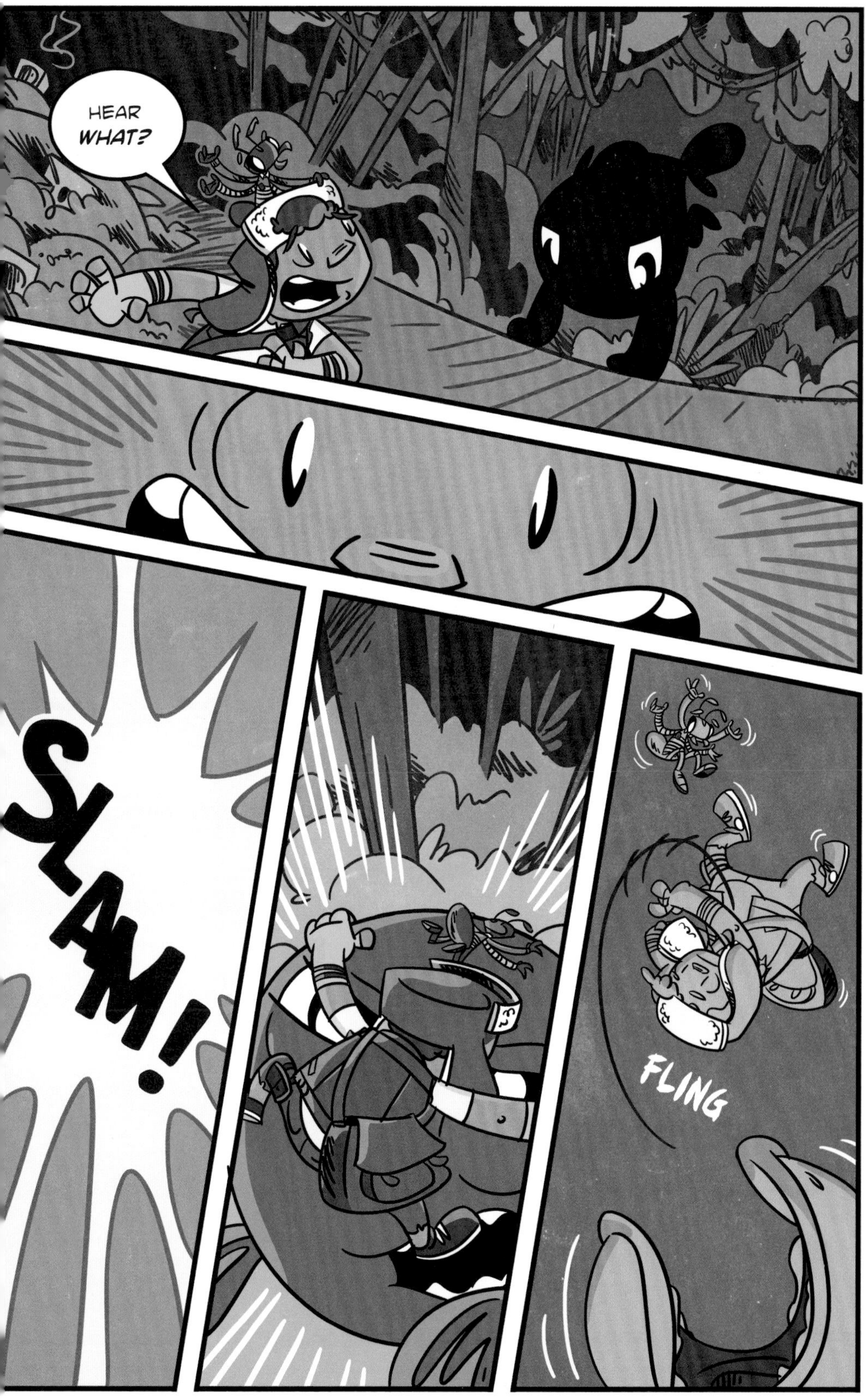
HEAR WHAT?
SLAM!
FLING

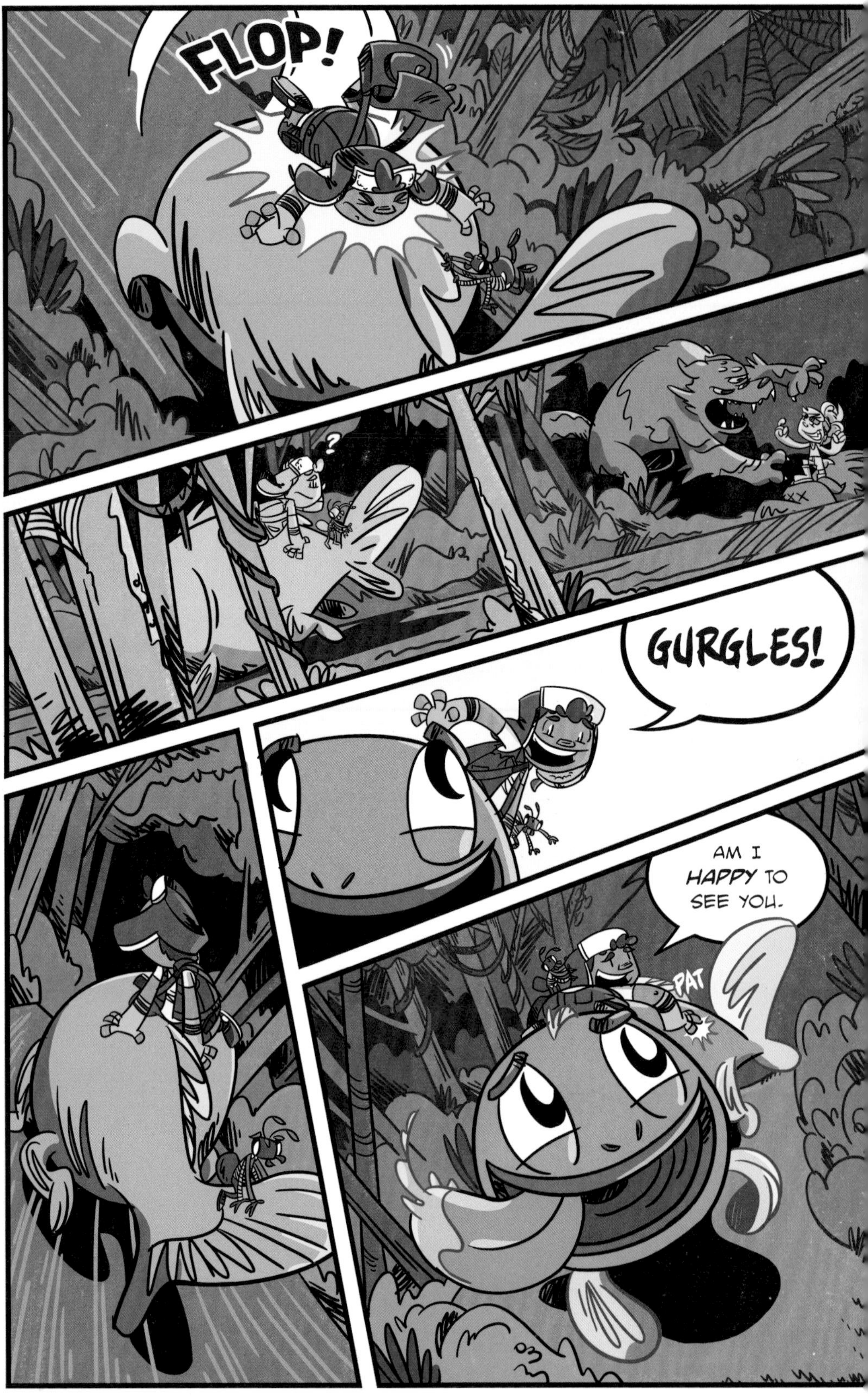
FLOP!
?
GURGLES!
AM I HAPPY TO SEE YOU.
PAT

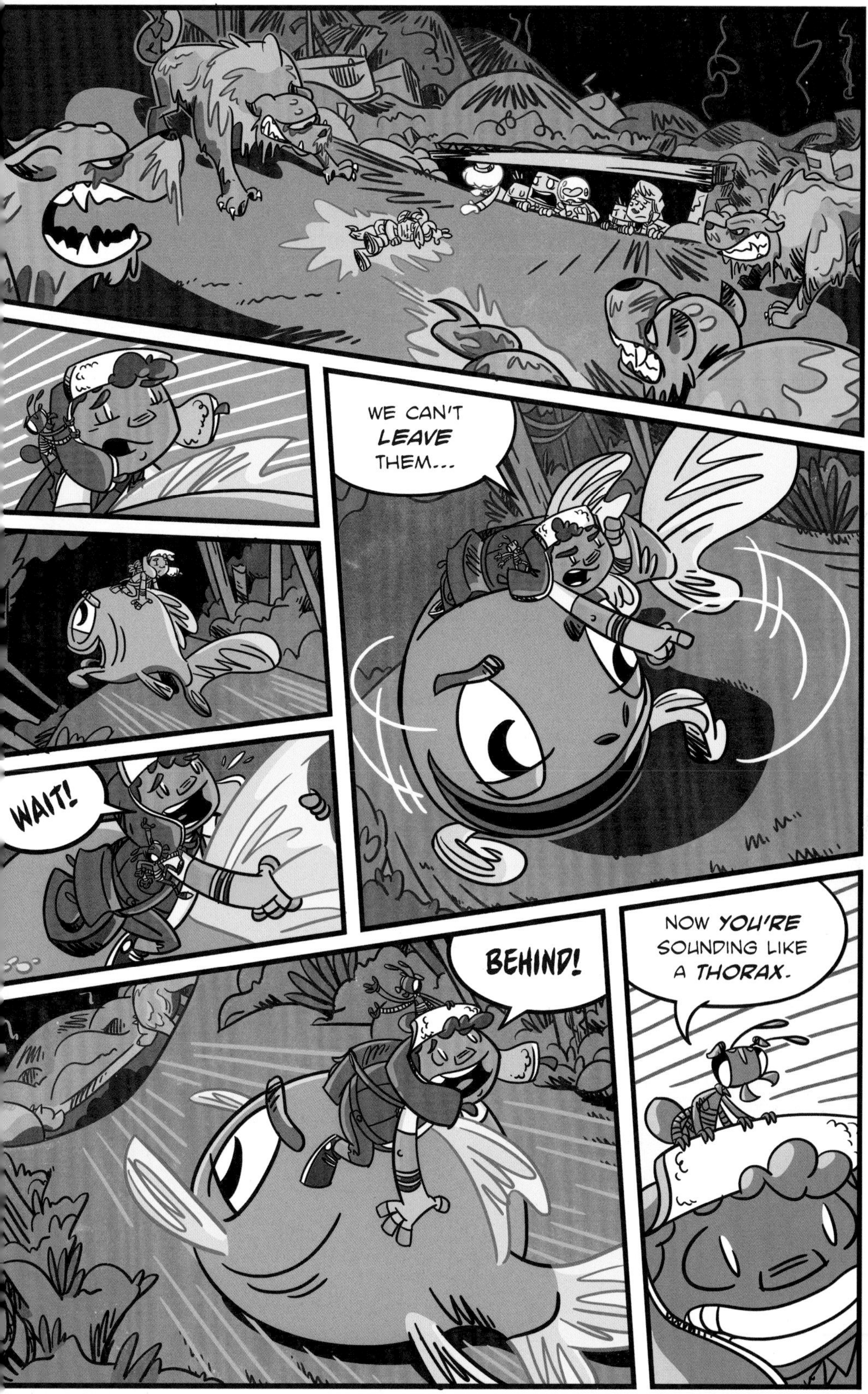
WE CAN'T LEAVE THEM...
WAIT!
BEHIND!
NOW YOU'RE SOUNDING LIKE A THORAX.

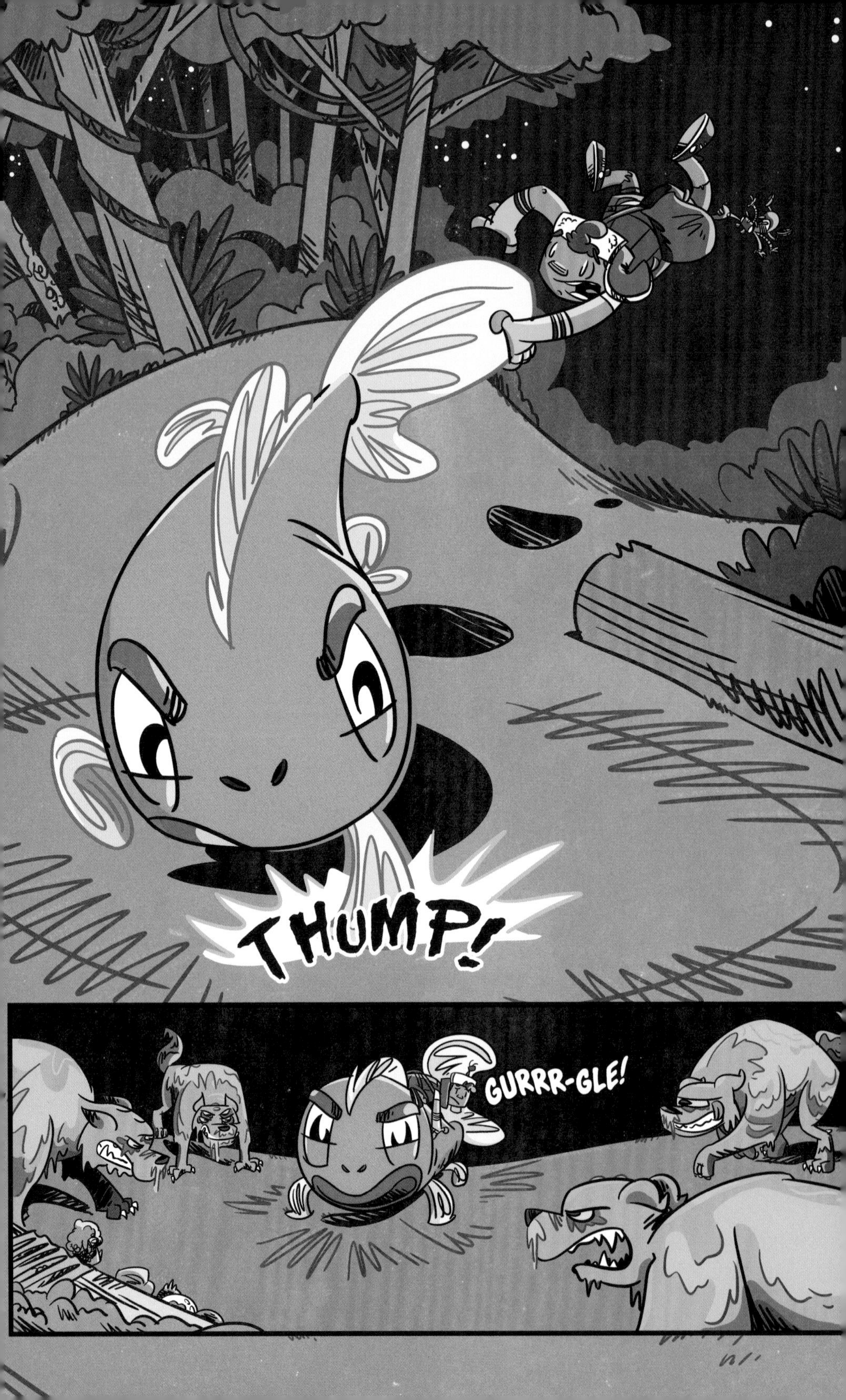
THUMP!
GURRR-GLE!

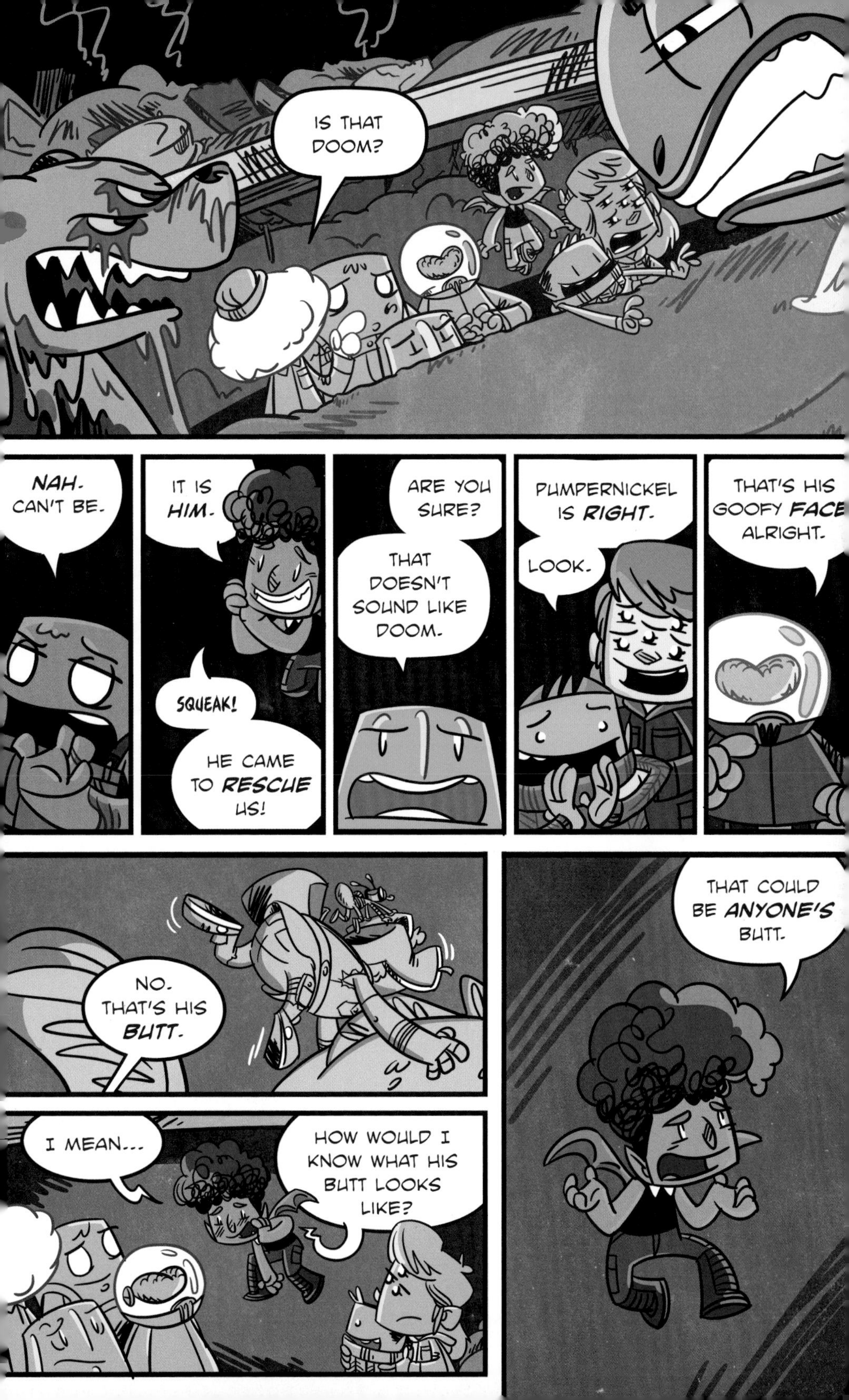
IS THAT DOOM?
NAH. CAN'T BE.
IT IS HIM.
SQUEAK!
HE CAME TO RESCUE US!
ARE YOU SURE?
THAT DOESN'T SOUND LIKE DOOM.
PUMPERNICKEL IS RIGHT.
LOOK.
THAT'S HIS GOOFY FACE ALRIGHT.
NO. THAT'S HIS BUTT.
THAT COULD BE ANYONE'S BUTT.
I MEAN...
HOW WOULD I KNOW WHAT HIS BUTT LOOKS LIKE?

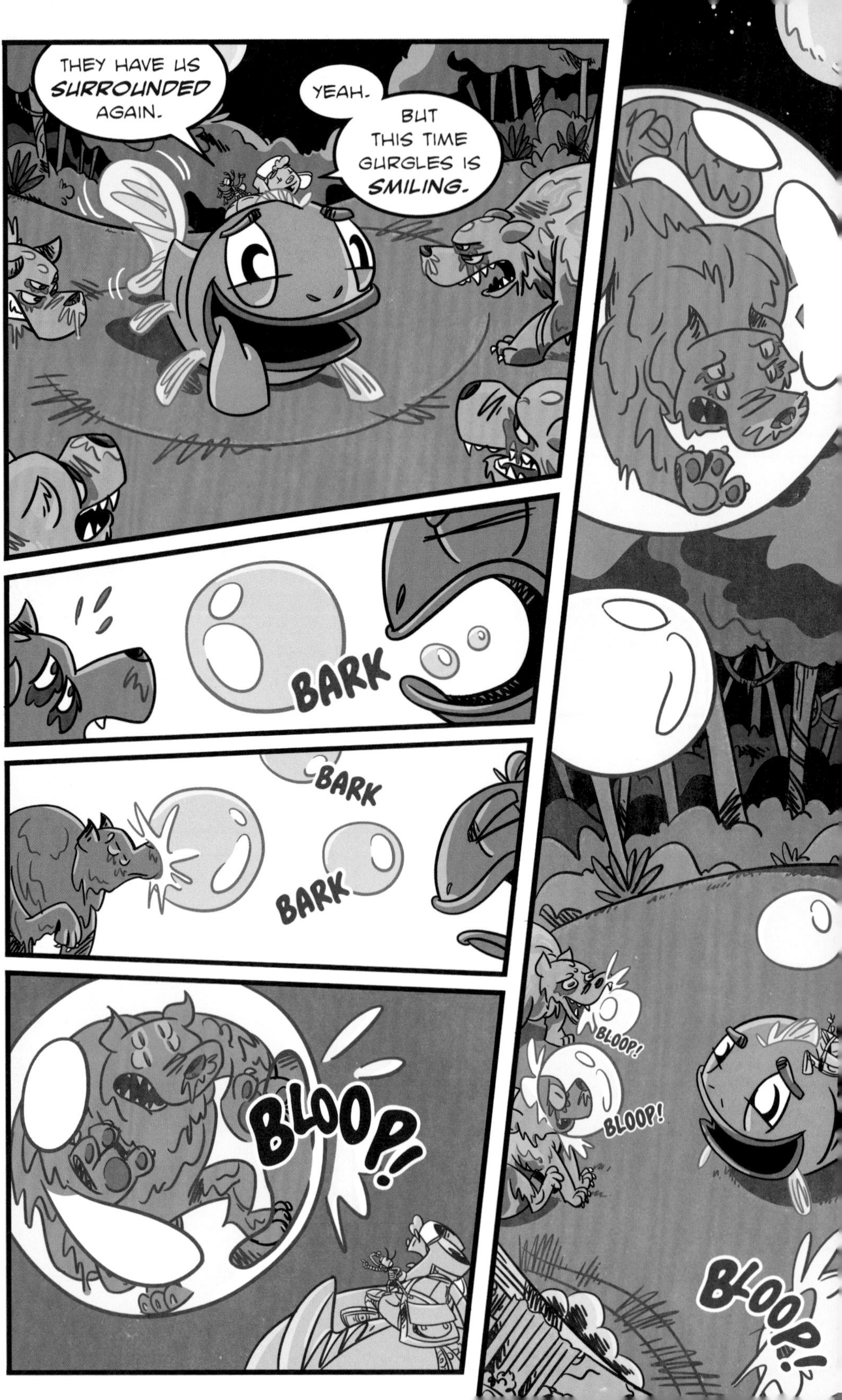
THEY HAVE US SURROUNDED AGAIN.
YEAH.
BUT THIS TIME GURGLES IS SMILING.
BARK
BARK
BARK
BLOOP!!
BLOOP!
BLOOP!
BLOOP!!

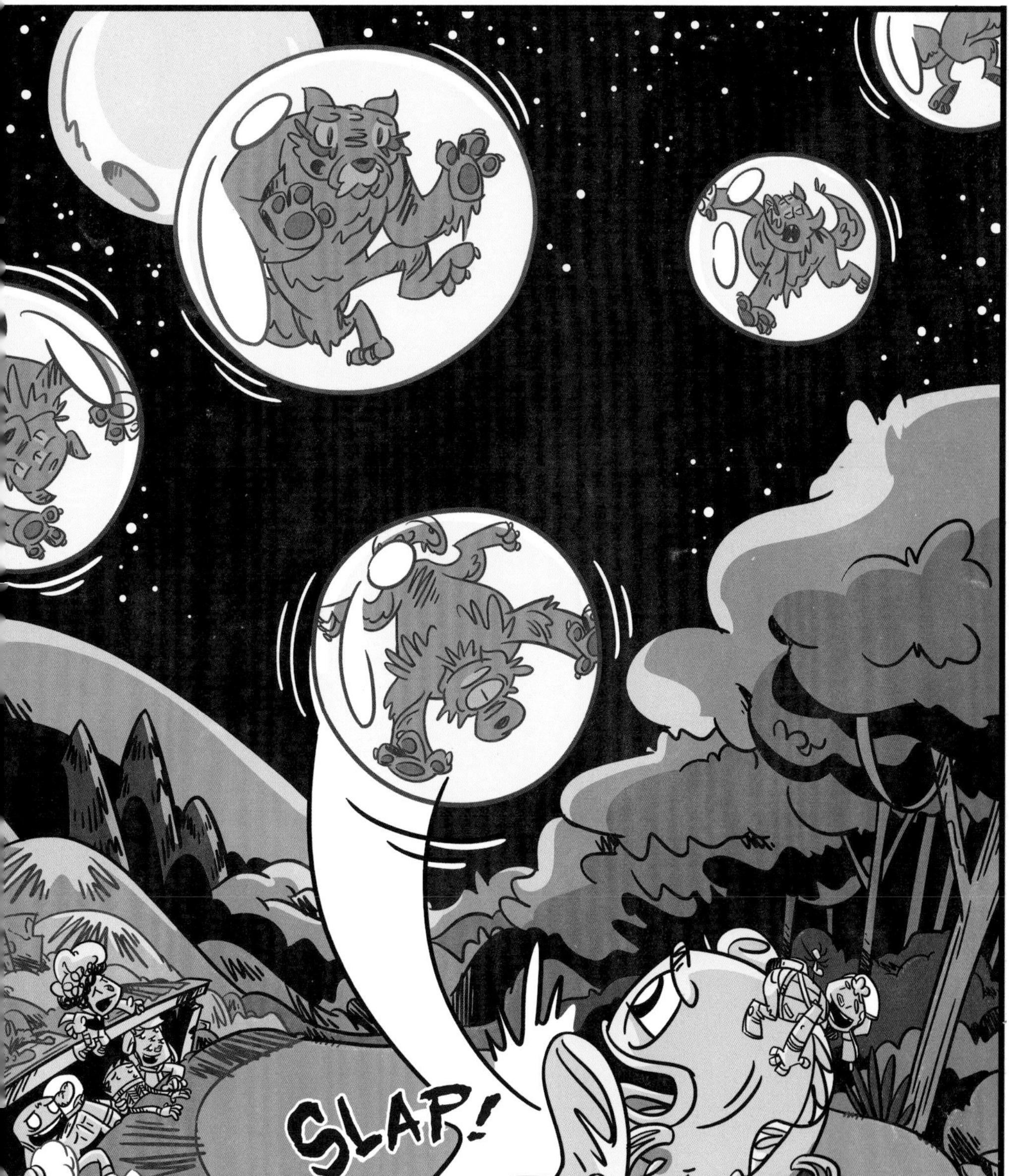
SLAP!

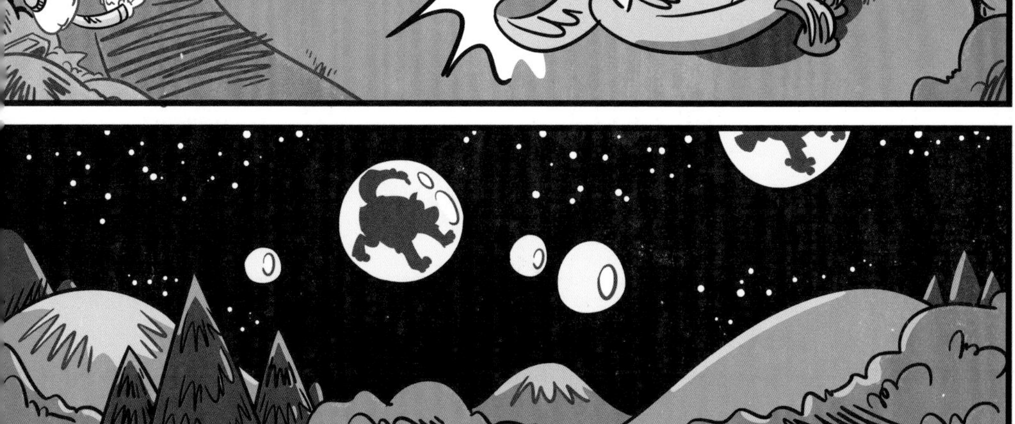

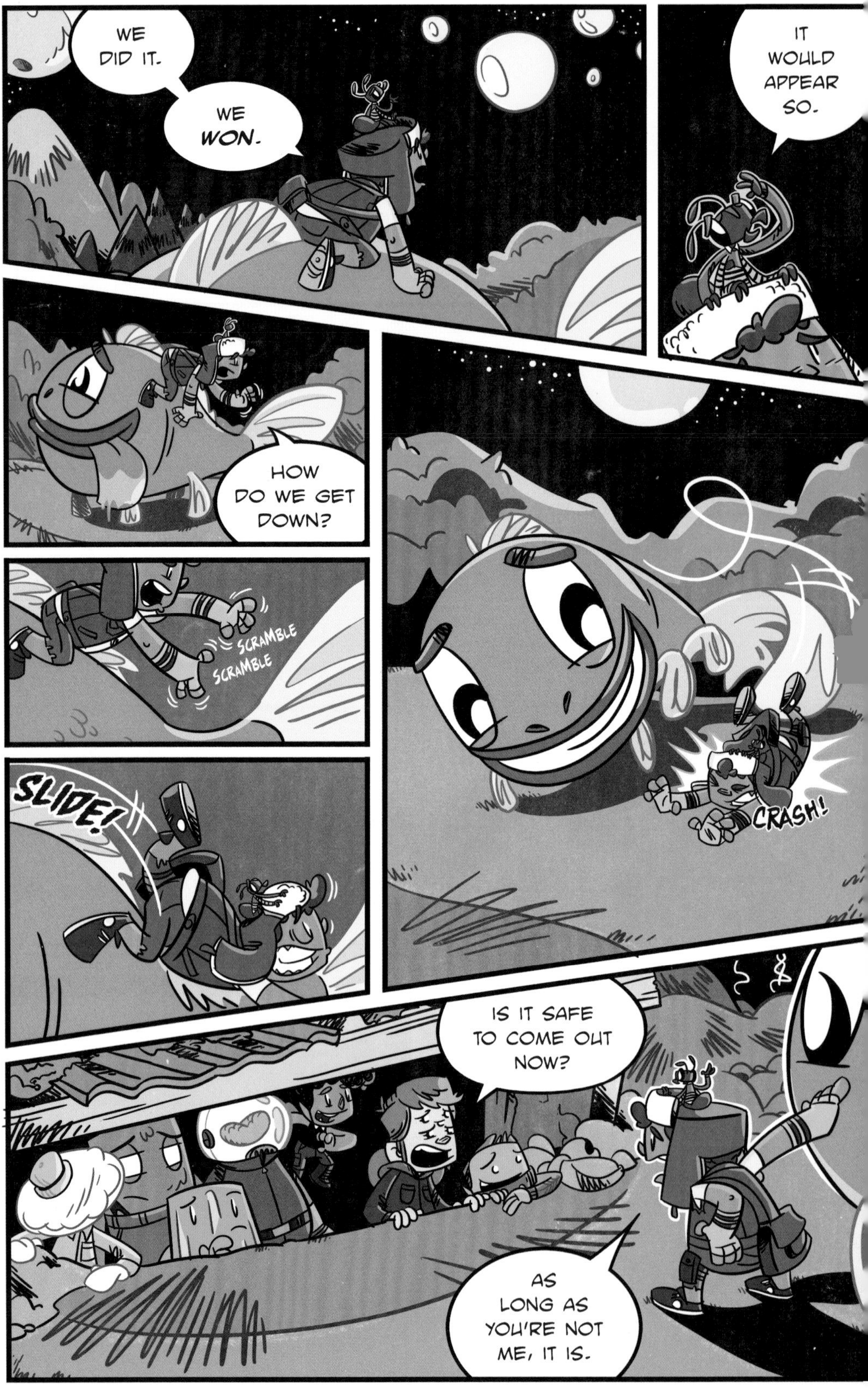
WE DID IT.
WE WON.
IT WOULD APPEAR SO.
HOW DO WE GET DOWN?
SCRAMBLE
SCRAMBLE
SLIDE!
CRASH!
IS IT SAFE TO COME OUT NOW?
AS LONG AS YOU'RE NOT ME, IT IS.

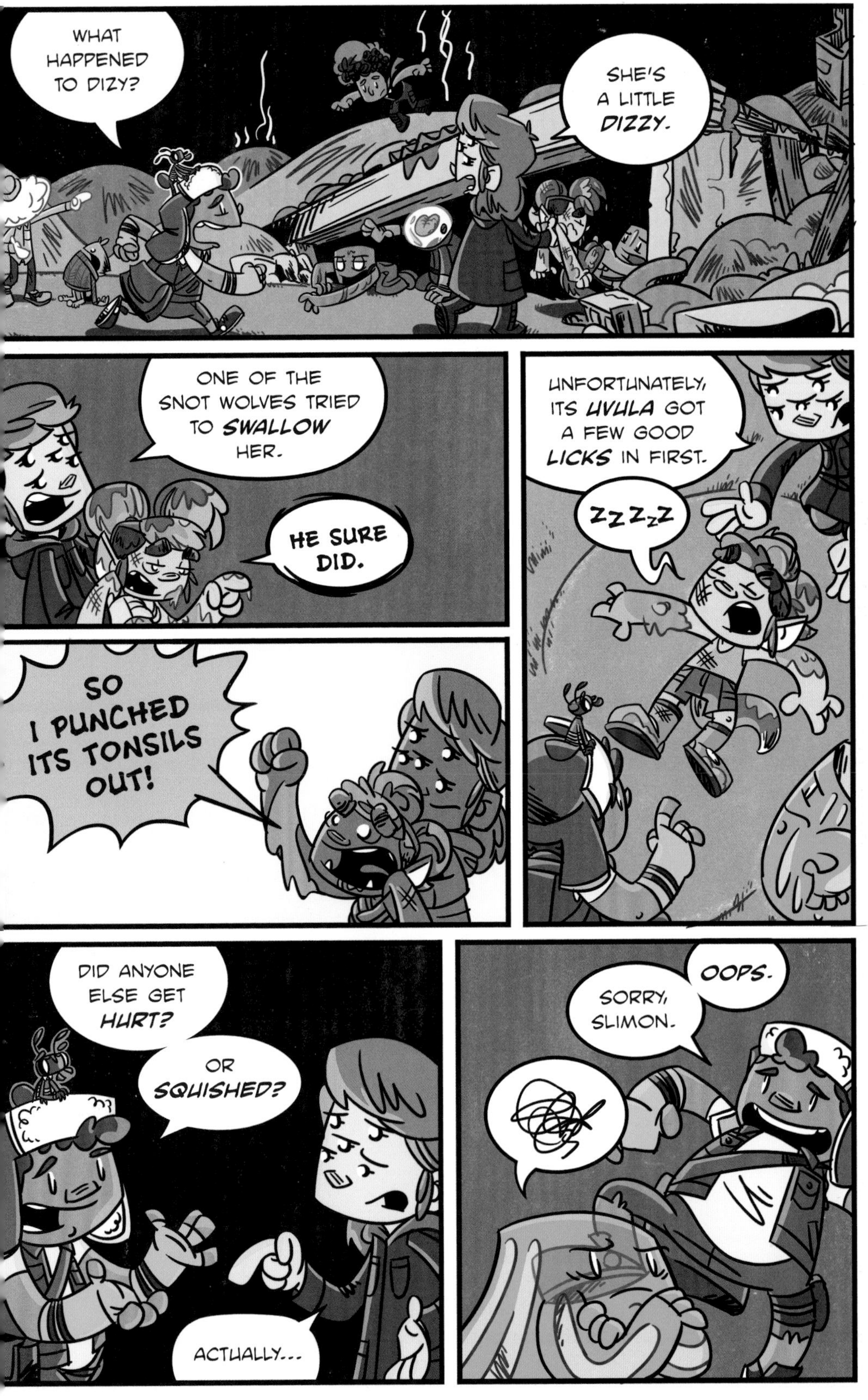
WHAT HAPPENED TO DIZY?
SHE'S A LITTLE DIZZY.
ONE OF THE SNOT WOLVES TRIED TO SWALLOW HER.
HE SURE DID.
UNFORTUNATELY, ITS UVULA GOT A FEW GOOD LICKS IN FIRST.
ZZZzZ
SO I PUNCHED ITS TONSILS OUT!
DID ANYONE ELSE GET HURT?
OR SQUISHED?
ACTUALLY...
OOPS.
SORRY, SLIMON.

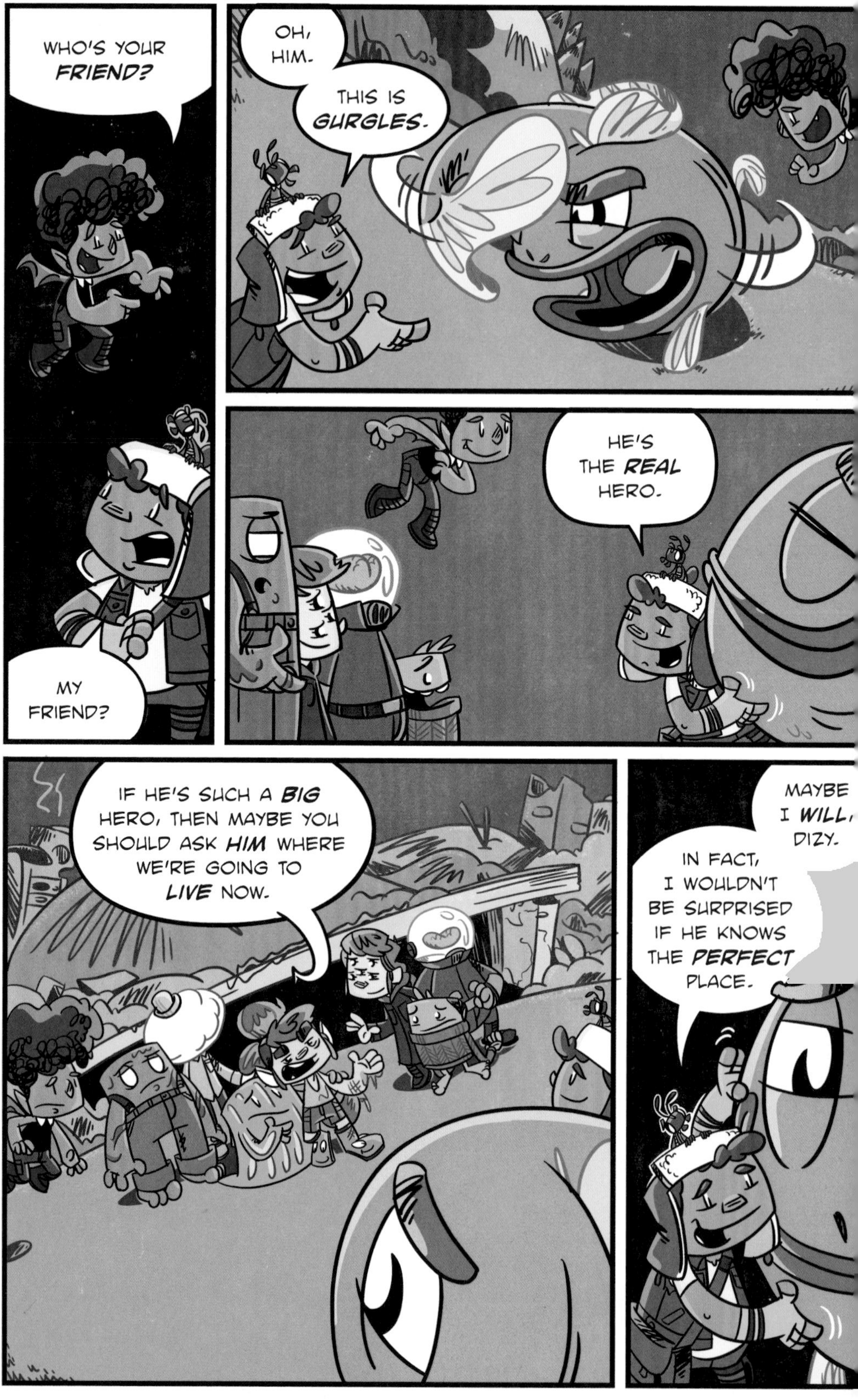

WHO'S YOUR *FRIEND?*
OH, HIM.
THIS IS *GURGLES.*
MY FRIEND?
HE'S THE *REAL* HERO.
IF HE'S SUCH A *BIG* HERO, THEN MAYBE YOU SHOULD ASK *HIM* WHERE WE'RE GOING TO *LIVE* NOW.
MAYBE I *WILL,* DIZY.
IN FACT, I WOULDN'T BE SURPRISED IF HE KNOWS THE *PERFECT* PLACE.

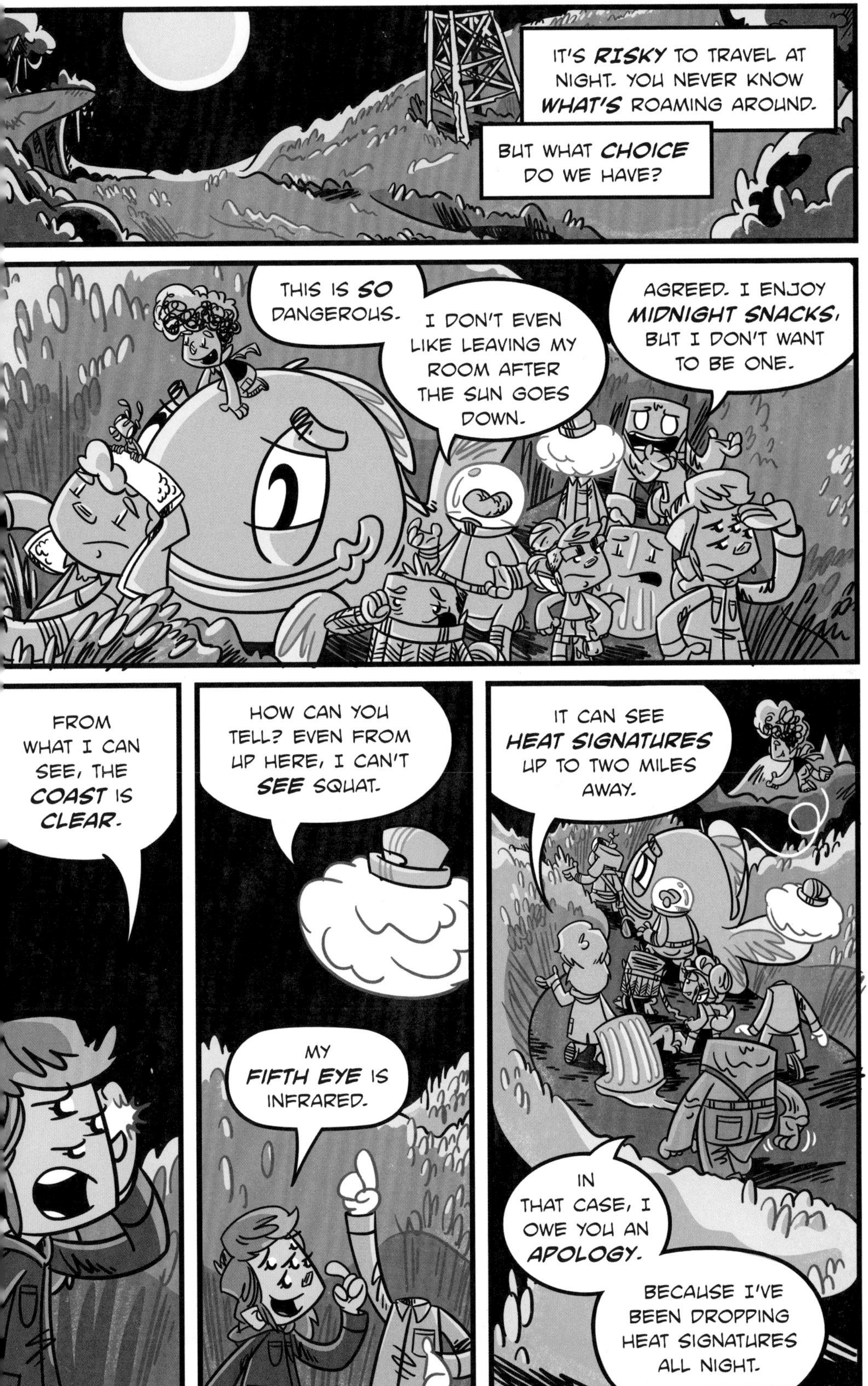
IT'S RISKY TO TRAVEL AT NIGHT. YOU NEVER KNOW WHAT'S ROAMING AROUND.
BUT WHAT CHOICE DO WE HAVE?
THIS IS SO DANGEROUS.
I DON'T EVEN LIKE LEAVING MY ROOM AFTER THE SUN GOES DOWN.
AGREED. I ENJOY MIDNIGHT SNACKS, BUT I DON'T WANT TO BE ONE.
FROM WHAT I CAN SEE, THE COAST IS CLEAR.
HOW CAN YOU TELL? EVEN FROM UP HERE, I CAN'T SEE SQUAT.
MY FIFTH EYE IS INFRARED.
IT CAN SEE HEAT SIGNATURES UP TO TWO MILES AWAY.
IN THAT CASE, I OWE YOU AN APOLOGY.
BECAUSE I'VE BEEN DROPPING HEAT SIGNATURES ALL NIGHT.

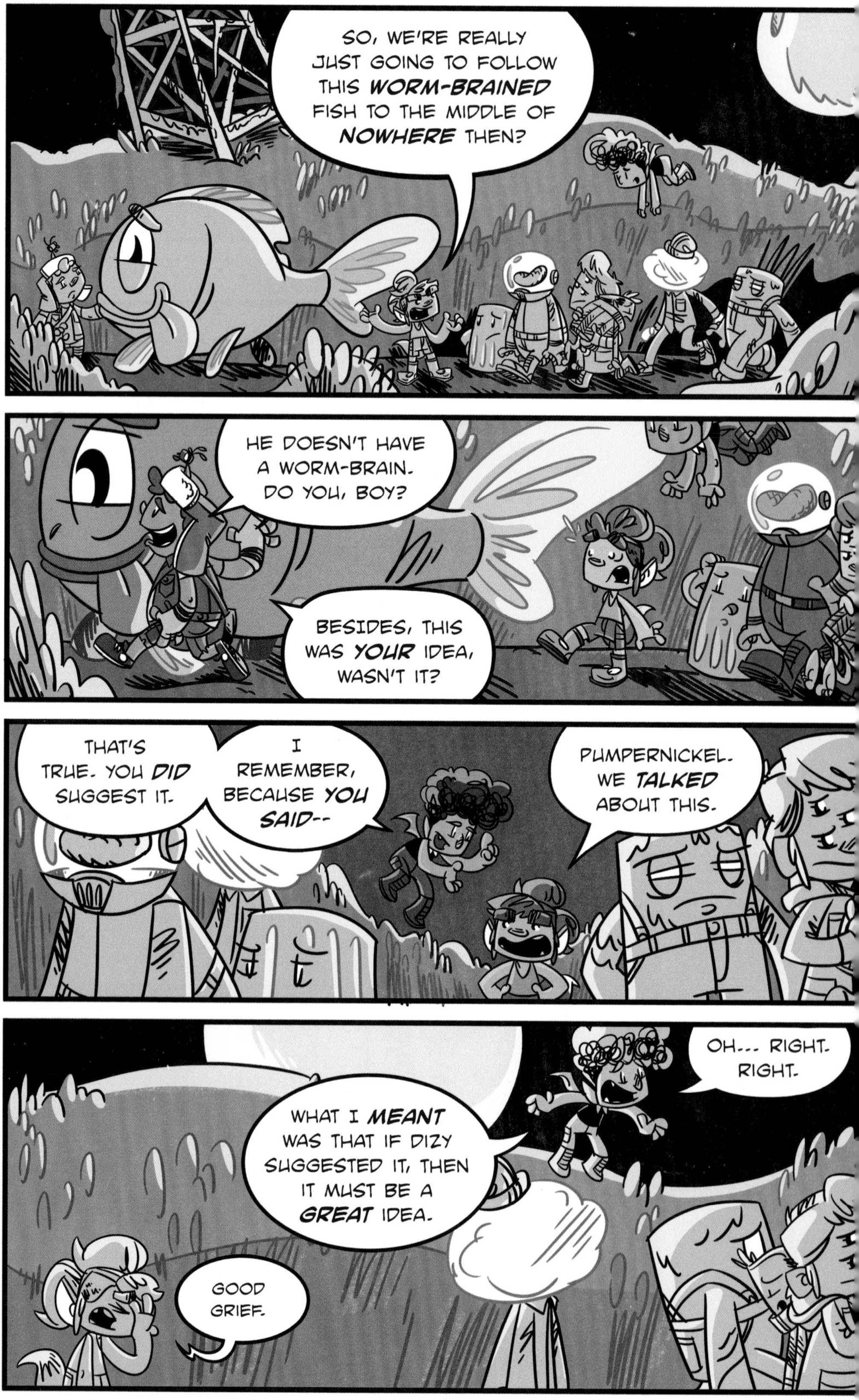
SO, WE'RE REALLY JUST GOING TO FOLLOW THIS WORM-BRAINED FISH TO THE MIDDLE OF NOWHERE THEN?
HE DOESN'T HAVE A WORM-BRAIN. DO YOU, BOY?
BESIDES, THIS WAS YOUR IDEA, WASN'T IT?
THAT'S TRUE. YOU DID SUGGEST IT.
I REMEMBER, BECAUSE YOU SAID--
PUMPERNICKEL. WE TALKED ABOUT THIS.
OH... RIGHT. RIGHT.
WHAT I MEANT WAS THAT IF DIZY SUGGESTED IT, THEN IT MUST BE A GREAT IDEA.
GOOD GRIEF.

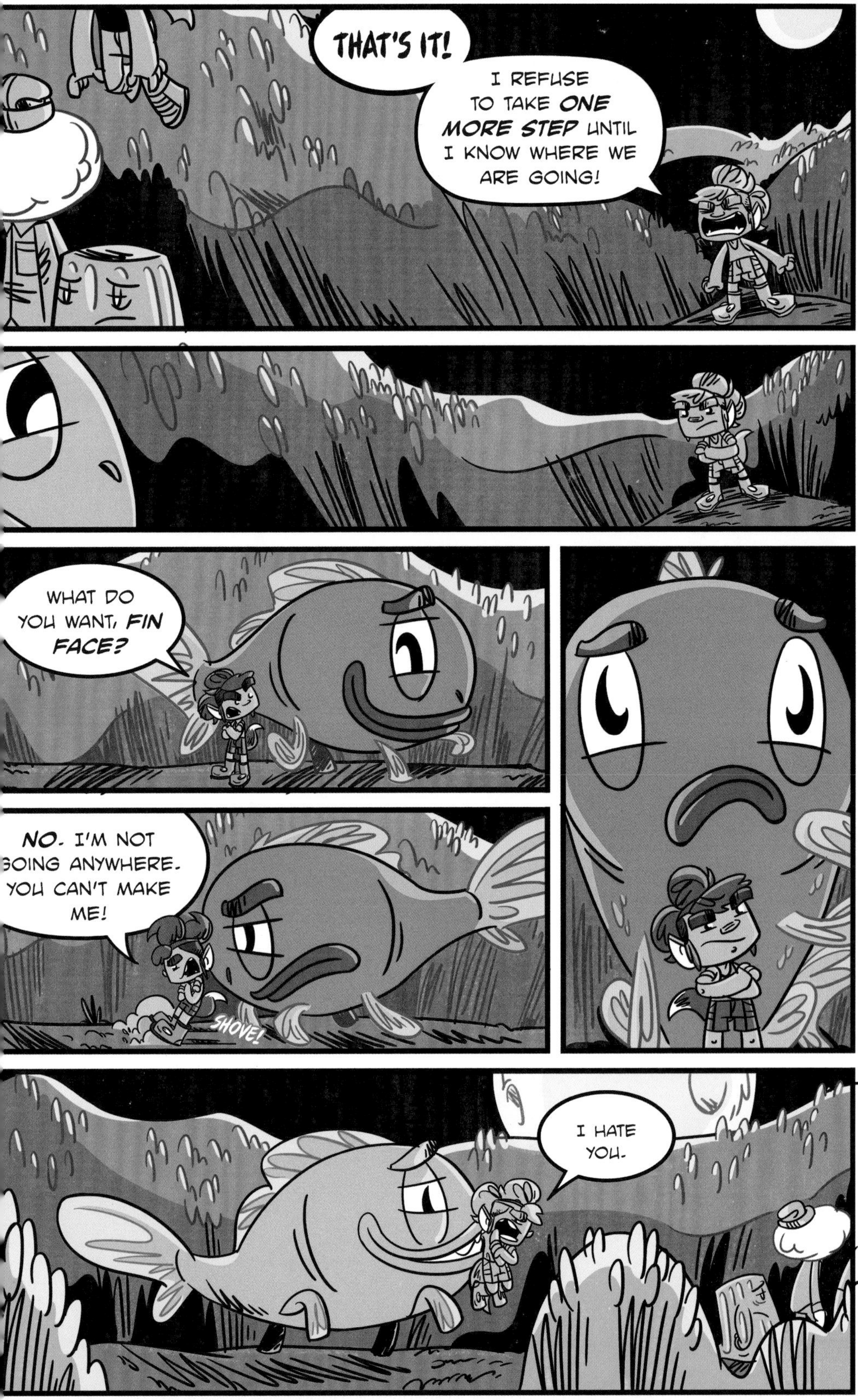
THAT'S IT!
I REFUSE TO TAKE ONE MORE STEP UNTIL I KNOW WHERE WE ARE GOING!
WHAT DO YOU WANT, FIN FACE?
NO. I'M NOT GOING ANYWHERE. YOU CAN'T MAKE ME!
SHOVE!
I HATE YOU.

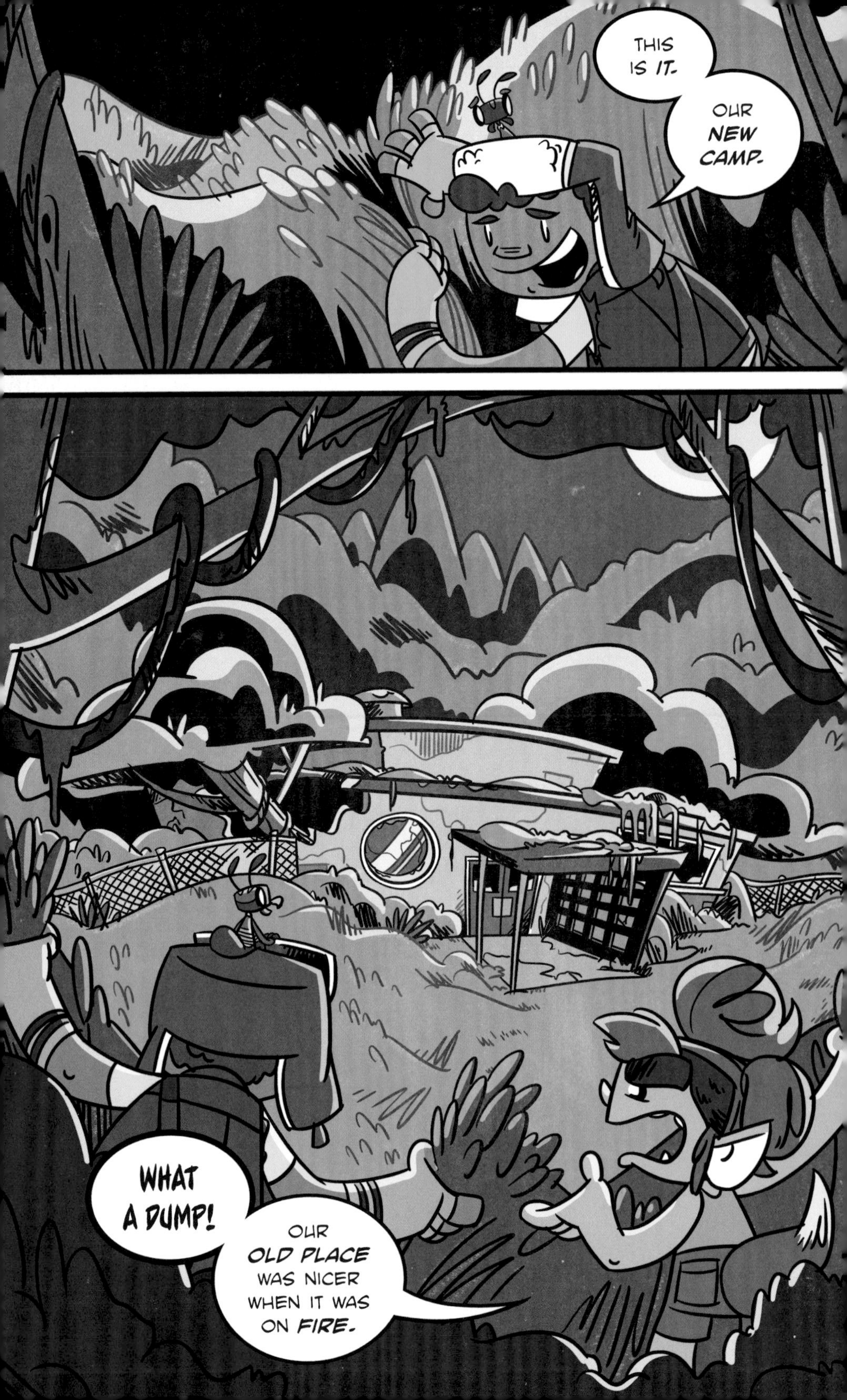
THIS IS IT.
OUR NEW CAMP.
WHAT A DUMP!
OUR OLD PLACE WAS NICER WHEN IT WAS ON FIRE.

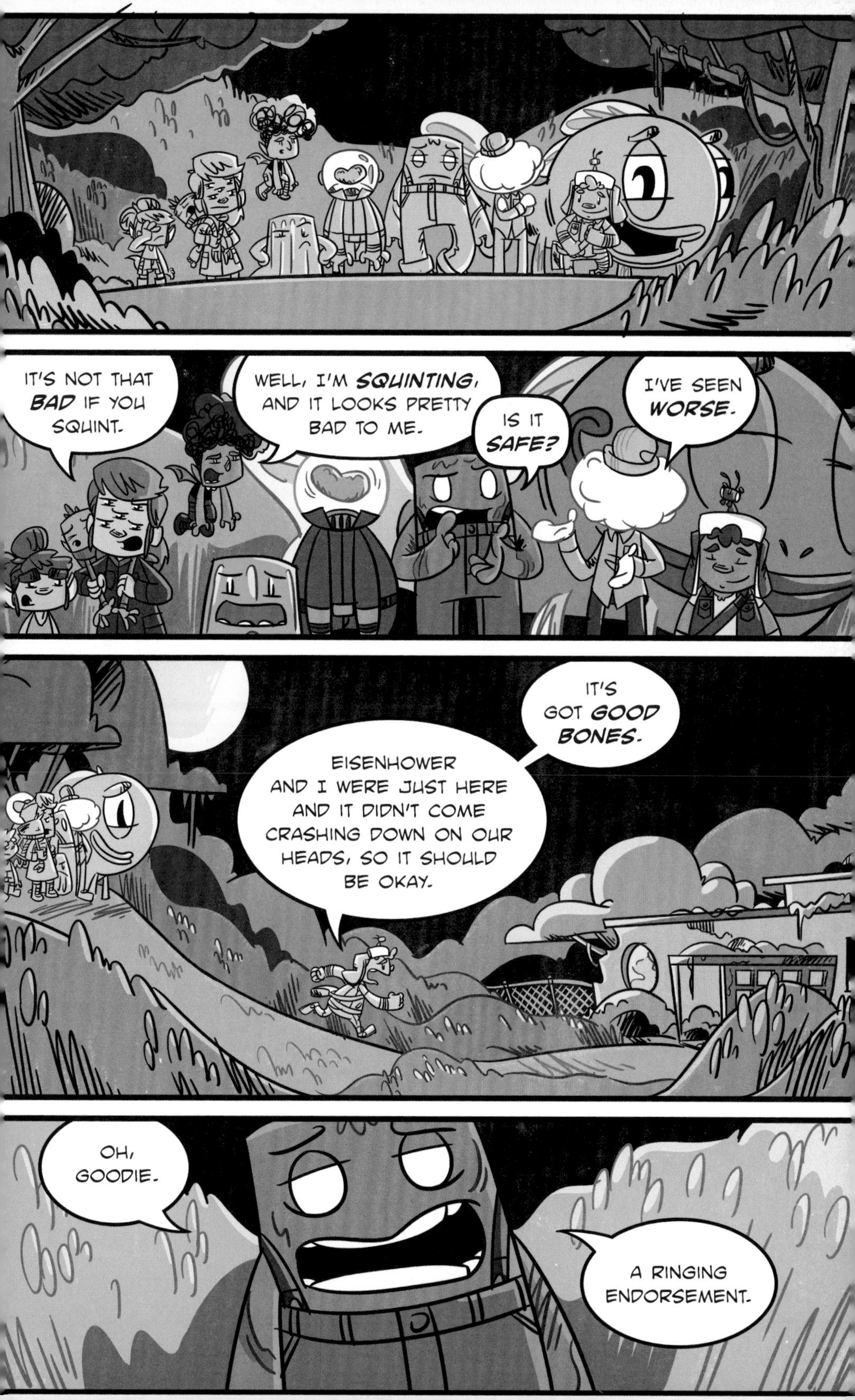
IT'S NOT THAT BAD IF YOU SQUINT.
WELL, I'M SQUINTING, AND IT LOOKS PRETTY BAD TO ME.
IS IT SAFE?
I'VE SEEN WORSE.
IT'S GOT GOOD BONES.
EISENHOWER AND I WERE JUST HERE AND IT DIDN'T COME CRASHING DOWN ON OUR HEADS, SO IT SHOULD BE OKAY.
OH, GOODIE.
A RINGING ENDORSEMENT.

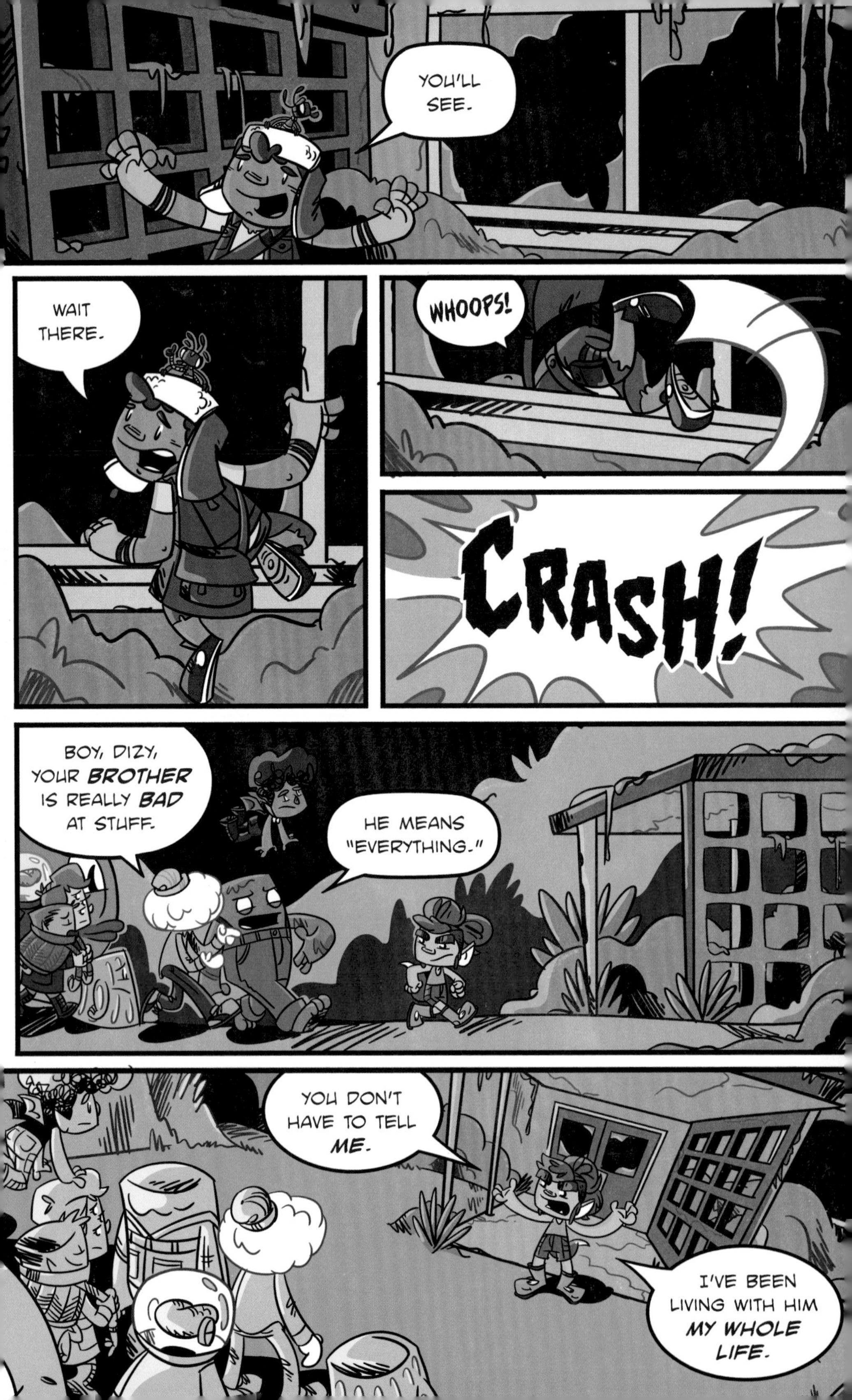
YOU'LL SEE.
WAIT THERE.
WHOOPS!
CRASH!
BOY, DIZY, YOUR **BROTHER** IS REALLY **BAD** AT STUFF.
HE MEANS "EVERYTHING."
YOU DON'T HAVE TO TELL **ME**.
I'VE BEEN LIVING WITH HIM **MY WHOLE LIFE**.

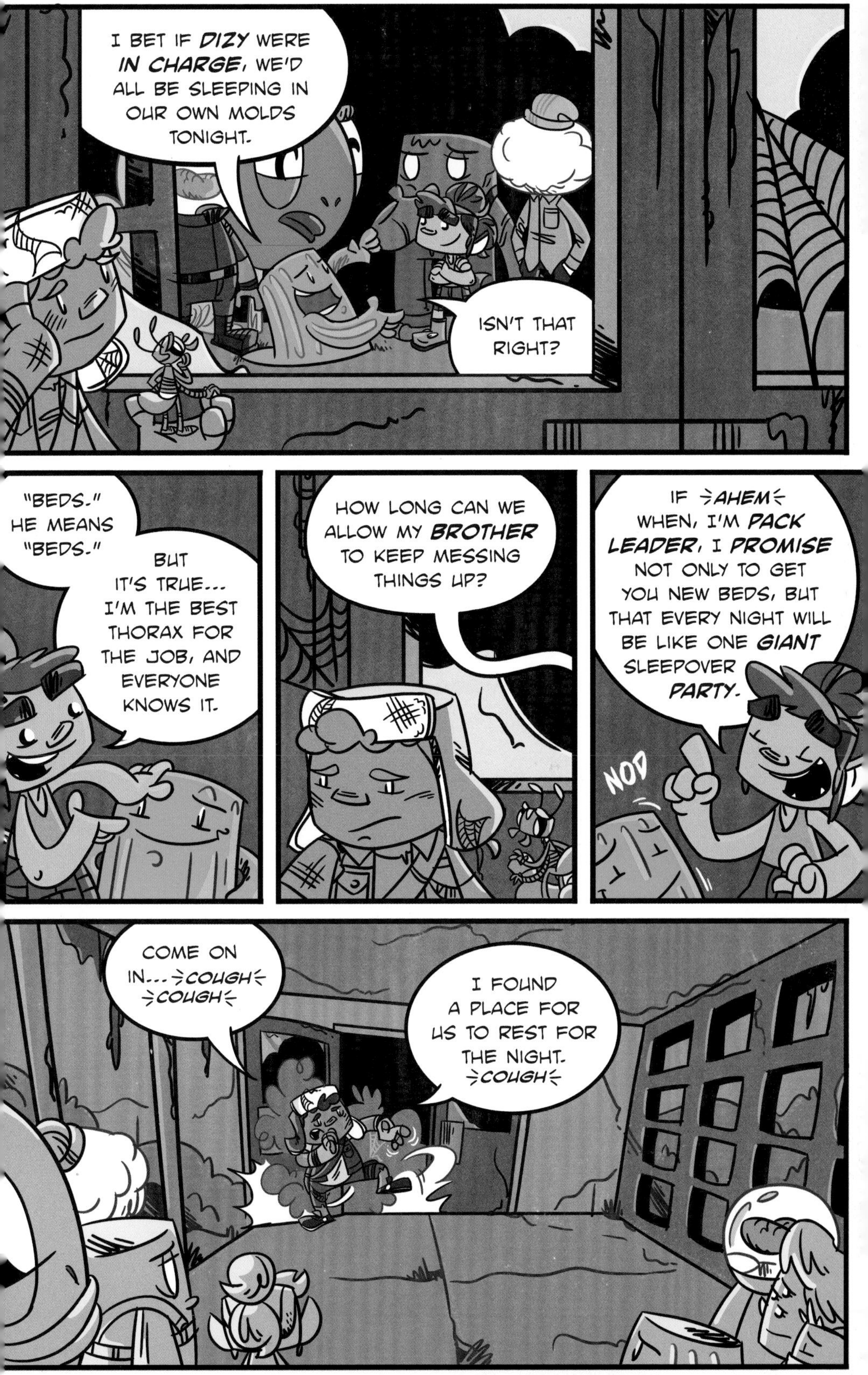
I BET IF DIZY WERE IN CHARGE, WE'D ALL BE SLEEPING IN OUR OWN MOLDS TONIGHT.
ISN'T THAT RIGHT?
"BEDS." HE MEANS "BEDS."
BUT IT'S TRUE... I'M THE BEST THORAX FOR THE JOB, AND EVERYONE KNOWS IT.
HOW LONG CAN WE ALLOW MY BROTHER TO KEEP MESSING THINGS UP?
IF ⩤AHEM⩥ WHEN, I'M PACK LEADER, I PROMISE NOT ONLY TO GET YOU NEW BEDS, BUT THAT EVERY NIGHT WILL BE LIKE ONE GIANT SLEEPOVER PARTY.
NOD
COME ON IN... ⩤COUGH⩥ ⩤COUGH⩥
I FOUND A PLACE FOR US TO REST FOR THE NIGHT. ⩤COUGH⩥

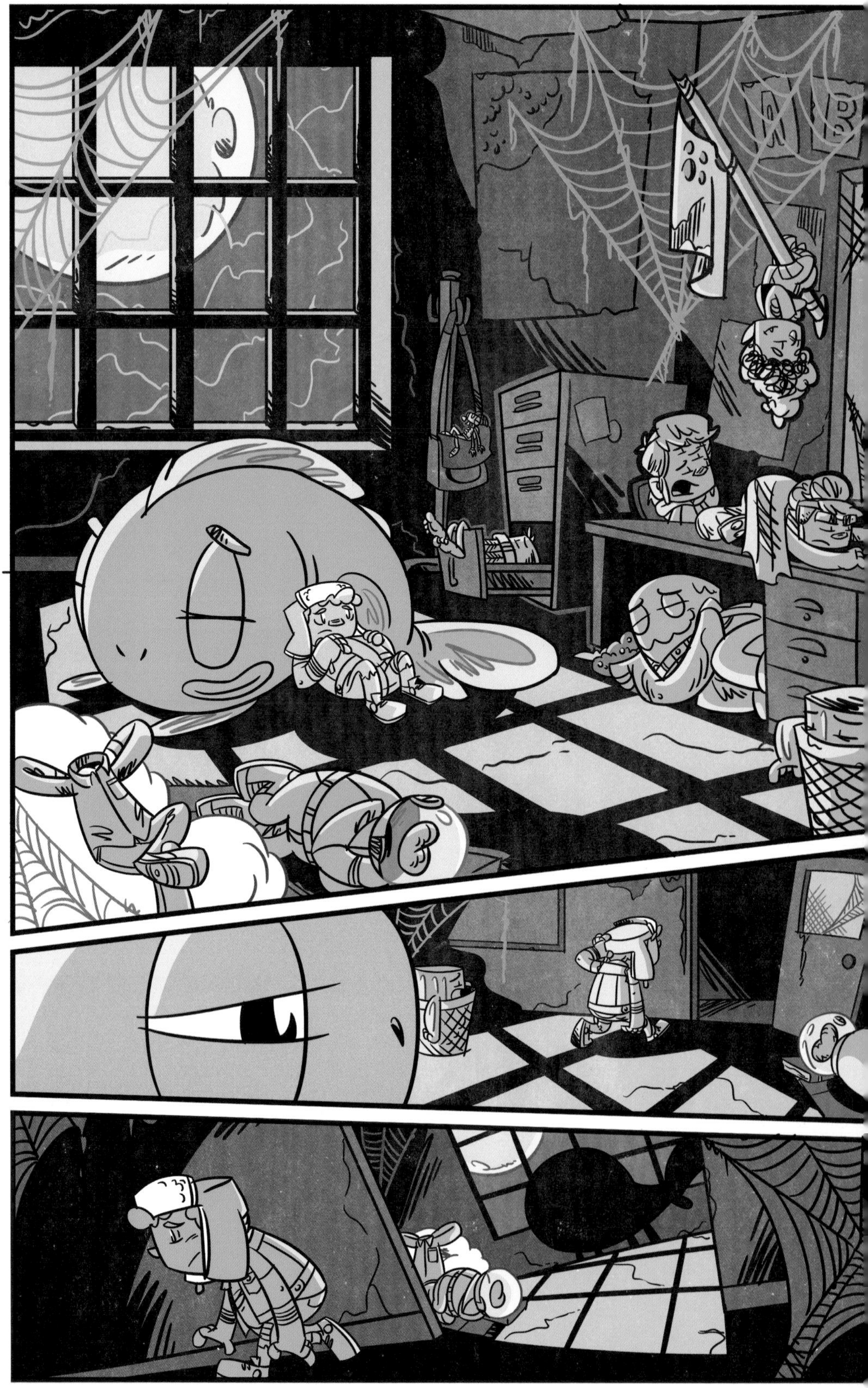

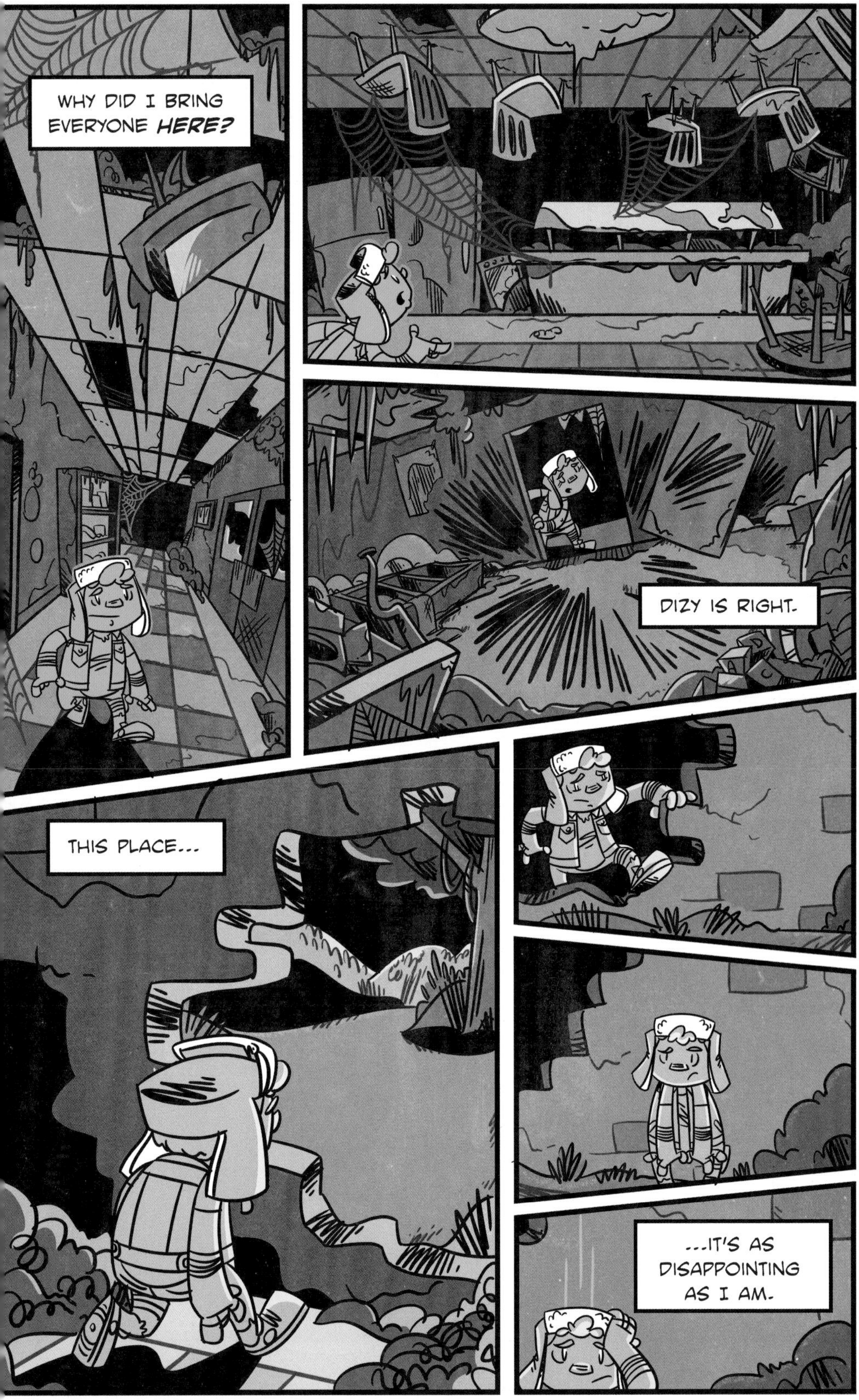
WHY DID I BRING EVERYONE *HERE?*
DIZY IS RIGHT.
THIS PLACE...
...IT'S AS DISAPPOINTING AS I AM.

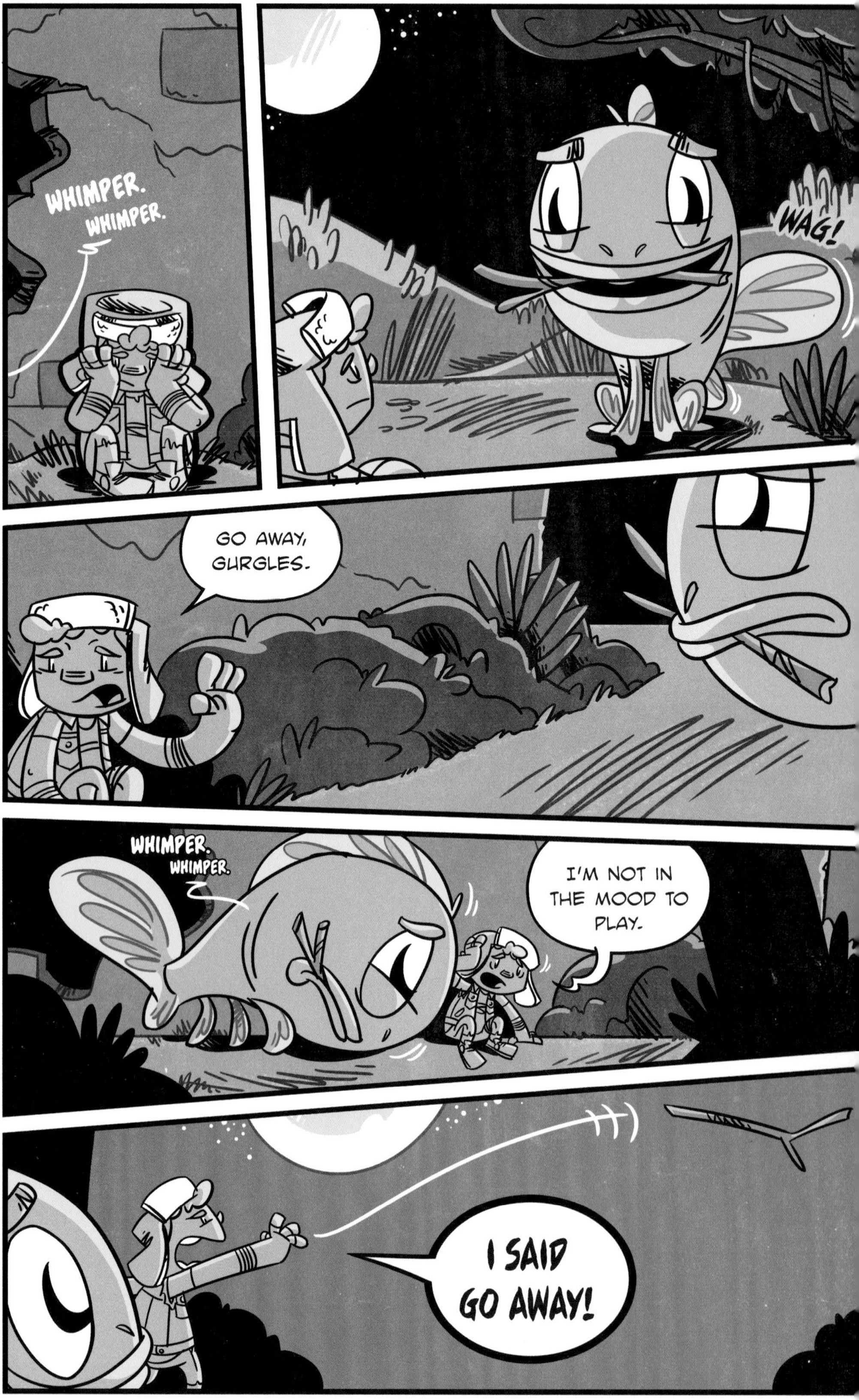
WHIMPER.
WHIMPER.
WAG!
GO AWAY, GURGLES.
WHIMPER.
WHIMPER.
I'M NOT IN THE MOOD TO PLAY.
I SAID GO AWAY!

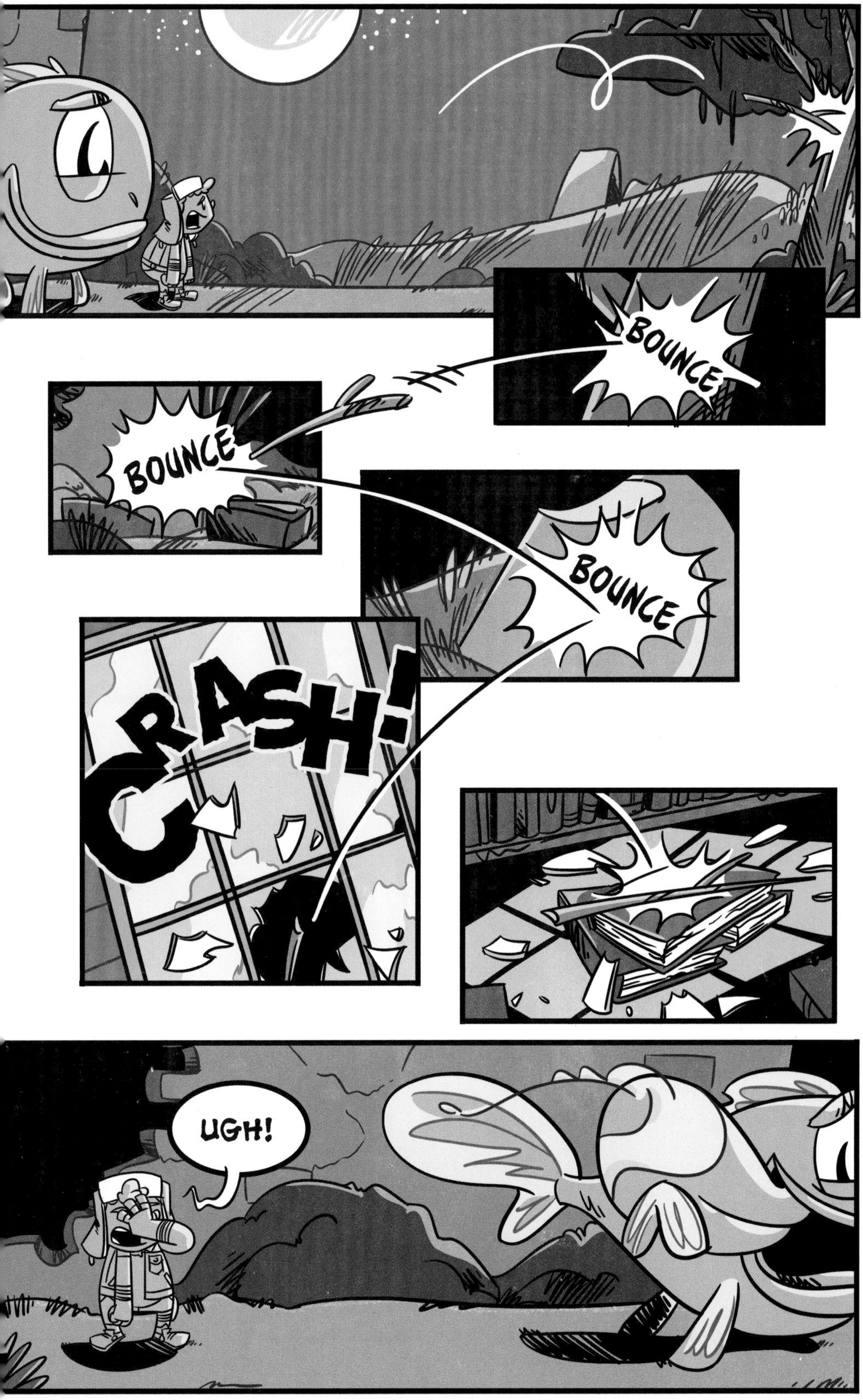
BOUNCE
BOUNCE
BOUNCE
CRASH!
UGH!

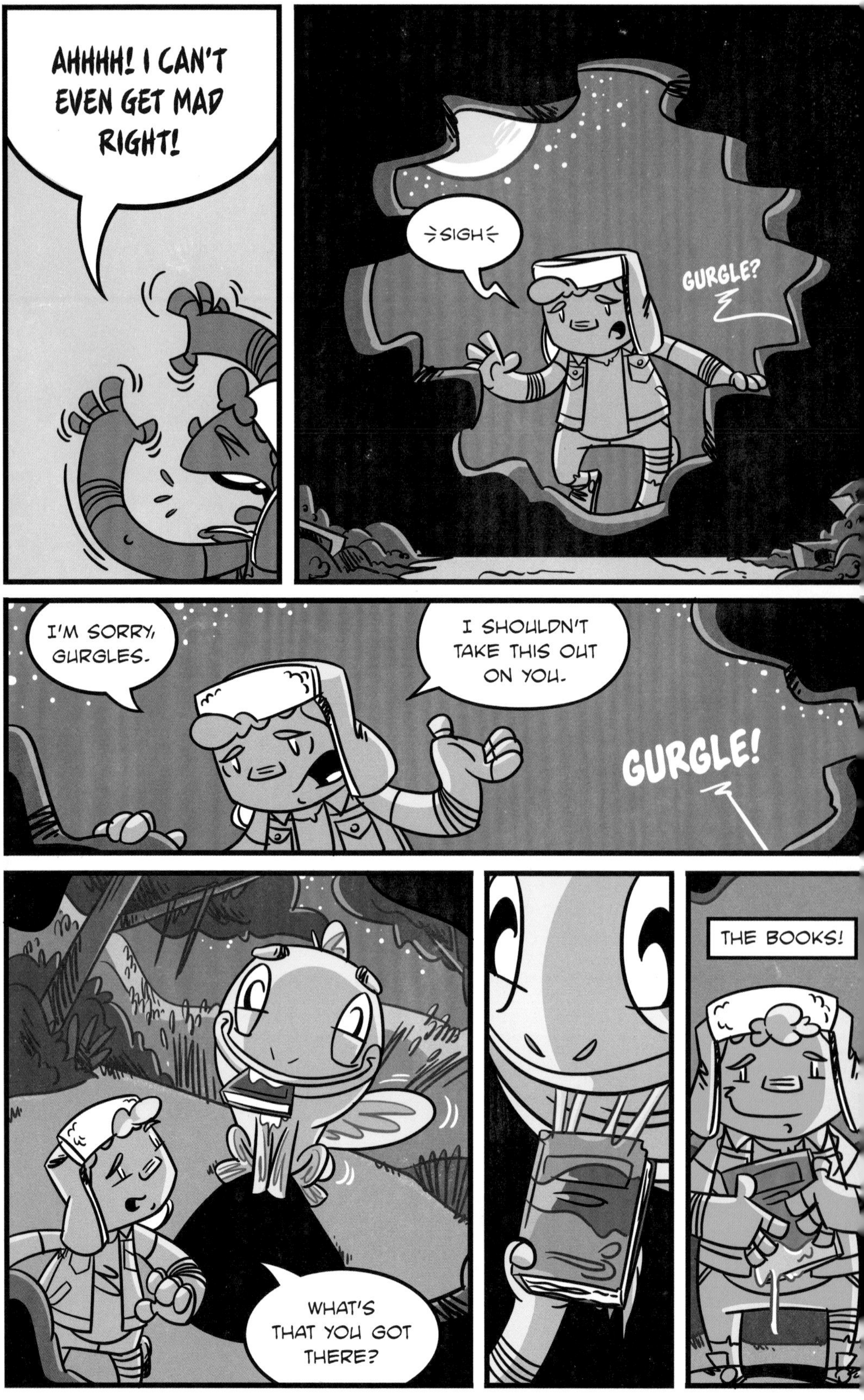
AHHHH! I CAN'T EVEN GET MAD RIGHT!
SIGH
GURGLE?
I'M SORRY, GURGLES.
I SHOULDN'T TAKE THIS OUT ON YOU.
GURGLE!
WHAT'S THAT YOU GOT THERE?
THE BOOKS!

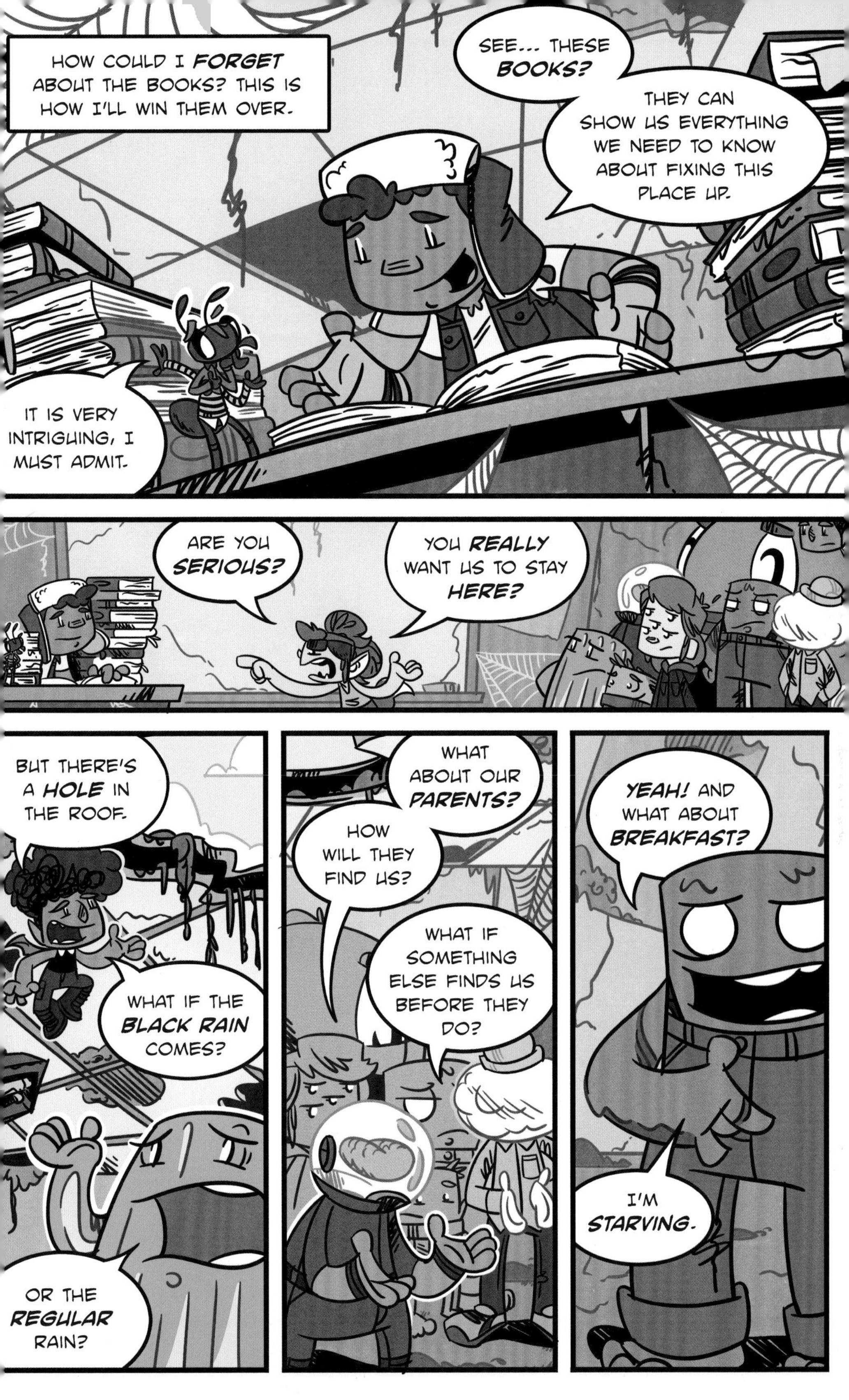
HOW COULD I FORGET ABOUT THE BOOKS? THIS IS HOW I'LL WIN THEM OVER.
SEE... THESE BOOKS?
THEY CAN SHOW US EVERYTHING WE NEED TO KNOW ABOUT FIXING THIS PLACE UP.
IT IS VERY INTRIGUING, I MUST ADMIT.
ARE YOU SERIOUS?
YOU REALLY WANT US TO STAY HERE?
BUT THERE'S A HOLE IN THE ROOF.
WHAT IF THE BLACK RAIN COMES?
OR THE REGULAR RAIN?
WHAT ABOUT OUR PARENTS?
HOW WILL THEY FIND US?
WHAT IF SOMETHING ELSE FINDS US BEFORE THEY DO?
YEAH! AND WHAT ABOUT BREAKFAST?
I'M STARVING.

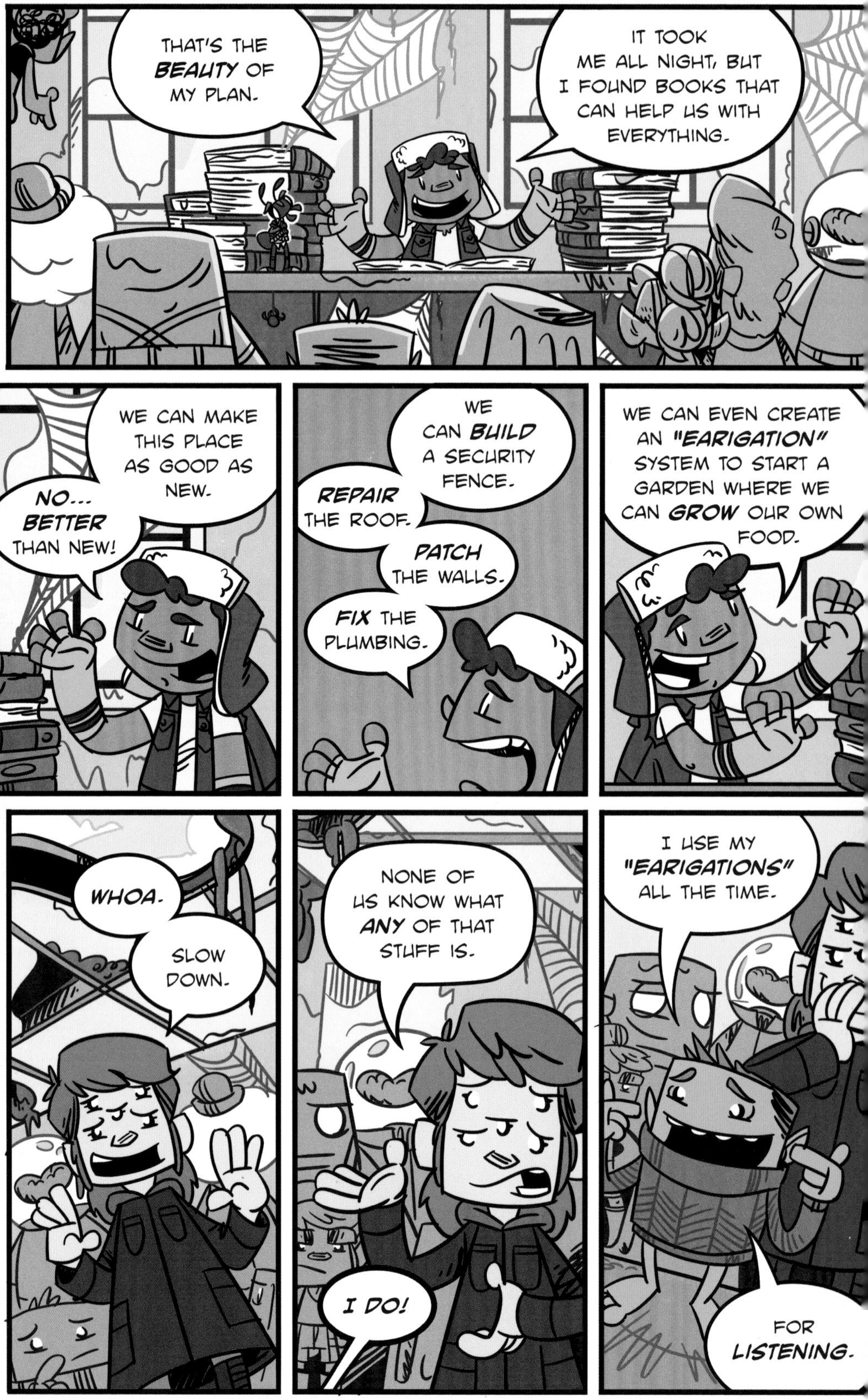
THAT'S THE BEAUTY OF MY PLAN.
IT TOOK ME ALL NIGHT, BUT I FOUND BOOKS THAT CAN HELP US WITH EVERYTHING.
WE CAN MAKE THIS PLACE AS GOOD AS NEW.
NO... BETTER THAN NEW!
WE CAN BUILD A SECURITY FENCE.
REPAIR THE ROOF.
PATCH THE WALLS.
FIX THE PLUMBING.
WE CAN EVEN CREATE AN "EARIGATION" SYSTEM TO START A GARDEN WHERE WE CAN GROW OUR OWN FOOD.
WHOA.
SLOW DOWN.
NONE OF US KNOW WHAT ANY OF THAT STUFF IS.
I DO!
I USE MY "EARIGATIONS" ALL THE TIME.
FOR LISTENING.

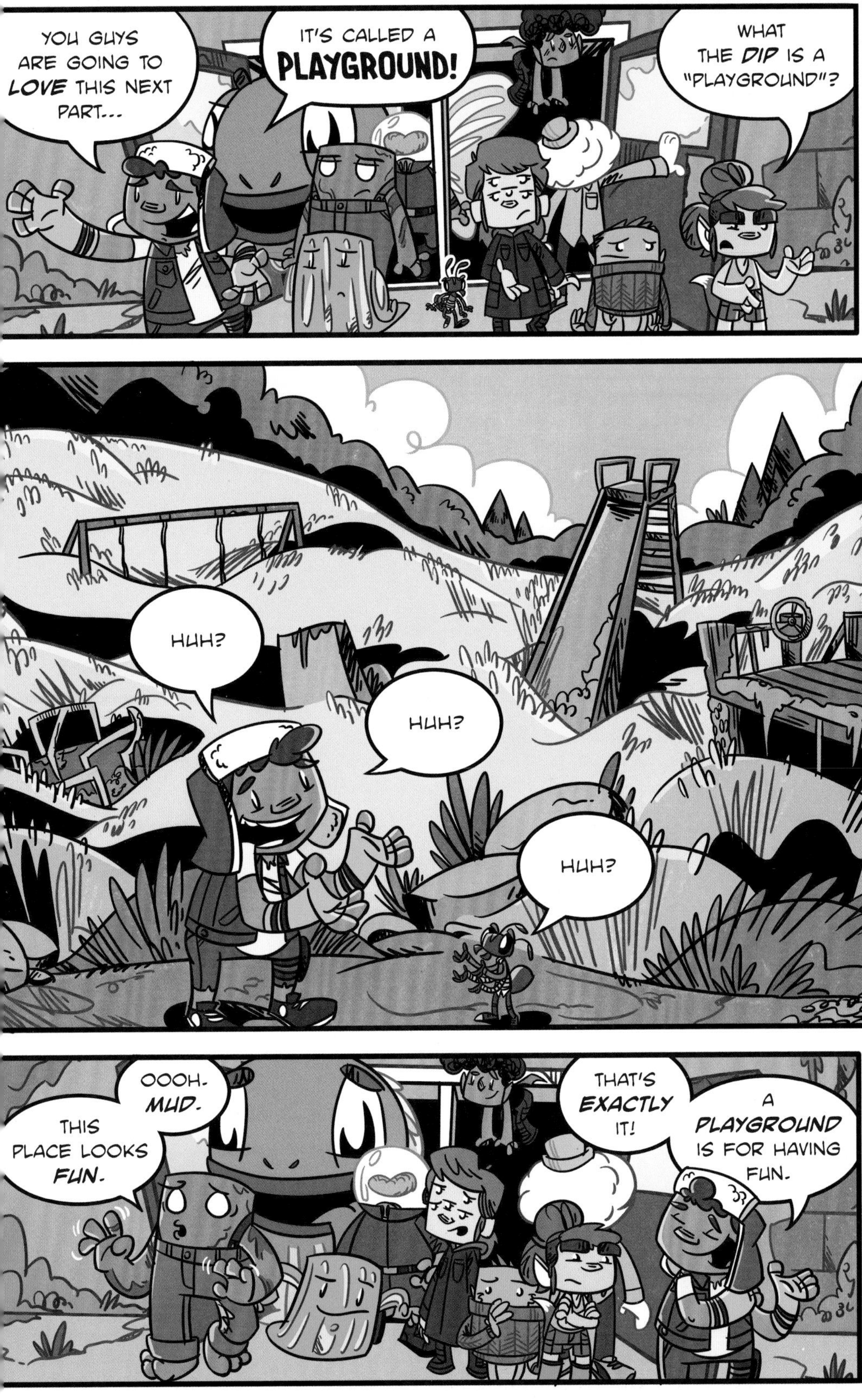
YOU GUYS ARE GOING TO LOVE THIS NEXT PART...
IT'S CALLED A PLAYGROUND!
WHAT THE DIP IS A "PLAYGROUND"?
HUH?
HUH?
HUH?
THIS PLACE LOOKS FUN.
OOOH. MUD.
THAT'S EXACTLY IT!
A PLAYGROUND IS FOR HAVING FUN.

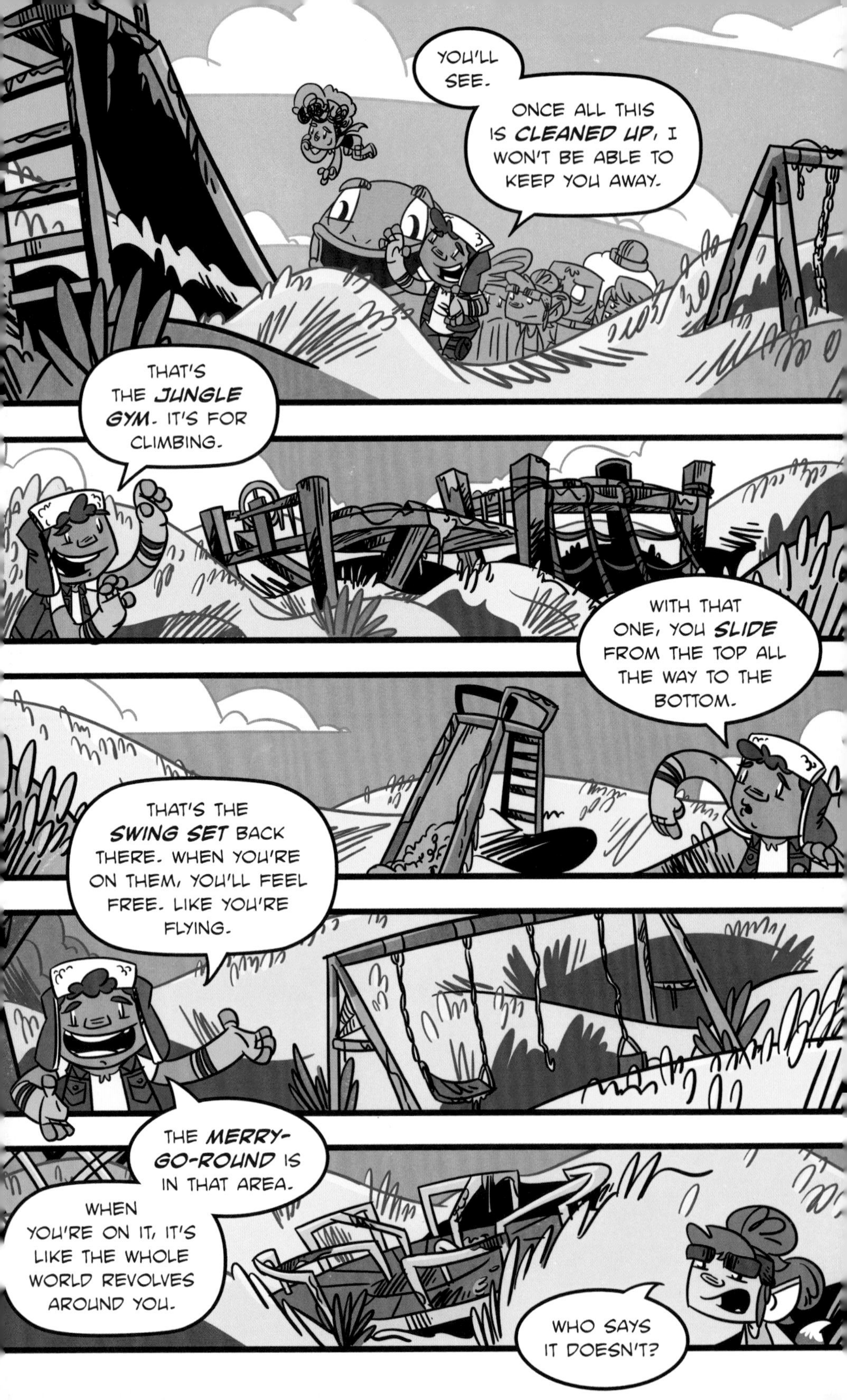

YOU'LL SEE.
ONCE ALL THIS IS CLEANED UP, I WON'T BE ABLE TO KEEP YOU AWAY.
THAT'S THE JUNGLE GYM. IT'S FOR CLIMBING.
WITH THAT ONE, YOU SLIDE FROM THE TOP ALL THE WAY TO THE BOTTOM.
THAT'S THE SWING SET BACK THERE. WHEN YOU'RE ON THEM, YOU'LL FEEL FREE. LIKE YOU'RE FLYING.
THE MERRY-GO-ROUND IS IN THAT AREA.
WHEN YOU'RE ON IT, IT'S LIKE THE WHOLE WORLD REVOLVES AROUND YOU.
WHO SAYS IT DOESN'T?

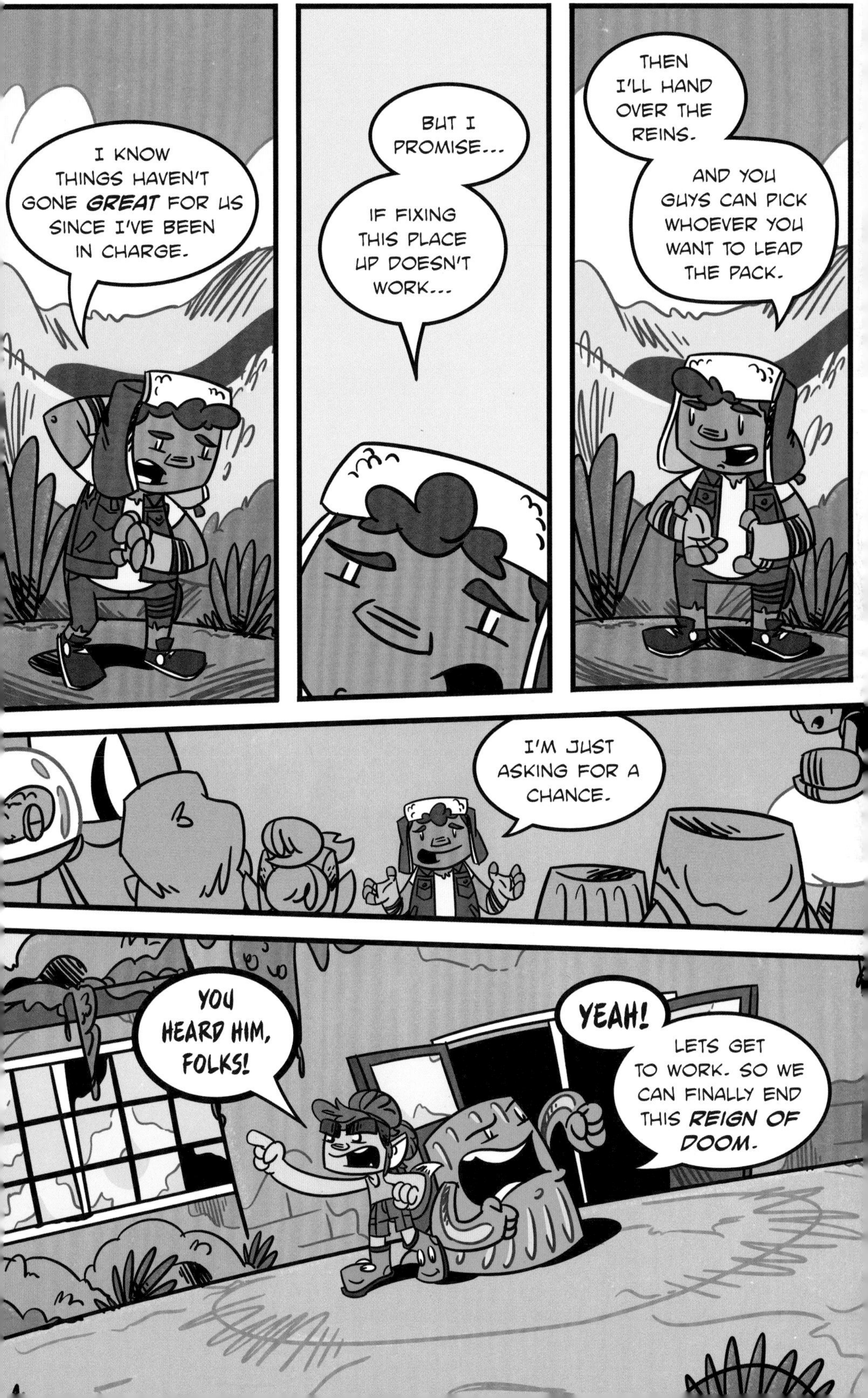
I KNOW THINGS HAVEN'T GONE GREAT FOR US SINCE I'VE BEEN IN CHARGE.
BUT I PROMISE...
IF FIXING THIS PLACE UP DOESN'T WORK...
THEN I'LL HAND OVER THE REINS.
AND YOU GUYS CAN PICK WHOEVER YOU WANT TO LEAD THE PACK.
I'M JUST ASKING FOR A CHANCE.
YOU HEARD HIM, FOLKS!
YEAH!
LETS GET TO WORK. SO WE CAN FINALLY END THIS REIGN OF DOOM.

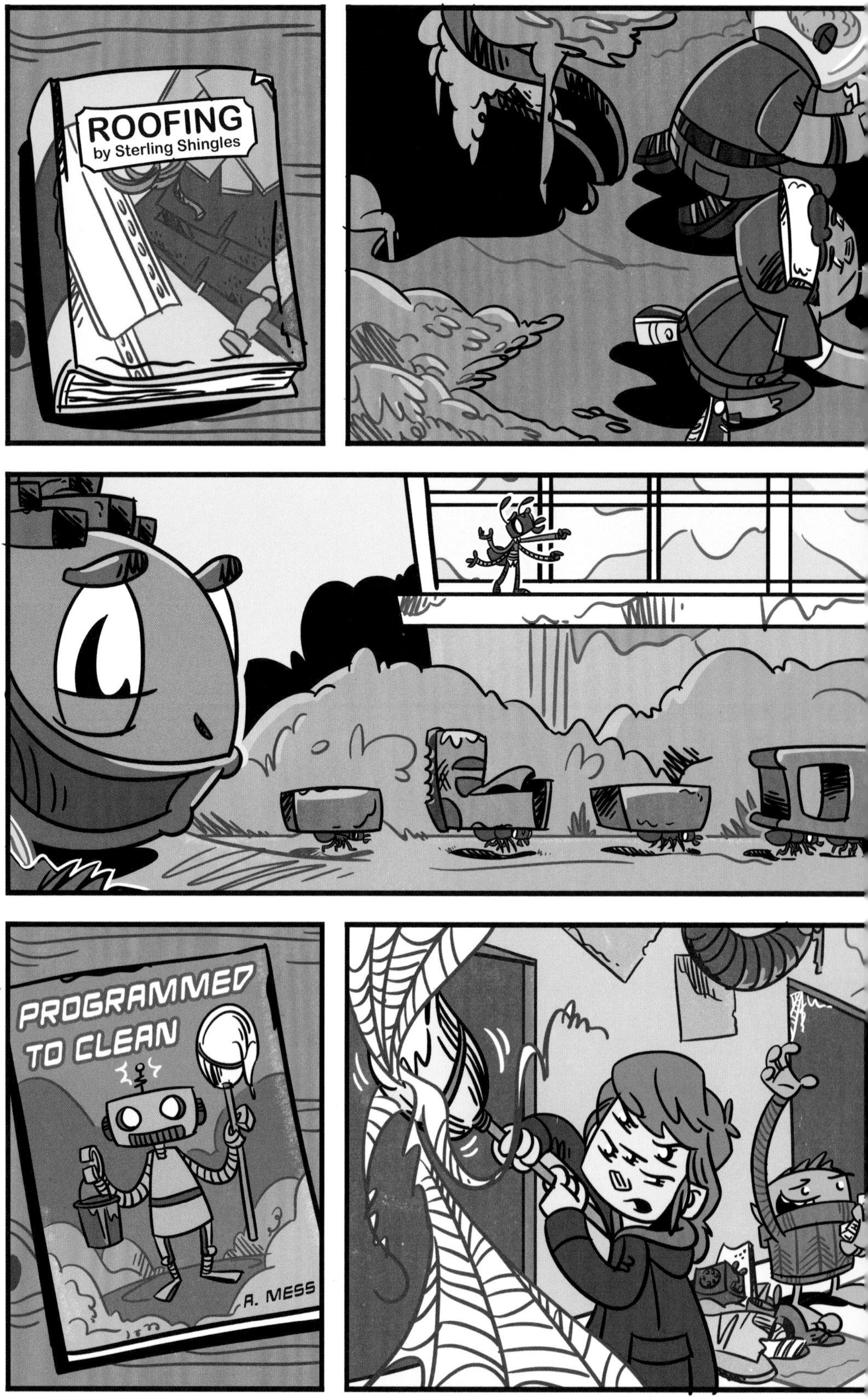
ROOFING
by Sterling Shingles
PROGRAMMED TO CLEAN
A. MESS

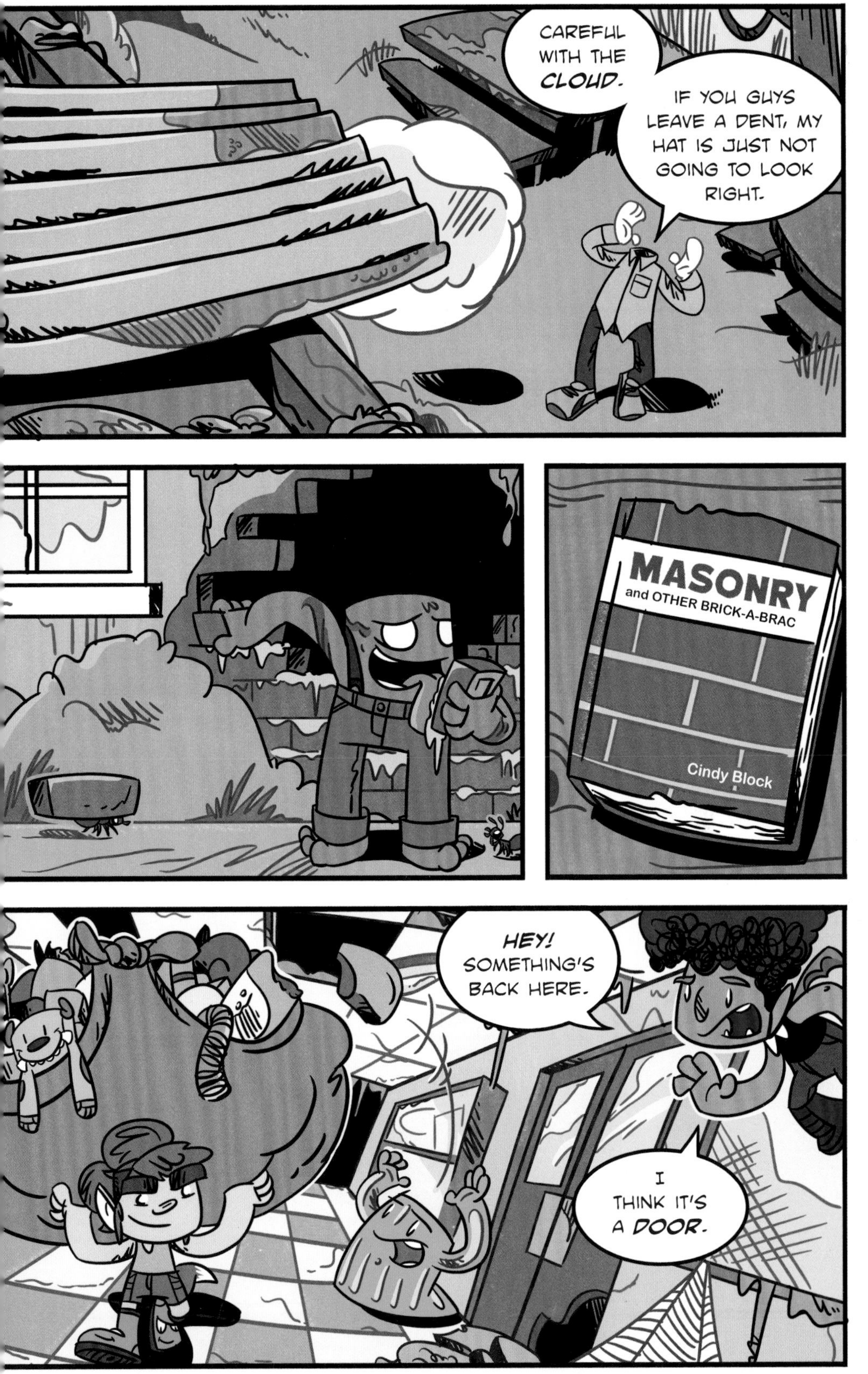
CAREFUL WITH THE *CLOUD*.
IF YOU GUYS LEAVE A DENT, MY HAT IS JUST NOT GOING TO LOOK RIGHT.
MASONRY
and OTHER BRICK-A-BRAC
Cindy Block
HEY! SOMETHING'S BACK HERE.
I THINK IT'S A *DOOR*.

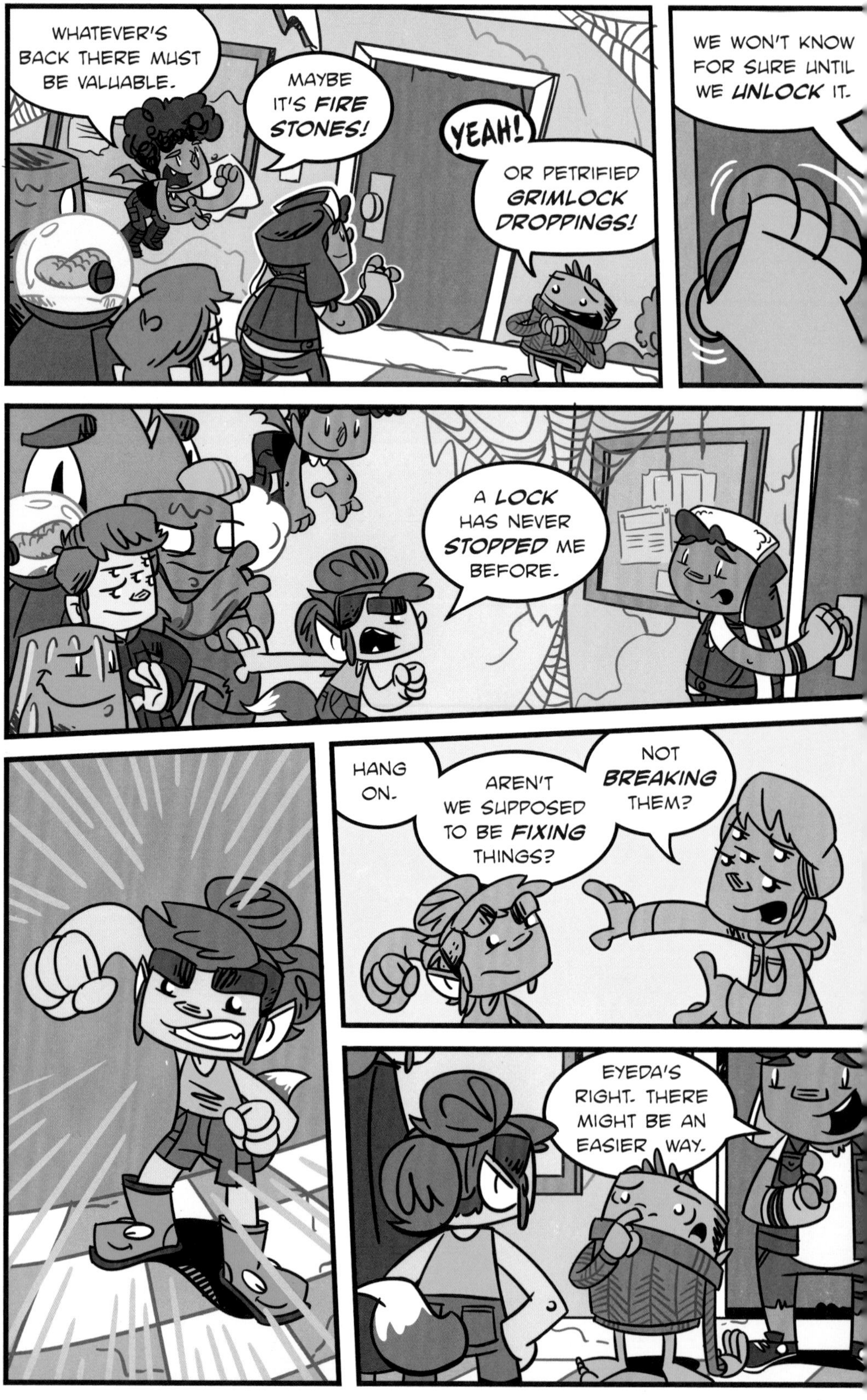

WHATEVER'S BACK THERE MUST BE VALUABLE.
MAYBE IT'S FIRE STONES!
YEAH!
OR PETRIFIED GRIMLOCK DROPPINGS!
WE WON'T KNOW FOR SURE UNTIL WE UNLOCK IT.
A LOCK HAS NEVER STOPPED ME BEFORE.
HANG ON.
AREN'T WE SUPPOSED TO BE FIXING THINGS?
NOT BREAKING THEM?
EYEDA'S RIGHT. THERE MIGHT BE AN EASIER WAY.

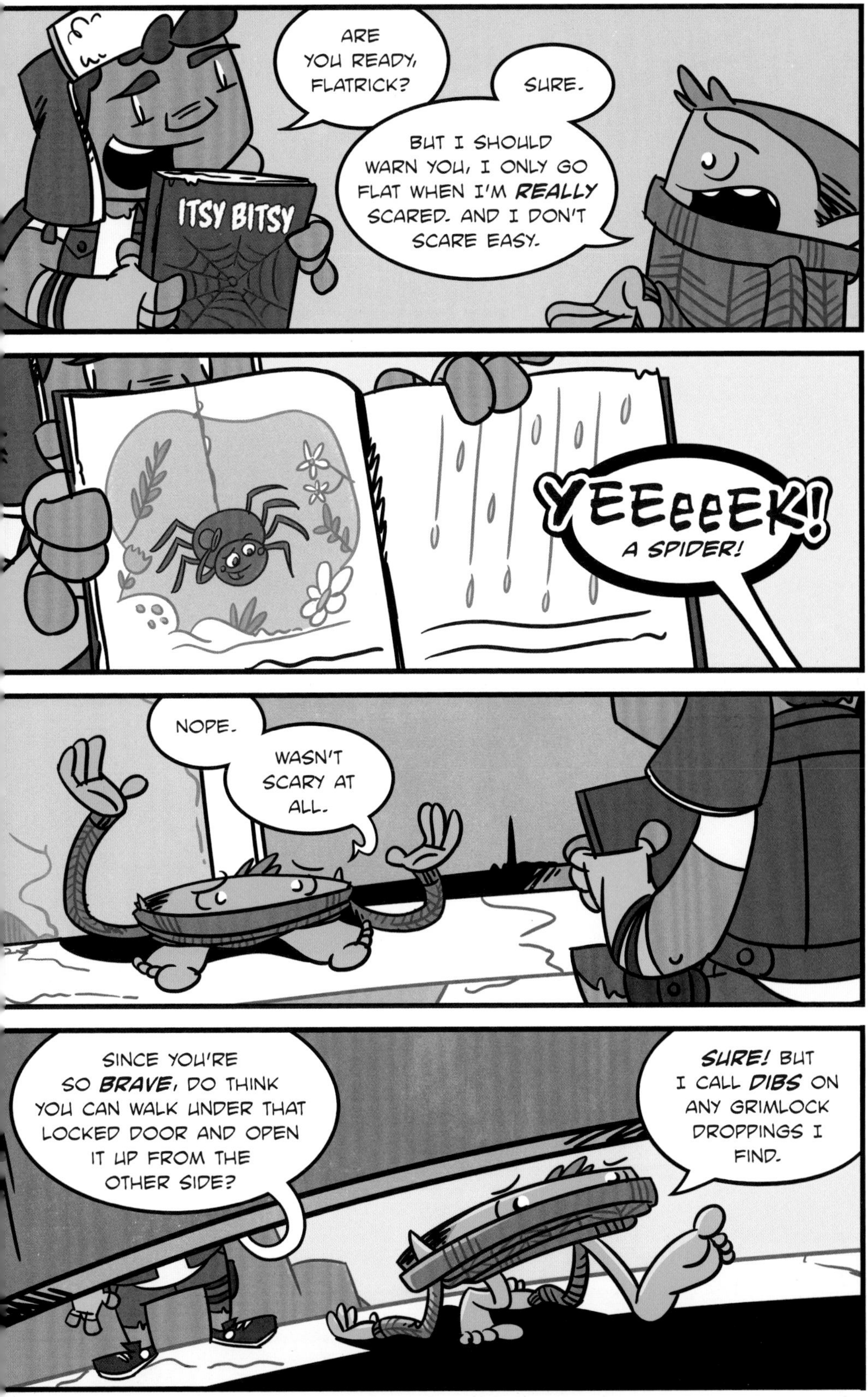
ARE YOU READY, FLATRICK?
SURE.
BUT I SHOULD WARN YOU, I ONLY GO FLAT WHEN I'M REALLY SCARED. AND I DON'T SCARE EASY.
ITSY BITSY
YEEeeEK! A SPIDER!
NOPE.
WASN'T SCARY AT ALL.
SINCE YOU'RE SO BRAVE, DO THINK YOU CAN WALK UNDER THAT LOCKED DOOR AND OPEN IT UP FROM THE OTHER SIDE?
SURE! BUT I CALL DIBS ON ANY GRIMLOCK DROPPINGS I FIND.

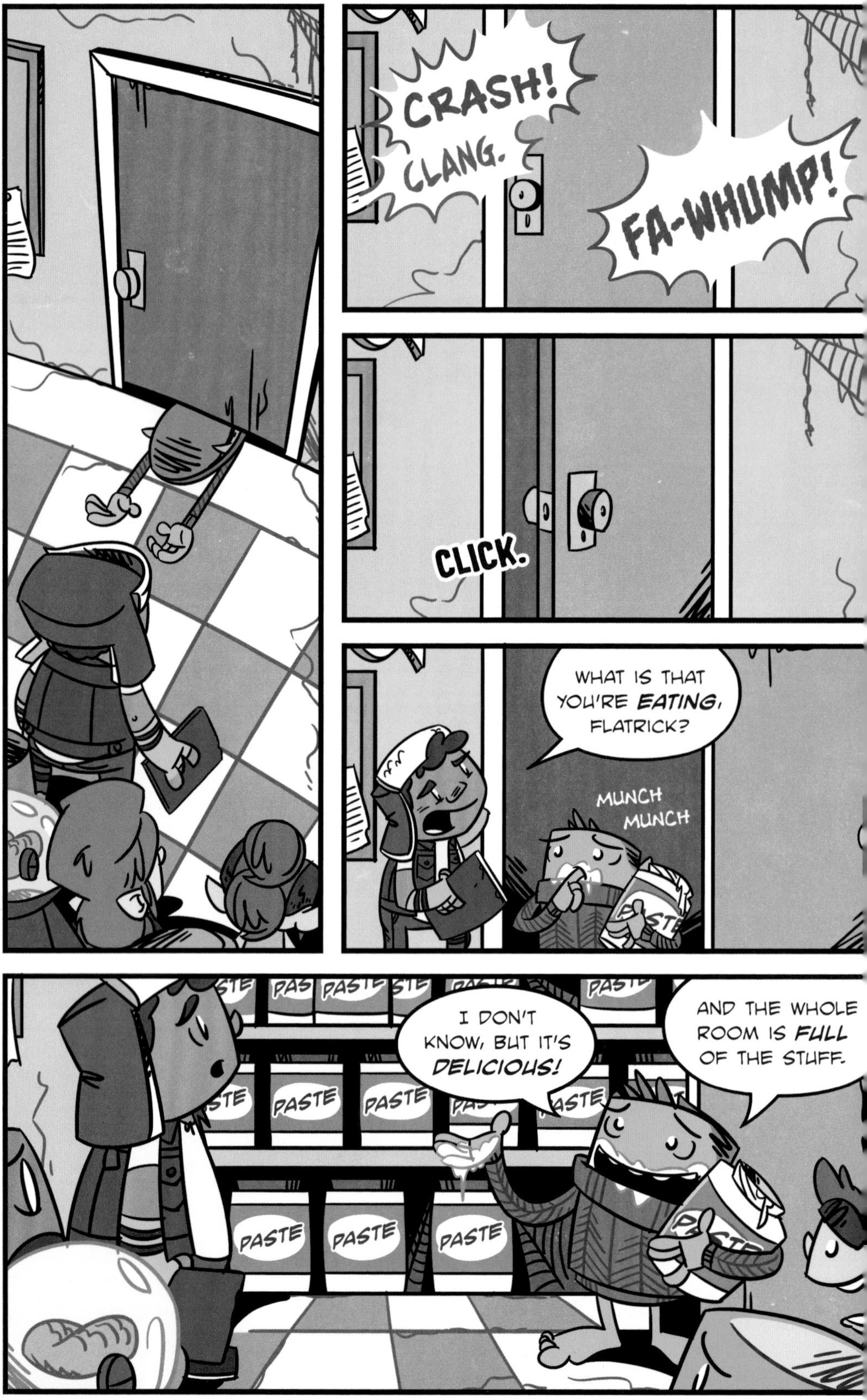
CRASH!
CLANG.
FA-WHUMP!
CLICK.
WHAT IS THAT YOU'RE *EATING*, FLATRICK?
MUNCH MUNCH
PASTE
I DON'T KNOW, BUT IT'S *DELICIOUS!*
AND THE WHOLE ROOM IS *FULL* OF THE STUFF.

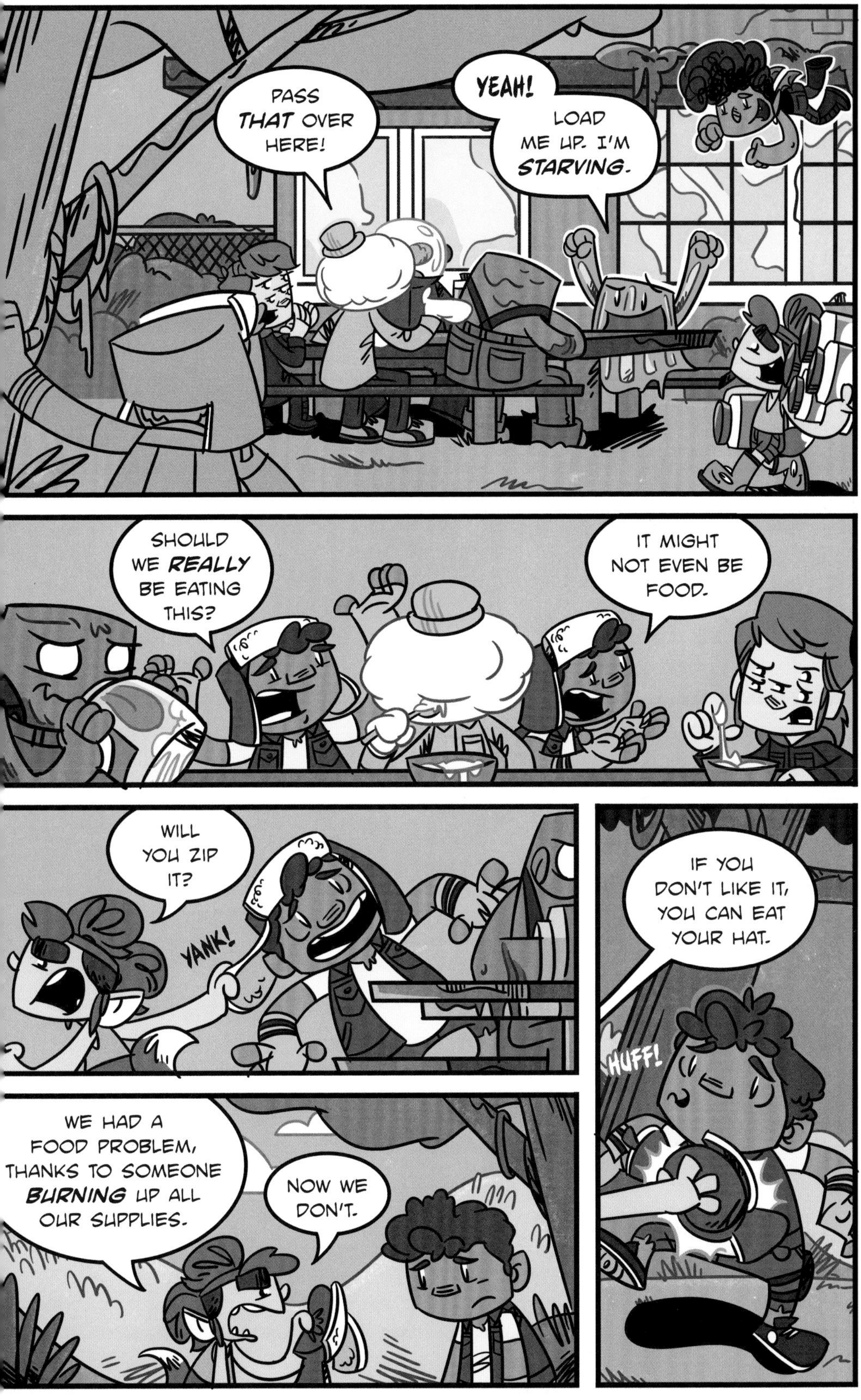
PASS THAT OVER HERE!
YEAH!
LOAD ME UP. I'M STARVING.
SHOULD WE REALLY BE EATING THIS?
IT MIGHT NOT EVEN BE FOOD.
WILL YOU ZIP IT?
YANK!
IF YOU DON'T LIKE IT, YOU CAN EAT YOUR HAT.
HUFF!
WE HAD A FOOD PROBLEM, THANKS TO SOMEONE BURNING UP ALL OUR SUPPLIES.
NOW WE DON'T.

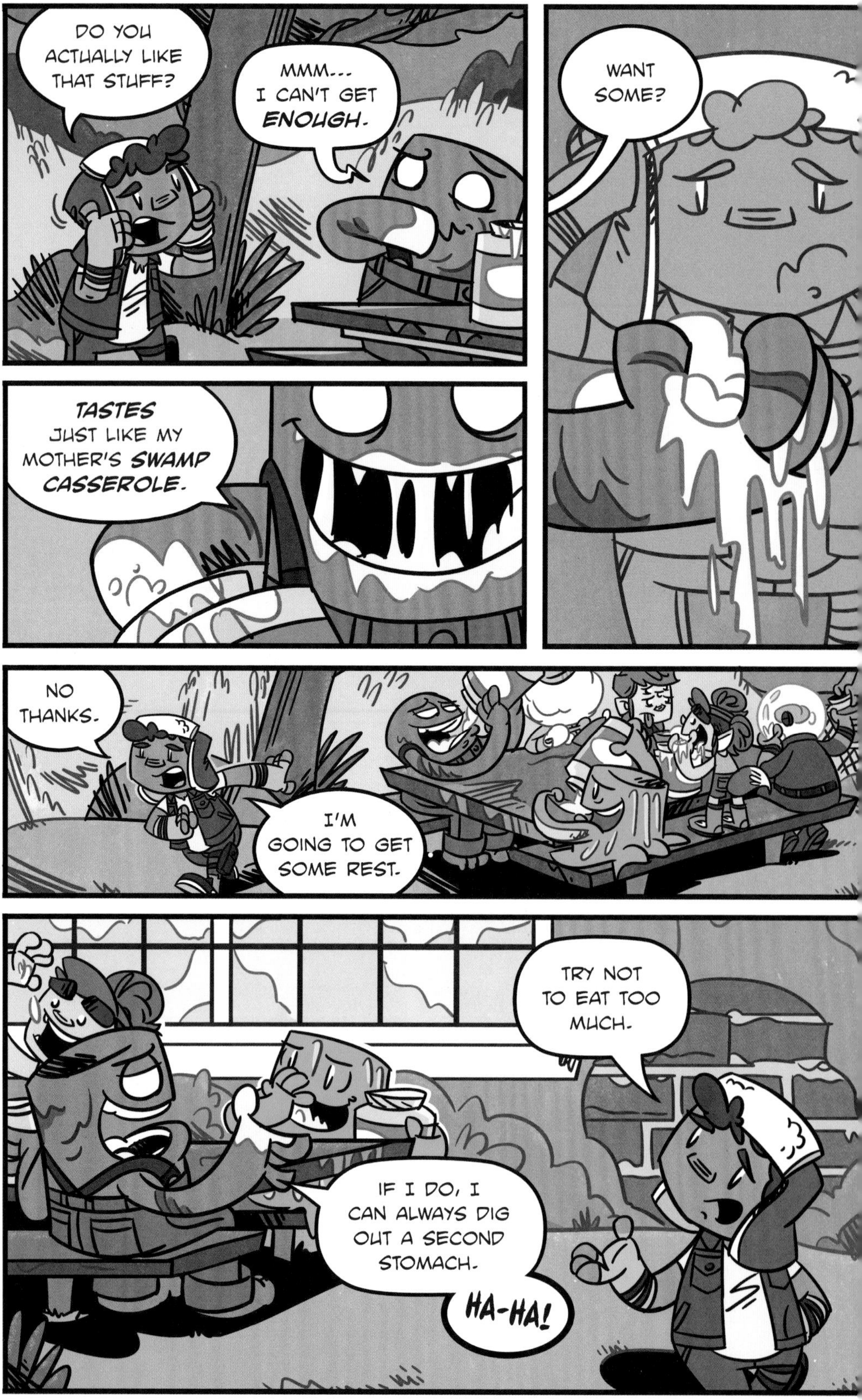
DO YOU ACTUALLY LIKE THAT STUFF?
MMM... I CAN'T GET ENOUGH.
WANT SOME?
TASTES JUST LIKE MY MOTHER'S SWAMP CASSEROLE.
NO THANKS.
I'M GOING TO GET SOME REST.
TRY NOT TO EAT TOO MUCH.
IF I DO, I CAN ALWAYS DIG OUT A SECOND STOMACH.
HA-HA!

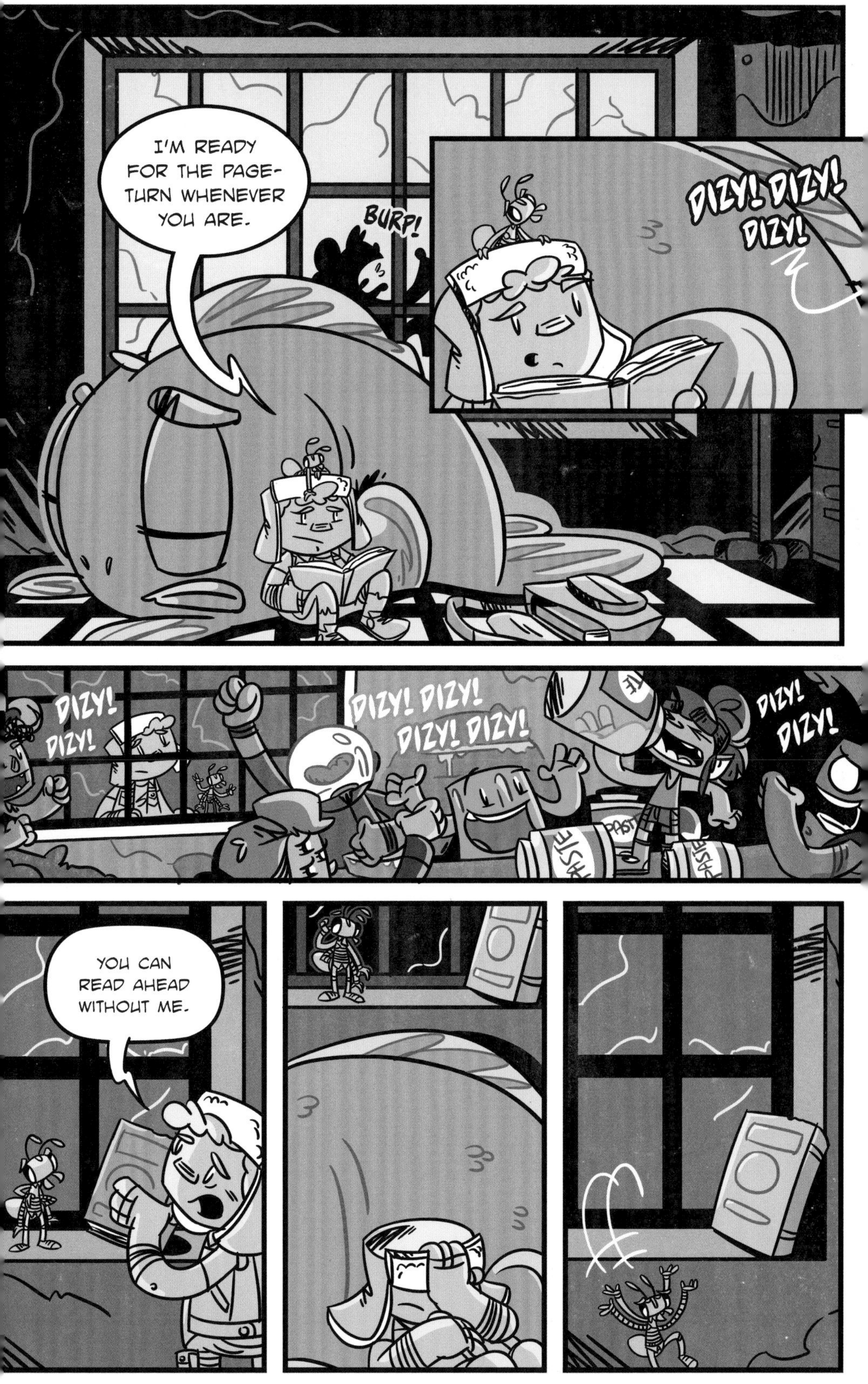
I'M READY FOR THE PAGE-TURN WHENEVER YOU ARE.
BURP!
DIZY! DIZY! DIZY!
DIZY! DIZY!
DIZY! DIZY! DIZY! DIZY!
DIZY! DIZY!
PASTE
PASTE
PASTE
YOU CAN READ AHEAD WITHOUT ME.

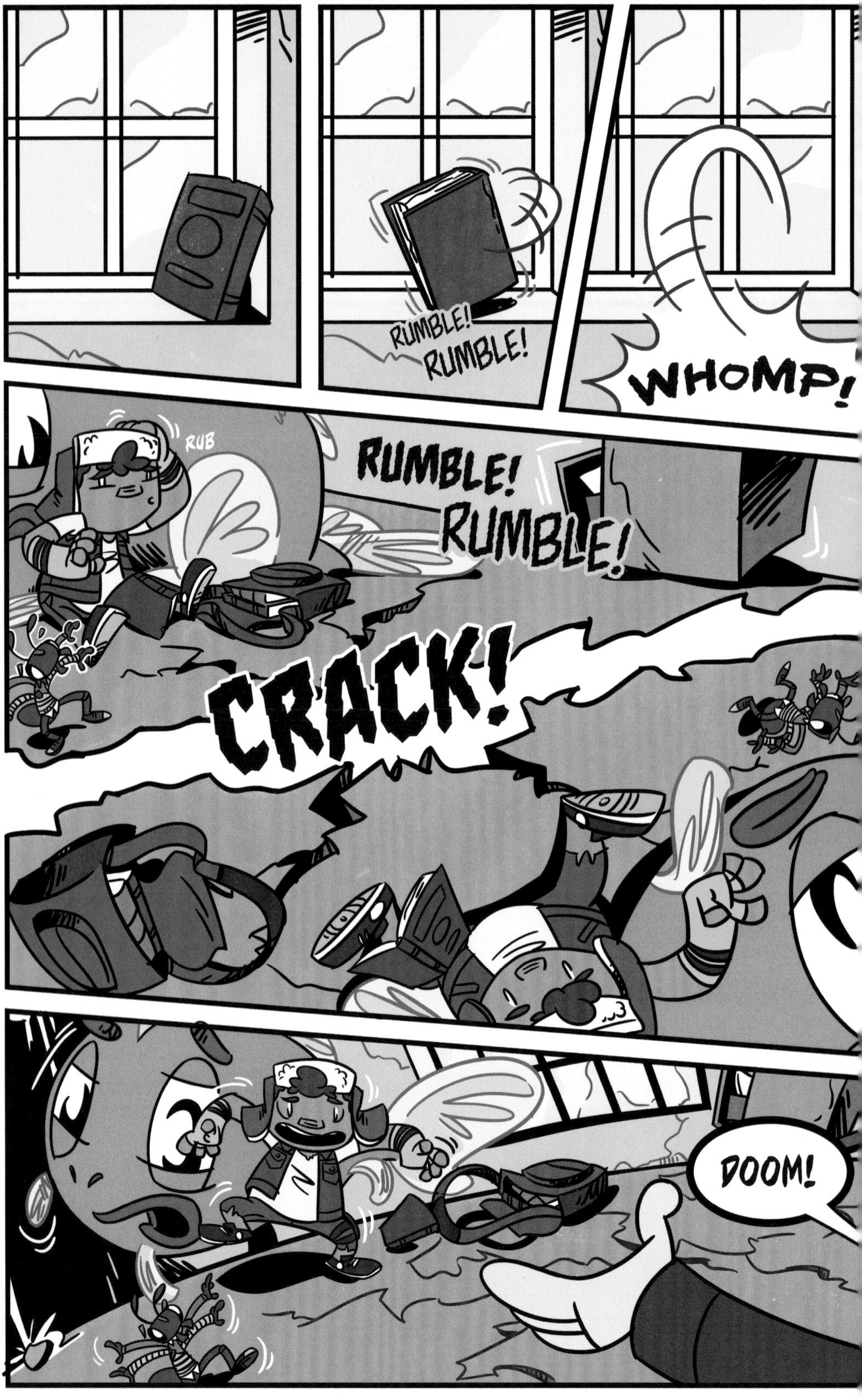
RUMBLE!
RUMBLE!
WHOMP!
RUB
RUMBLE!
RUMBLE!
CRACK!
DOOM!

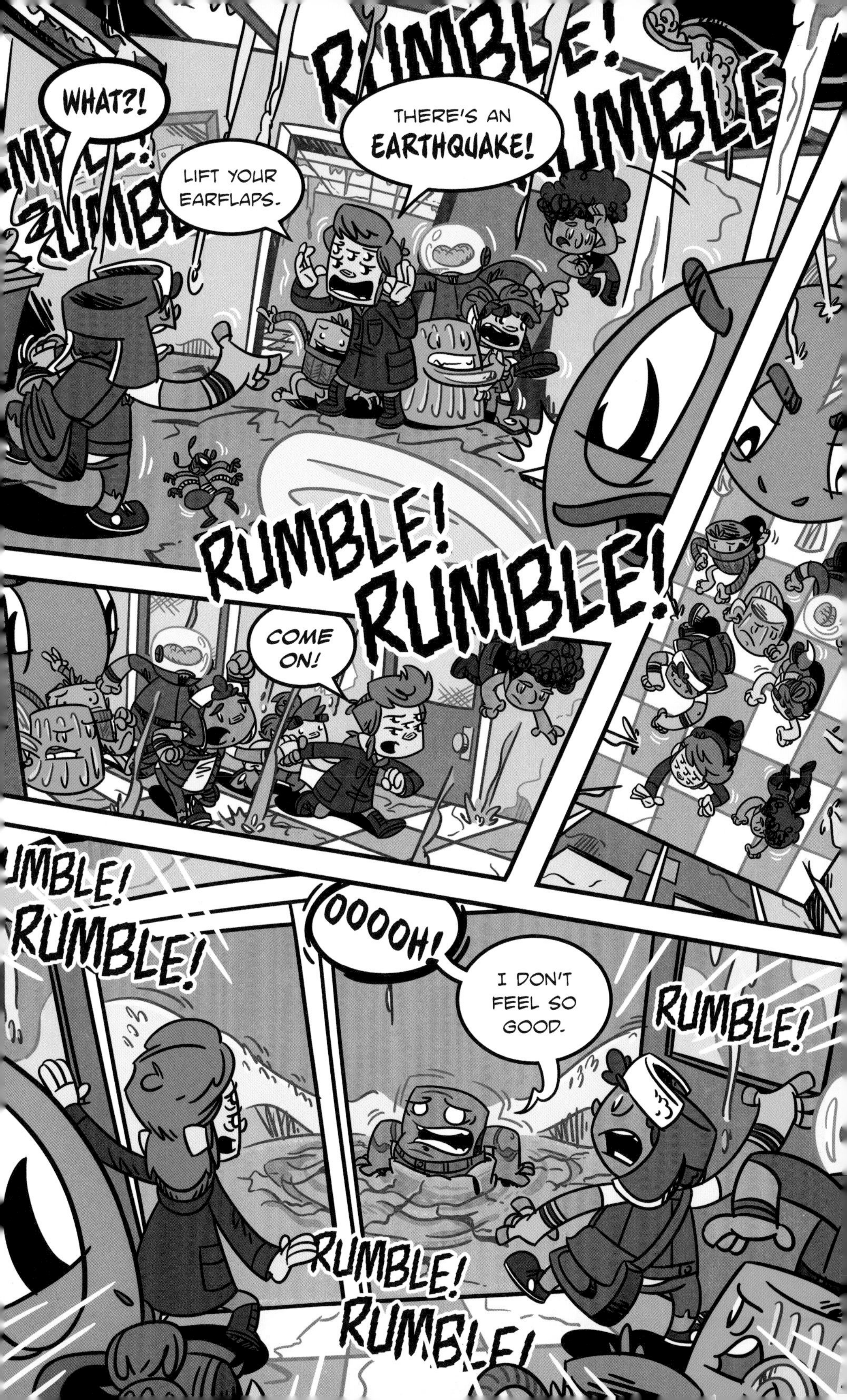

RUMBLE! RUMBLE
WHAT?!
LIFT YOUR EARFLAPS.
THERE'S AN EARTHQUAKE!
RUMBLE! RUMBLE!
COME ON!
UMBLE! RUMBLE!
OOOOH!
I DON'T FEEL SO GOOD.
RUMBLE!
RUMBLE! RUMBLE!

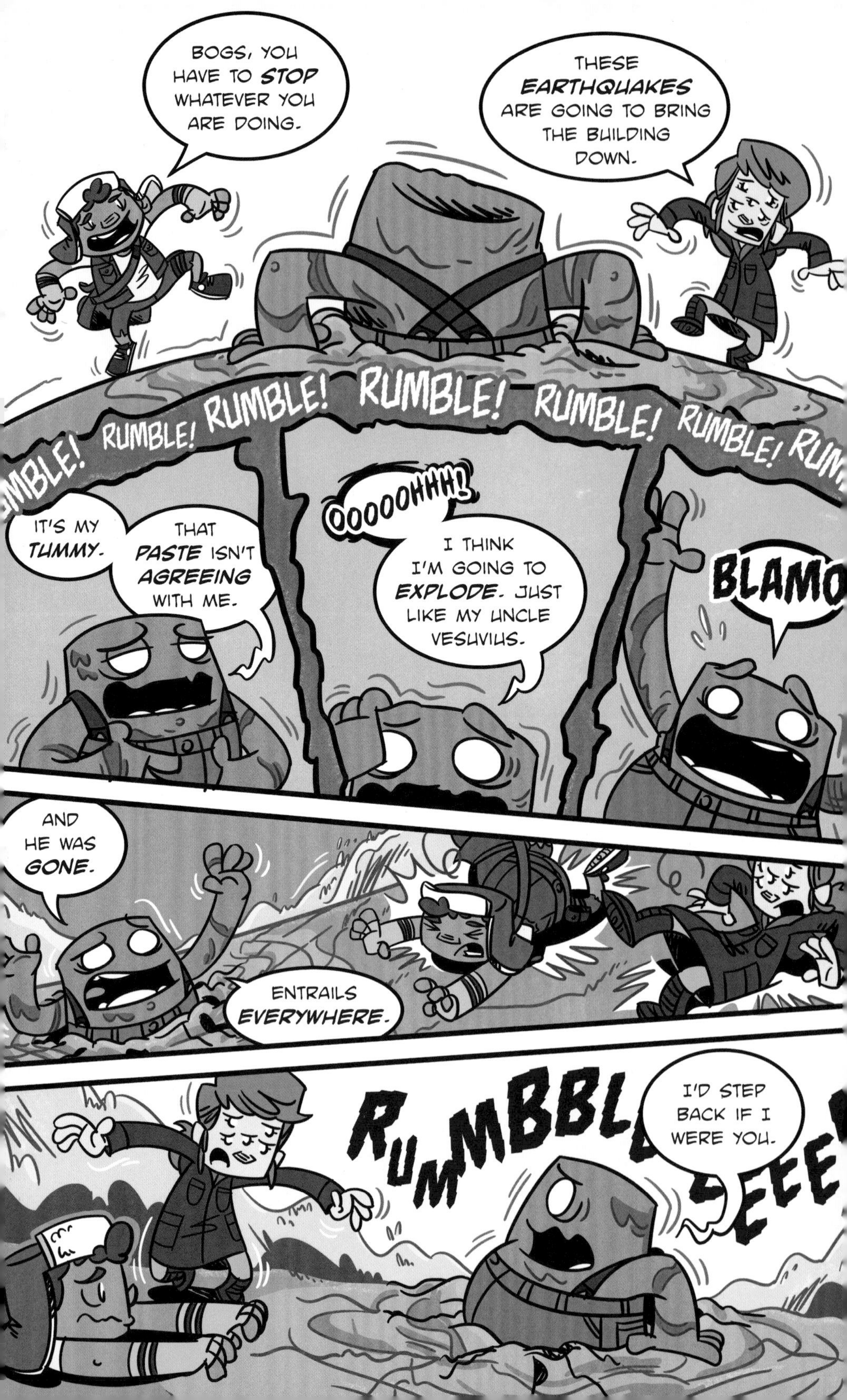
BOGS, YOU HAVE TO STOP WHATEVER YOU ARE DOING.
THESE EARTHQUAKES ARE GOING TO BRING THE BUILDING DOWN.
RUMBLE! RUMBLE! RUMBLE! RUMBLE! RUMBLE!
IT'S MY TUMMY.
THAT PASTE ISN'T AGREEING WITH ME.
OOOOOHHH!
I THINK I'M GOING TO EXPLODE. JUST LIKE MY UNCLE VESUVIUS.
BLAMO
AND HE WAS GONE.
ENTRAILS EVERYWHERE.
I'D STEP BACK IF I WERE YOU.

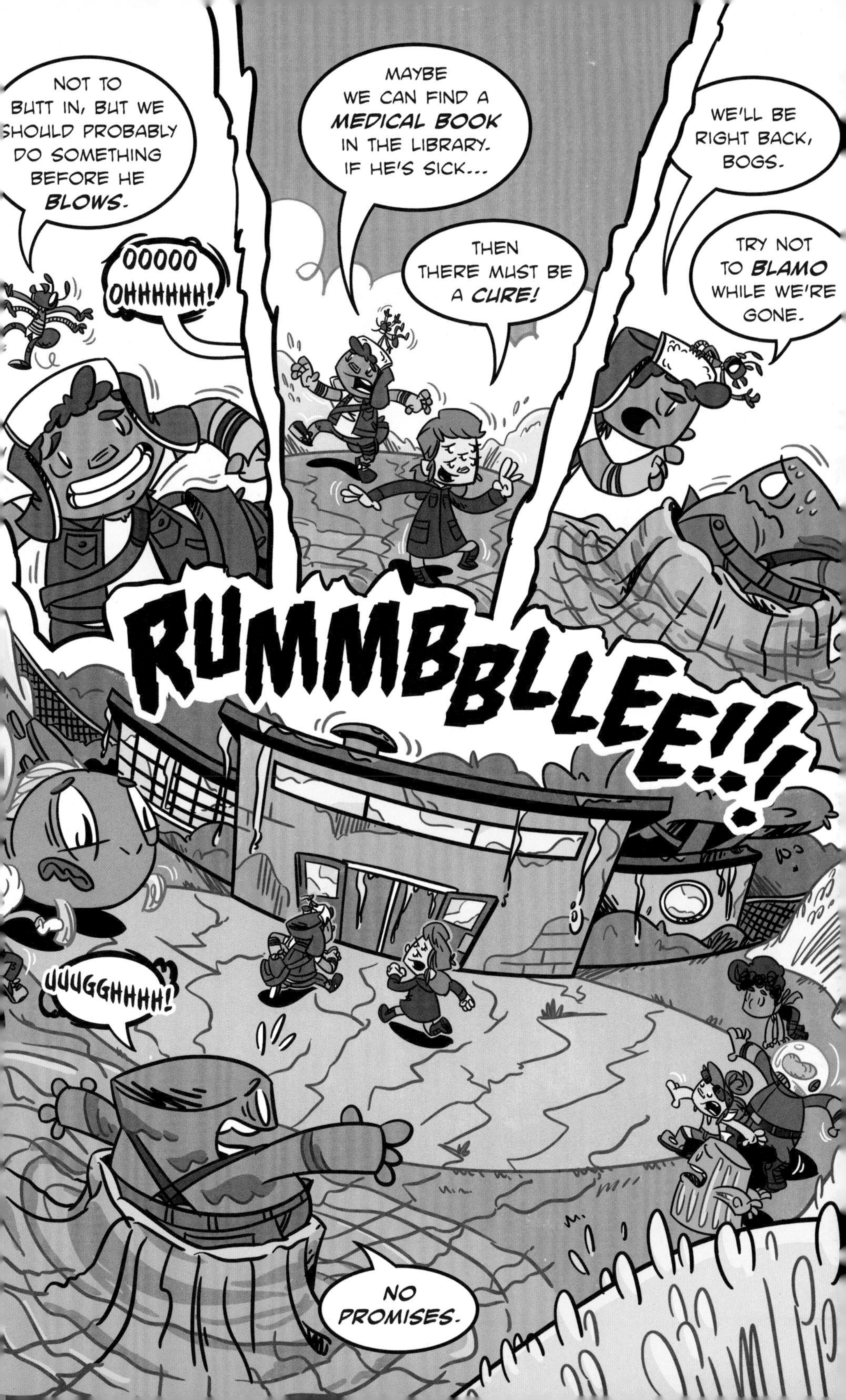
NOT TO BUTT IN, BUT WE SHOULD PROBABLY DO SOMETHING BEFORE HE BLOWS.
OOOOO OHHHHHH!
MAYBE WE CAN FIND A MEDICAL BOOK IN THE LIBRARY. IF HE'S SICK...
THEN THERE MUST BE A CURE!
WE'LL BE RIGHT BACK, BOGS.
TRY NOT TO BLAMO WHILE WE'RE GONE.
RUMMBBLLEE!!!
UUUGGHHHH!
NO PROMISES.

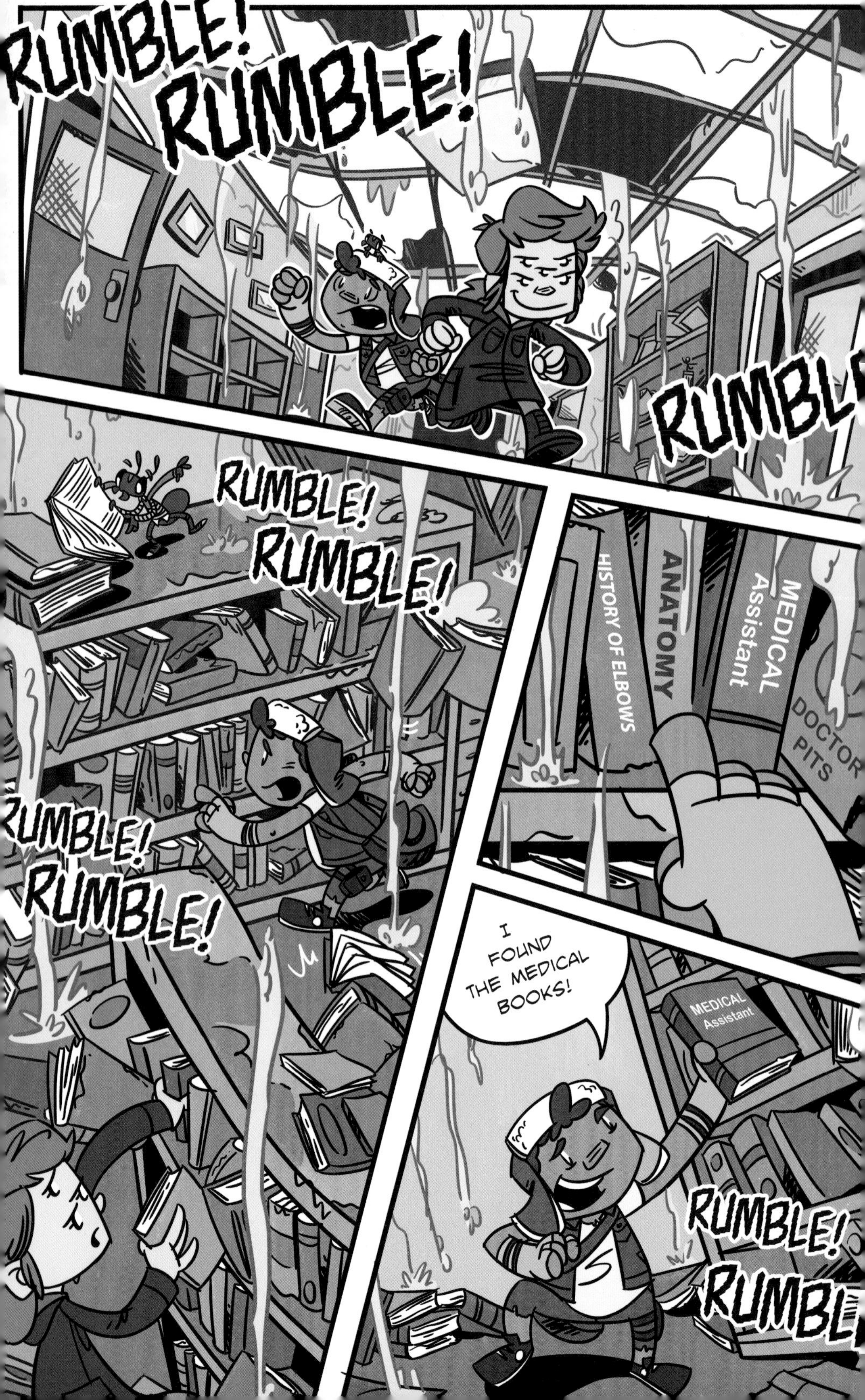
RUMBLE! RUMBLE!
RUMBLE
RUMBLE! RUMBLE!
RUMBLE! RUMBLE!
HISTORY OF ELBOWS
ANATOMY
MEDICAL Assistant
DOCTOR PITS
I FOUND THE MEDICAL BOOKS!
MEDICAL Assistant
RUMBLE! RUMBL

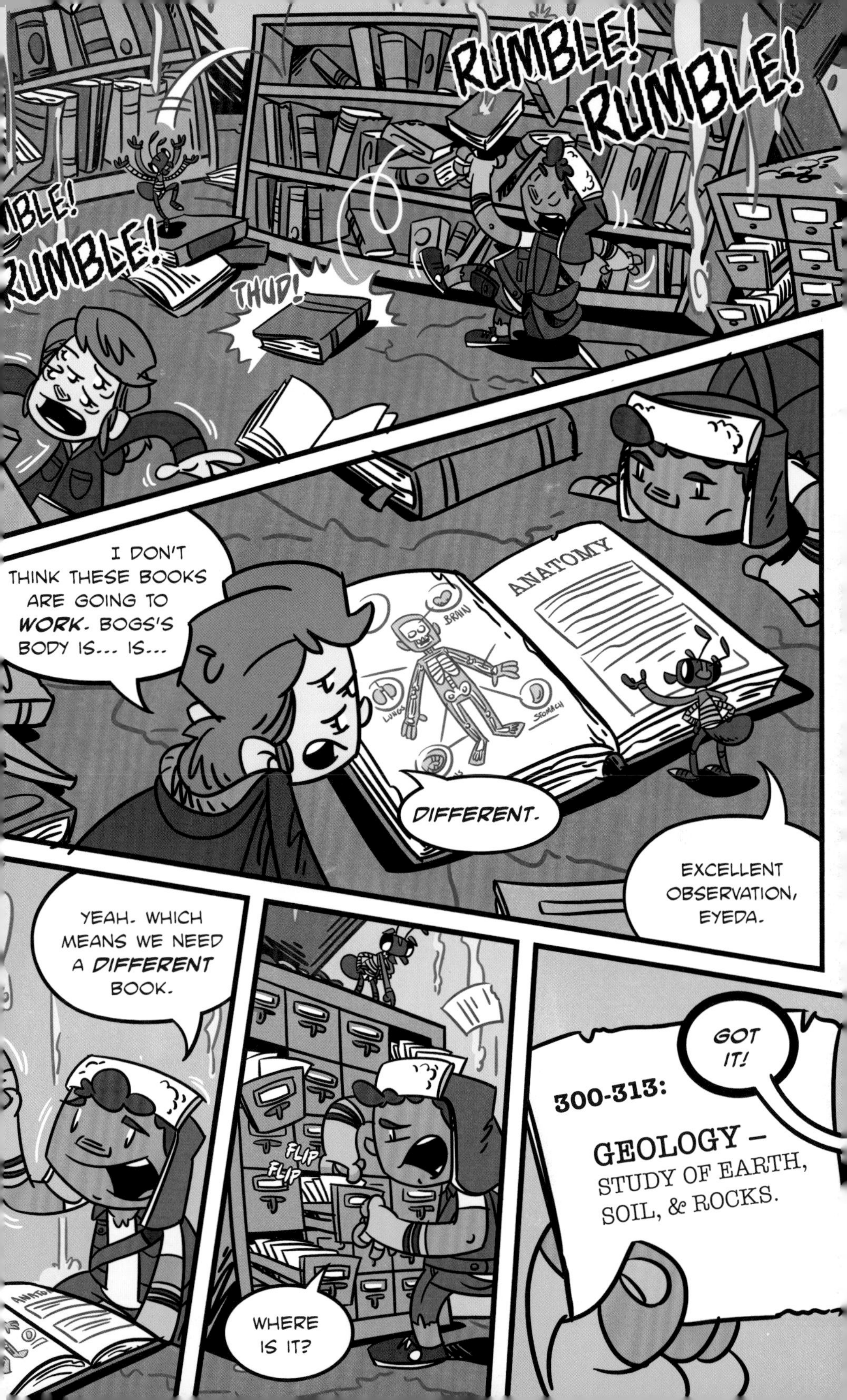
RUMBLE! RUMBLE!
RUMBLE! RUMBLE!
THUD!
I DON'T THINK THESE BOOKS ARE GOING TO WORK. BOGS'S BODY IS... IS...
ANATOMY
BRAIN
LUNGS
STOMACH
DIFFERENT.
EXCELLENT OBSERVATION, EYEDA.
YEAH. WHICH MEANS WE NEED A DIFFERENT BOOK.
FLIP FLIP
WHERE IS IT?
GOT IT!
300-313:
GEOLOGY – STUDY OF EARTH, SOIL, & ROCKS.

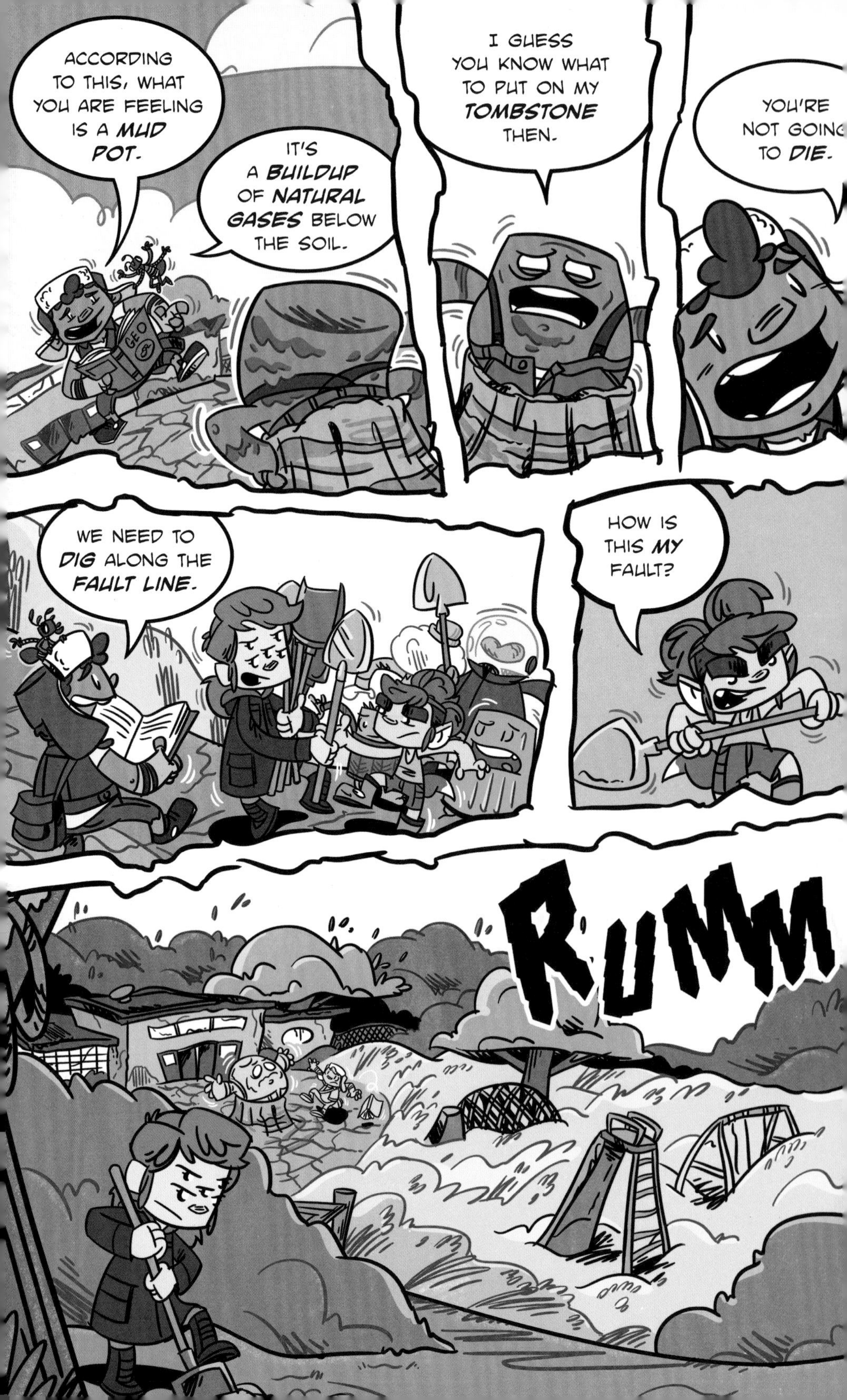
ACCORDING TO THIS, WHAT YOU ARE FEELING IS A MUD POT.
IT'S A BUILDUP OF NATURAL GASES BELOW THE SOIL.
GEO
I GUESS YOU KNOW WHAT TO PUT ON MY TOMBSTONE THEN.
YOU'RE NOT GOING TO DIE.
WE NEED TO DIG ALONG THE FAULT LINE.
HOW IS THIS MY FAULT?
RUMM

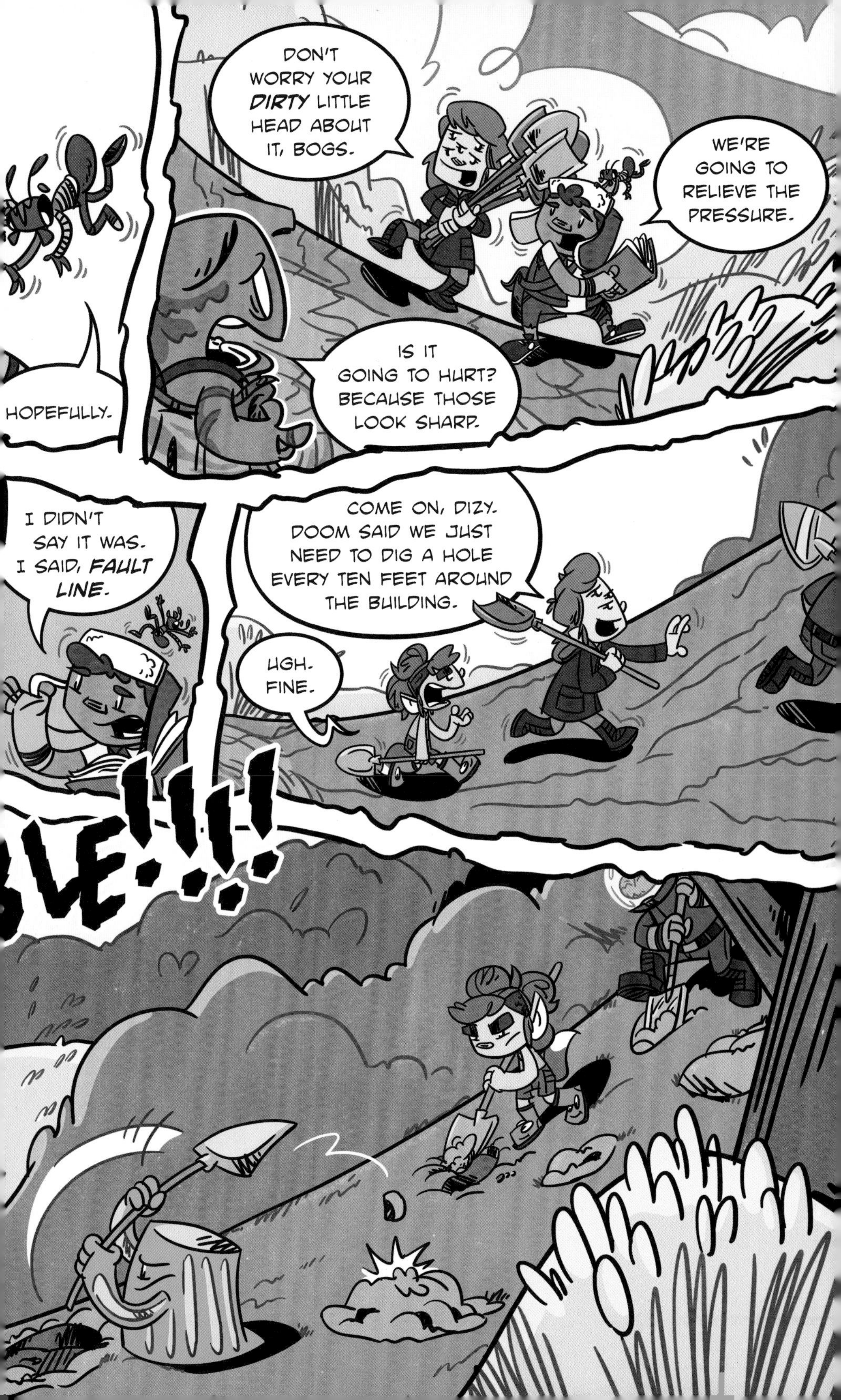
DON'T WORRY YOUR DIRTY LITTLE HEAD ABOUT IT, BOGS.
WE'RE GOING TO RELIEVE THE PRESSURE.
HOPEFULLY.
IS IT GOING TO HURT? BECAUSE THOSE LOOK SHARP.
I DIDN'T SAY IT WAS. I SAID, FAULT LINE.
COME ON, DIZY. DOOM SAID WE JUST NEED TO DIG A HOLE EVERY TEN FEET AROUND THE BUILDING.
UGH. FINE.
BLE!!!!

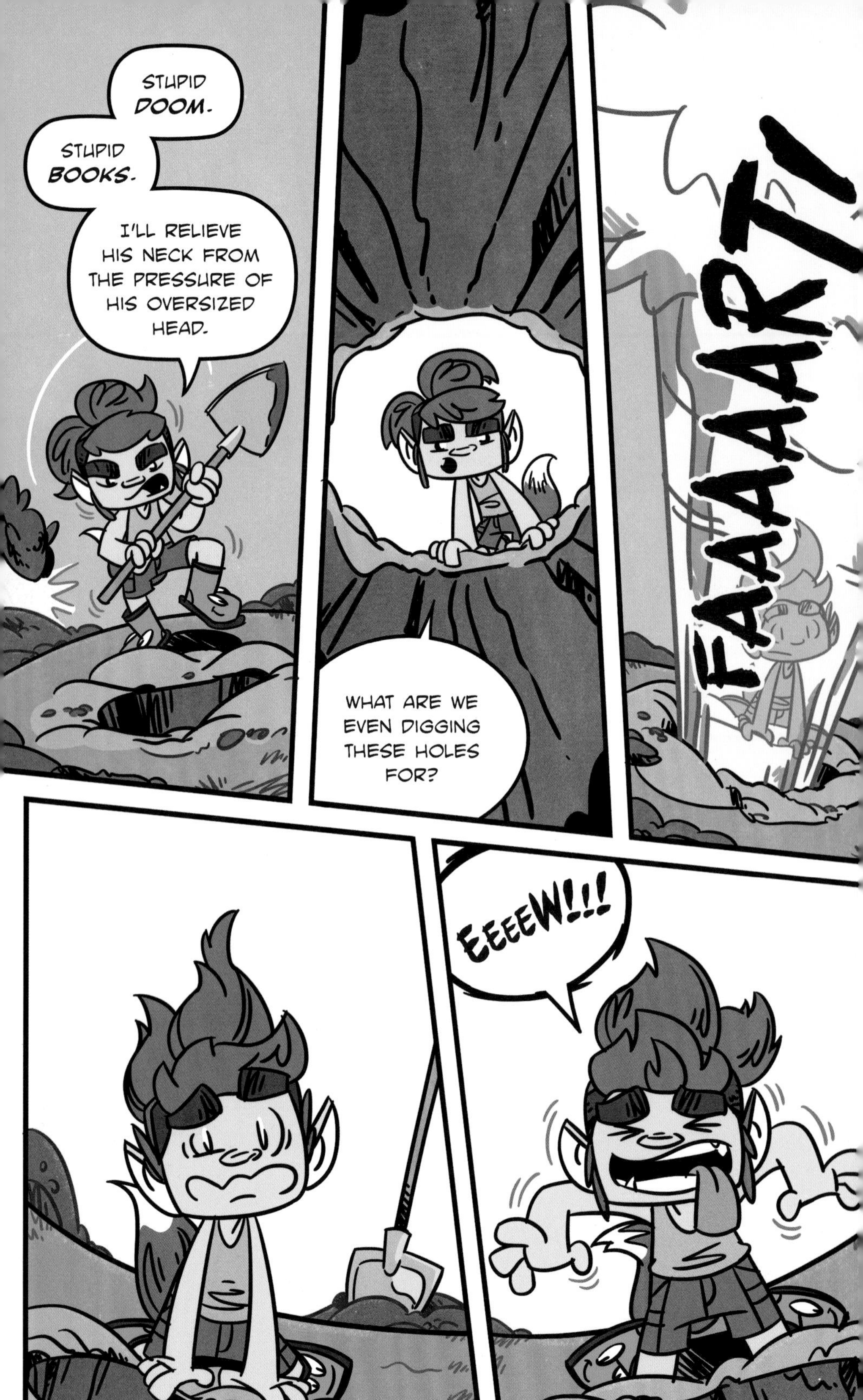
STUPID DOOM.
STUPID BOOKS.
I'LL RELIEVE HIS NECK FROM THE PRESSURE OF HIS OVERSIZED HEAD.
WHAT ARE WE EVEN DIGGING THESE HOLES FOR?
FAAAART!
EEEEW!!!

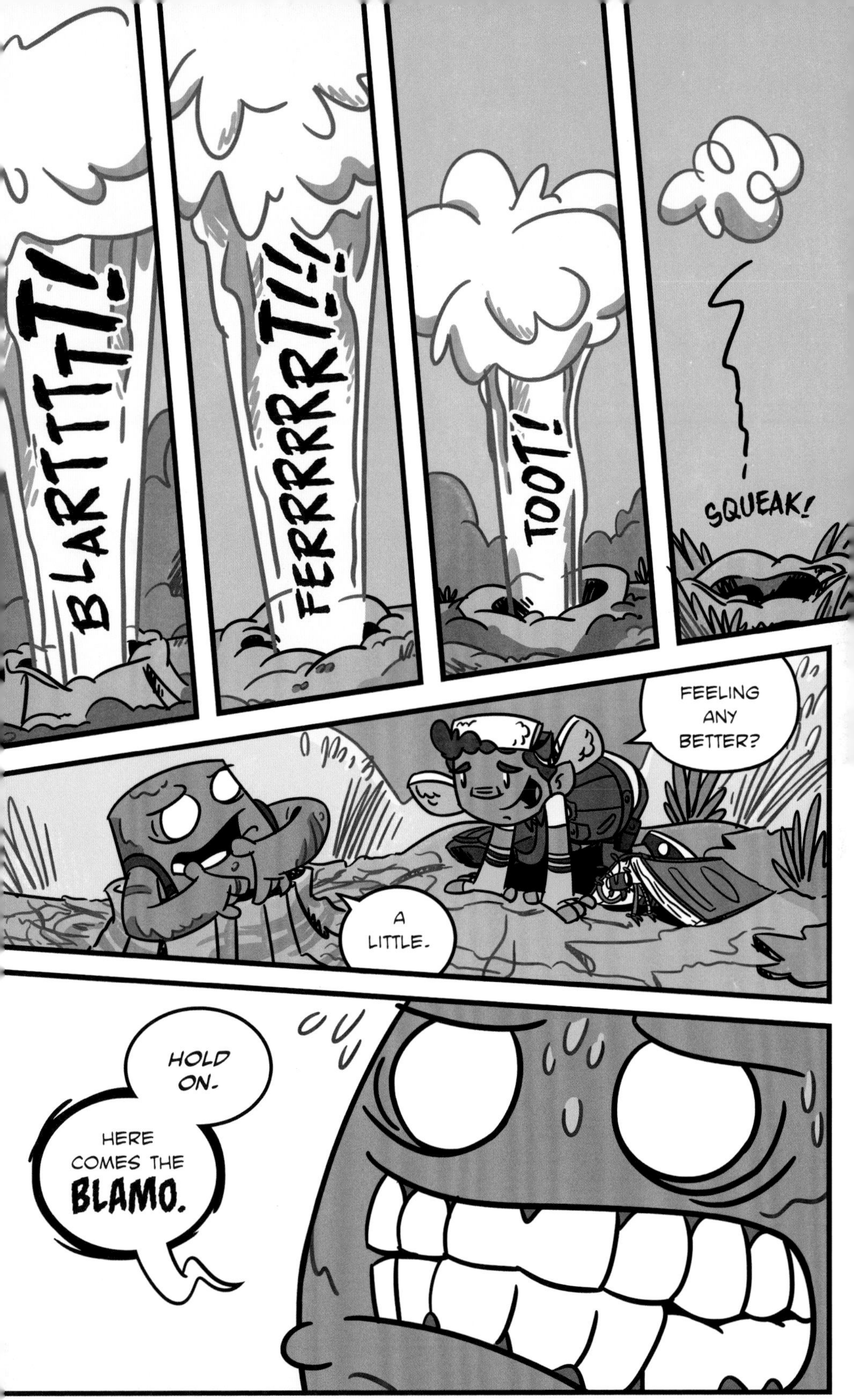
BLARTTTTT!!
FERRRRRRT!!
TOOT!
SQUEAK!
FEELING ANY BETTER?
A LITTLE.
HOLD ON.
HERE COMES THE BLAMO.

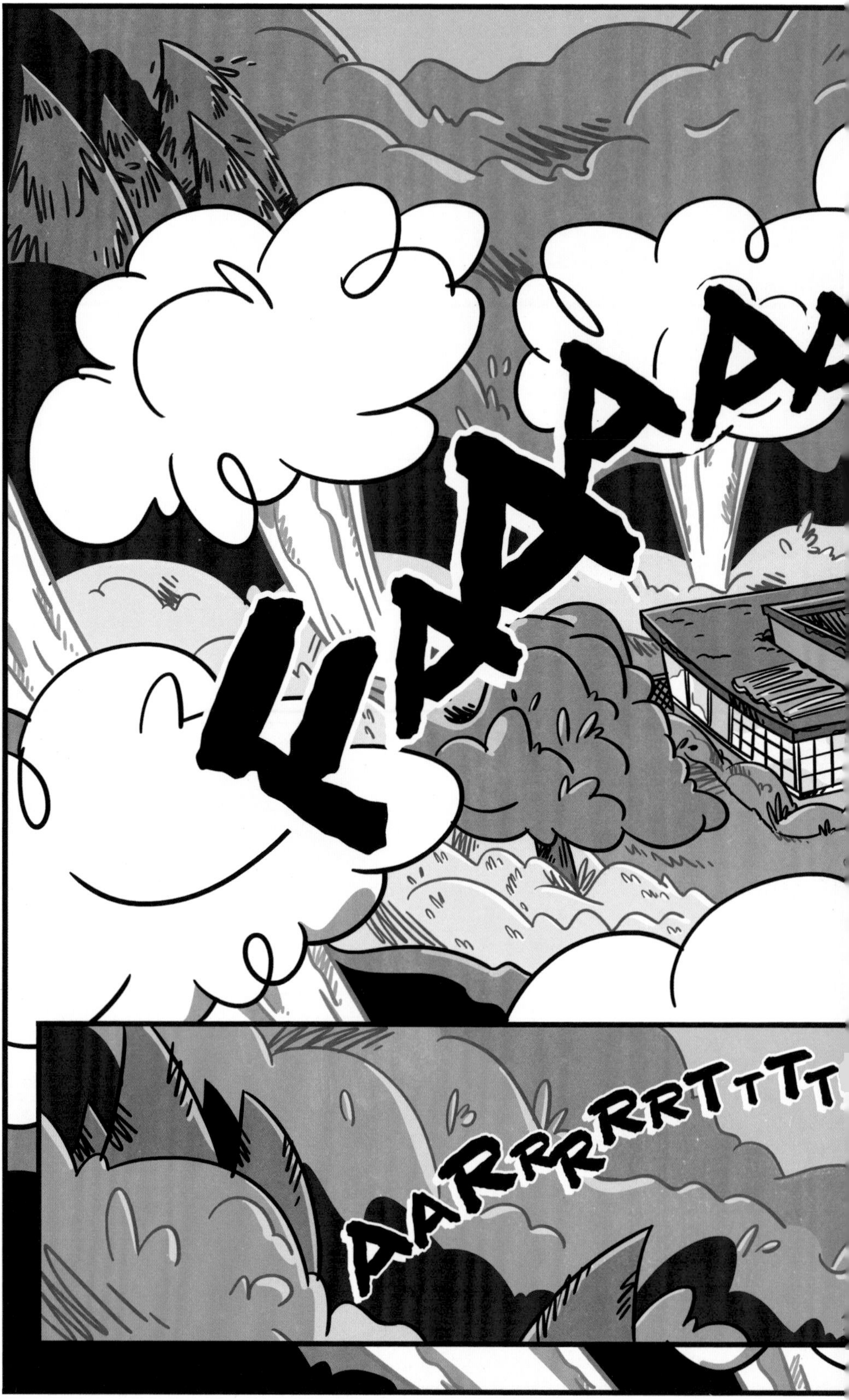

AARRRRRTTTT

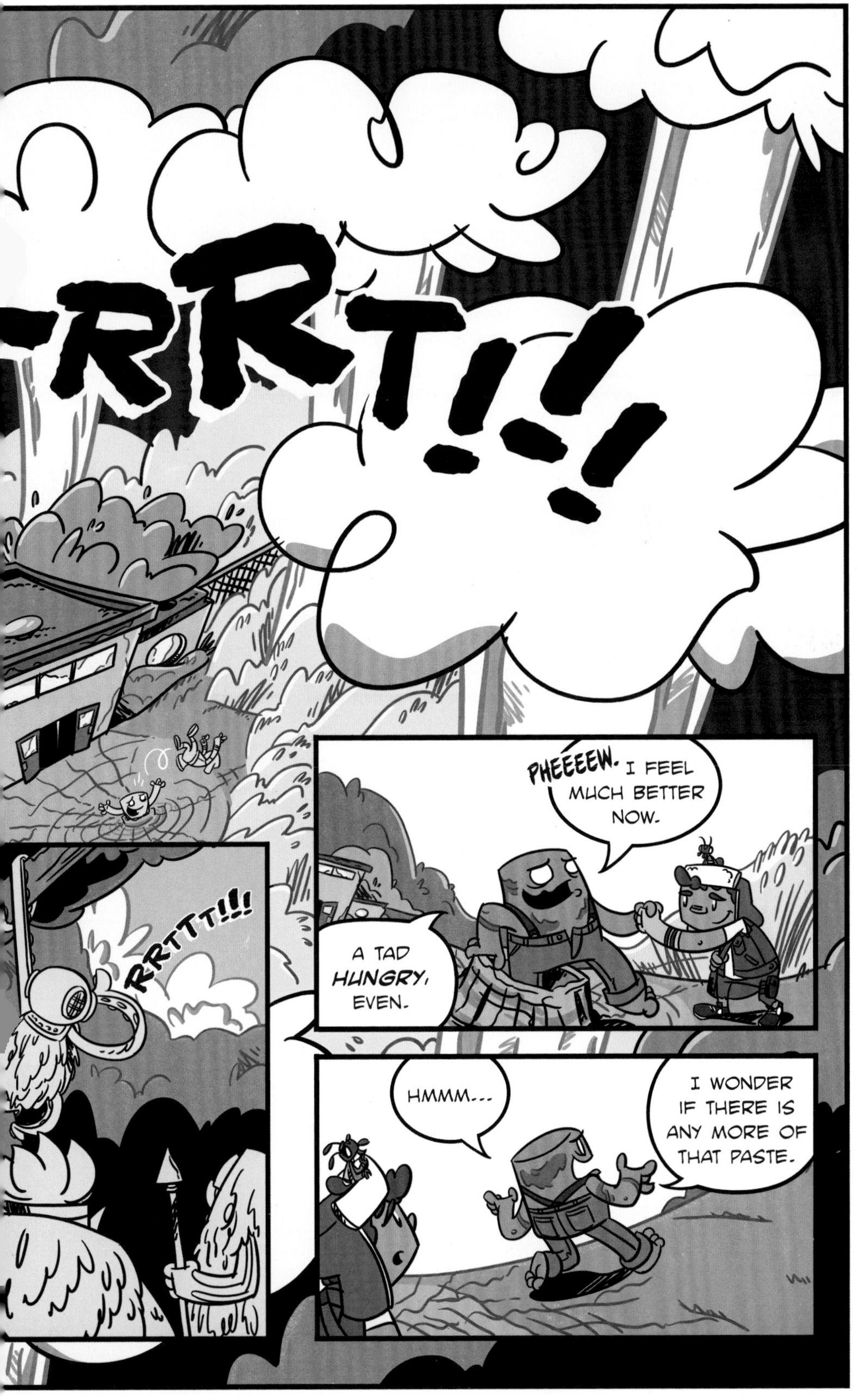
RRT!!!
PHEEEEW. I FEEL MUCH BETTER NOW.
A TAD HUNGRY, EVEN.
RRTTTT!!!
HMMM...
I WONDER IF THERE IS ANY MORE OF THAT PASTE.

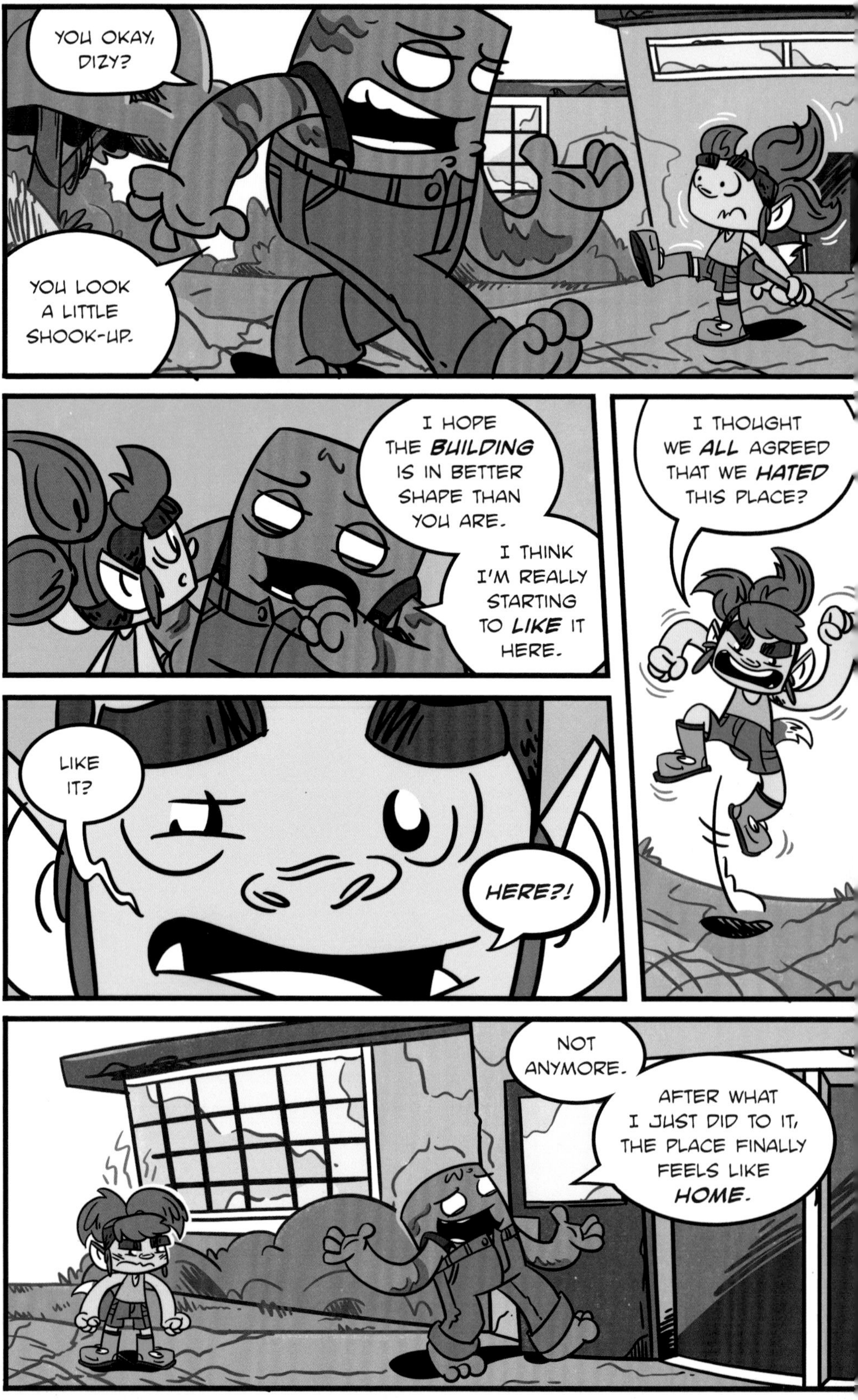
YOU OKAY, DIZY?
YOU LOOK A LITTLE SHOOK-UP.
I HOPE THE BUILDING IS IN BETTER SHAPE THAN YOU ARE.
I THINK I'M REALLY STARTING TO LIKE IT HERE.
I THOUGHT WE ALL AGREED THAT WE HATED THIS PLACE?
LIKE IT?
HERE?!
NOT ANYMORE.
AFTER WHAT I JUST DID TO IT, THE PLACE FINALLY FEELS LIKE HOME.

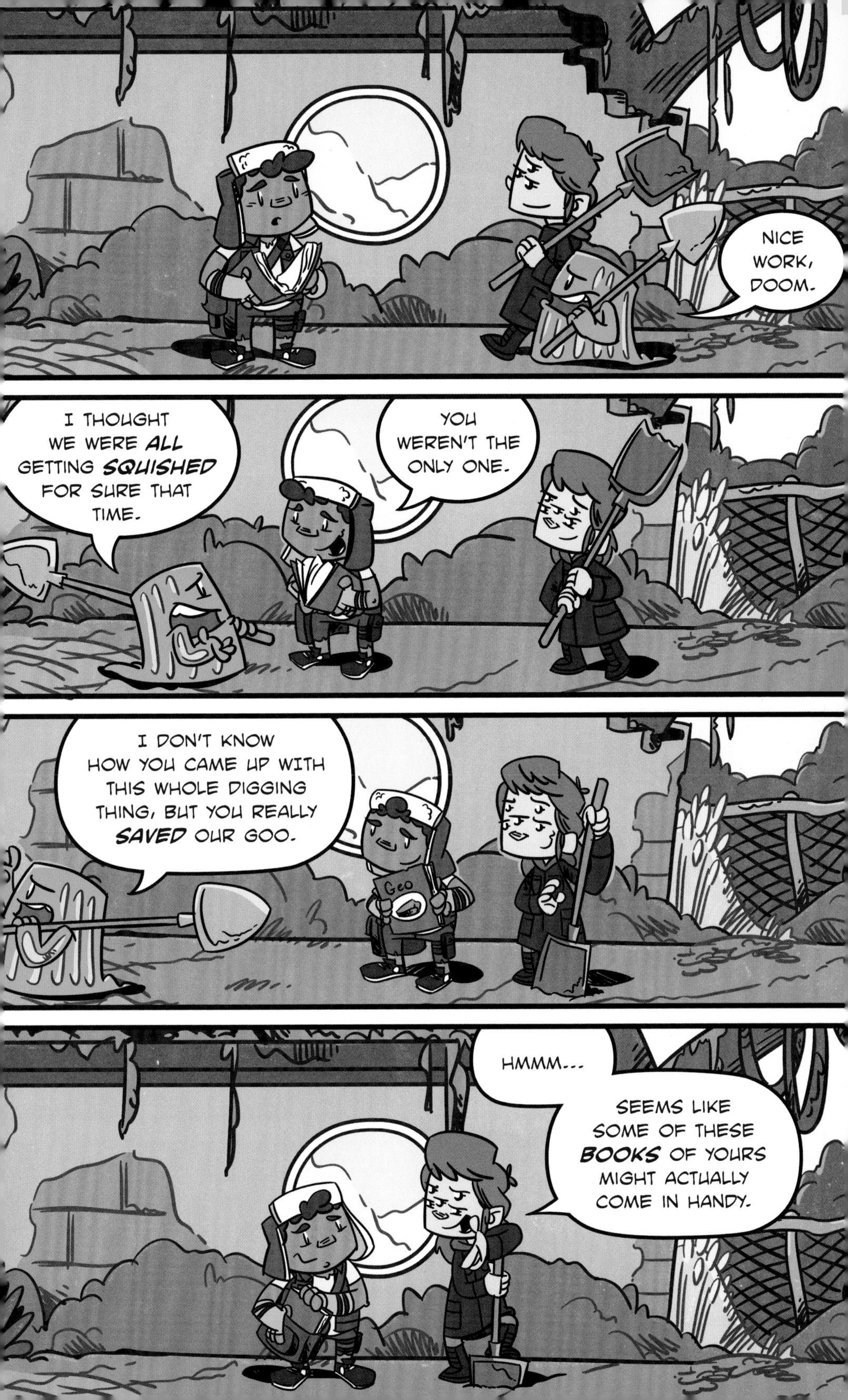
NICE WORK, DOOM.
I THOUGHT WE WERE ALL GETTING SQUISHED FOR SURE THAT TIME.
YOU WEREN'T THE ONLY ONE.
I DON'T KNOW HOW YOU CAME UP WITH THIS WHOLE DIGGING THING, BUT YOU REALLY SAVED OUR GOO.
Geo
HMMM...
SEEMS LIKE SOME OF THESE BOOKS OF YOURS MIGHT ACTUALLY COME IN HANDY.

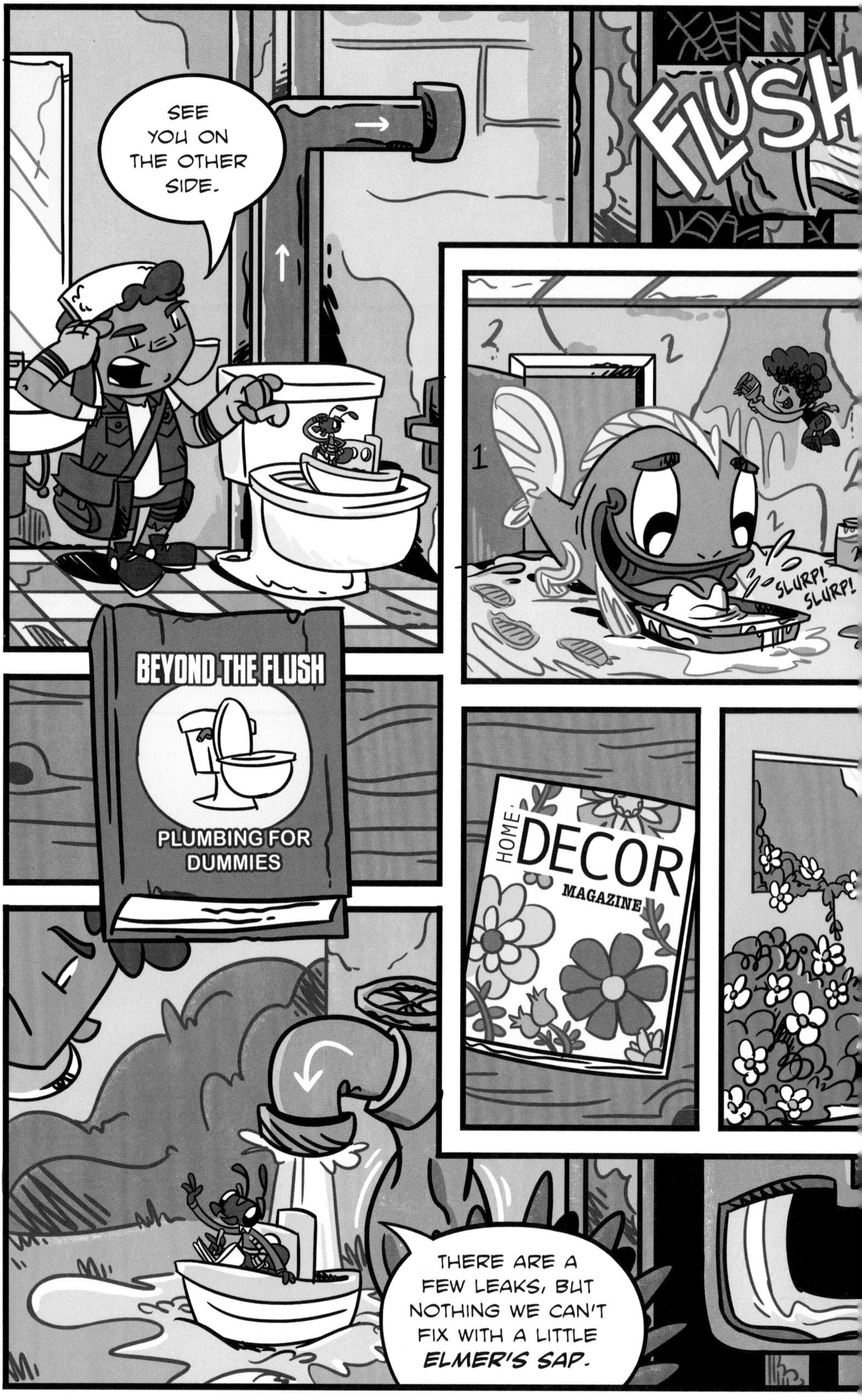
SEE YOU ON THE OTHER SIDE.
FLUSH
SLURP! SLURP!
BEYOND THE FLUSH
PLUMBING FOR DUMMIES
HOME DECOR MAGAZINE
THERE ARE A FEW LEAKS, BUT NOTHING WE CAN'T FIX WITH A LITTLE ELMER'S SAP.

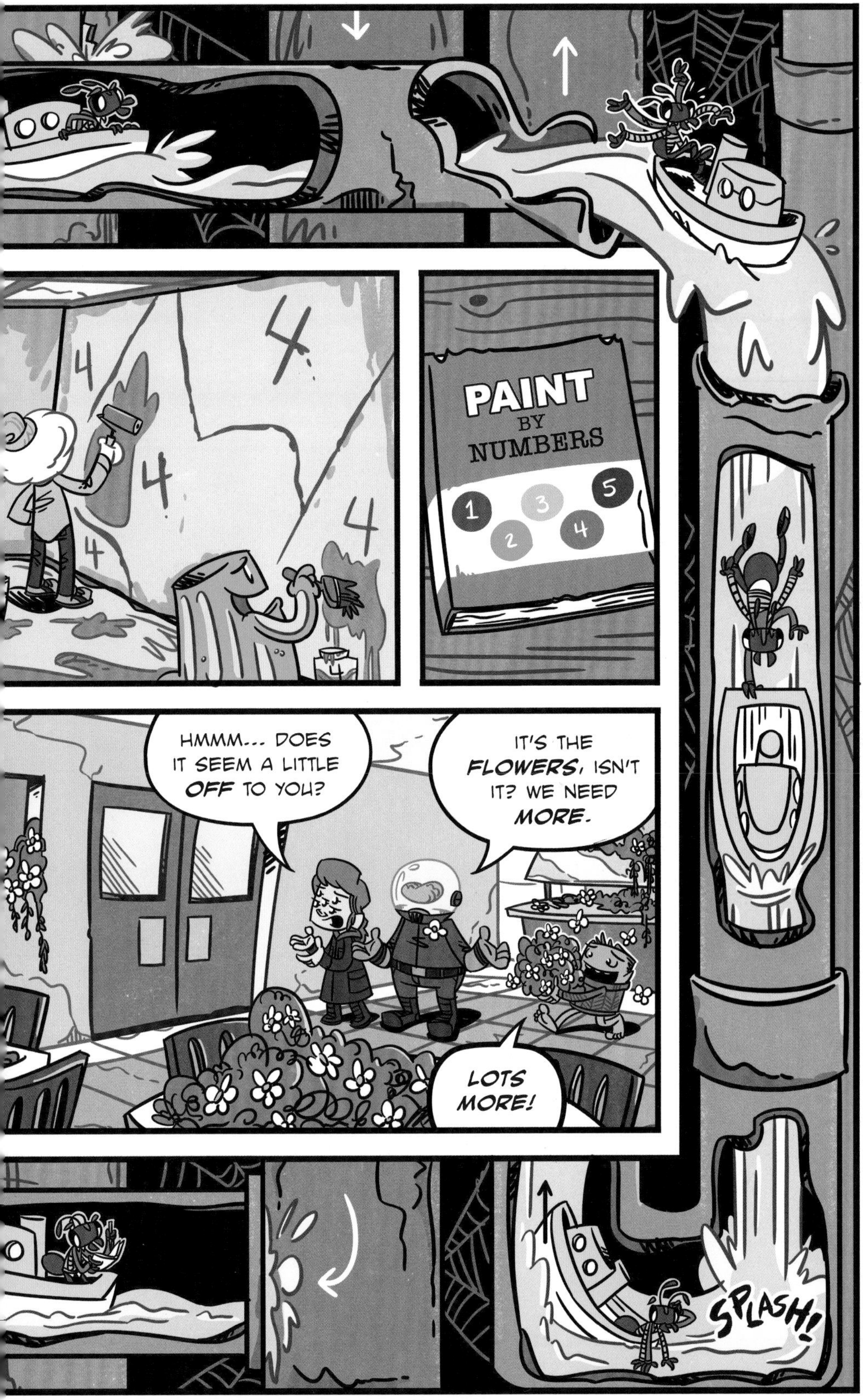
PAINT BY NUMBERS
1 2 3 4 5
HMMM... DOES IT SEEM A LITTLE OFF TO YOU?
IT'S THE FLOWERS, ISN'T IT? WE NEED MORE.
LOTS MORE!
SPLASH!

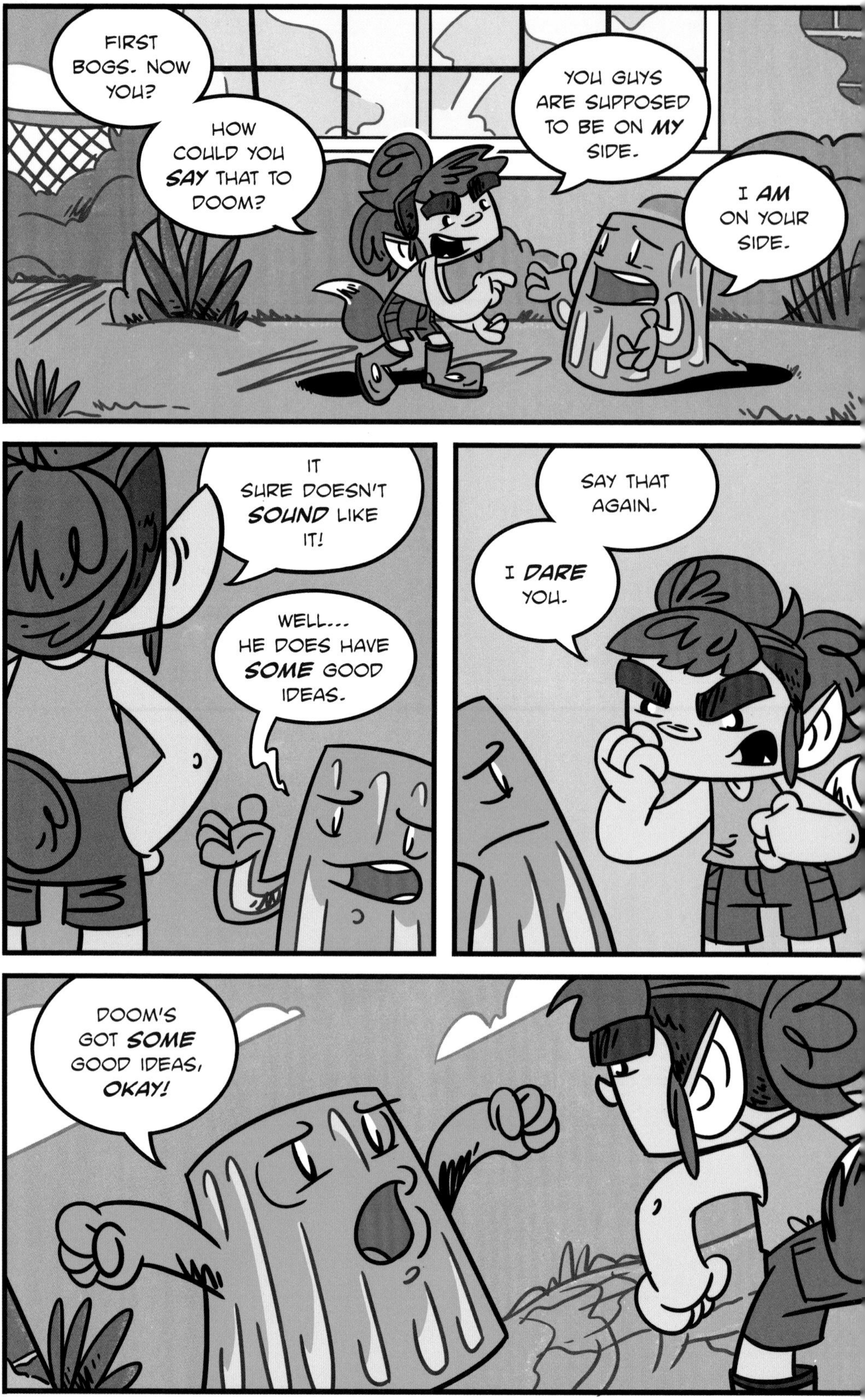
FIRST BOGS. NOW YOU?
HOW COULD YOU SAY THAT TO DOOM?
YOU GUYS ARE SUPPOSED TO BE ON MY SIDE.
I AM ON YOUR SIDE.
IT SURE DOESN'T SOUND LIKE IT!
WELL... HE DOES HAVE SOME GOOD IDEAS.
SAY THAT AGAIN.
I DARE YOU.
DOOM'S GOT SOME GOOD IDEAS, OKAY!

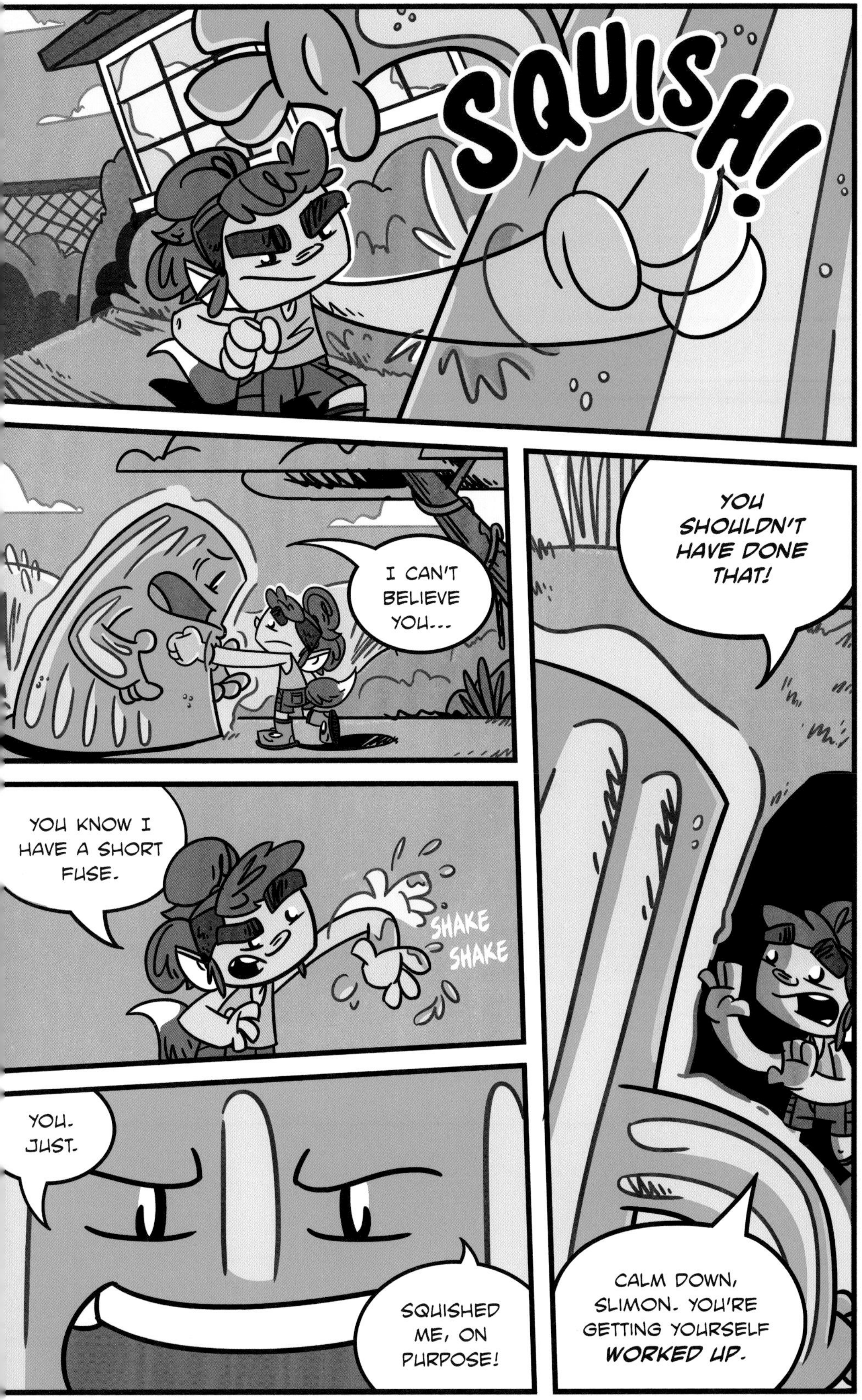
SQUISH!
I CAN'T BELIEVE YOU...
YOU SHOULDN'T HAVE DONE THAT!
YOU KNOW I HAVE A SHORT FUSE.
SHAKE SHAKE
YOU. JUST.
SQUISHED ME, ON PURPOSE!
CALM DOWN, SLIMON. YOU'RE GETTING YOURSELF WORKED UP.

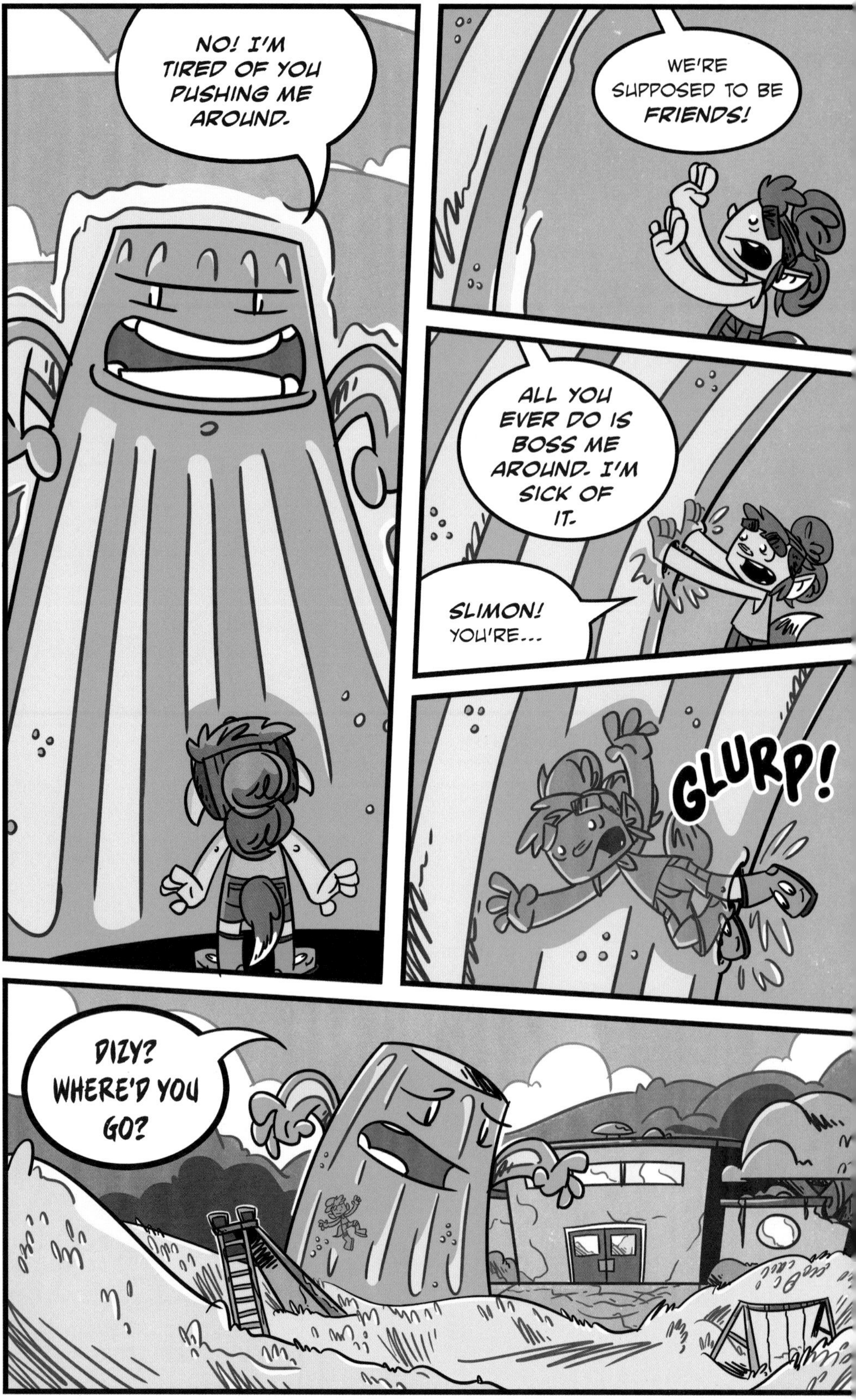
NO! I'M TIRED OF YOU PUSHING ME AROUND.
WE'RE SUPPOSED TO BE FRIENDS!
ALL YOU EVER DO IS BOSS ME AROUND. I'M SICK OF IT.
SLIMON! YOU'RE...
GLURP!
DIZY? WHERE'D YOU GO?

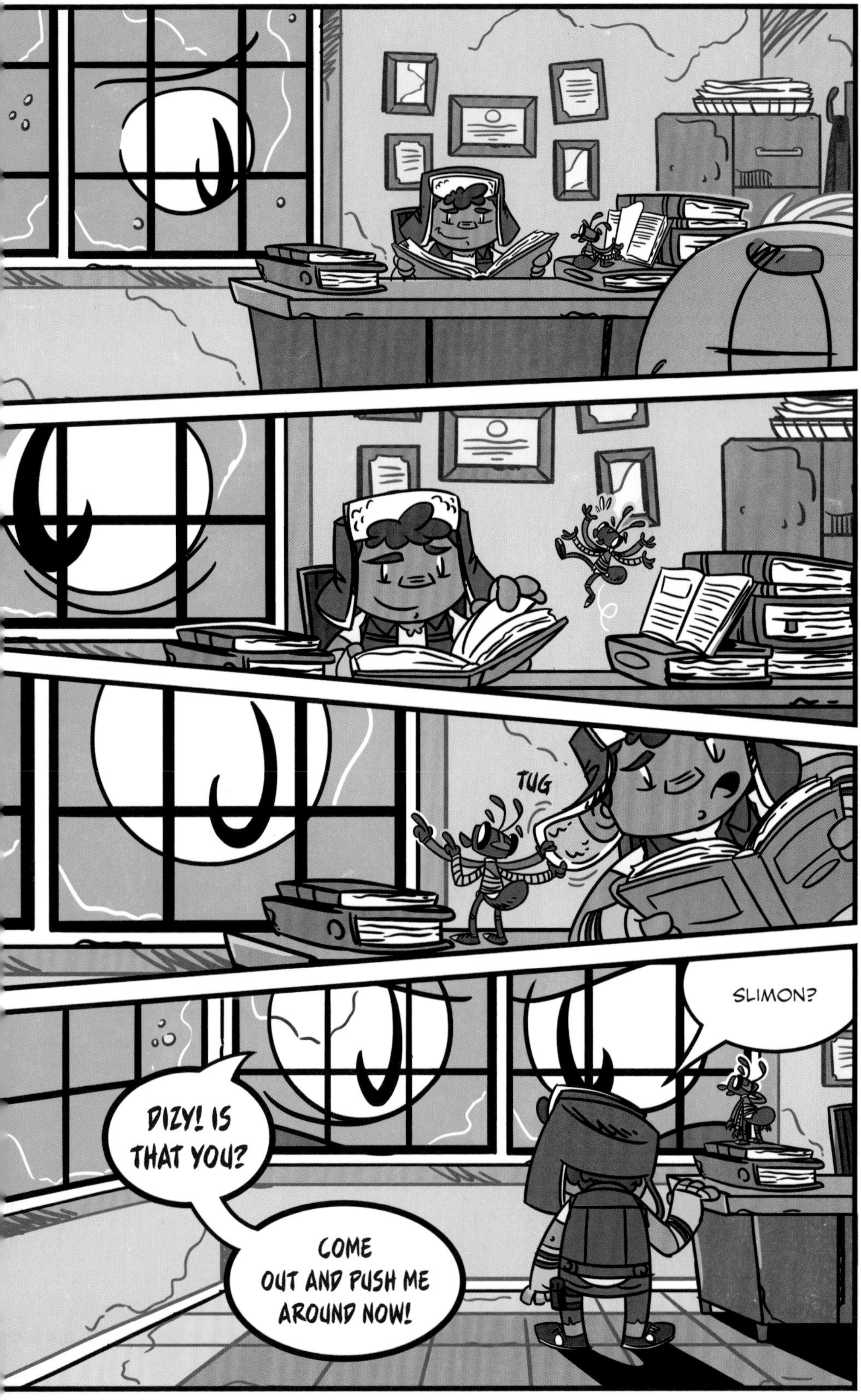
TUG
SLIMON?
DIZY! IS THAT YOU?
COME OUT AND PUSH ME AROUND NOW!

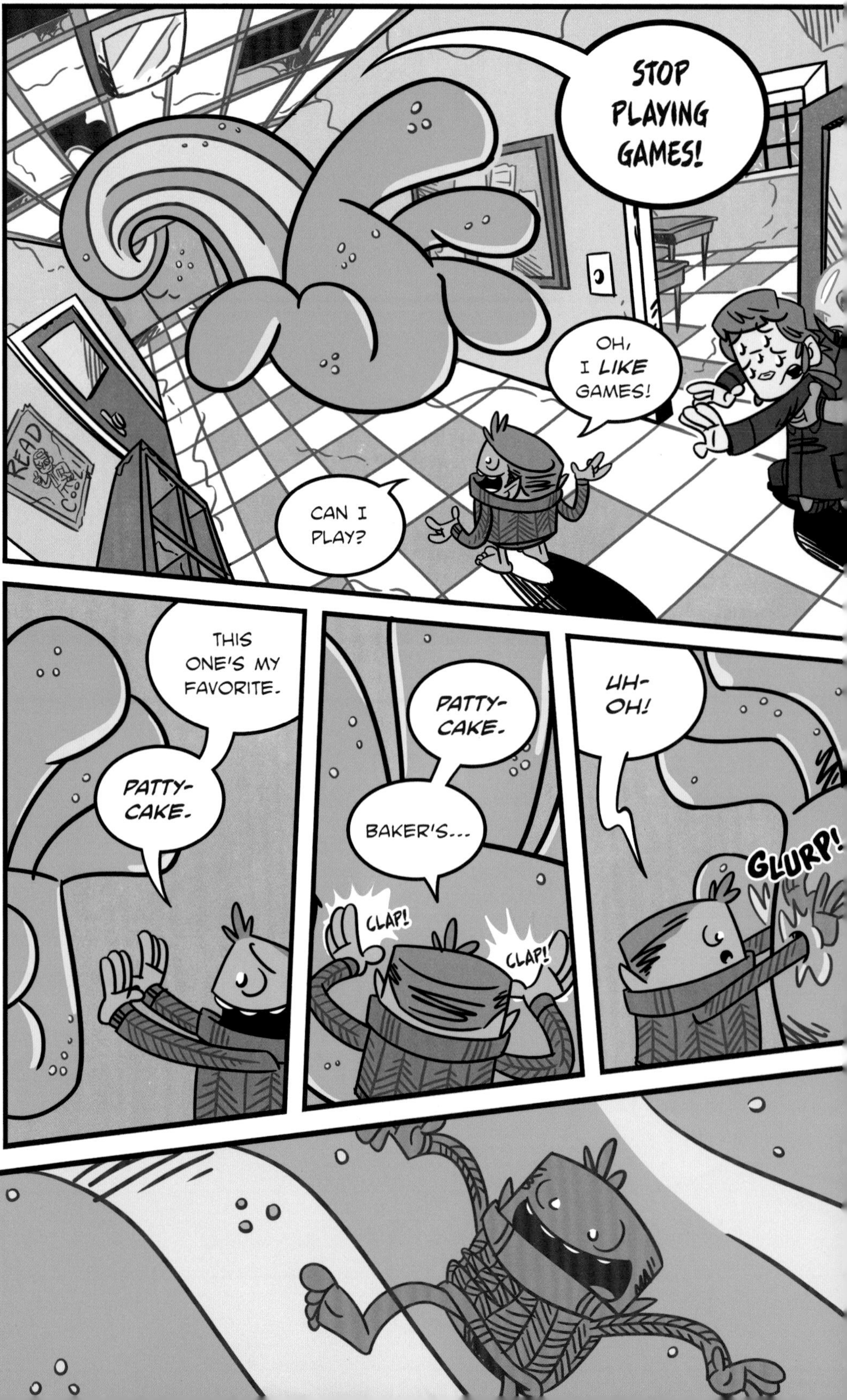
STOP PLAYING GAMES!
OH, I LIKE GAMES!
CAN I PLAY?
THIS ONE'S MY FAVORITE.
PATTY-CAKE.
PATTY-CAKE.
BAKER'S...
CLAP!
CLAP!
UH-OH!
GLURP!

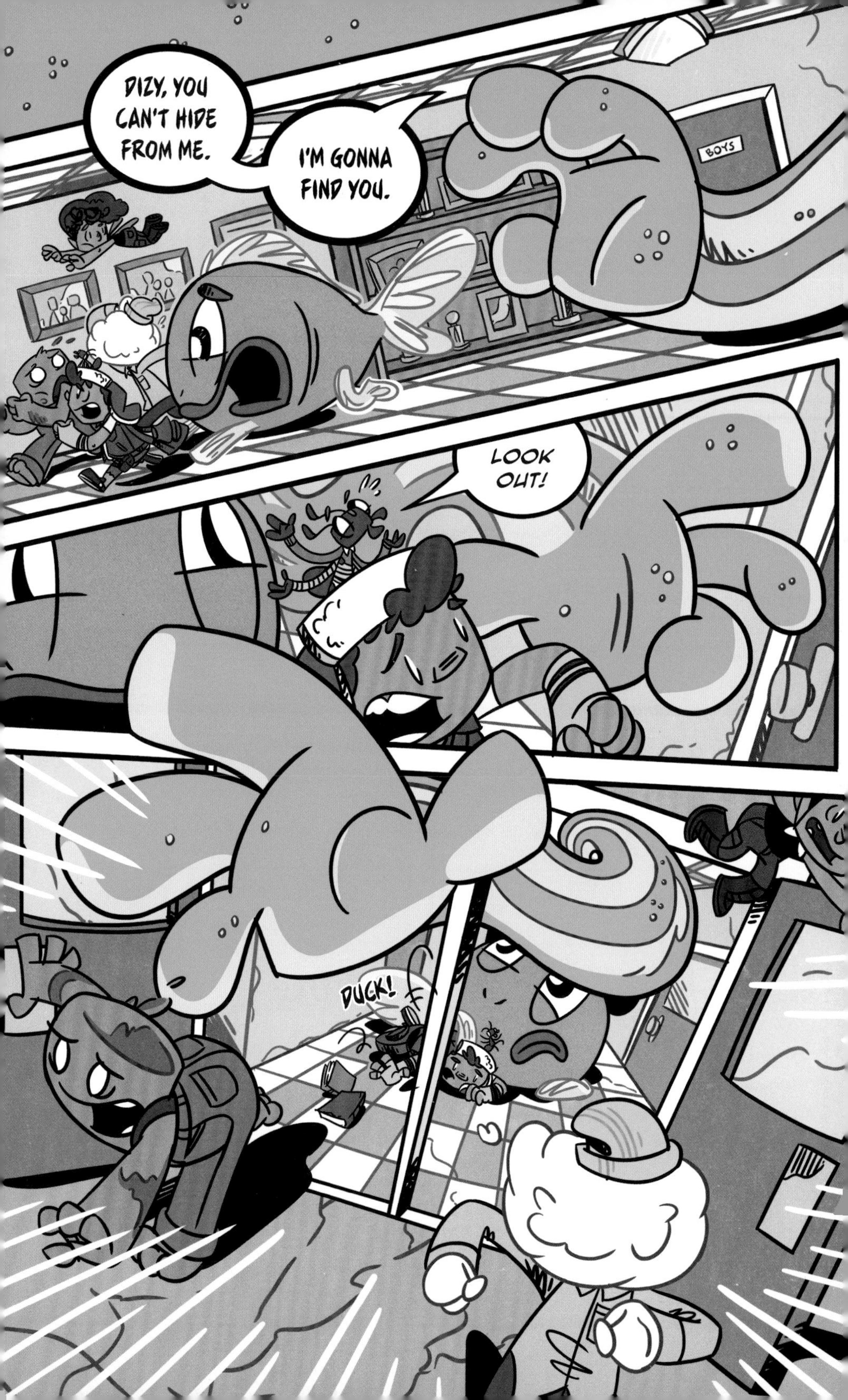
DIZY, YOU CAN'T HIDE FROM ME.
I'M GONNA FIND YOU.
BOYS
LOOK OUT!
DUCK!

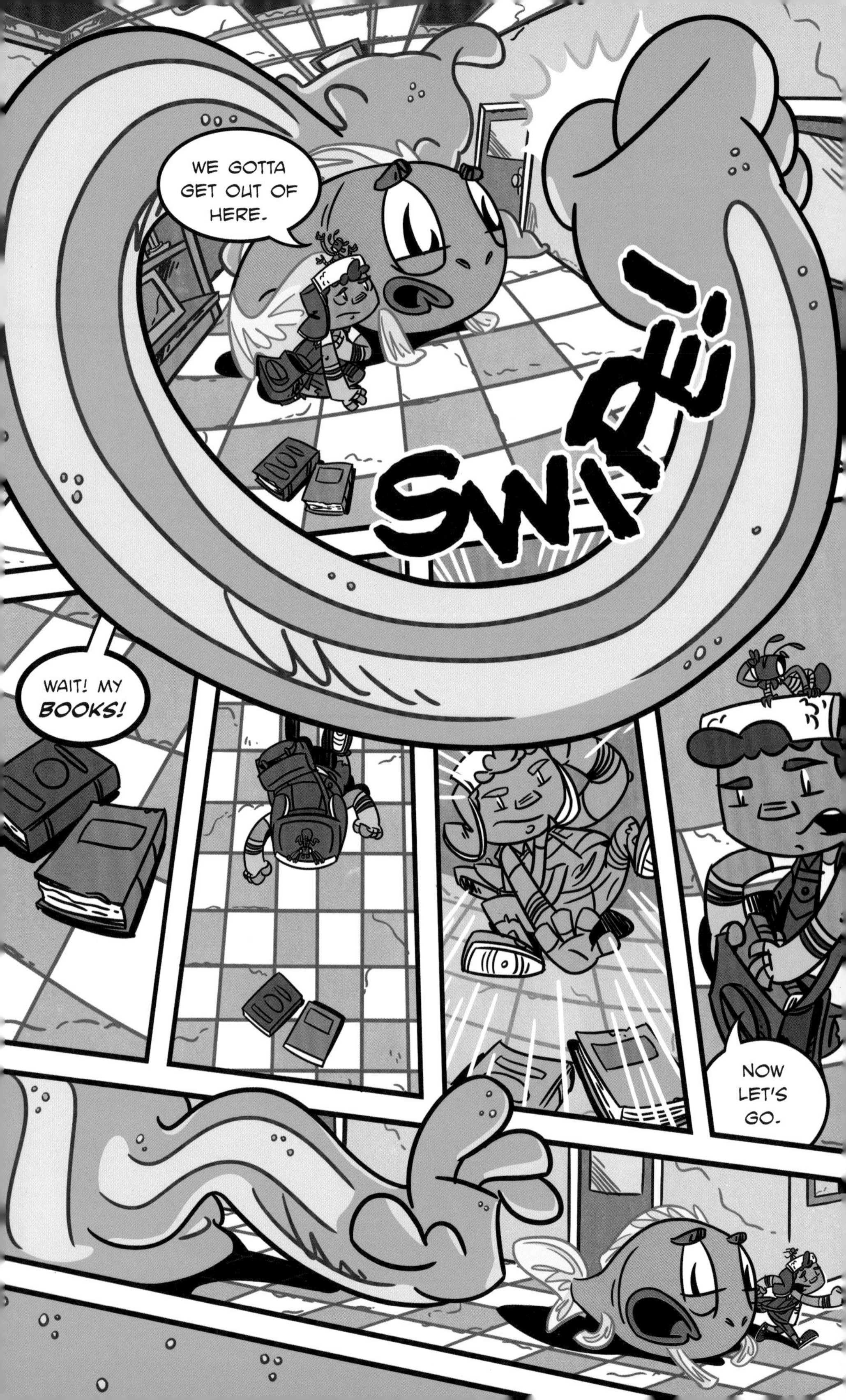
WE GOTTA GET OUT OF HERE.
SWIPE!
WAIT! MY BOOKS!
NOW LET'S GO.

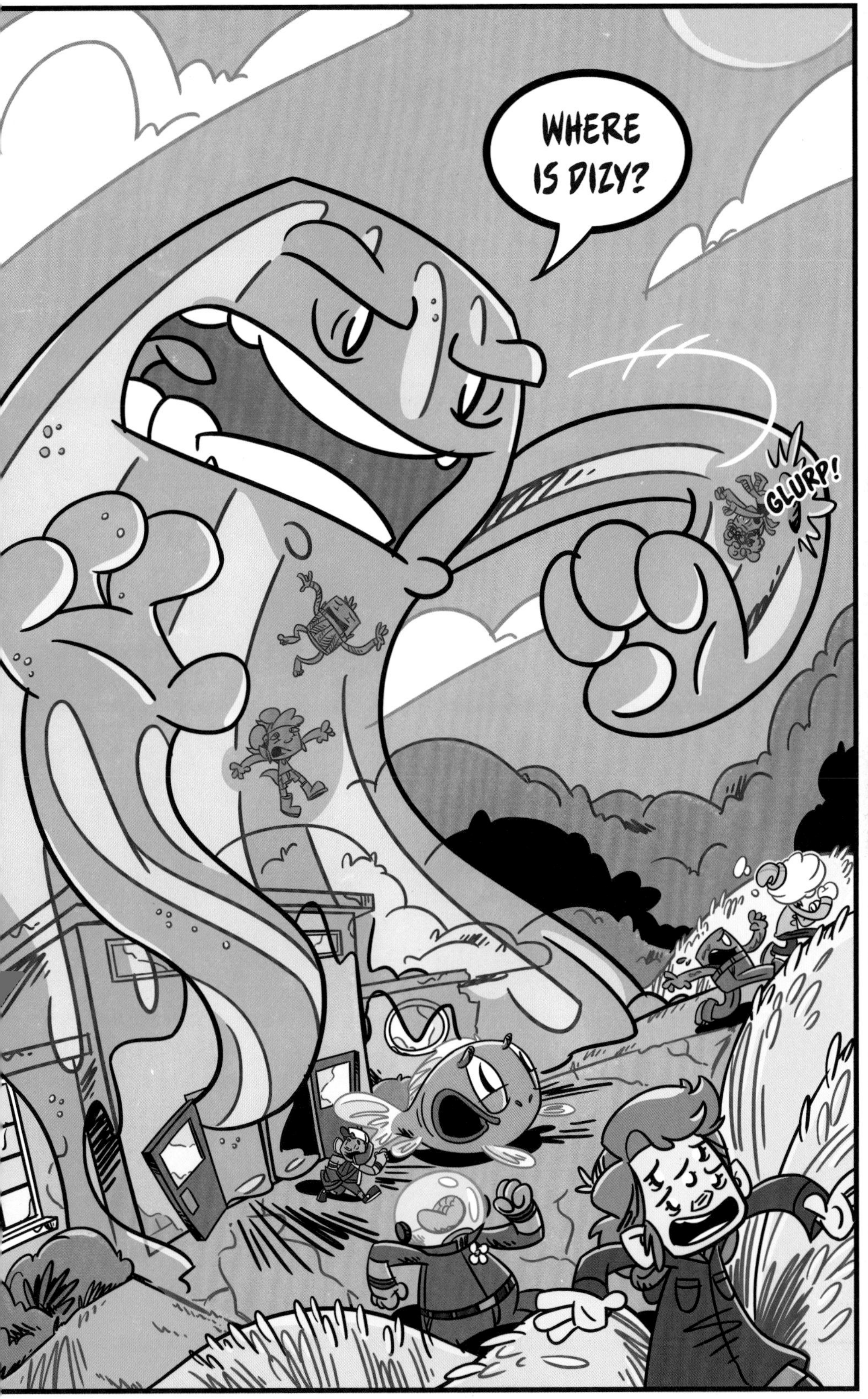
WHERE IS DIZY?
GLURP!

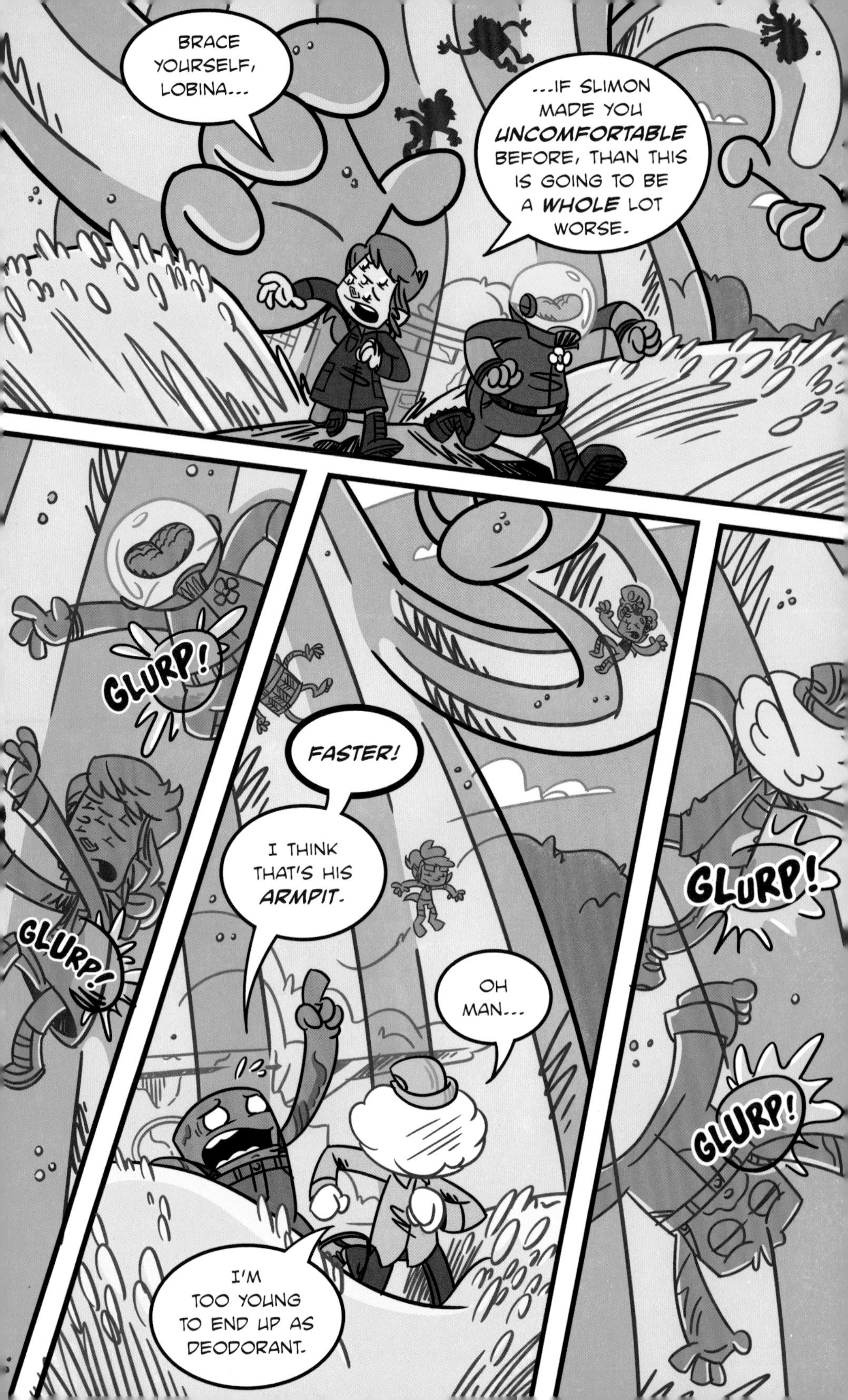
BRACE YOURSELF, LOBINA...
...IF SLIMON MADE YOU *UNCOMFORTABLE* BEFORE, THAN THIS IS GOING TO BE A *WHOLE* LOT WORSE.
GLURP!
GLURP!
FASTER!
I THINK THAT'S HIS *ARMPIT*.
OH MAN...
I'M TOO YOUNG TO END UP AS DEODORANT.
GLURP!
GLURP!

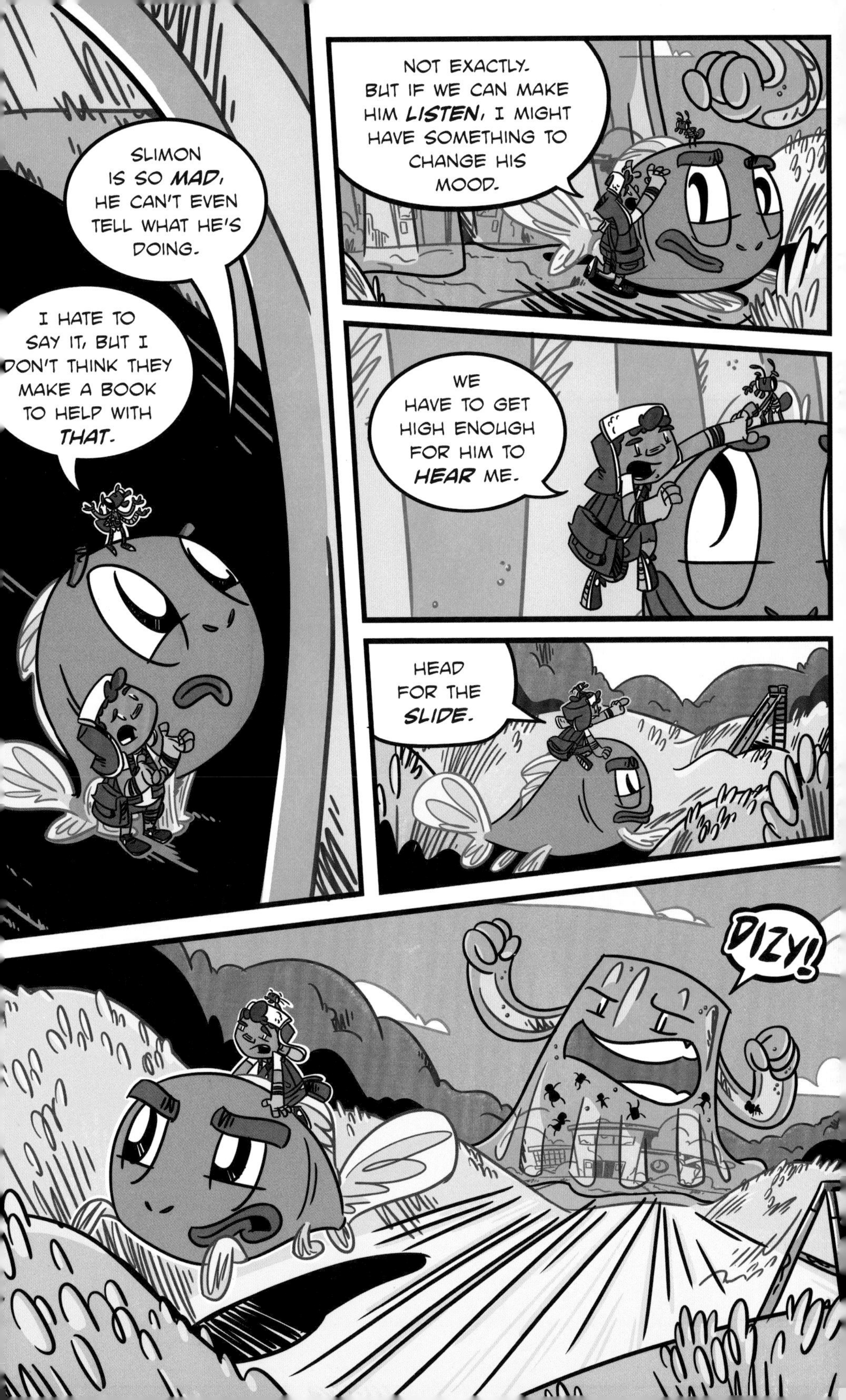
SLIMON IS SO MAD, HE CAN'T EVEN TELL WHAT HE'S DOING.
I HATE TO SAY IT, BUT I DON'T THINK THEY MAKE A BOOK TO HELP WITH THAT.
NOT EXACTLY. BUT IF WE CAN MAKE HIM LISTEN, I MIGHT HAVE SOMETHING TO CHANGE HIS MOOD.
WE HAVE TO GET HIGH ENOUGH FOR HIM TO HEAR ME.
HEAD FOR THE SLIDE.
DIZY!

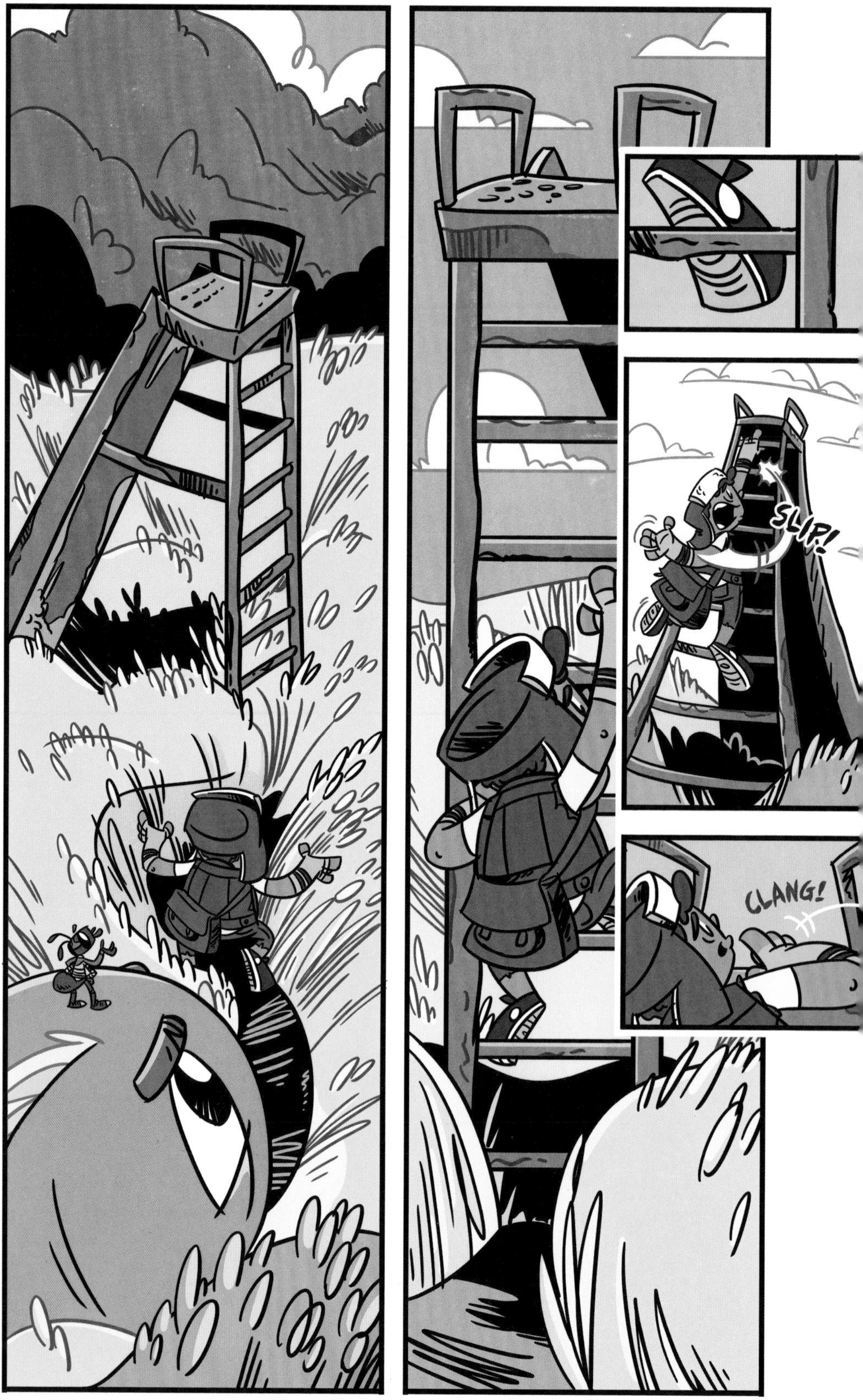

SLIP!
CLANG!

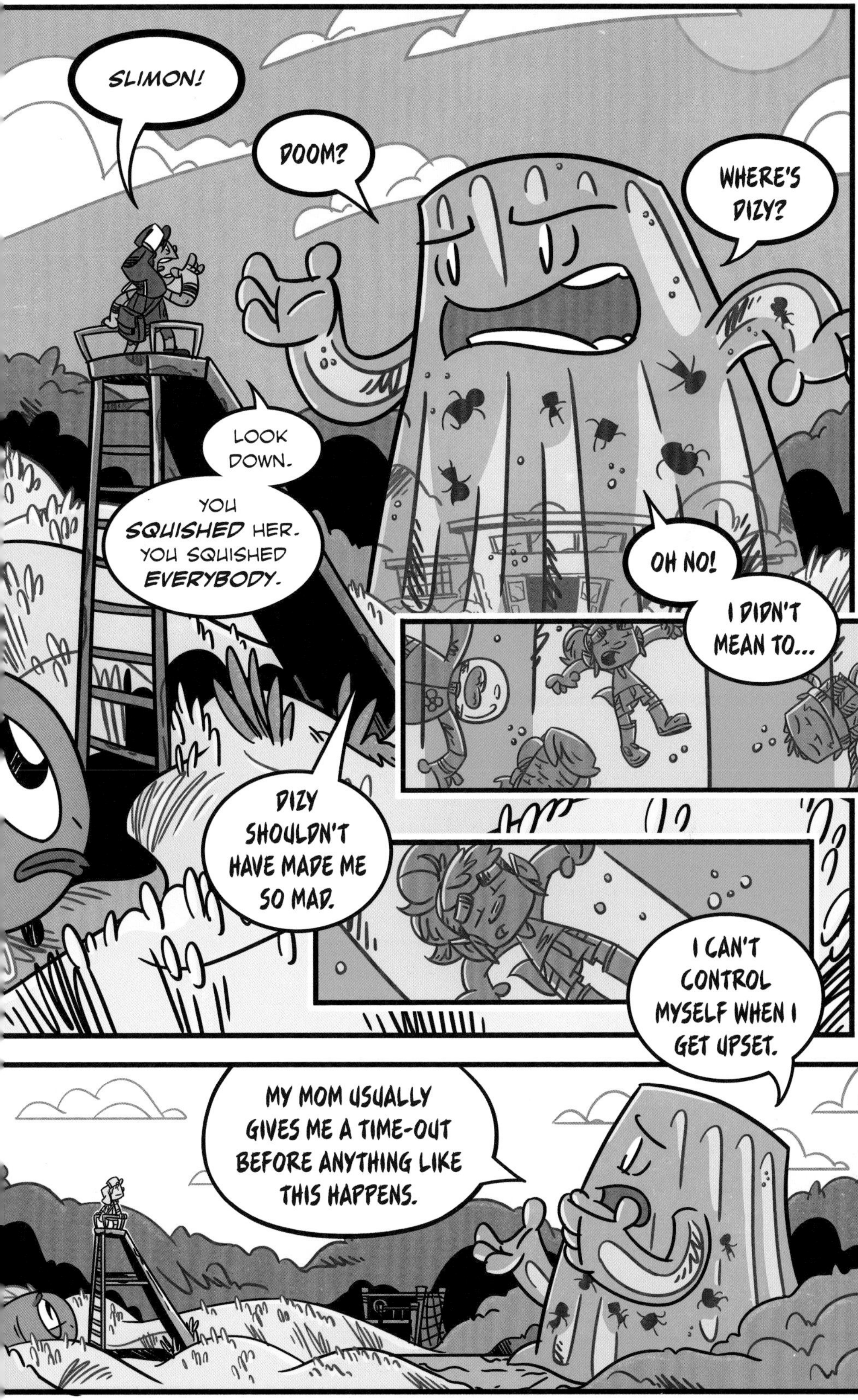
SLIMON!
DOOM?
WHERE'S DIZY?
LOOK DOWN.
YOU *SQUISHED* HER. YOU SQUISHED *EVERYBODY*.
OH NO!
I DIDN'T MEAN TO...
DIZY SHOULDN'T HAVE MADE ME SO MAD.
I CAN'T CONTROL MYSELF WHEN I GET UPSET.
MY MOM USUALLY GIVES ME A TIME-OUT BEFORE ANYTHING LIKE THIS HAPPENS.

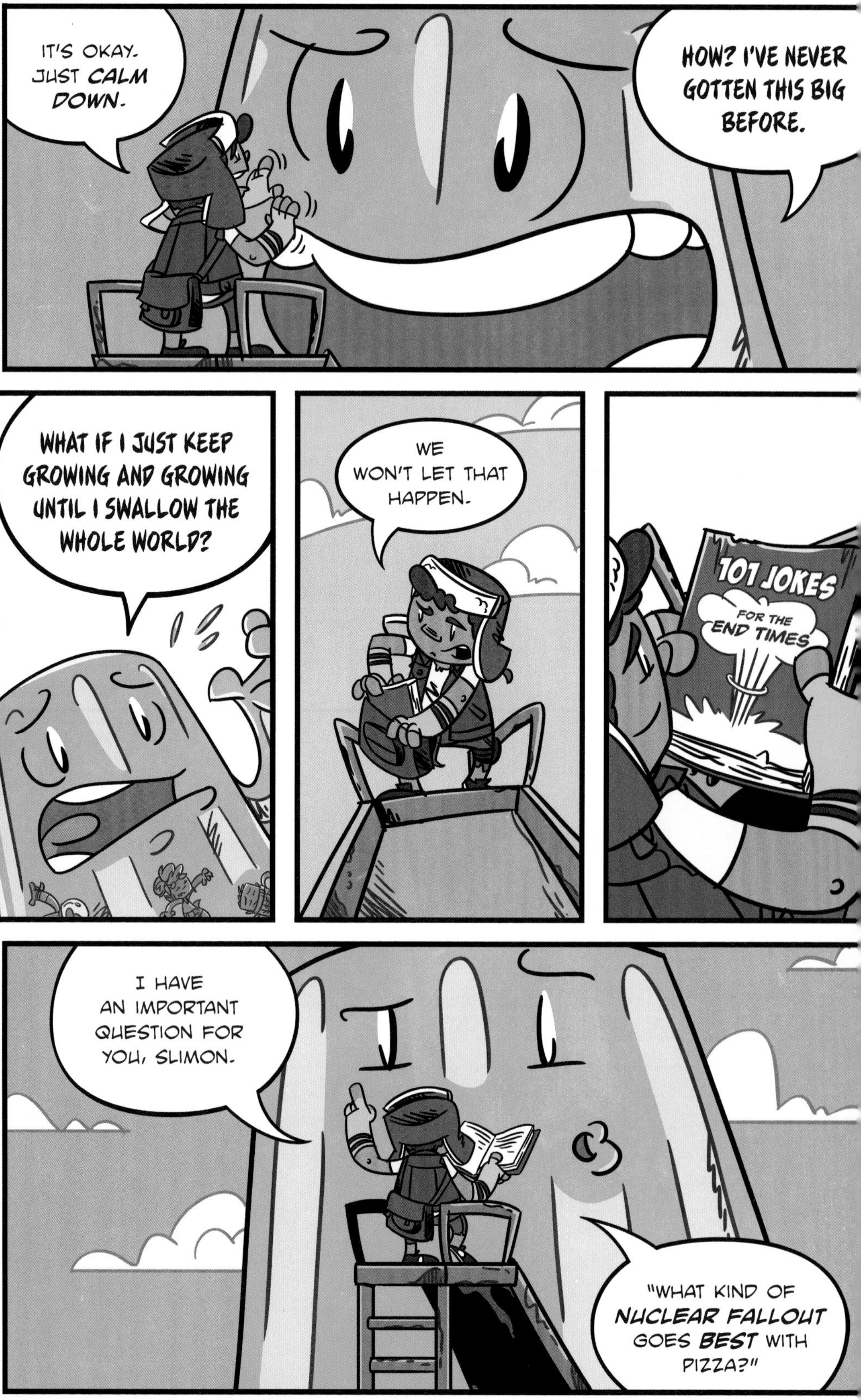
IT'S OKAY. JUST CALM DOWN.
HOW? I'VE NEVER GOTTEN THIS BIG BEFORE.
WHAT IF I JUST KEEP GROWING AND GROWING UNTIL I SWALLOW THE WHOLE WORLD?
WE WON'T LET THAT HAPPEN.
101 JOKES FOR THE END TIMES
I HAVE AN IMPORTANT QUESTION FOR YOU, SLIMON.
"WHAT KIND OF NUCLEAR FALLOUT GOES BEST WITH PIZZA?"

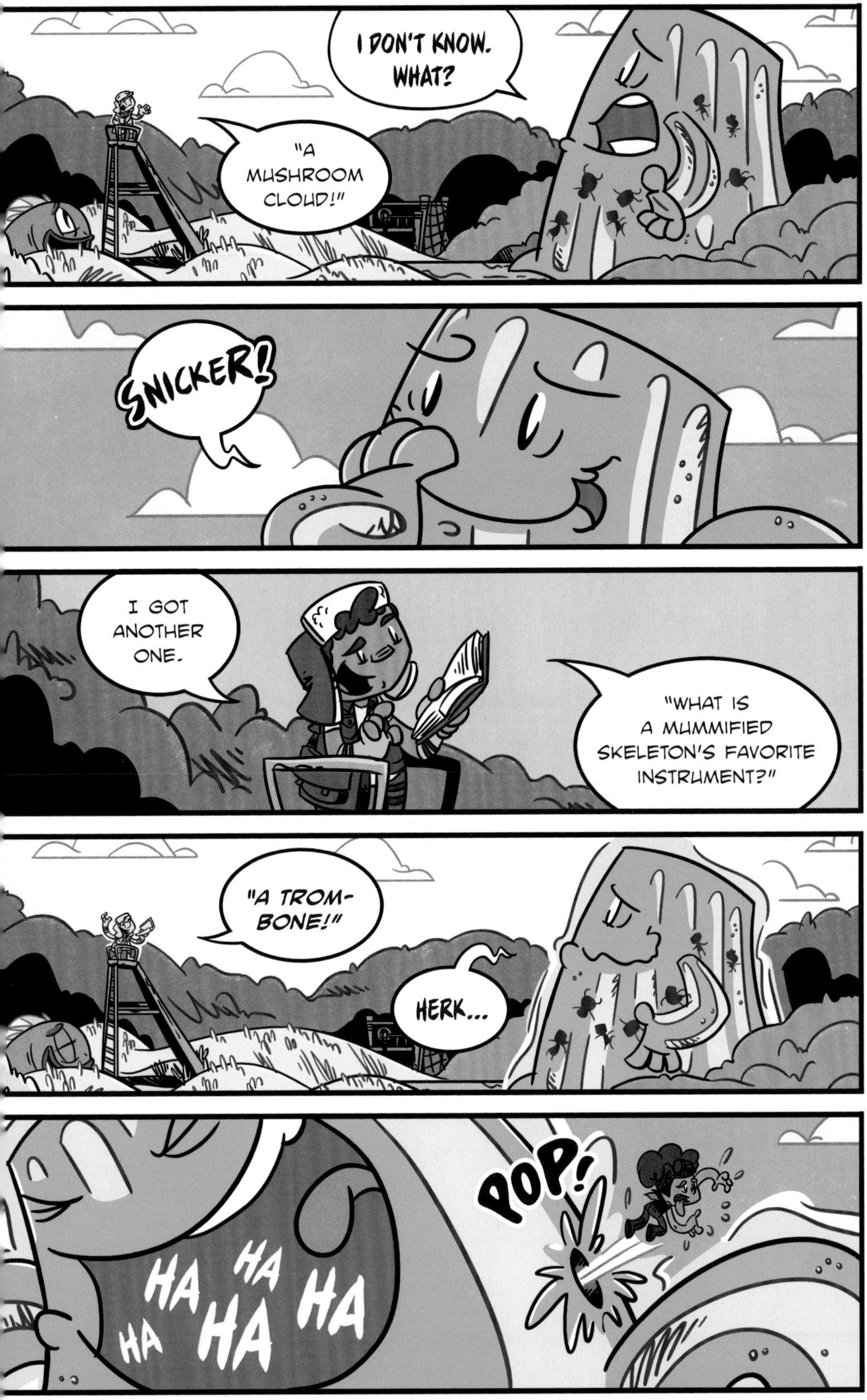
I DON'T KNOW. WHAT?
"A MUSHROOM CLOUD!"
SNICKER!
I GOT ANOTHER ONE.
"WHAT IS A MUMMIFIED SKELETON'S FAVORITE INSTRUMENT?"
"A TROM-BONE!"
HERK...
HA HA HA HA HA HA
POP!

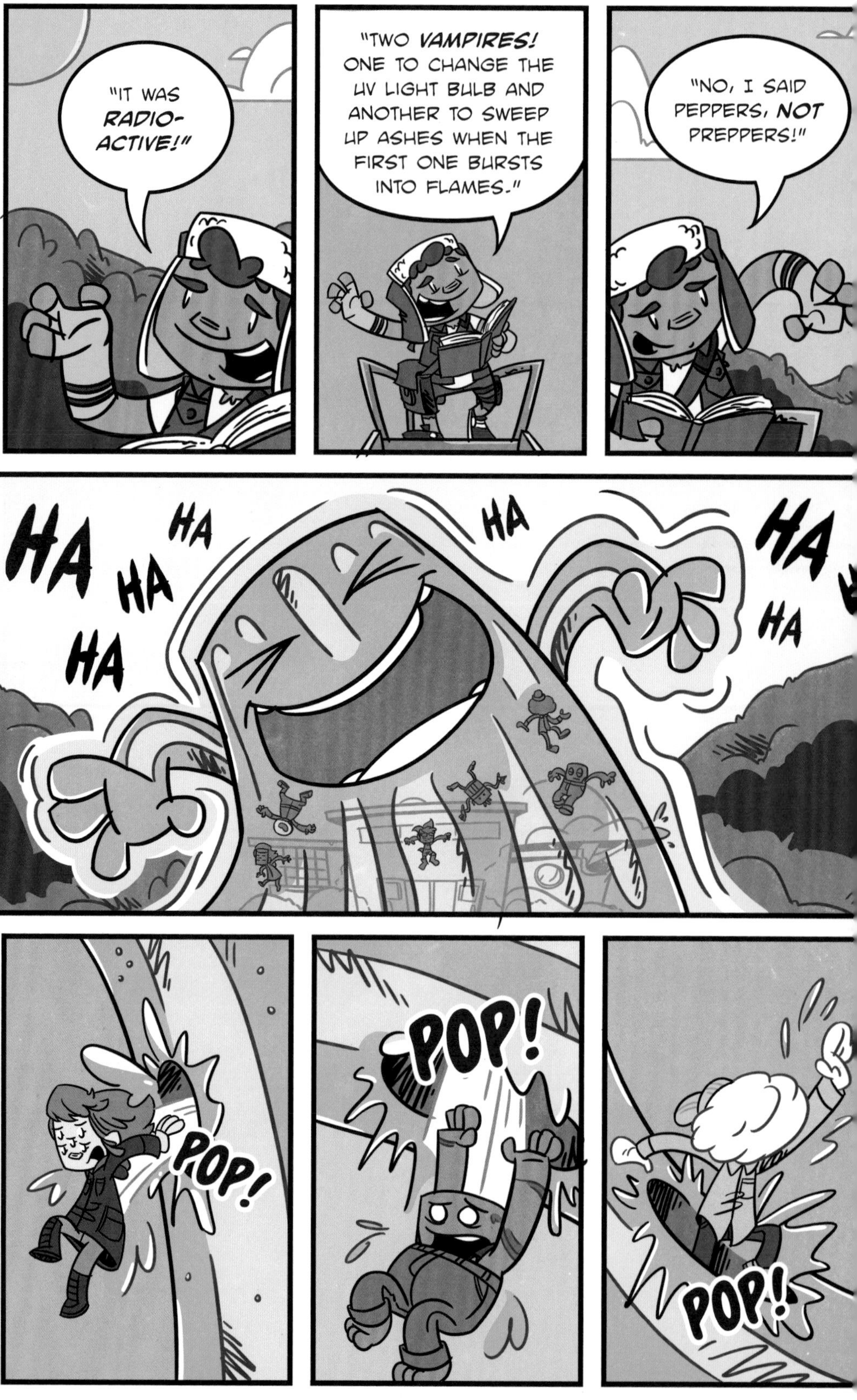
"IT WAS RADIO-ACTIVE!"
"TWO VAMPIRES! ONE TO CHANGE THE UV LIGHT BULB AND ANOTHER TO SWEEP UP ASHES WHEN THE FIRST ONE BURSTS INTO FLAMES."
"NO, I SAID PEPPERS, NOT PREPPERS!"
HA HA HA HA HA HA HA
POP!
POP!
POP!

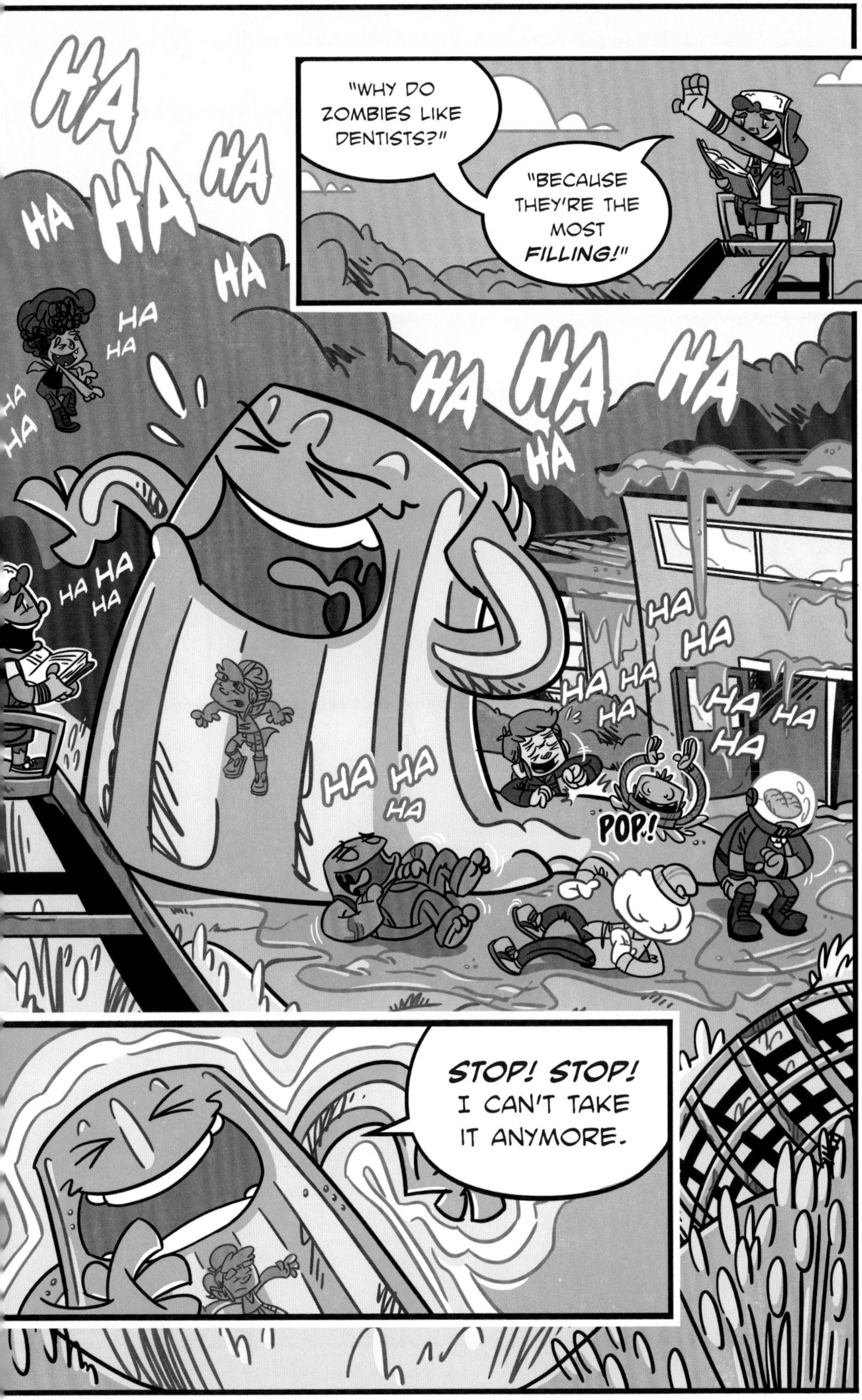
HA HA HA HA HA HA
"WHY DO ZOMBIES LIKE DENTISTS?"
"BECAUSE THEY'RE THE MOST FILLING!"
HA HA
HA HA
HA HA HA
HA HA HA HA
HA HA HA
HA HA
HA HA HA
HA HA HA
POP!
STOP! STOP! I CAN'T TAKE IT ANYMORE.

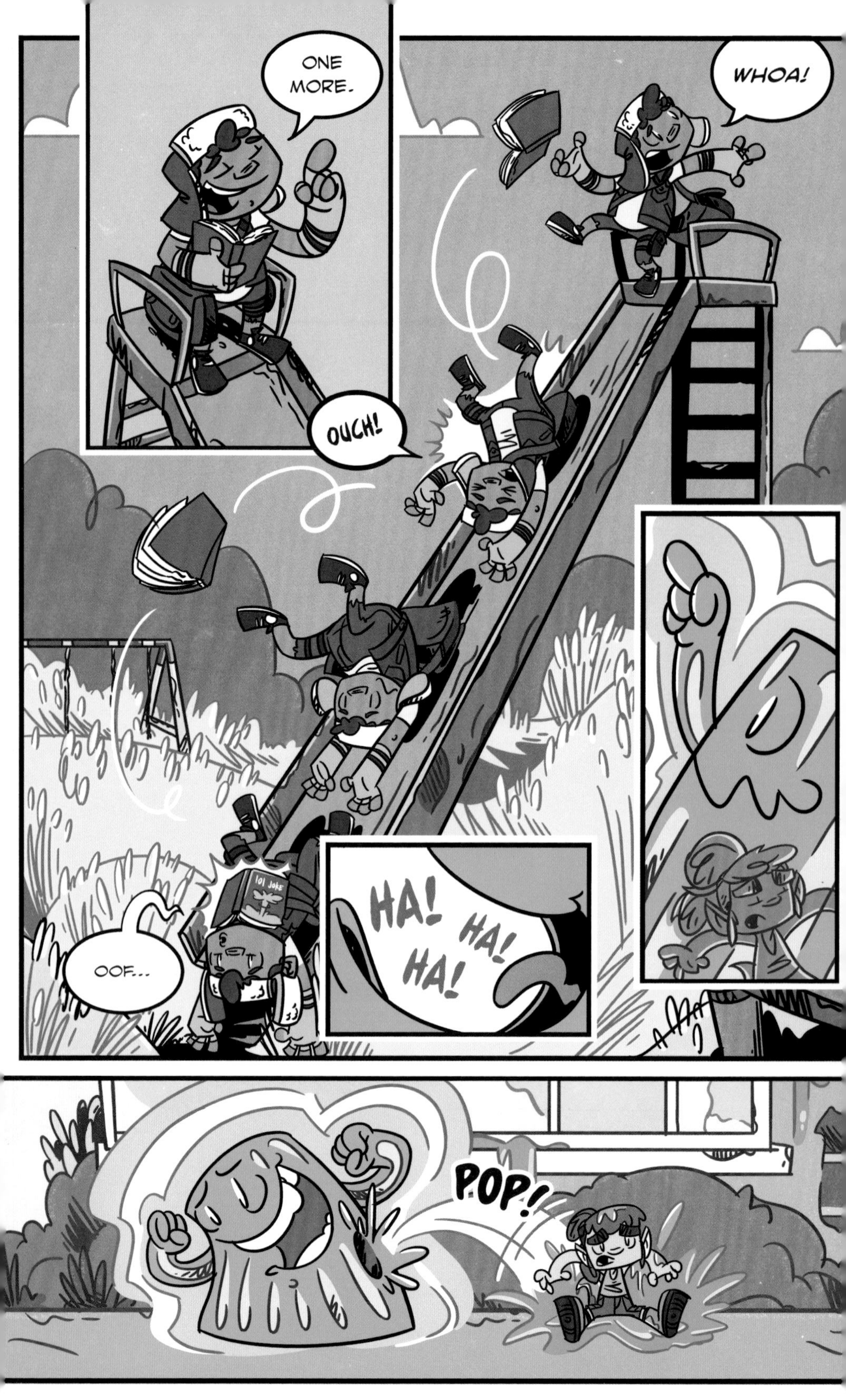

ONE MORE.
WHOA!
OUCH!
OOF...
101 JOKE
HA! HA! HA!
POP!

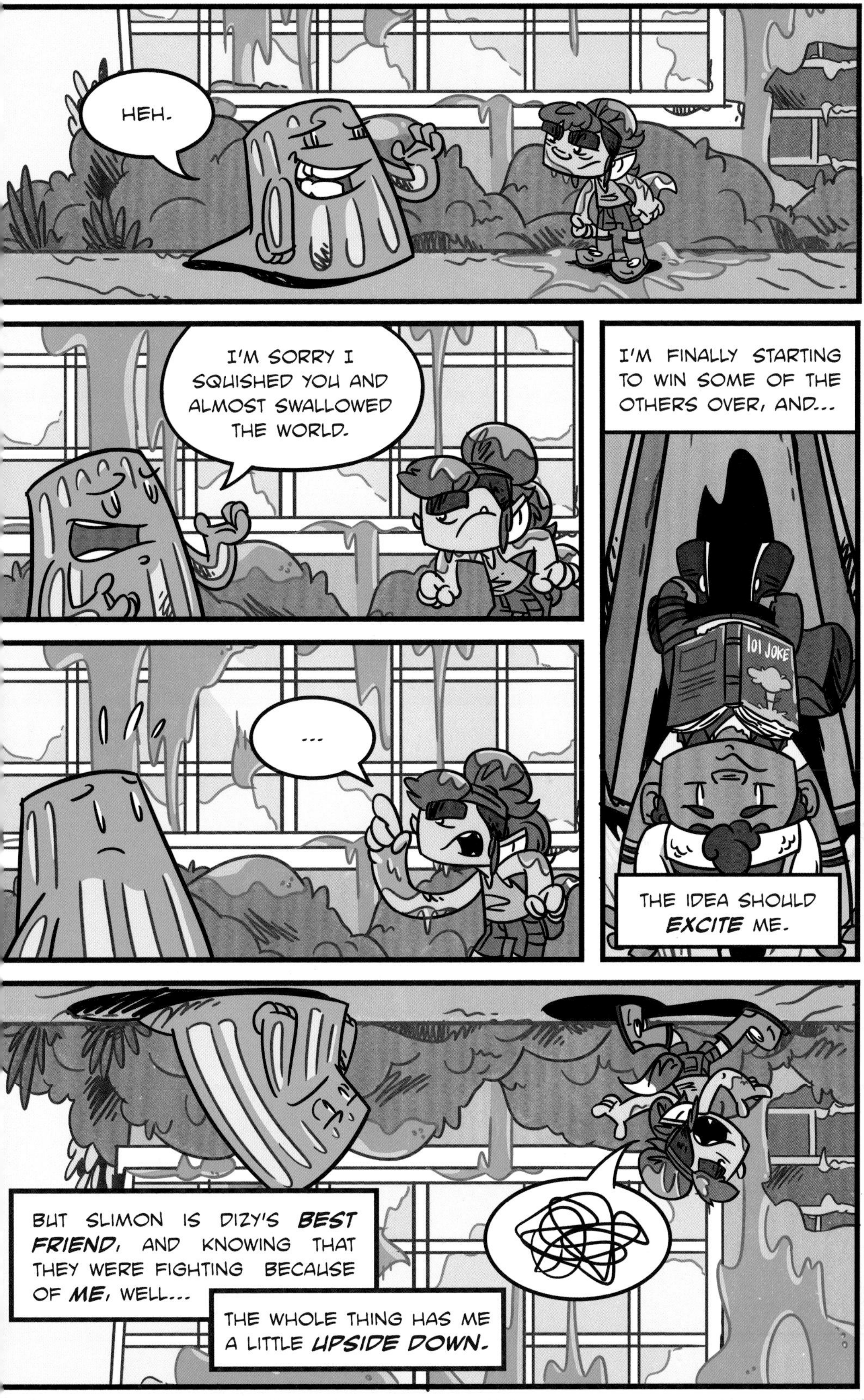
HEH.
I'M SORRY I SQUISHED YOU AND ALMOST SWALLOWED THE WORLD.
...
I'M FINALLY STARTING TO WIN SOME OF THE OTHERS OVER, AND...
101 JOKE
THE IDEA SHOULD EXCITE ME.
BUT SLIMON IS DIZY'S BEST FRIEND, AND KNOWING THAT THEY WERE FIGHTING BECAUSE OF ME, WELL...
THE WHOLE THING HAS ME A LITTLE UPSIDE DOWN.

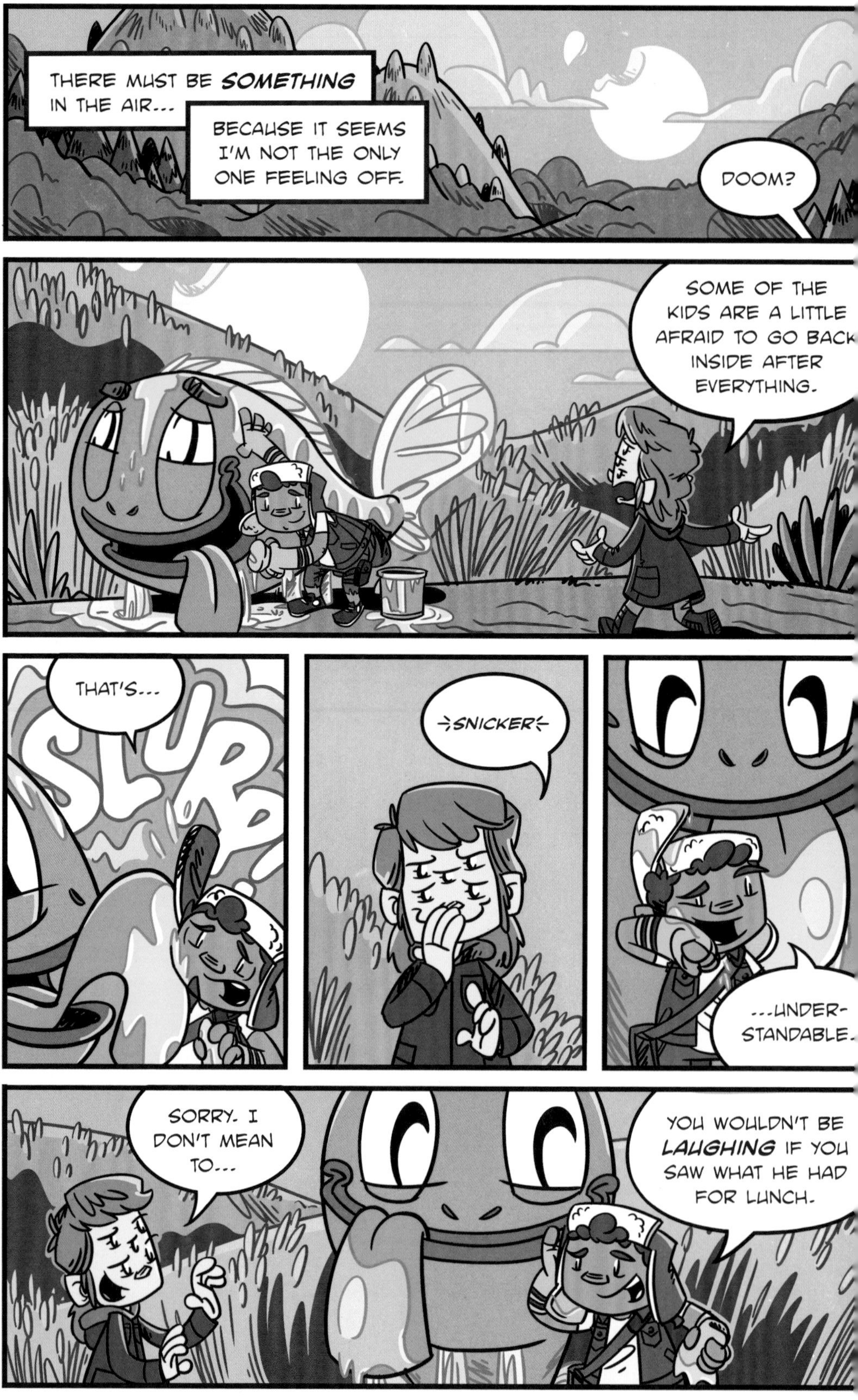
THERE MUST BE SOMETHING IN THE AIR...
BECAUSE IT SEEMS I'M NOT THE ONLY ONE FEELING OFF.
DOOM?
SOME OF THE KIDS ARE A LITTLE AFRAID TO GO BACK INSIDE AFTER EVERYTHING.
THAT'S...
SLURP
SNICKER
...UNDER-STANDABLE.
SORRY. I DON'T MEAN TO...
YOU WOULDN'T BE LAUGHING IF YOU SAW WHAT HE HAD FOR LUNCH.

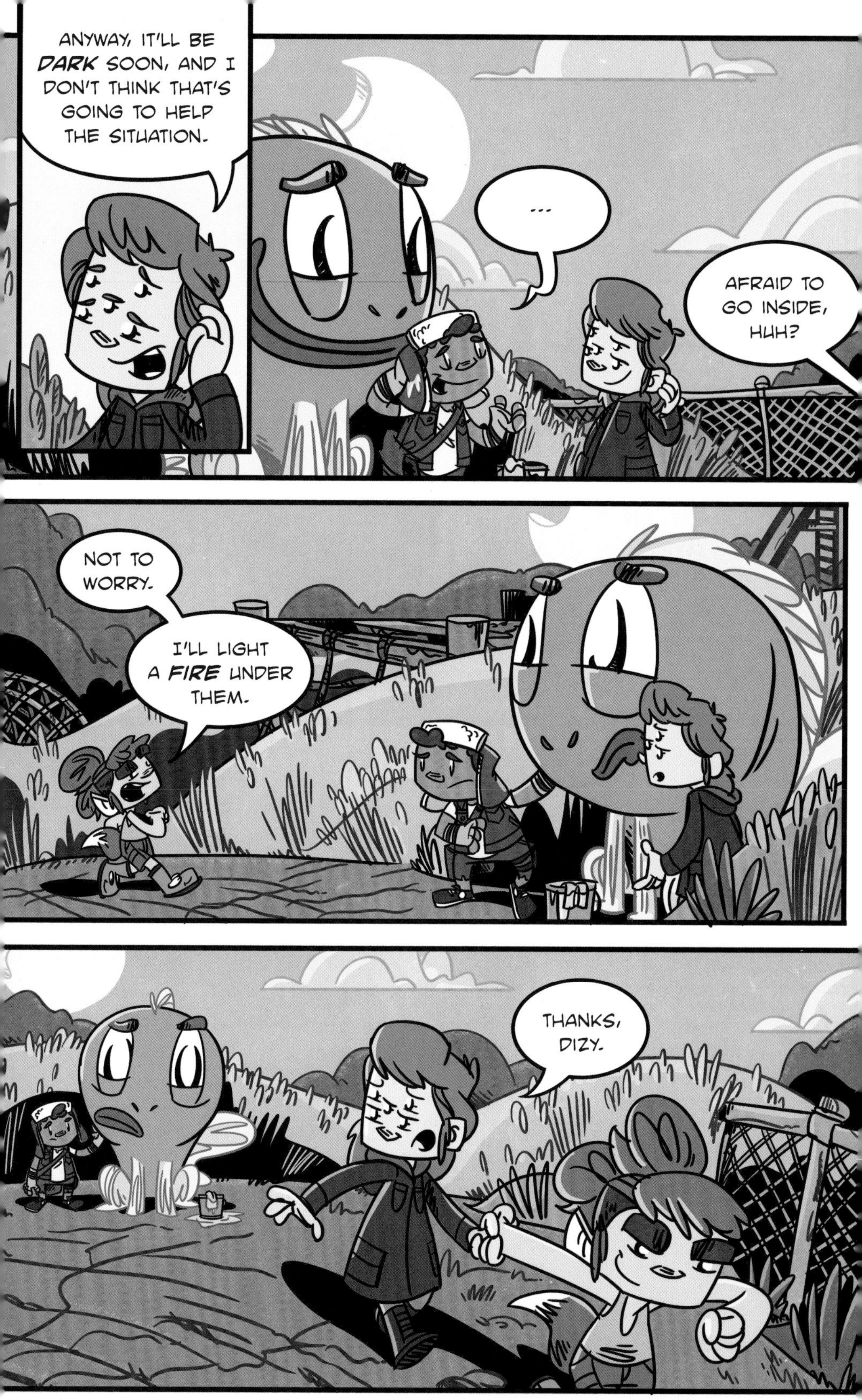
ANYWAY, IT'LL BE DARK SOON, AND I DON'T THINK THAT'S GOING TO HELP THE SITUATION.
...
AFRAID TO GO INSIDE, HUH?
NOT TO WORRY.
I'LL LIGHT A FIRE UNDER THEM.
THANKS, DIZY.

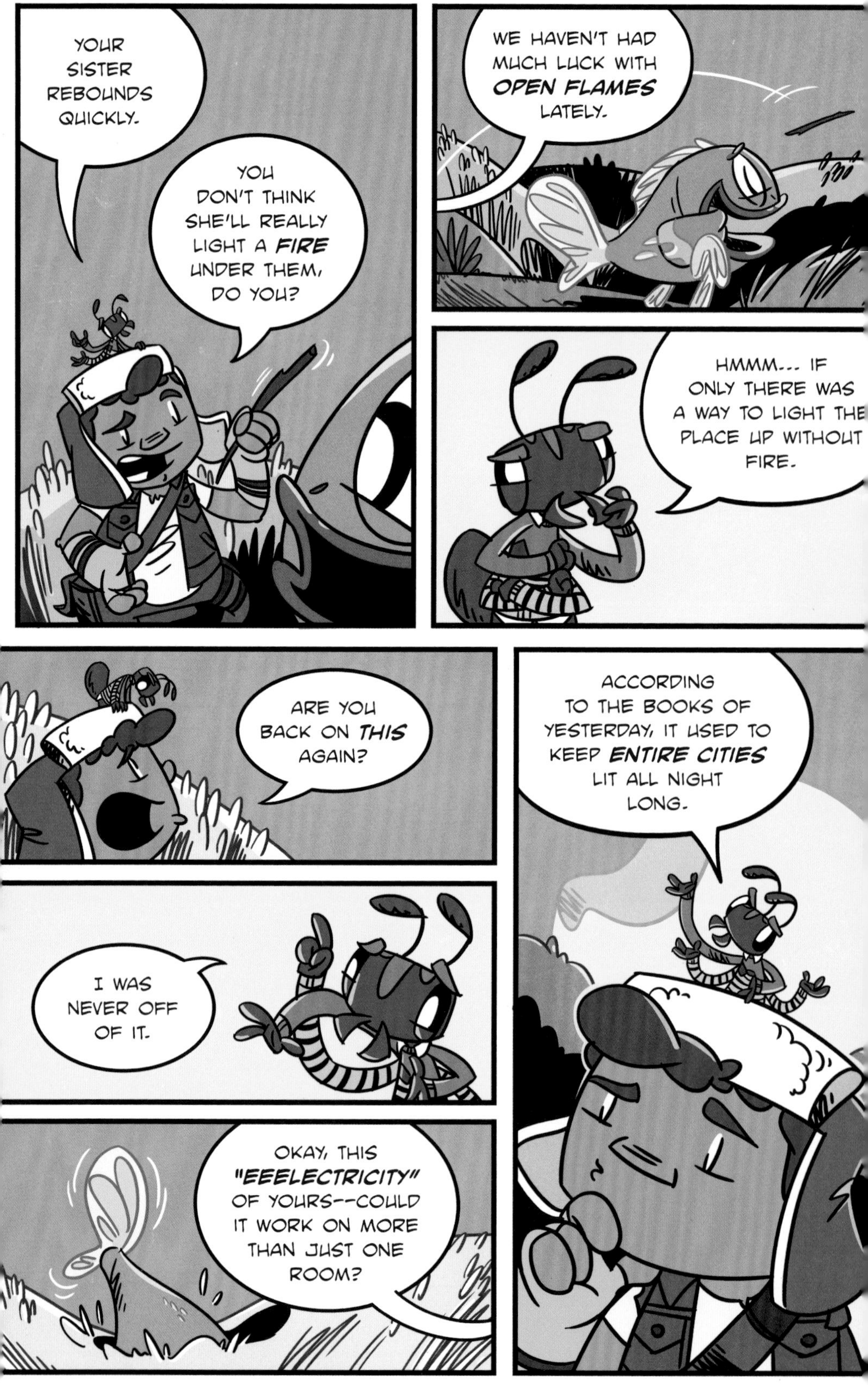

YOUR SISTER REBOUNDS QUICKLY.
YOU DON'T THINK SHE'LL REALLY LIGHT A FIRE UNDER THEM, DO YOU?
WE HAVEN'T HAD MUCH LUCK WITH OPEN FLAMES LATELY.
HMMM... IF ONLY THERE WAS A WAY TO LIGHT THE PLACE UP WITHOUT FIRE.
ARE YOU BACK ON THIS AGAIN?
I WAS NEVER OFF OF IT.
ACCORDING TO THE BOOKS OF YESTERDAY, IT USED TO KEEP ENTIRE CITIES LIT ALL NIGHT LONG.
OKAY, THIS "EEELECTRICITY" OF YOURS--COULD IT WORK ON MORE THAN JUST ONE ROOM?

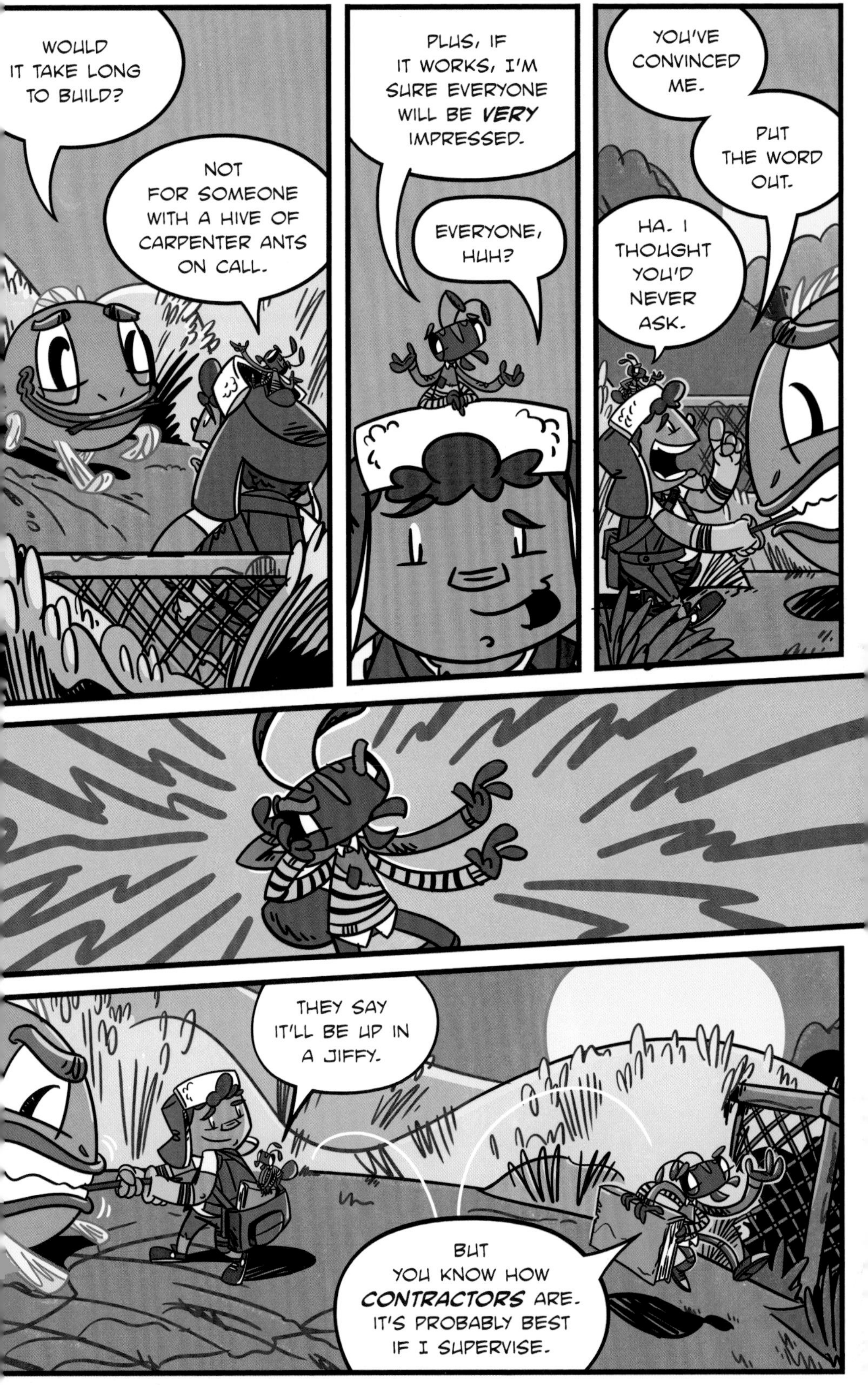
WOULD IT TAKE LONG TO BUILD?
NOT FOR SOMEONE WITH A HIVE OF CARPENTER ANTS ON CALL.
PLUS, IF IT WORKS, I'M SURE EVERYONE WILL BE *VERY* IMPRESSED.
EVERYONE, HUH?
YOU'VE CONVINCED ME.
PUT THE WORD OUT.
HA. I THOUGHT YOU'D NEVER ASK.
THEY SAY IT'LL BE UP IN A JIFFY.
BUT YOU KNOW HOW **CONTRACTORS** ARE. IT'S PROBABLY BEST IF I SUPERVISE.

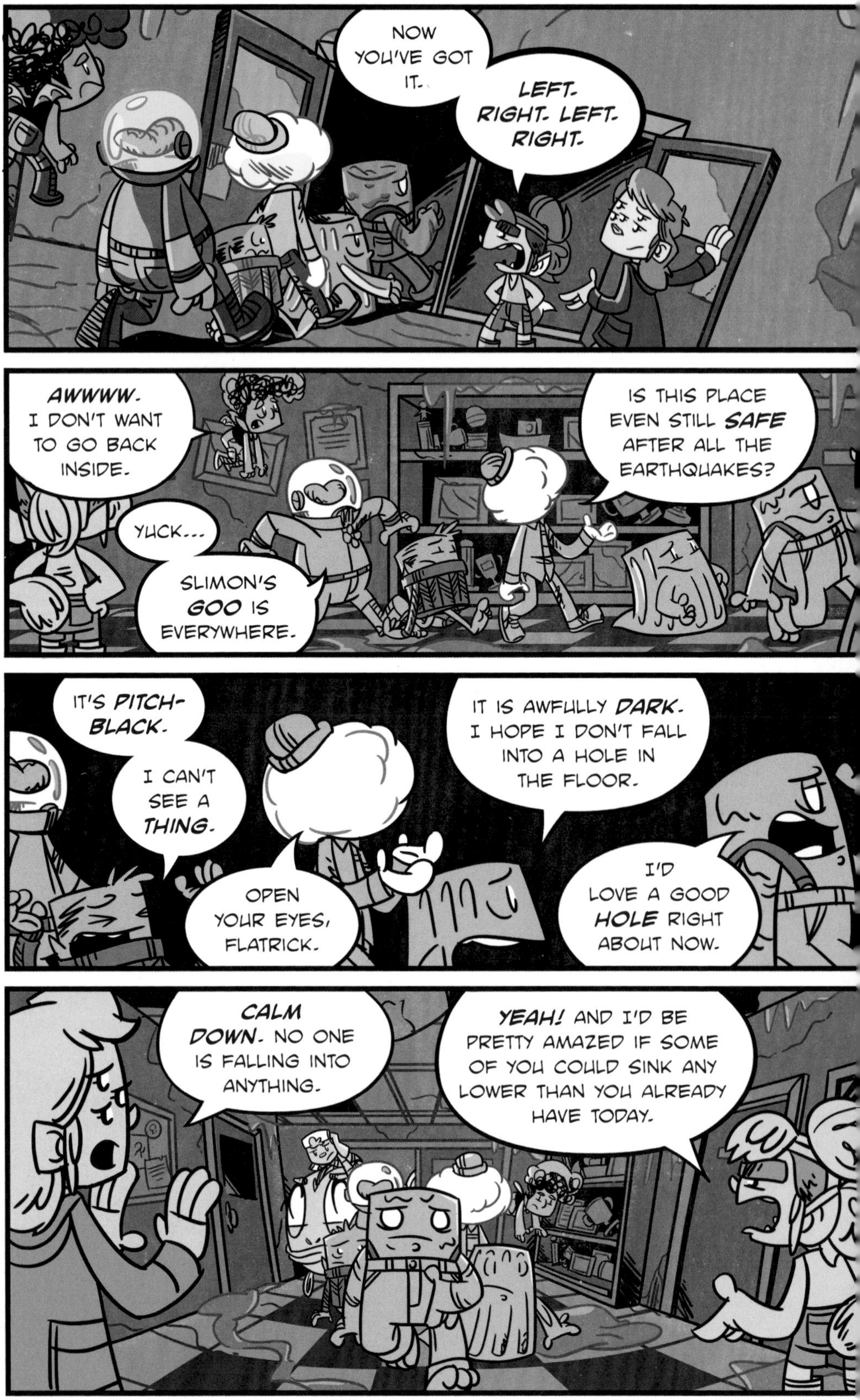
NOW YOU'VE GOT IT.
LEFT. RIGHT. LEFT. RIGHT.
AWWWW. I DON'T WANT TO GO BACK INSIDE.
IS THIS PLACE EVEN STILL SAFE AFTER ALL THE EARTHQUAKES?
YUCK...
SLIMON'S GOO IS EVERYWHERE.
IT'S PITCH-BLACK.
I CAN'T SEE A THING.
IT IS AWFULLY DARK. I HOPE I DON'T FALL INTO A HOLE IN THE FLOOR.
OPEN YOUR EYES, FLATRICK.
I'D LOVE A GOOD HOLE RIGHT ABOUT NOW.
CALM DOWN. NO ONE IS FALLING INTO ANYTHING.
YEAH! AND I'D BE PRETTY AMAZED IF SOME OF YOU COULD SINK ANY LOWER THAN YOU ALREADY HAVE TODAY.

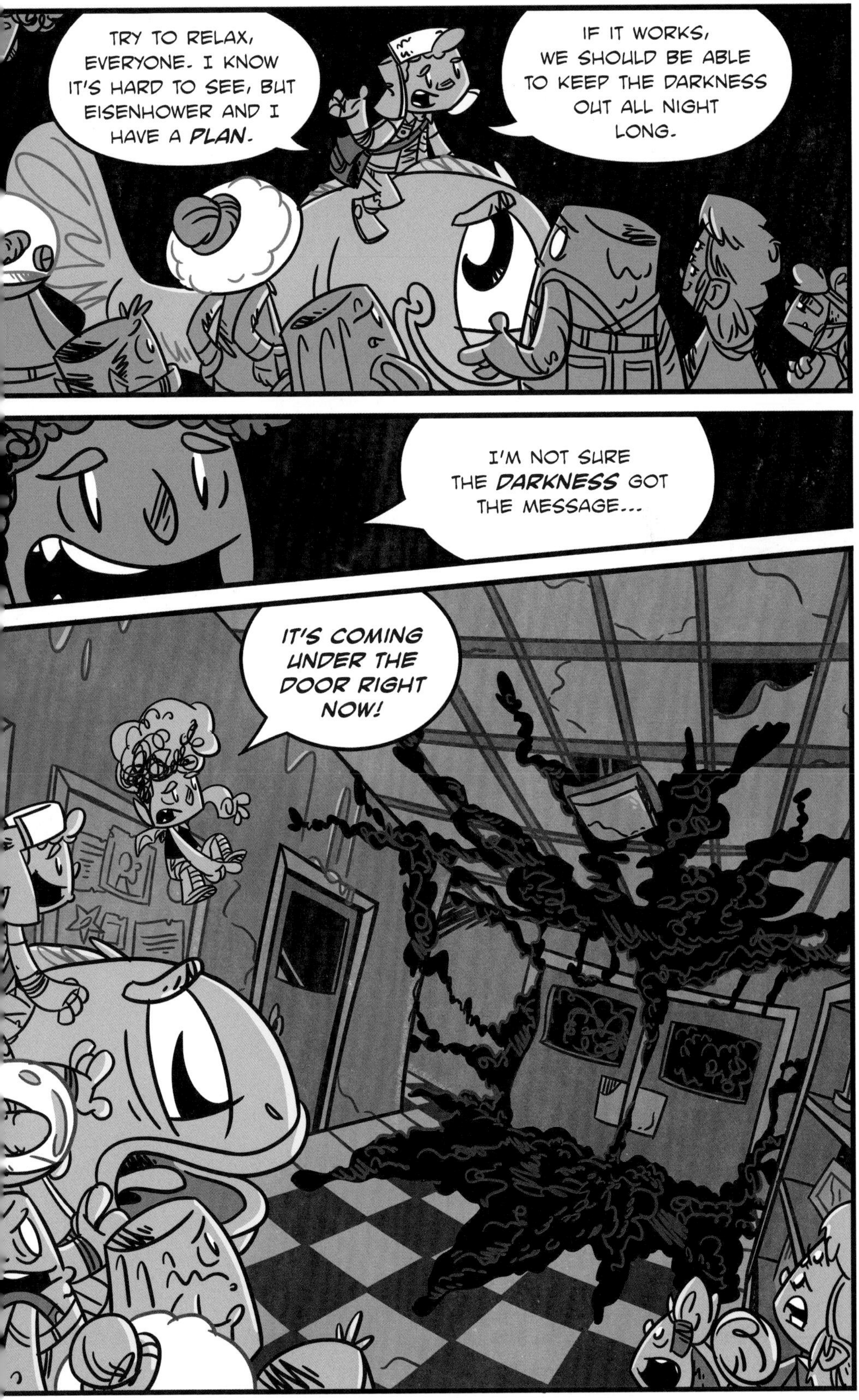
TRY TO RELAX, EVERYONE. I KNOW IT'S HARD TO SEE, BUT EISENHOWER AND I HAVE A PLAN.
IF IT WORKS, WE SHOULD BE ABLE TO KEEP THE DARKNESS OUT ALL NIGHT LONG.
I'M NOT SURE THE DARKNESS GOT THE MESSAGE...
IT'S COMING UNDER THE DOOR RIGHT NOW!

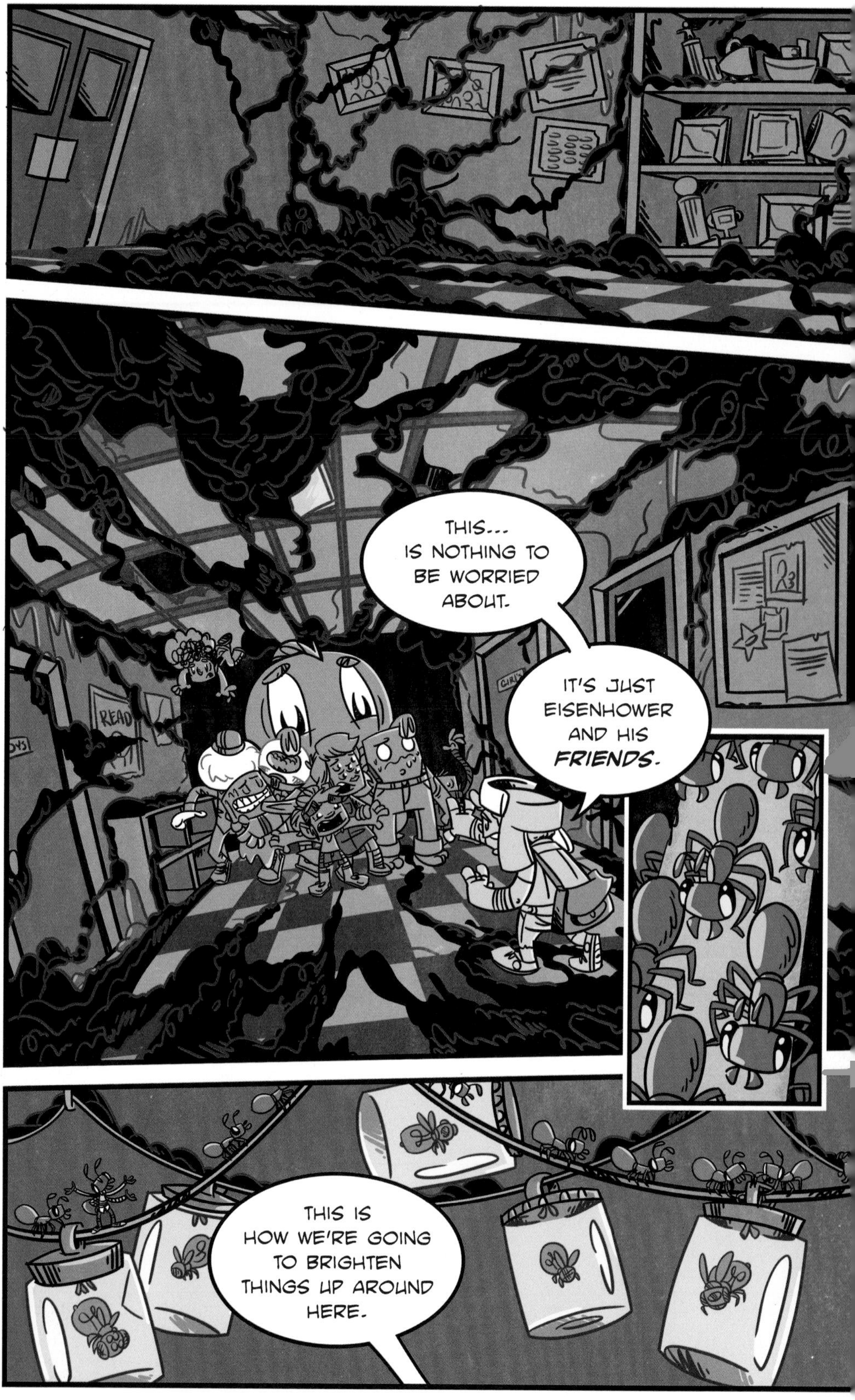

READ
THIS... IS NOTHING TO BE WORRIED ABOUT.
IT'S JUST EISENHOWER AND HIS *FRIENDS*.
THIS IS HOW WE'RE GOING TO BRIGHTEN THINGS UP AROUND HERE.

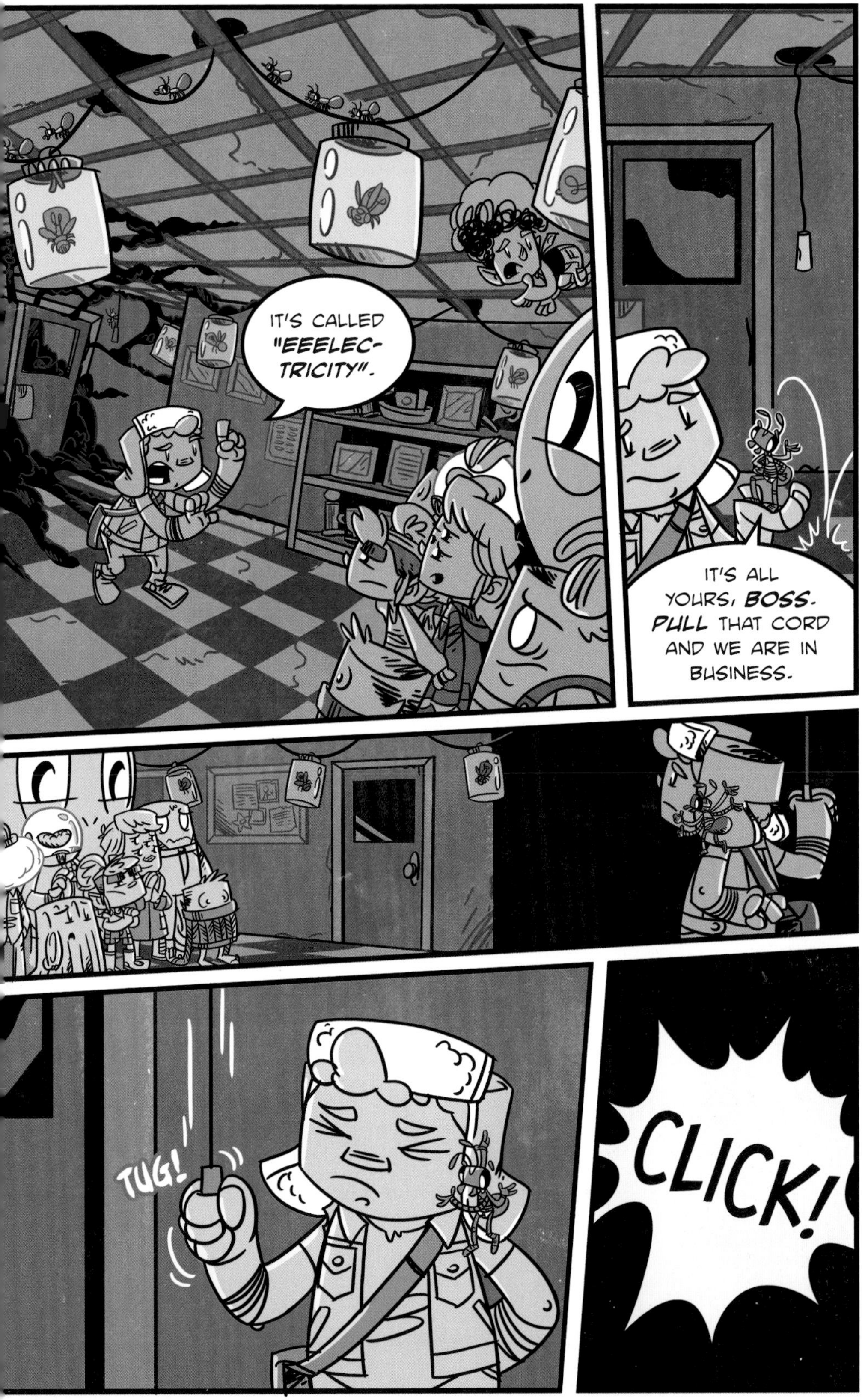
IT'S CALLED "EEELEC-TRICITY".
IT'S ALL YOURS, BOSS. PULL THAT CORD AND WE ARE IN BUSINESS.
TUG!
CLICK!

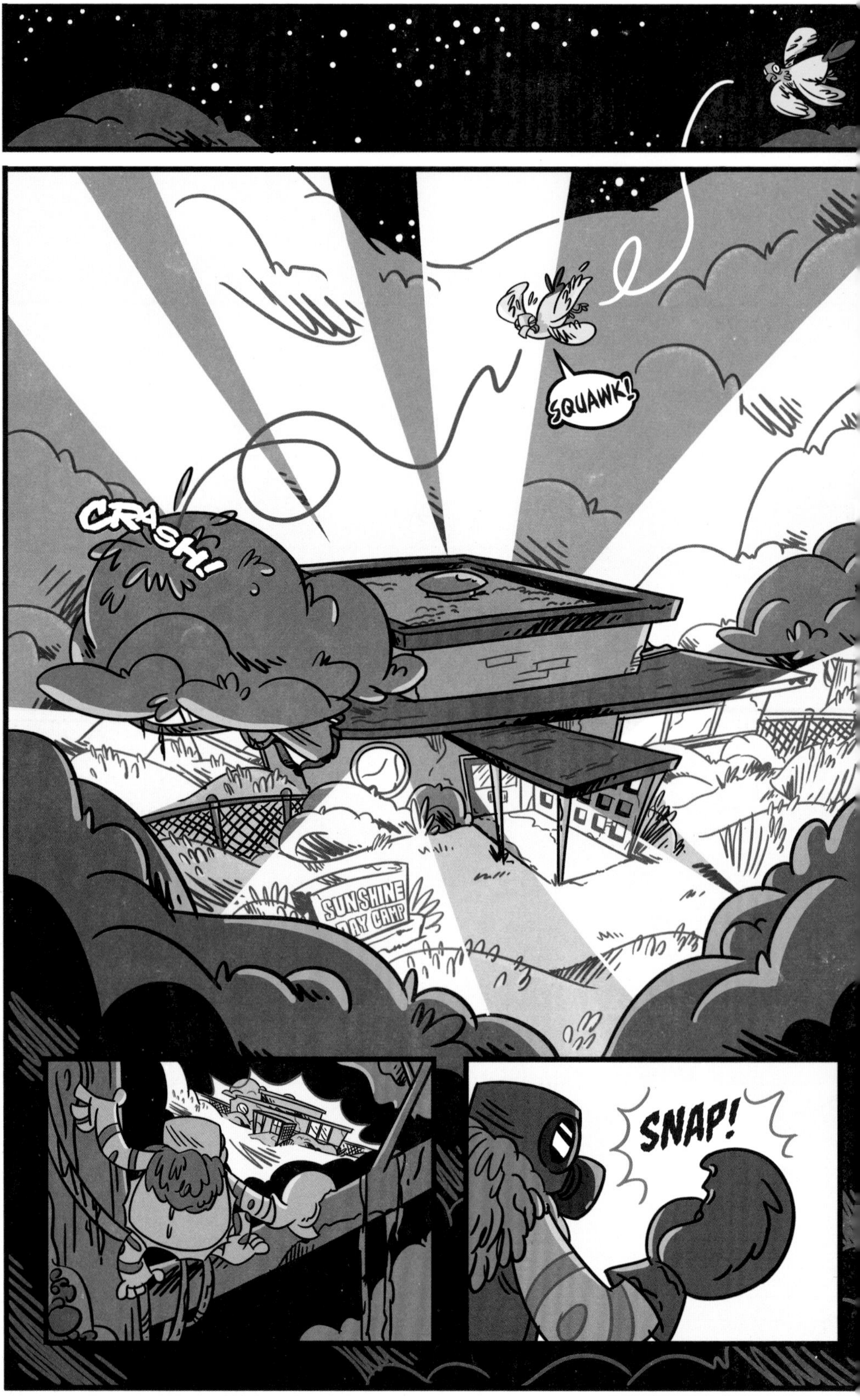
SQUAWK!
CRASH!
SUNSHINE DAY CAMP
SNAP!

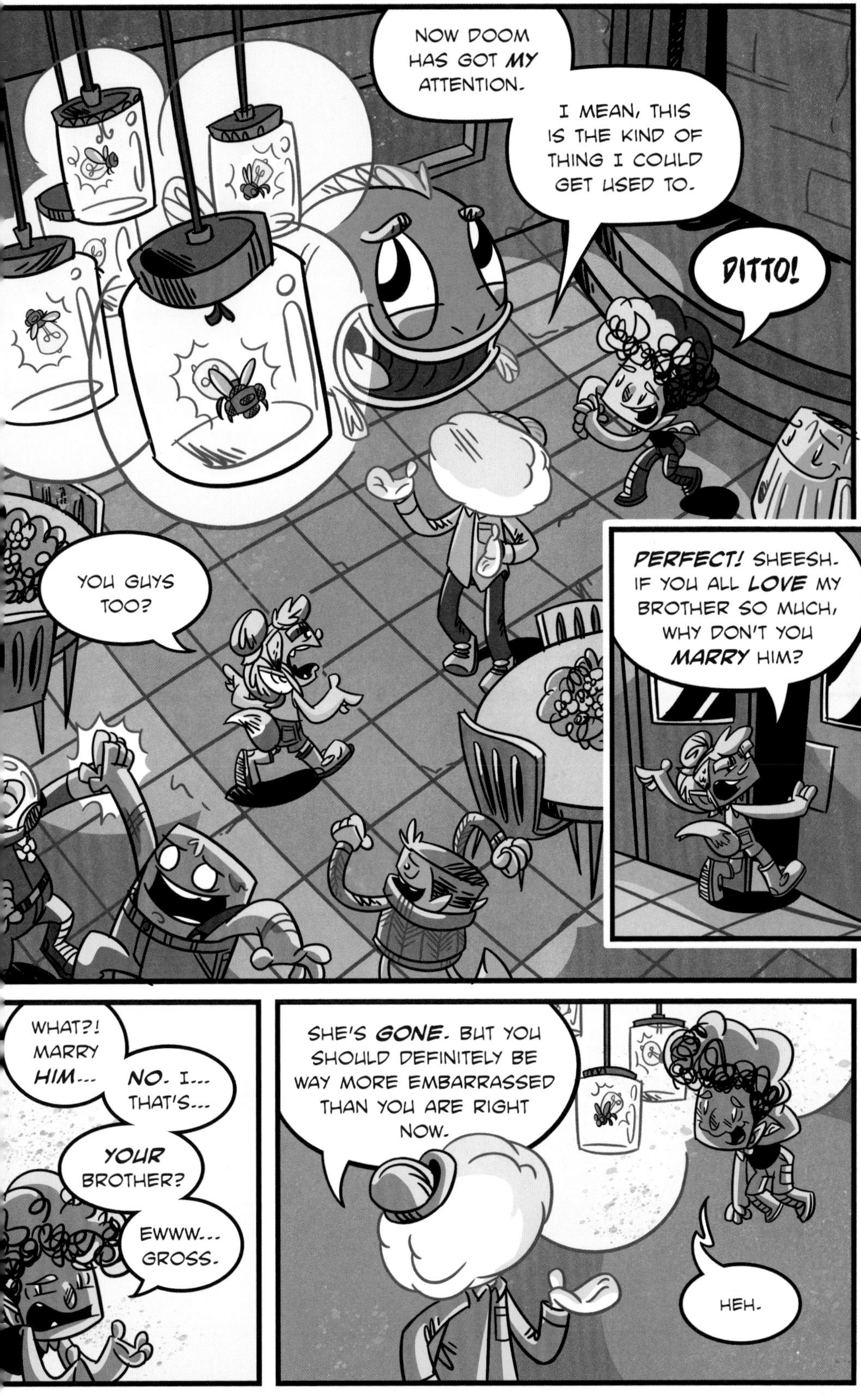
NOW DOOM HAS GOT *MY* ATTENTION.
I MEAN, THIS IS THE KIND OF THING I COULD GET USED TO.
DITTO!
YOU GUYS TOO?
PERFECT! SHEESH. IF YOU ALL *LOVE* MY BROTHER SO MUCH, WHY DON'T YOU *MARRY* HIM?
WHAT?! MARRY *HIM*...
NO. I... THAT'S...
YOUR BROTHER?
EWWW... GROSS.
SHE'S *GONE*. BUT YOU SHOULD DEFINITELY BE WAY MORE EMBARRASSED THAN YOU ARE RIGHT NOW.
HEH.

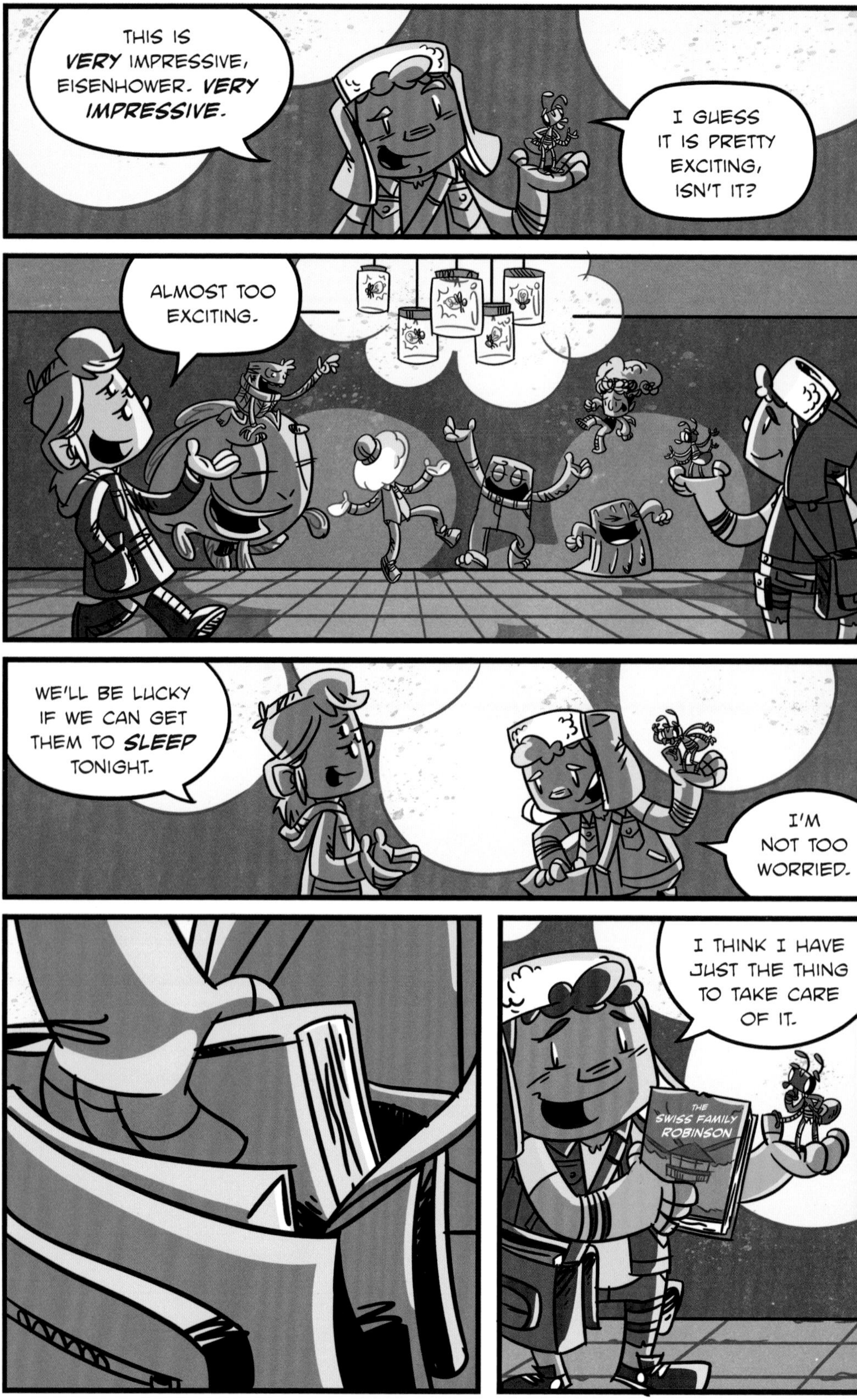

THIS IS VERY IMPRESSIVE, EISENHOWER. VERY IMPRESSIVE.
I GUESS IT IS PRETTY EXCITING, ISN'T IT?
ALMOST TOO EXCITING.
WE'LL BE LUCKY IF WE CAN GET THEM TO SLEEP TONIGHT.
I'M NOT TOO WORRIED.
I THINK I HAVE JUST THE THING TO TAKE CARE OF IT.
THE SWISS FAMILY ROBINSON

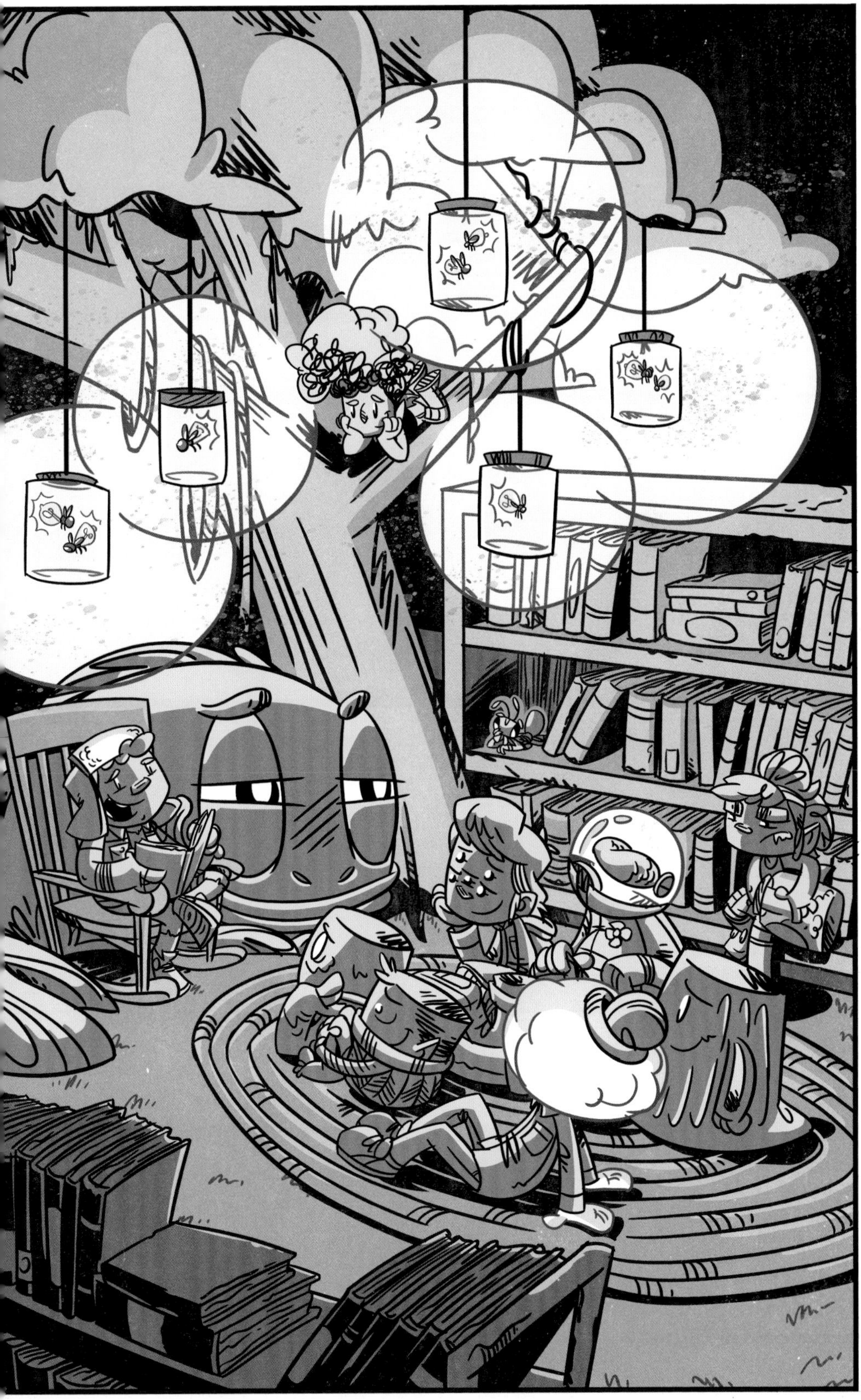

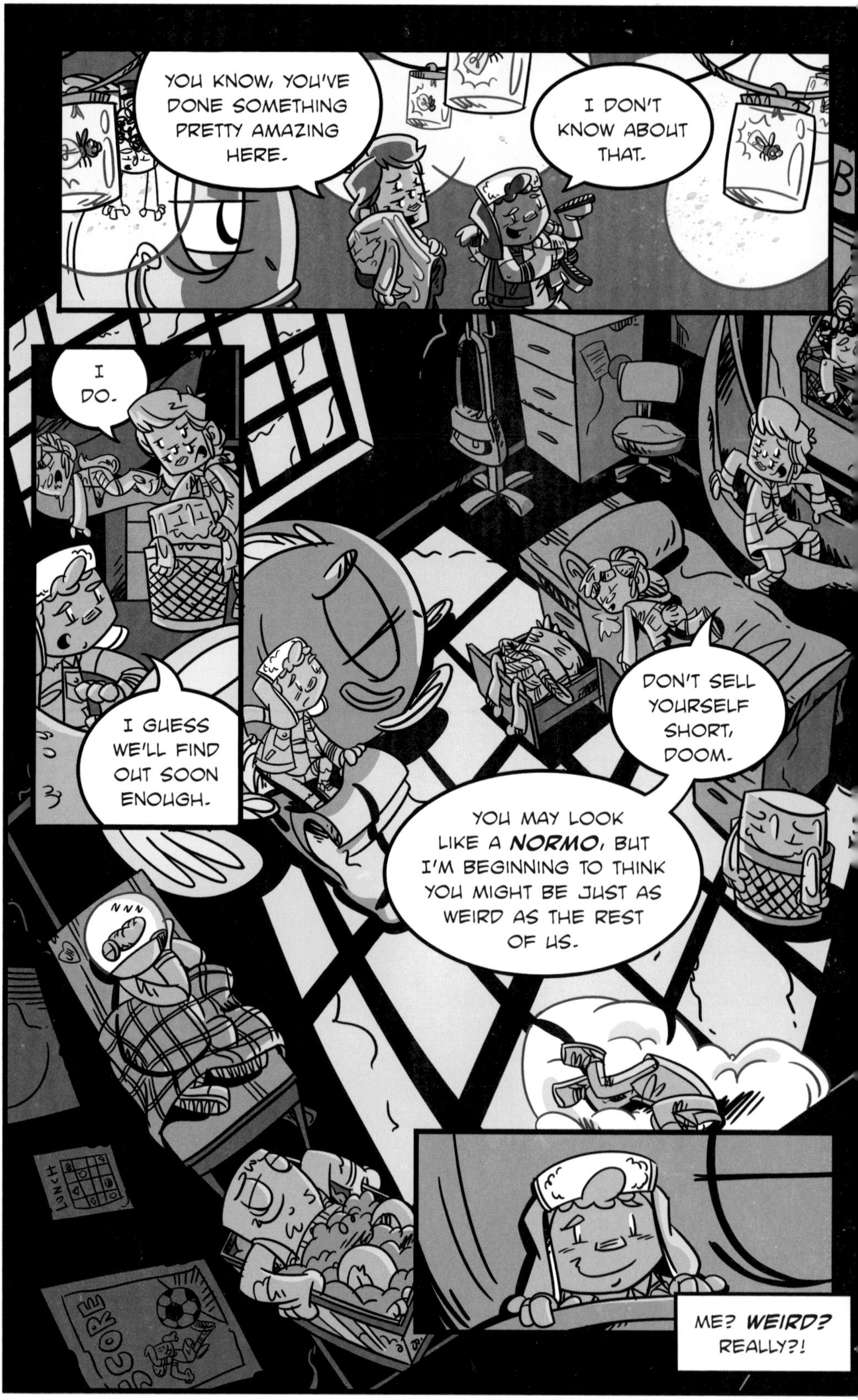
YOU KNOW, YOU'VE DONE SOMETHING PRETTY AMAZING HERE.
I DON'T KNOW ABOUT THAT.
I DO.
I GUESS WE'LL FIND OUT SOON ENOUGH.
DON'T SELL YOURSELF SHORT, DOOM.
YOU MAY LOOK LIKE A ***NORMO***, BUT I'M BEGINNING TO THINK YOU MIGHT BE JUST AS WEIRD AS THE REST OF US.
NNN
LUNCH
SCORE
ME? ***WEIRD?*** REALLY?!

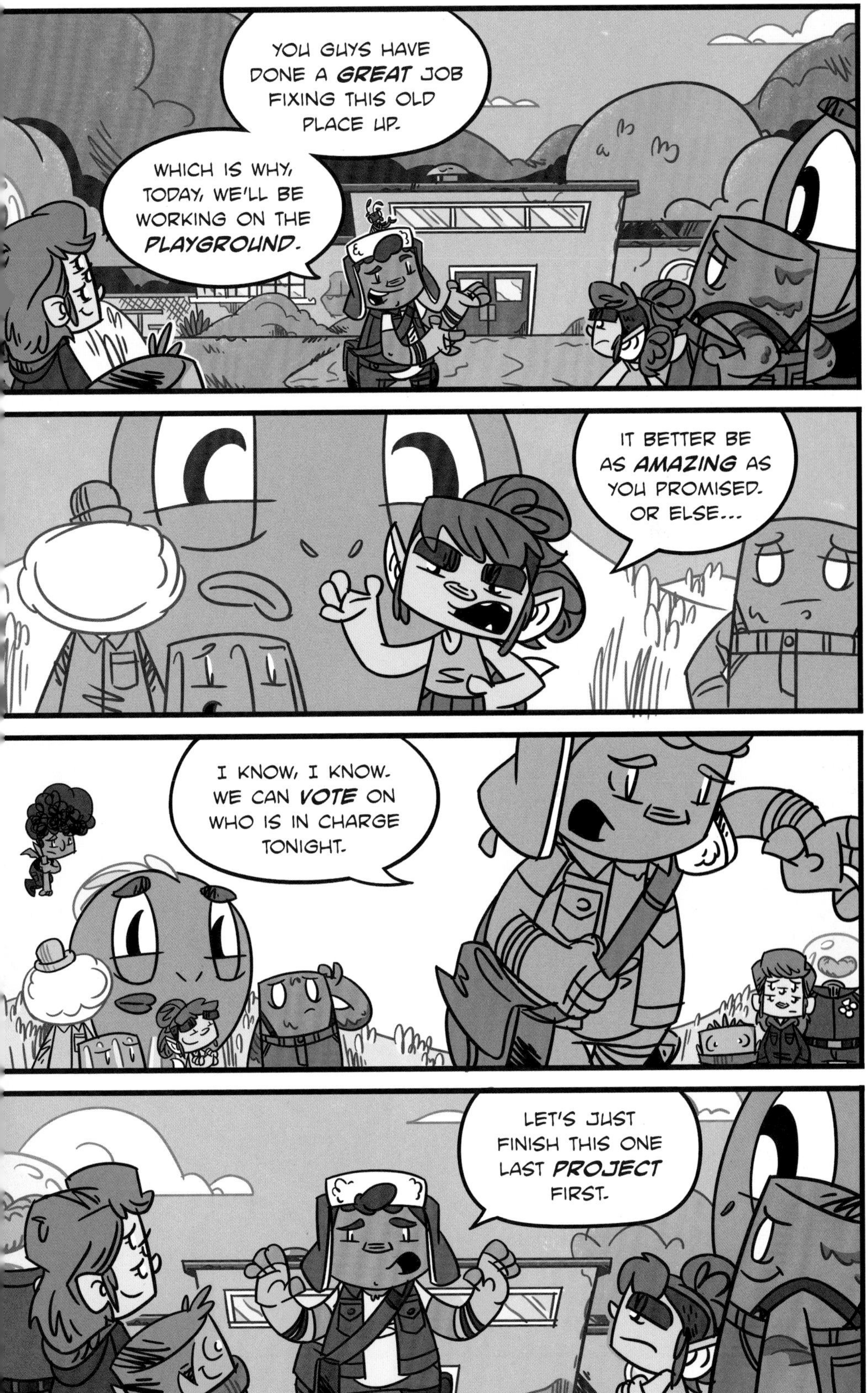
YOU GUYS HAVE DONE A GREAT JOB FIXING THIS OLD PLACE UP.
WHICH IS WHY, TODAY, WE'LL BE WORKING ON THE PLAYGROUND.
IT BETTER BE AS AMAZING AS YOU PROMISED. OR ELSE...
I KNOW, I KNOW. WE CAN VOTE ON WHO IS IN CHARGE TONIGHT.
LET'S JUST FINISH THIS ONE LAST PROJECT FIRST.

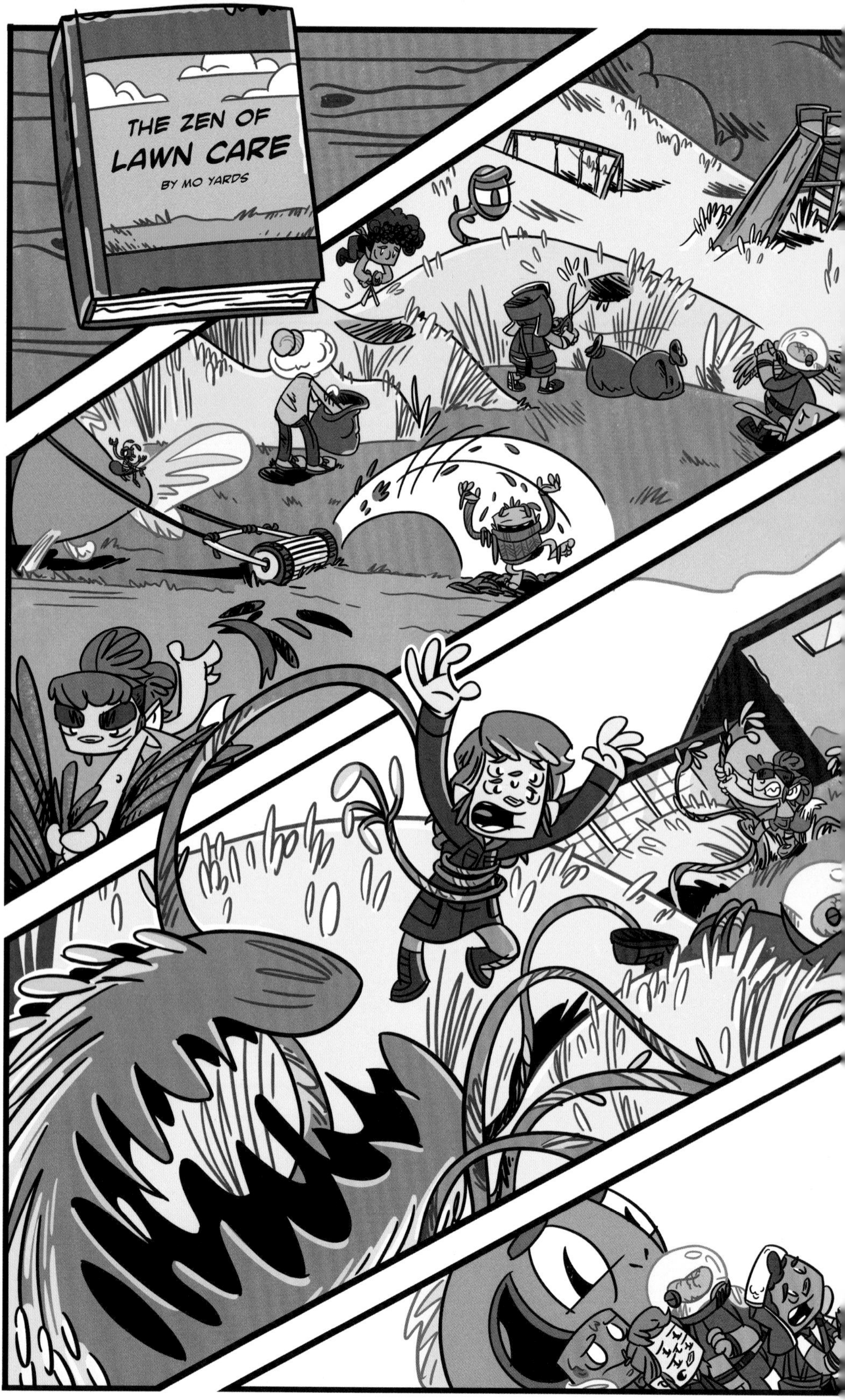
THE ZEN OF
LAWN CARE
BY MO YARDS

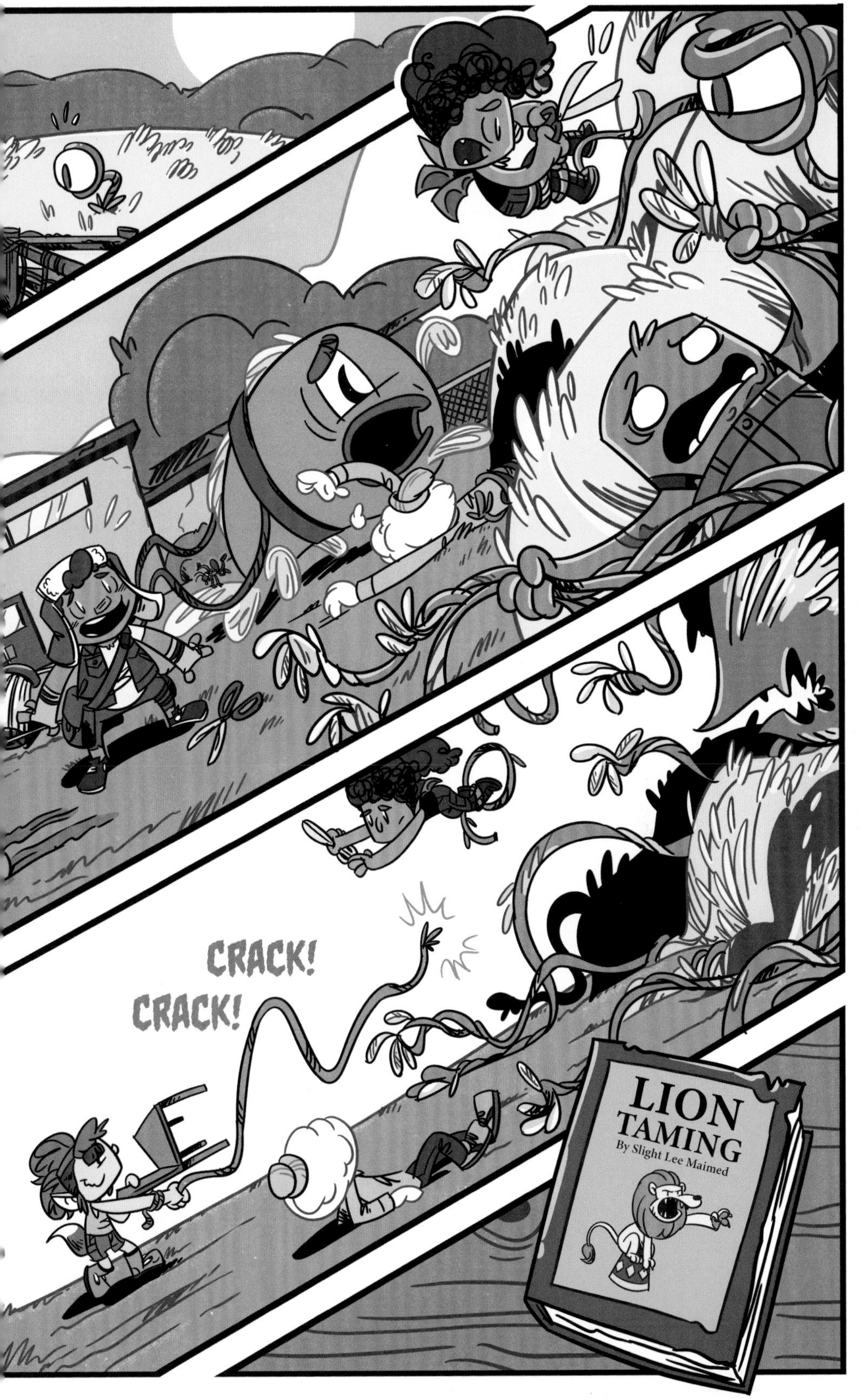
CRACK!
CRACK!
LION
TAMING
By Slight Lee Maimed

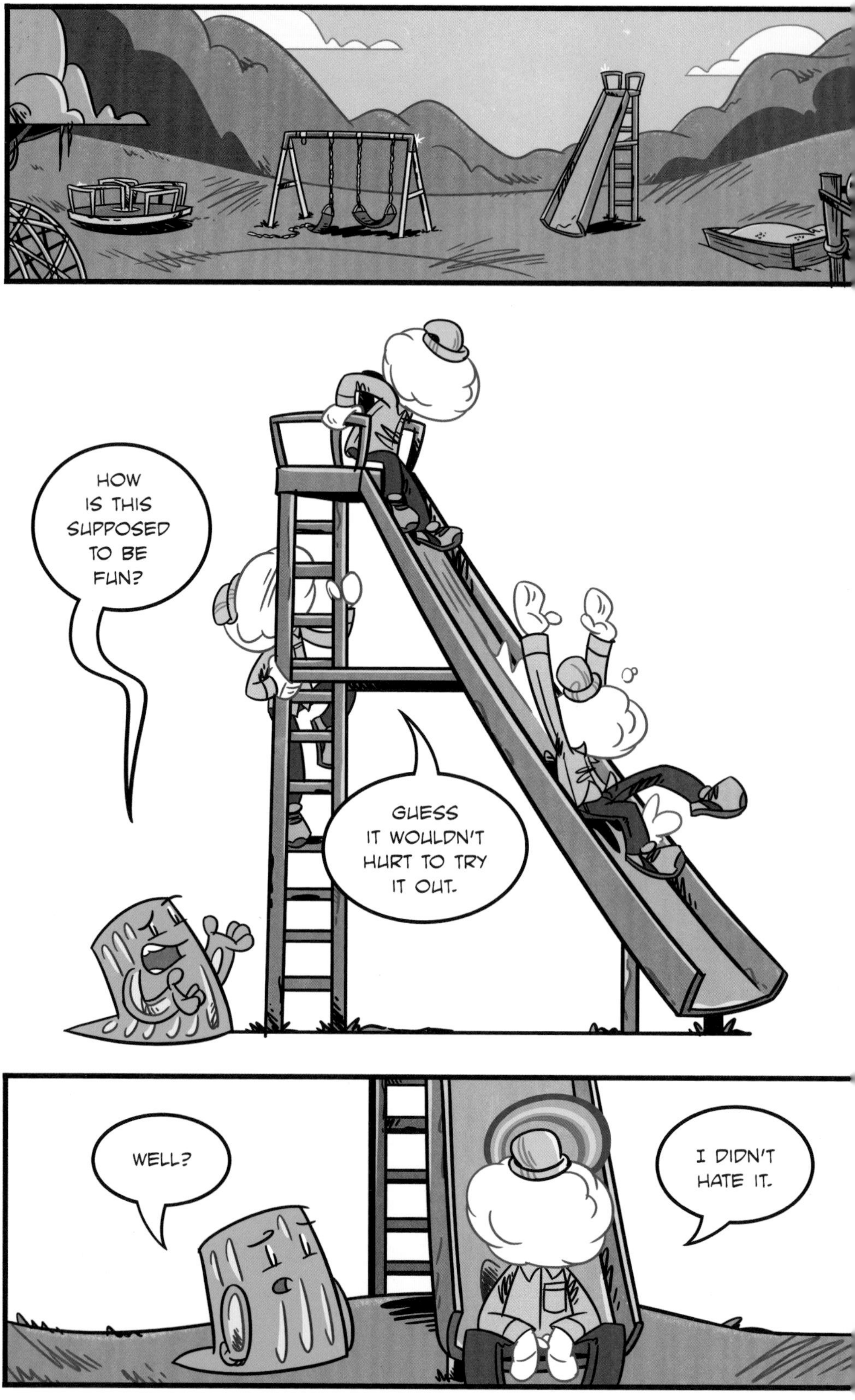
HOW IS THIS SUPPOSED TO BE FUN?
GUESS IT WOULDN'T HURT TO TRY IT OUT.
WELL?
I DIDN'T HATE IT.

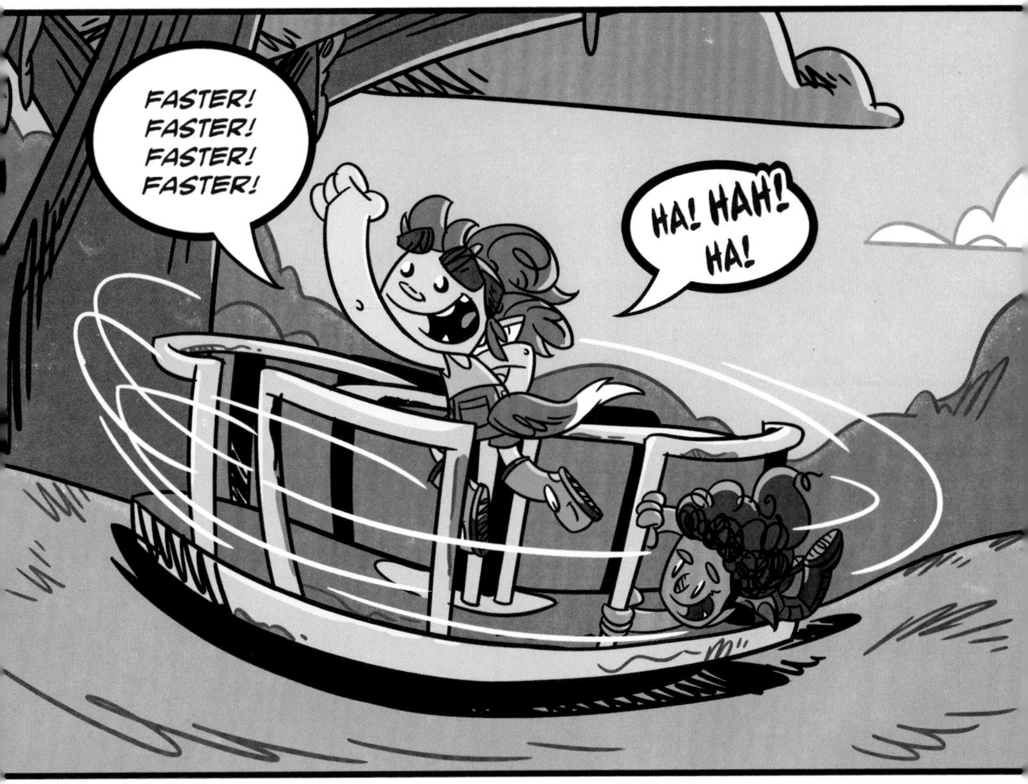
FASTER! FASTER! FASTER! FASTER!
HA! HAH! HA!

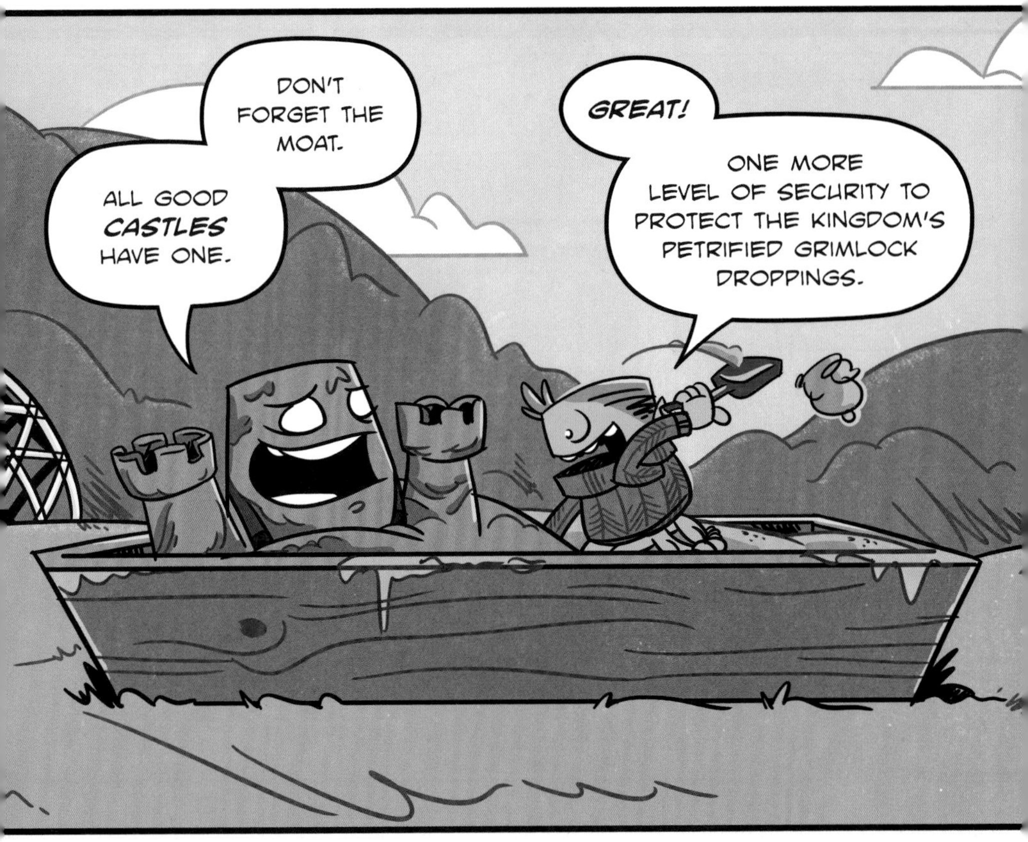
DON'T FORGET THE MOAT.
ALL GOOD CASTLES HAVE ONE.
GREAT!
ONE MORE LEVEL OF SECURITY TO PROTECT THE KINGDOM'S PETRIFIED GRIMLOCK DROPPINGS.

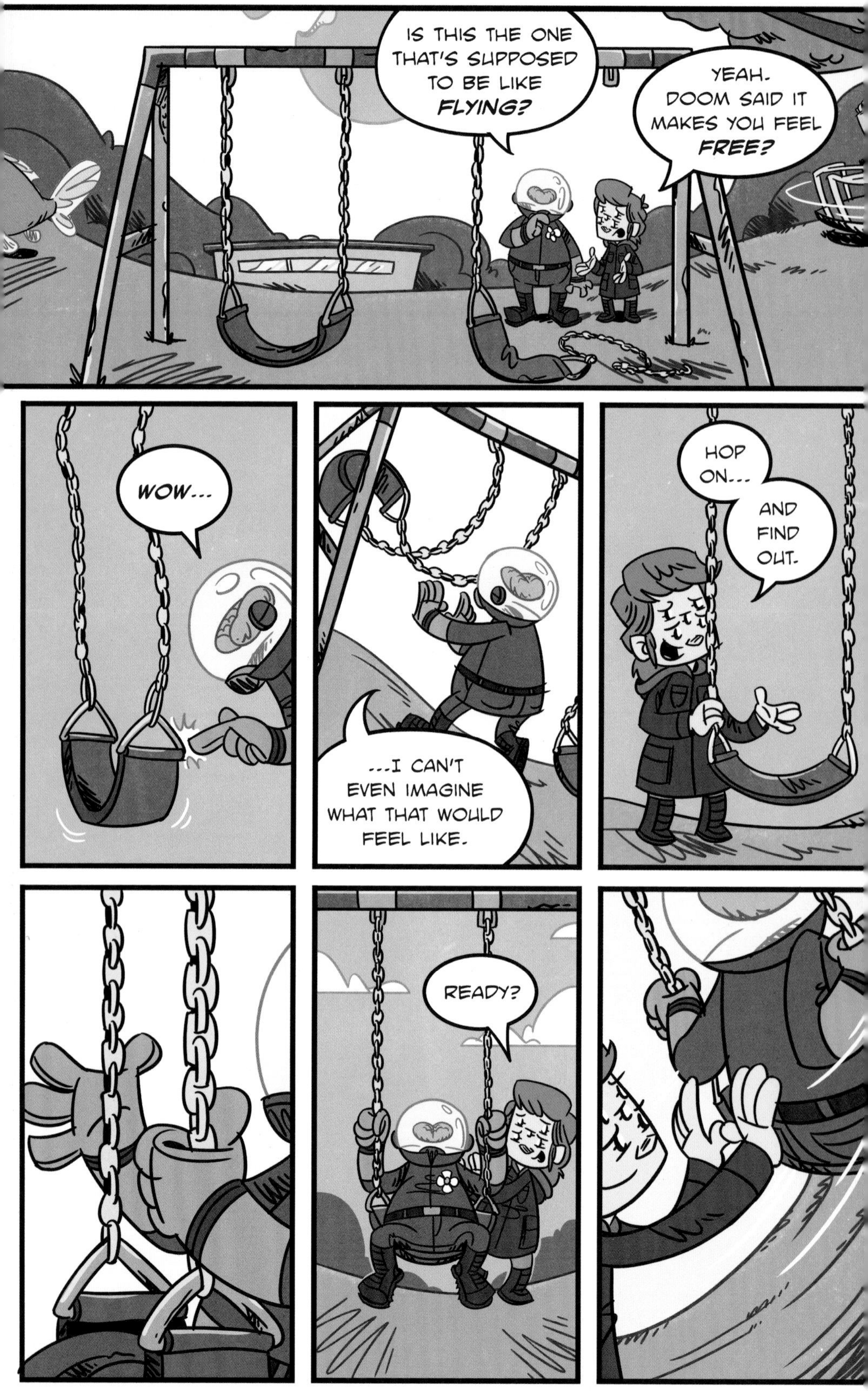
IS THIS THE ONE THAT'S SUPPOSED TO BE LIKE FLYING?
YEAH. DOOM SAID IT MAKES YOU FEEL FREE?
WOW...
...I CAN'T EVEN IMAGINE WHAT THAT WOULD FEEL LIKE.
HOP ON...
AND FIND OUT.
READY?

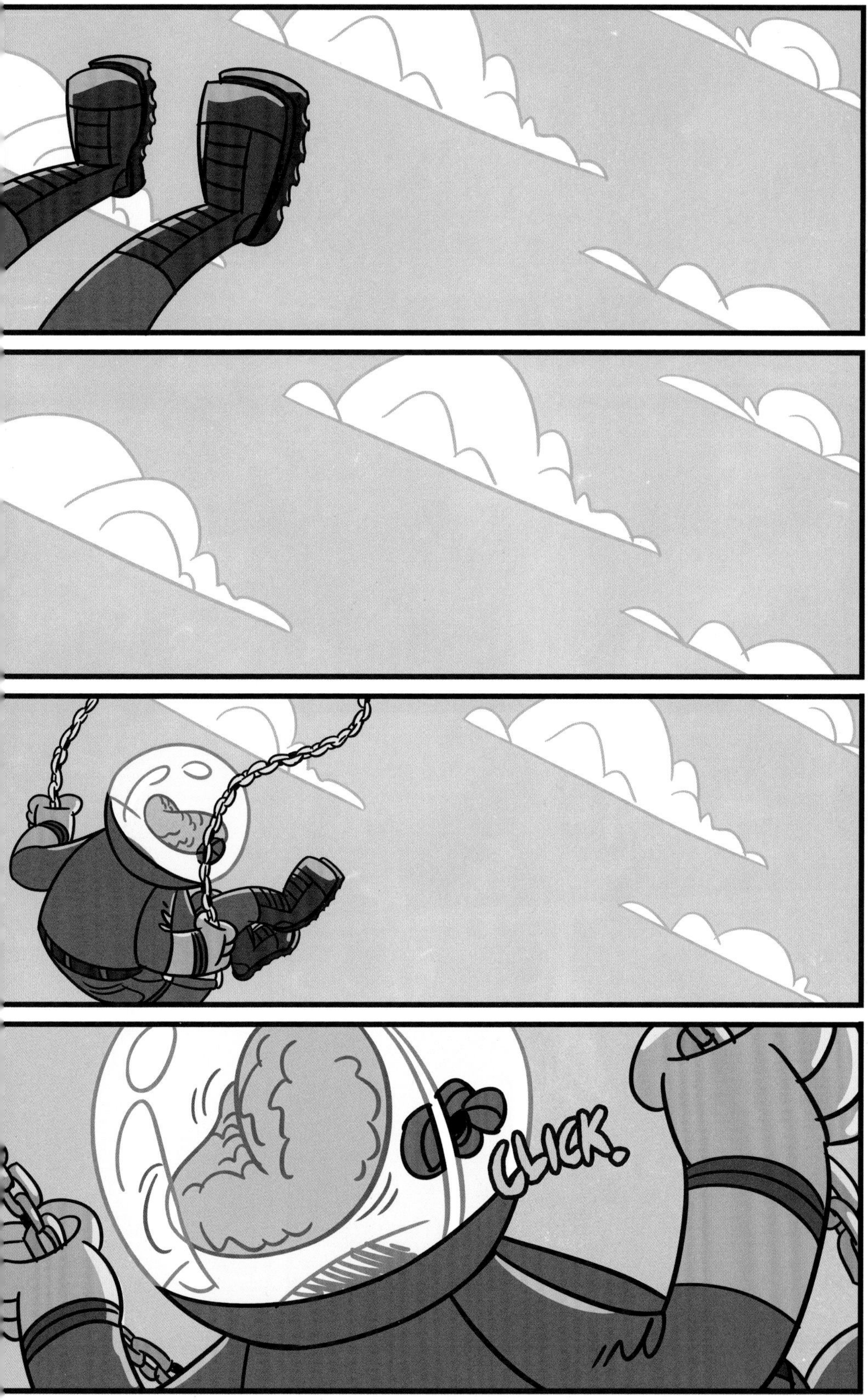
CLICK.

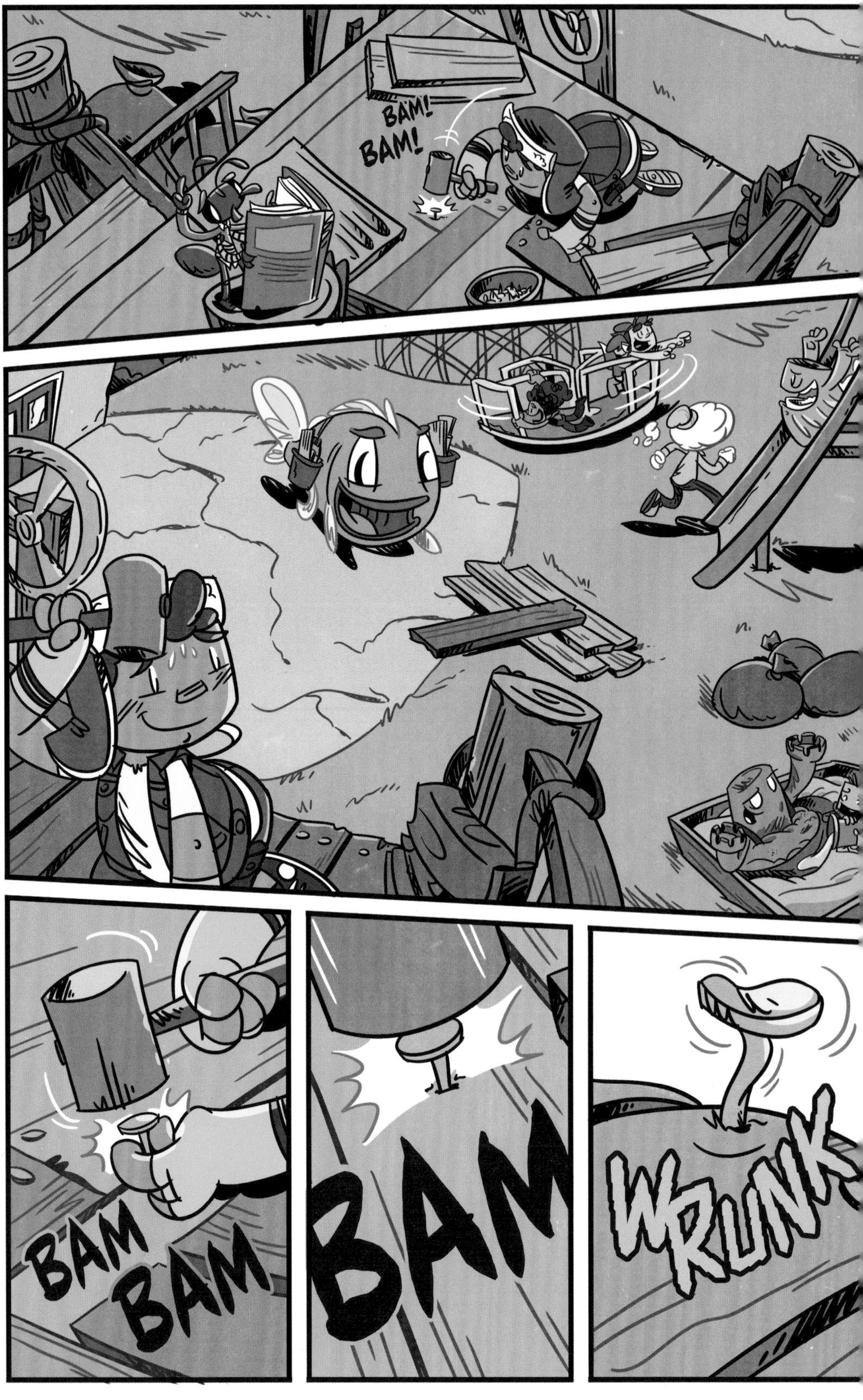

BAM!
BAM!
BAM
BAM
BAM
WRUNK!

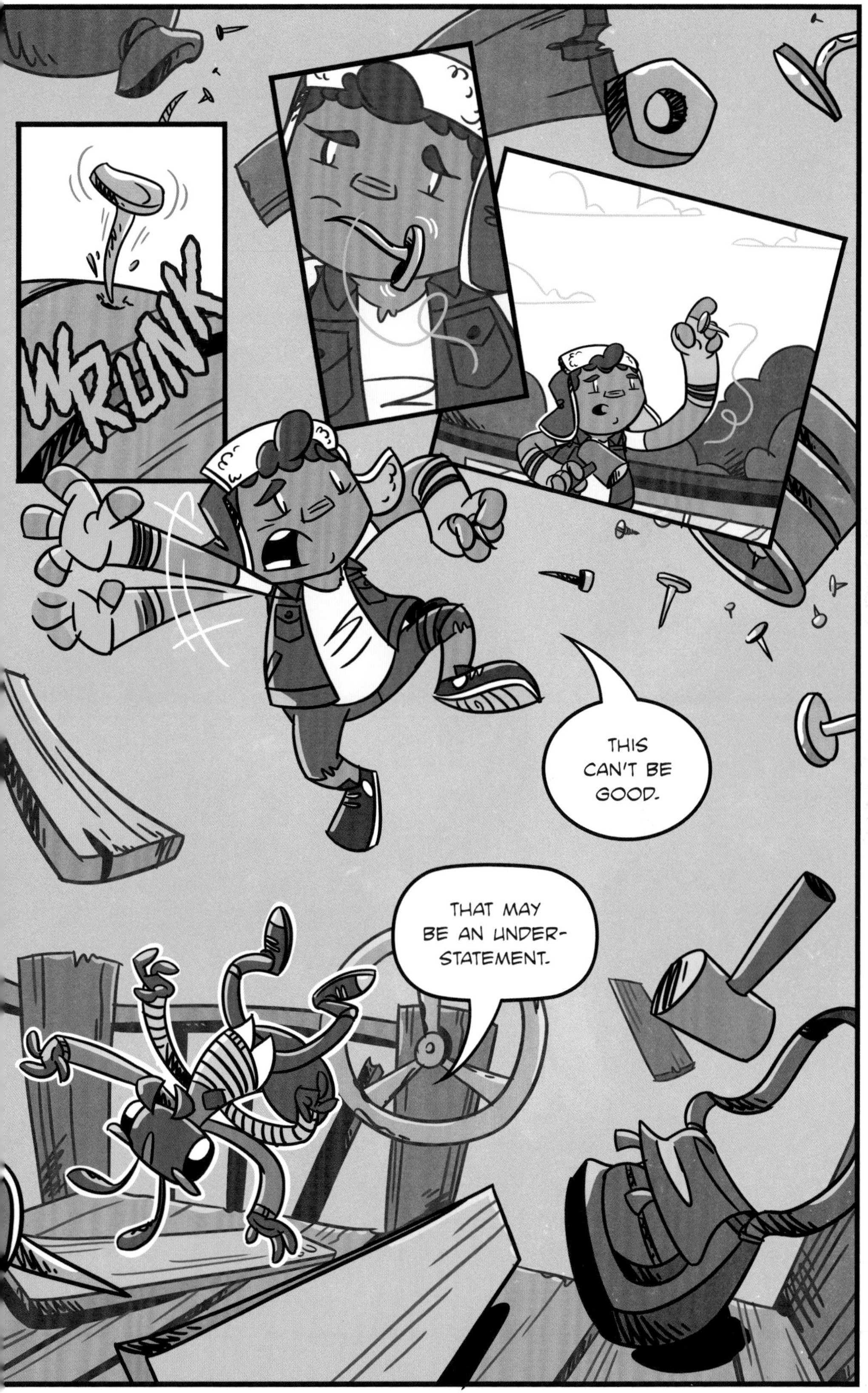
WRUNK
THIS CAN'T BE GOOD.
THAT MAY BE AN UNDER-STATEMENT.

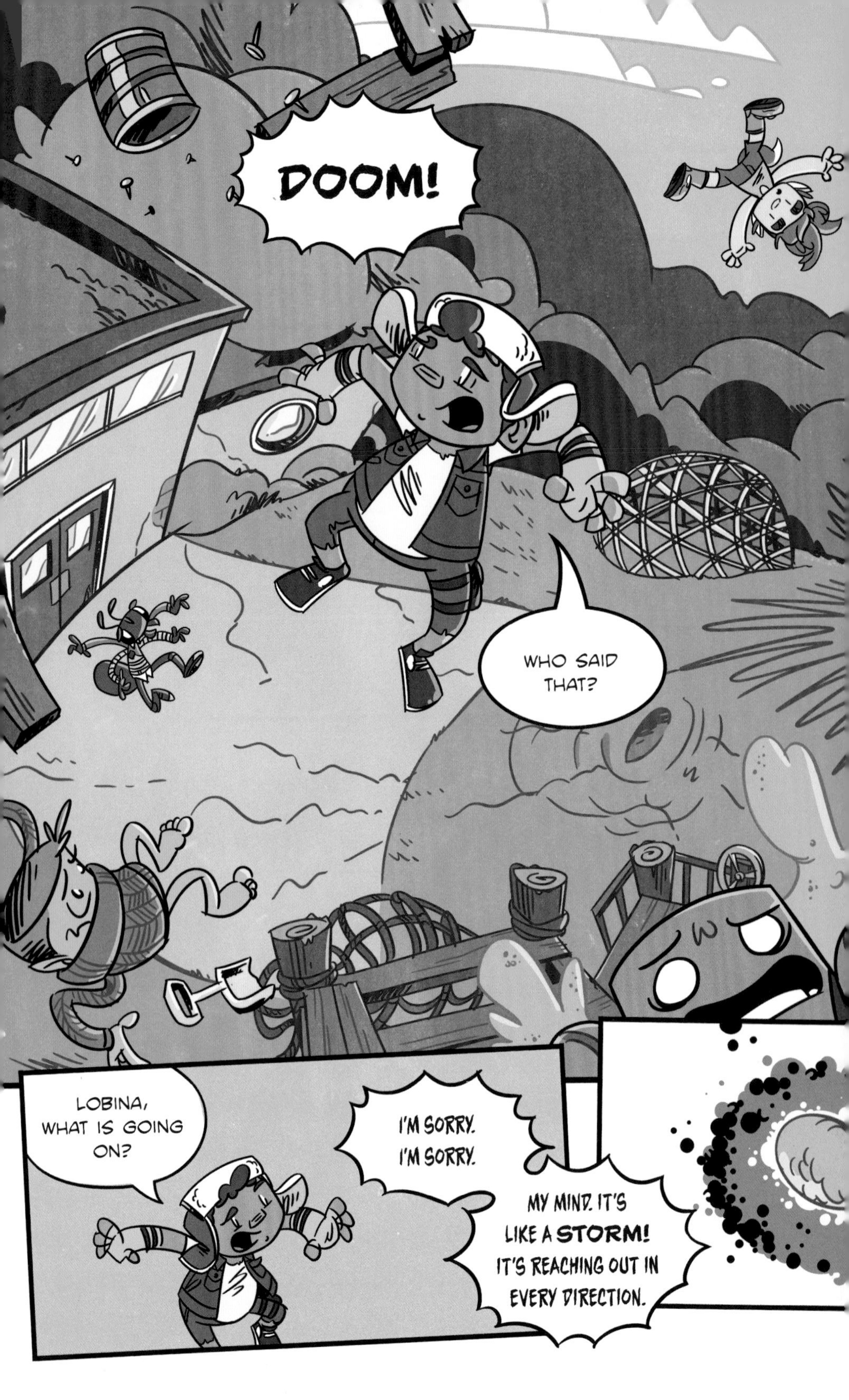
DOOM!
WHO SAID THAT?
LOBINA, WHAT IS GOING ON?
I'M SORRY. I'M SORRY.
MY MIND. IT'S LIKE A STORM! IT'S REACHING OUT IN EVERY DIRECTION.

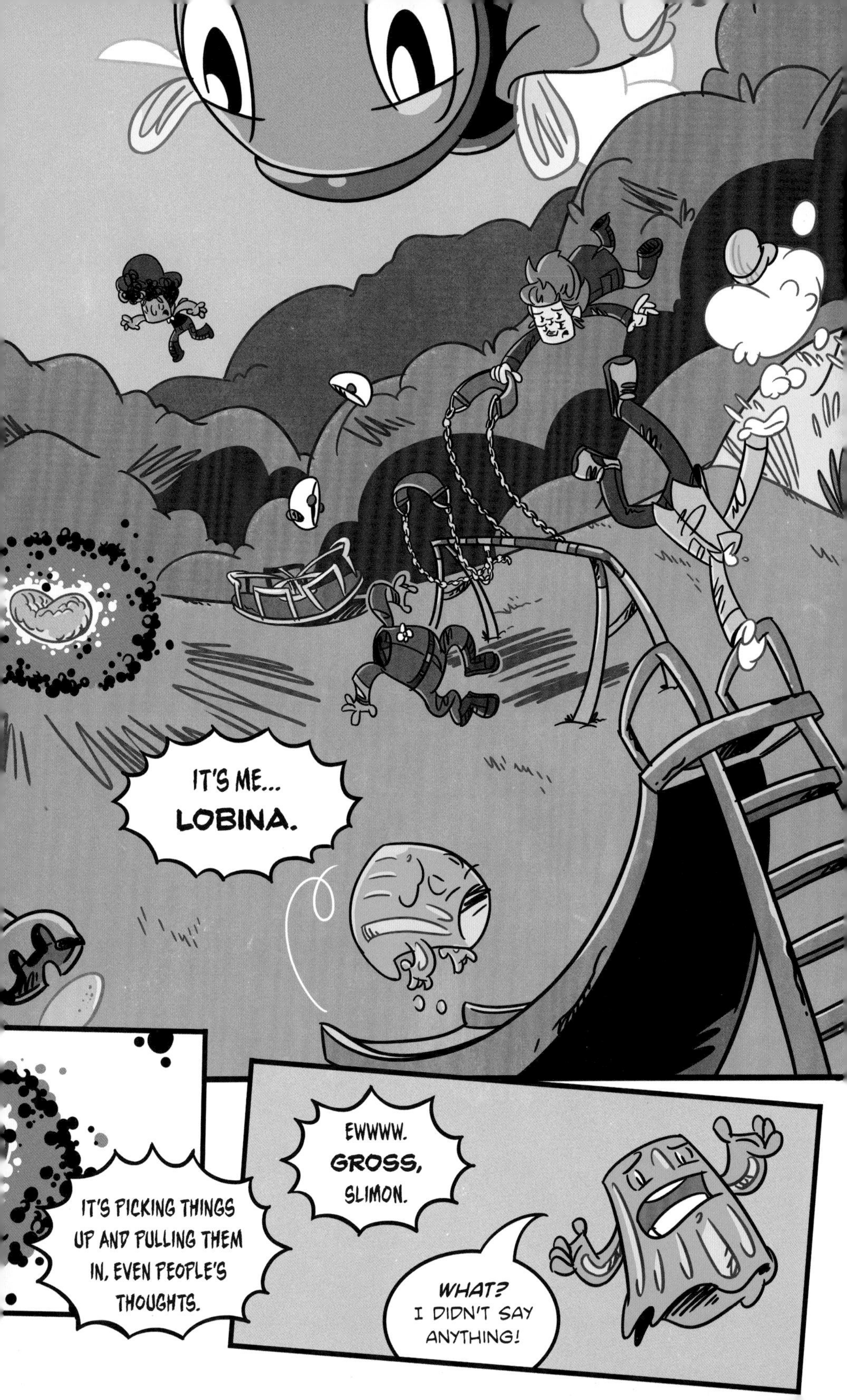
IT'S ME... LOBINA.
IT'S PICKING THINGS UP AND PULLING THEM IN, EVEN PEOPLE'S THOUGHTS.
EWWWW. GROSS, SLIMON.
WHAT? I DIDN'T SAY ANYTHING!

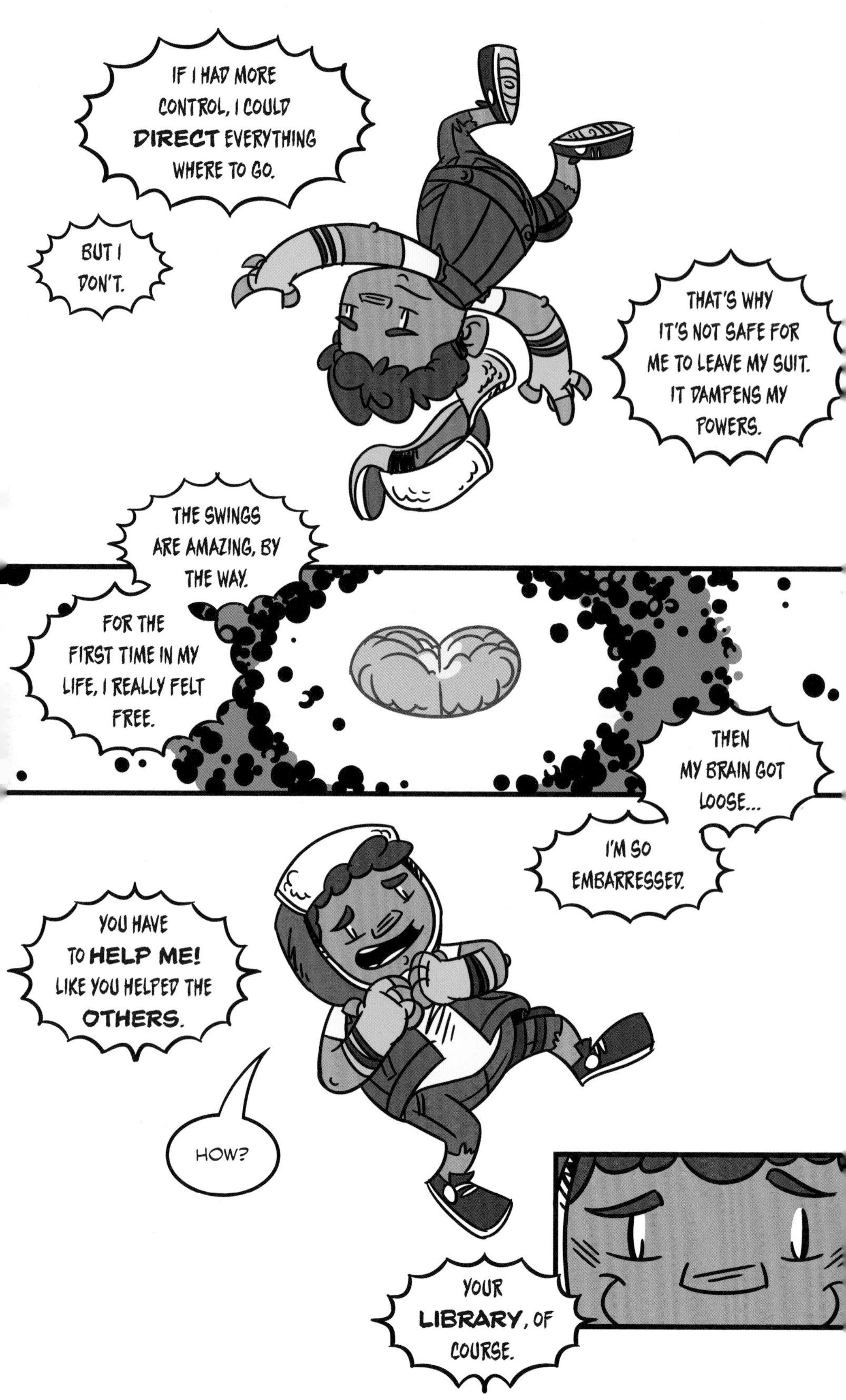
IF I HAD MORE CONTROL, I COULD **DIRECT** EVERYTHING WHERE TO GO.
BUT I DON'T.
THAT'S WHY IT'S NOT SAFE FOR ME TO LEAVE MY SUIT. IT DAMPENS MY POWERS.
THE SWINGS ARE AMAZING, BY THE WAY.
FOR THE FIRST TIME IN MY LIFE, I REALLY FELT FREE.
THEN MY BRAIN GOT LOOSE...
I'M SO EMBARRESSED.
YOU HAVE TO **HELP ME!** LIKE YOU HELPED THE **OTHERS**.
HOW?
YOUR **LIBRARY**, OF COURSE.

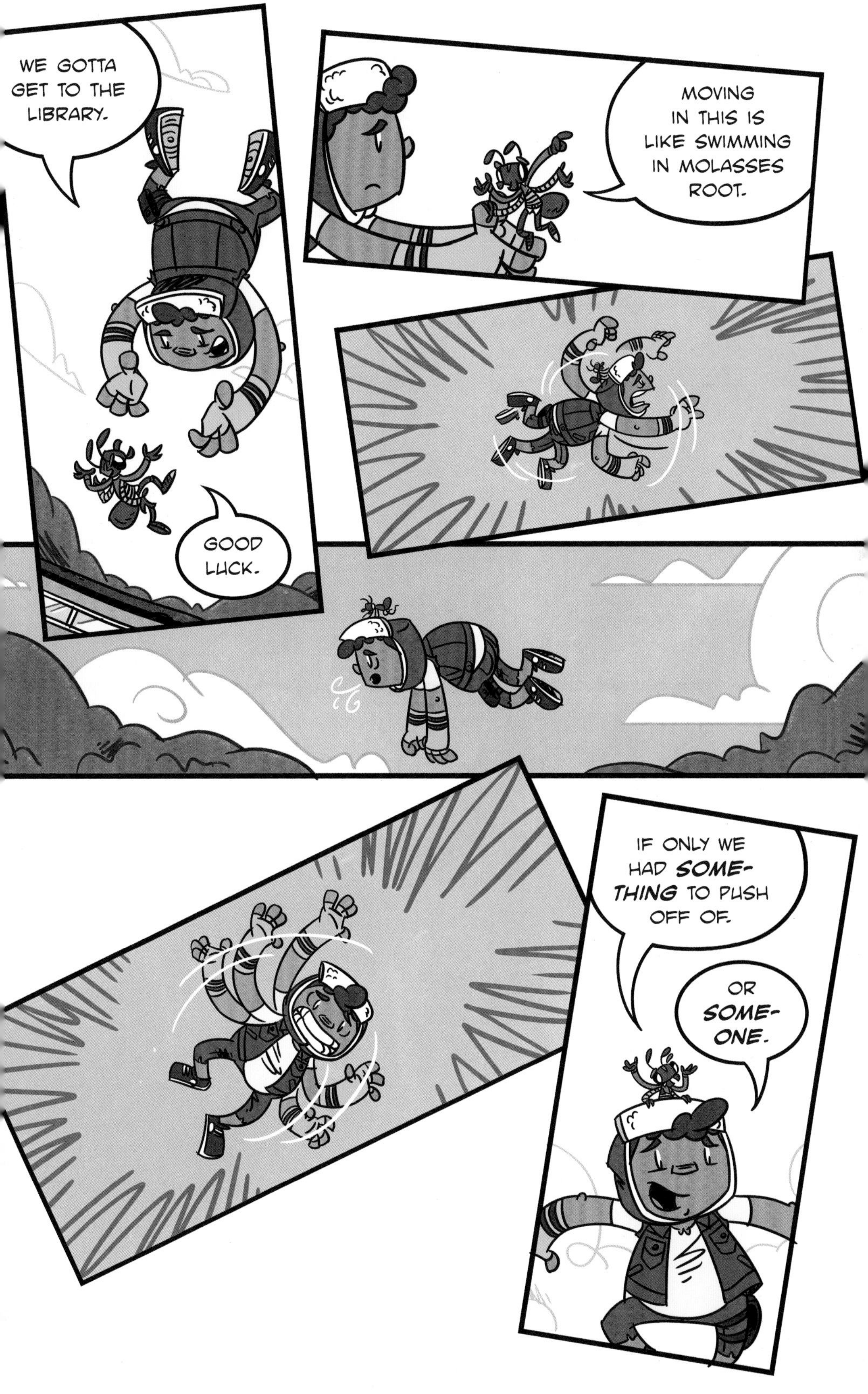
WE GOTTA GET TO THE LIBRARY.
MOVING IN THIS IS LIKE SWIMMING IN MOLASSES ROOT.
GOOD LUCK.
IF ONLY WE HAD SOMETHING TO PUSH OFF OF.
OR SOMEONE.

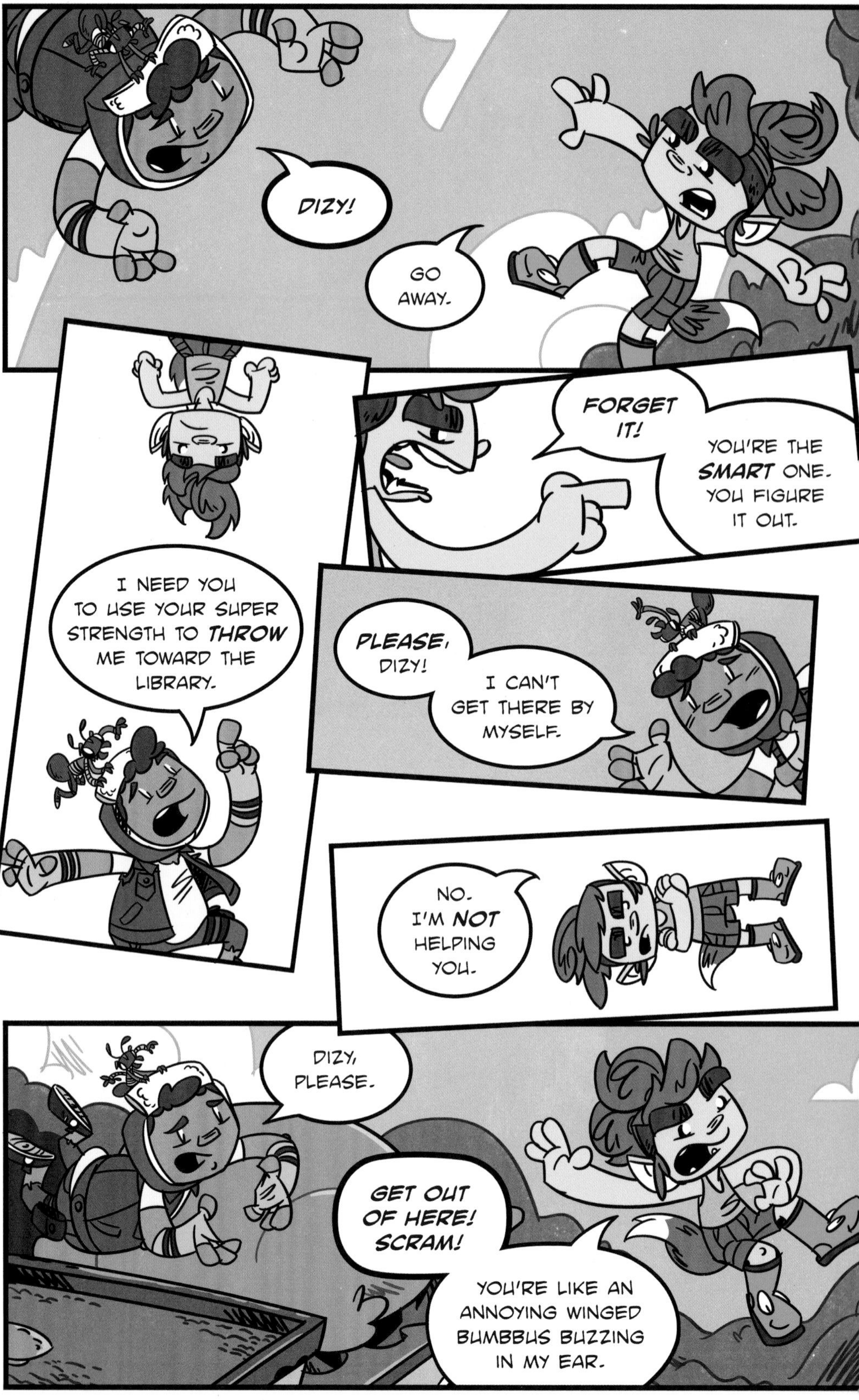
DIZY!
GO AWAY.
I NEED YOU TO USE YOUR SUPER STRENGTH TO THROW ME TOWARD THE LIBRARY.
FORGET IT!
YOU'RE THE SMART ONE. YOU FIGURE IT OUT.
PLEASE, DIZY!
I CAN'T GET THERE BY MYSELF.
NO. I'M NOT HELPING YOU.
DIZY, PLEASE.
GET OUT OF HERE! SCRAM!
YOU'RE LIKE AN ANNOYING WINGED BUMBBUS BUZZING IN MY EAR.

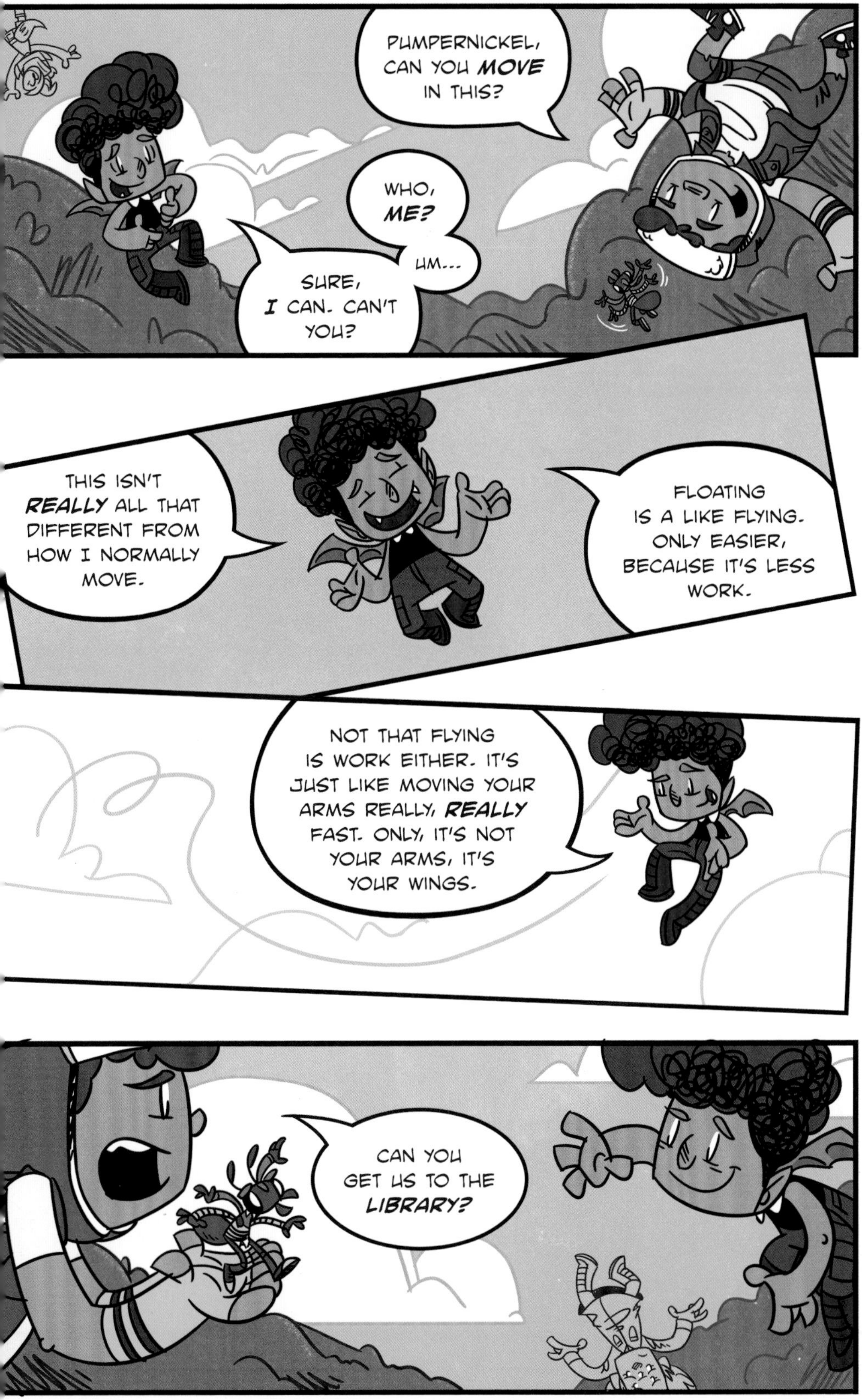
PUMPERNICKEL, CAN YOU MOVE IN THIS?
WHO, ME?
UM...
SURE, I CAN. CAN'T YOU?
THIS ISN'T REALLY ALL THAT DIFFERENT FROM HOW I NORMALLY MOVE.
FLOATING IS A LIKE FLYING. ONLY EASIER, BECAUSE IT'S LESS WORK.
NOT THAT FLYING IS WORK EITHER. IT'S JUST LIKE MOVING YOUR ARMS REALLY, REALLY FAST. ONLY, IT'S NOT YOUR ARMS, IT'S YOUR WINGS.
CAN YOU GET US TO THE LIBRARY?

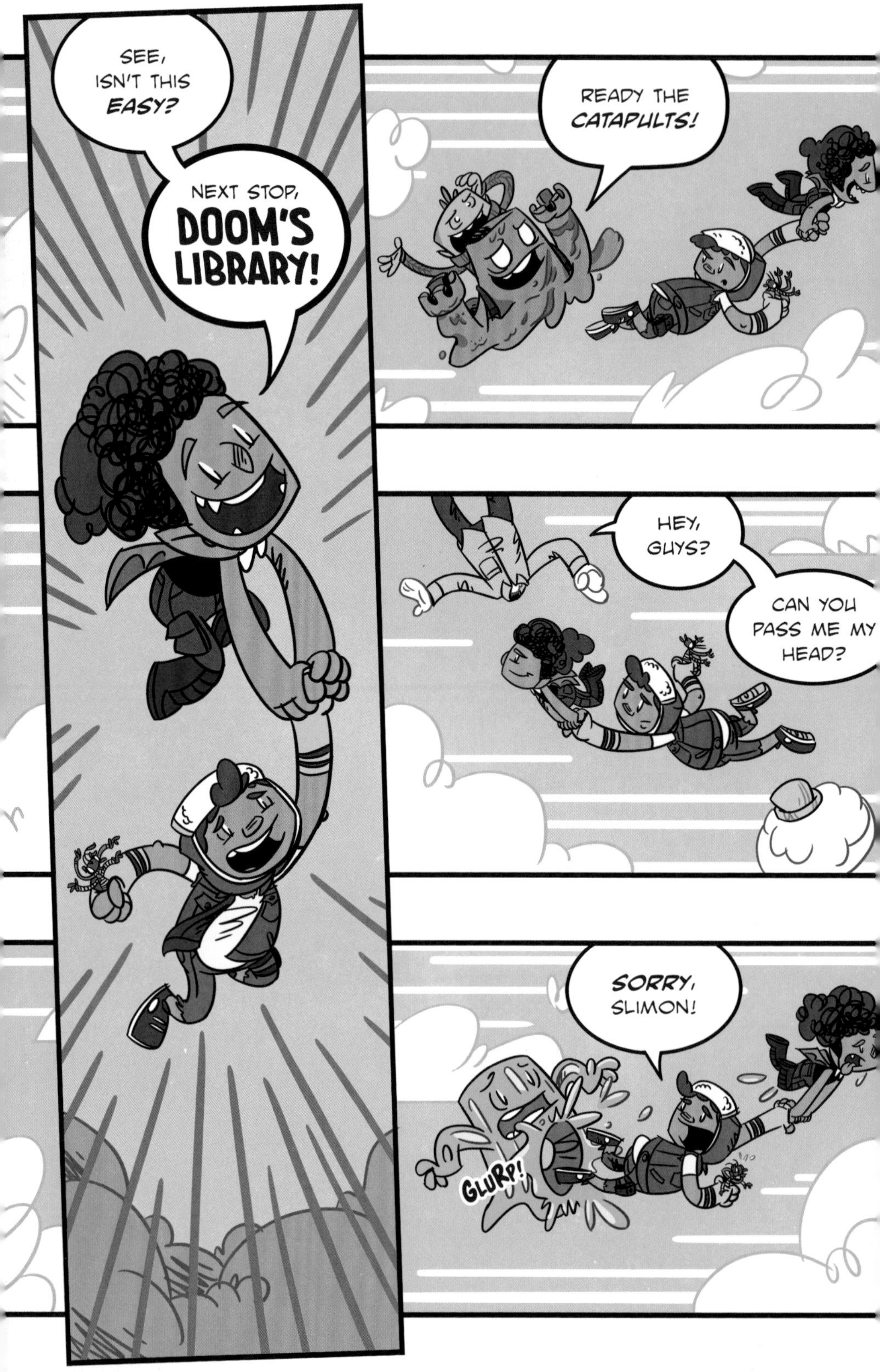
SEE, ISN'T THIS EASY?
NEXT STOP, DOOM'S LIBRARY!
READY THE CATAPULTS!
HEY, GUYS?
CAN YOU PASS ME MY HEAD?
SORRY, SLIMON!
GLURP!

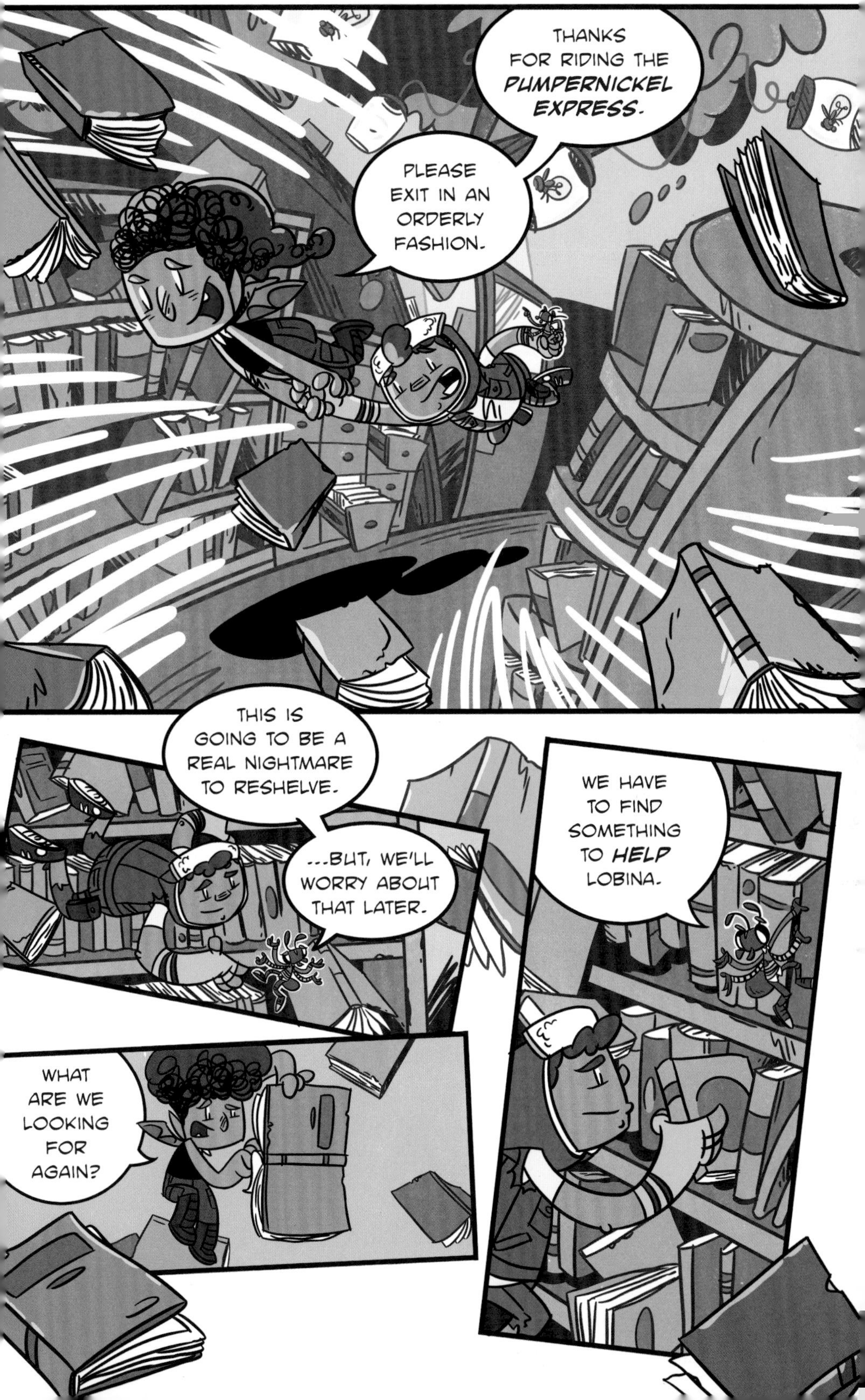
THANKS FOR RIDING THE *PUMPERNICKEL EXPRESS*.
PLEASE EXIT IN AN ORDERLY FASHION.
THIS IS GOING TO BE A REAL NIGHTMARE TO RESHELVE.
...BUT, WE'LL WORRY ABOUT THAT LATER.
WE HAVE TO FIND SOMETHING TO *HELP* LOBINA.
WHAT ARE WE LOOKING FOR AGAIN?

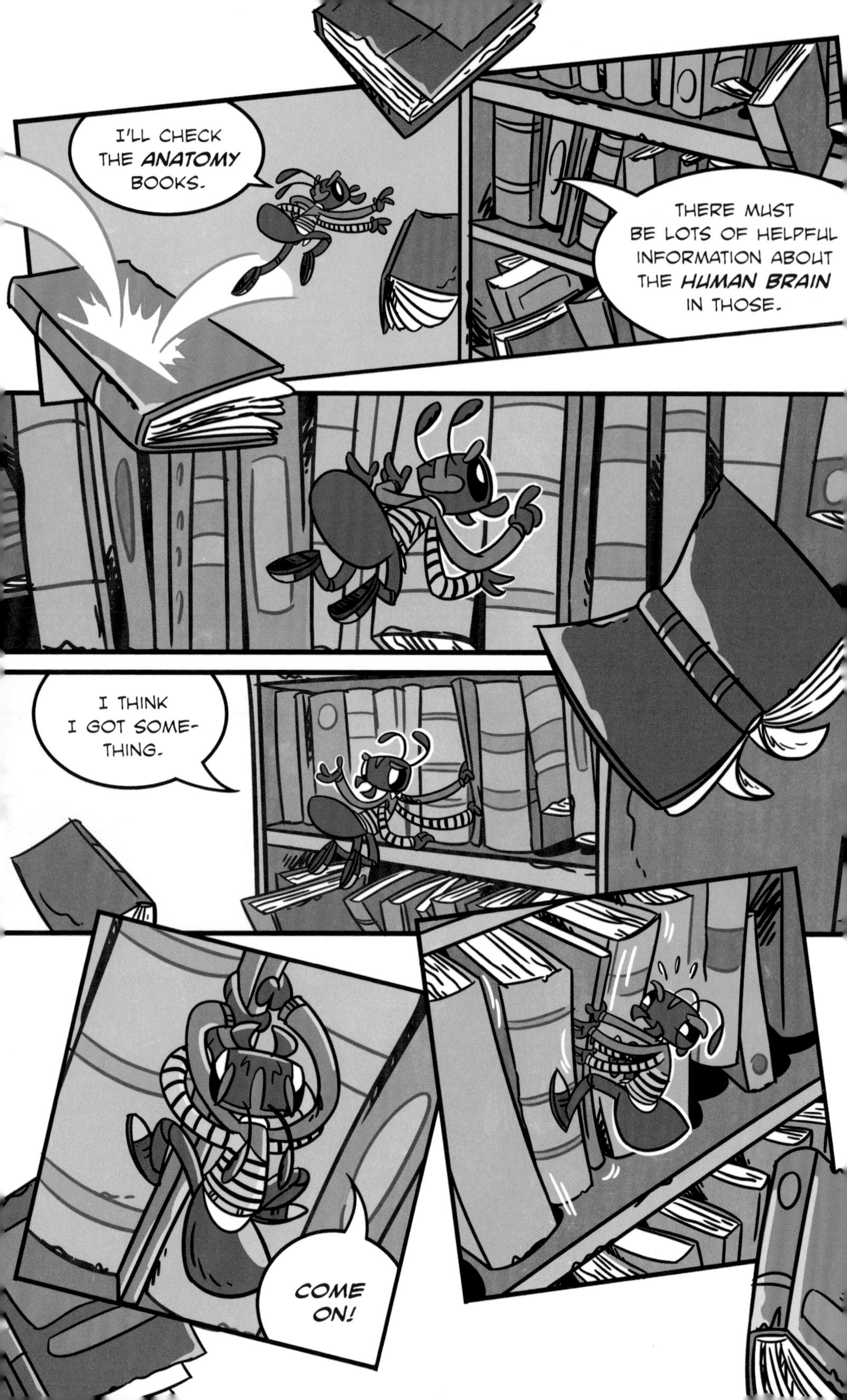
I'LL CHECK THE ANATOMY BOOKS.
THERE MUST BE LOTS OF HELPFUL INFORMATION ABOUT THE HUMAN BRAIN IN THOSE.
I THINK I GOT SOME- THING.
COME ON!

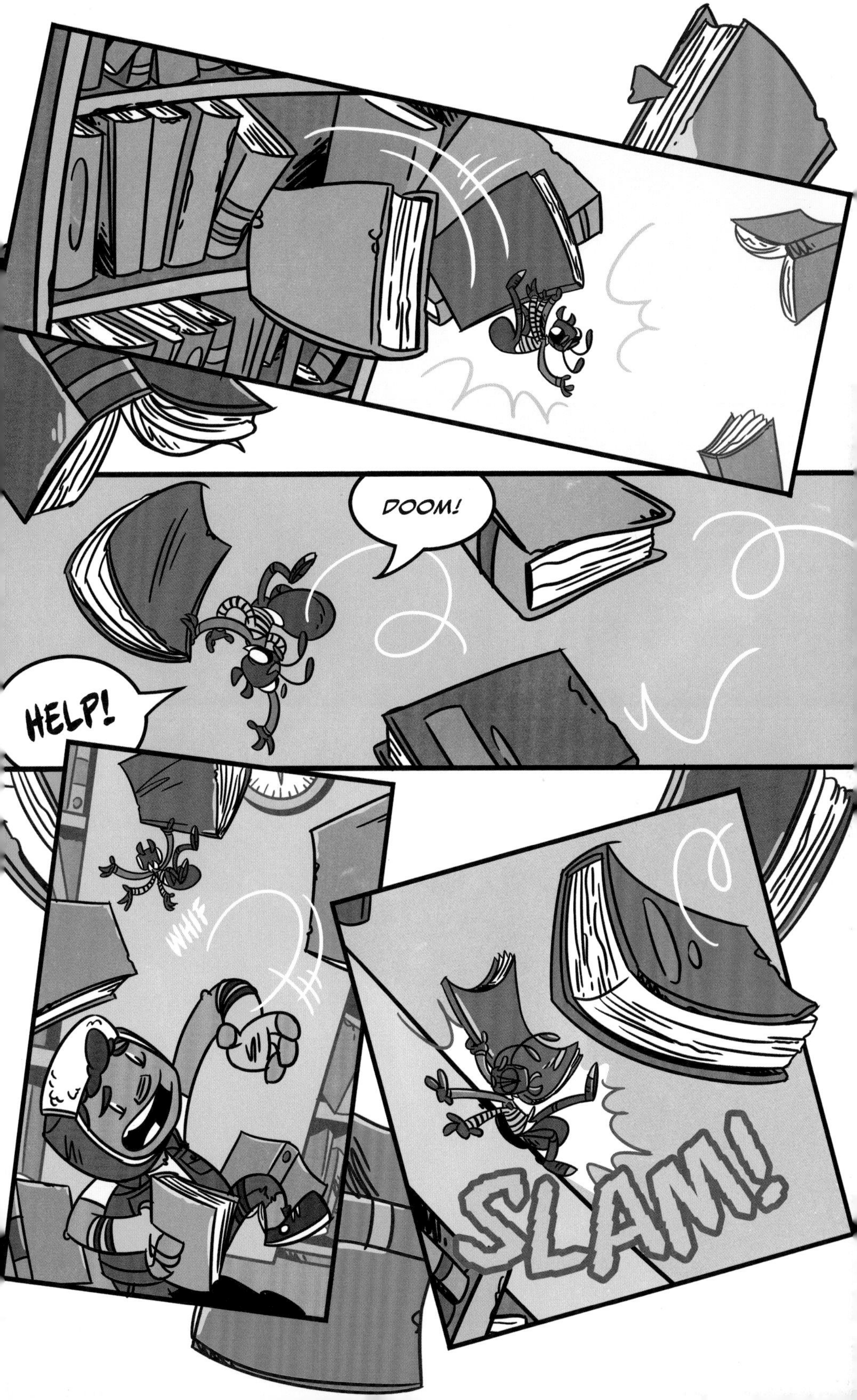

DOOM!
HELP!
WHIF
SLAM!

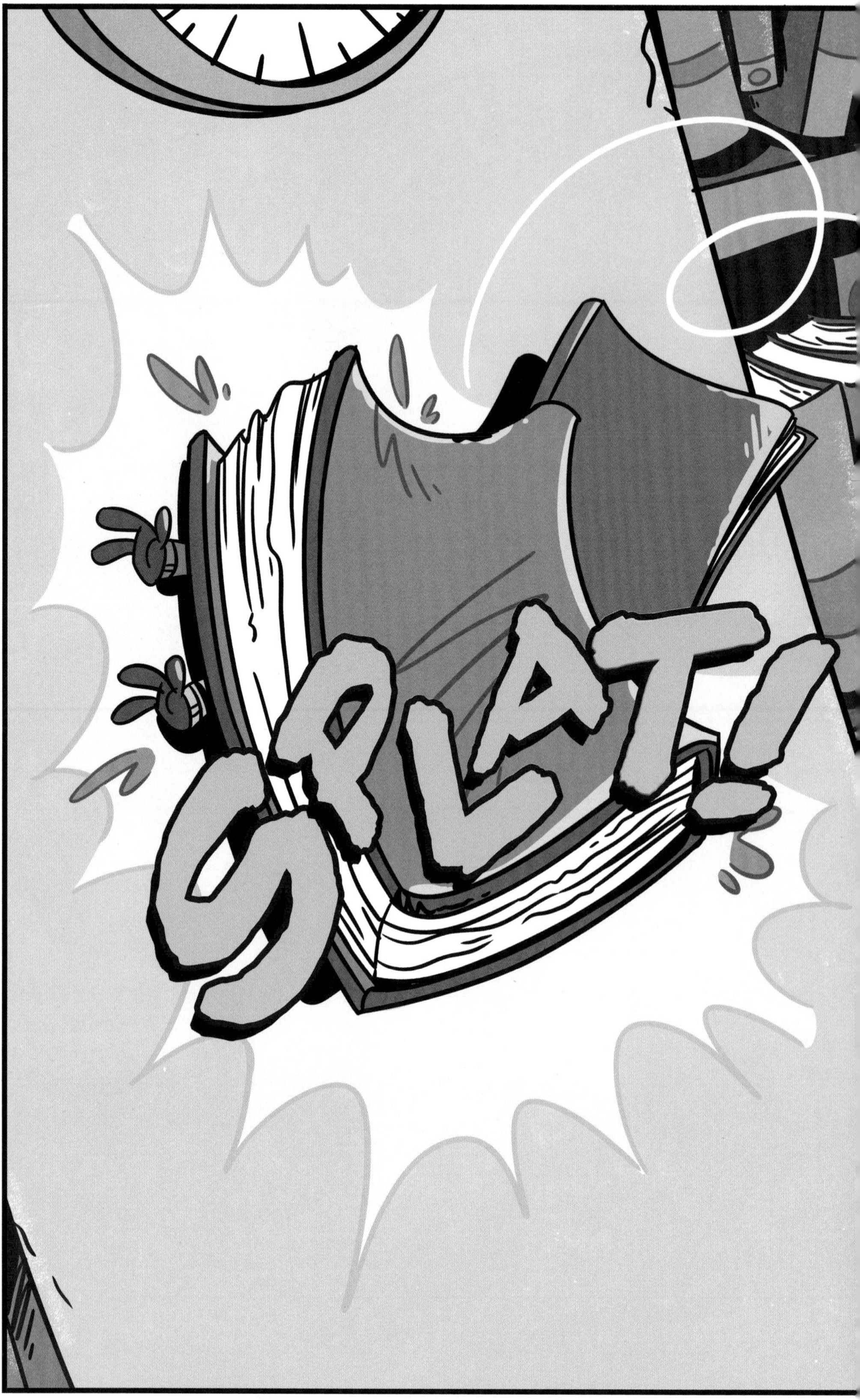
SPLAT!

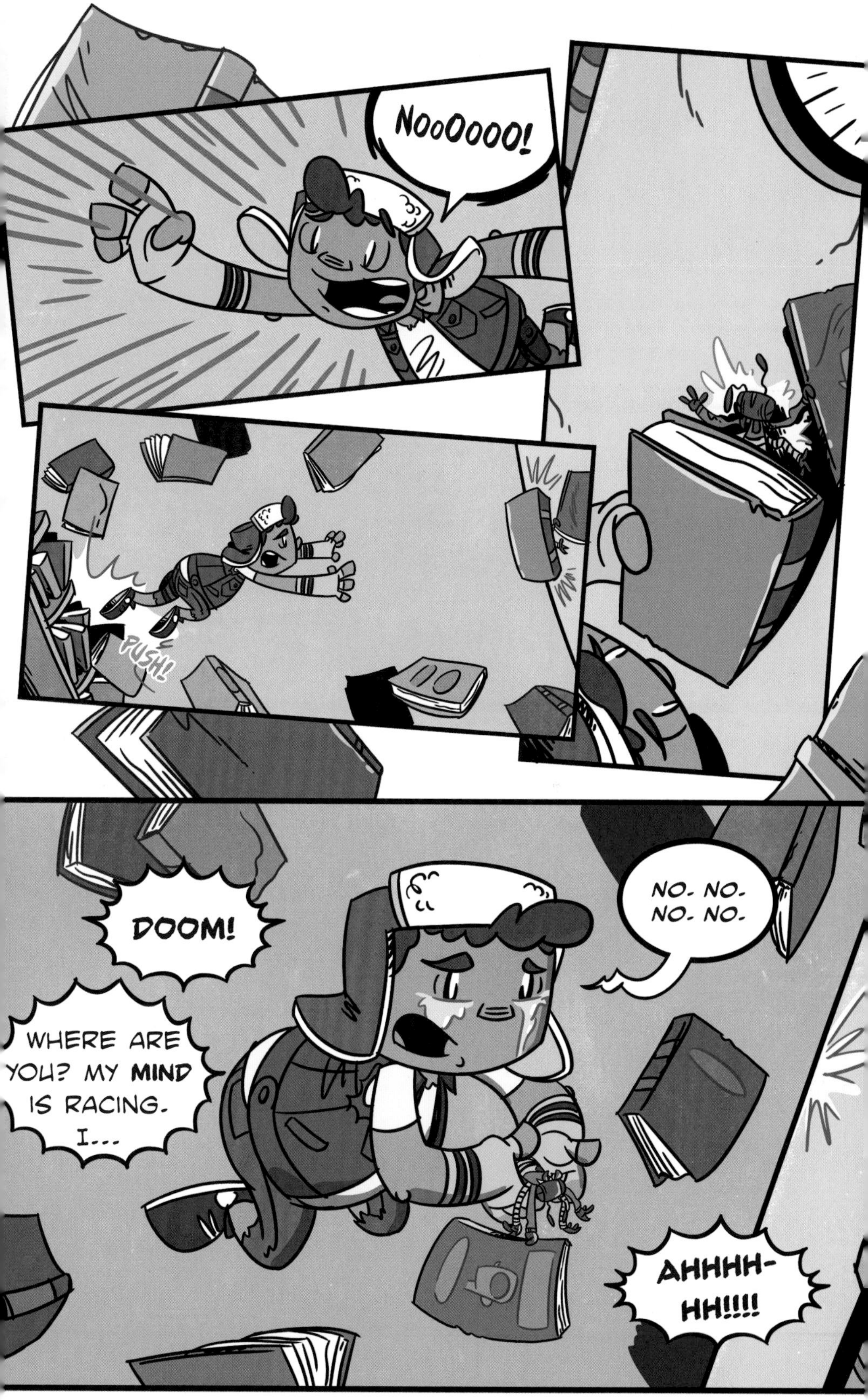
NOoOOOO!
PUSH!
DOOM!
WHERE ARE YOU? MY **MIND** IS RACING. I...
NO. NO. NO. NO.
AHHHH-HH!!!!

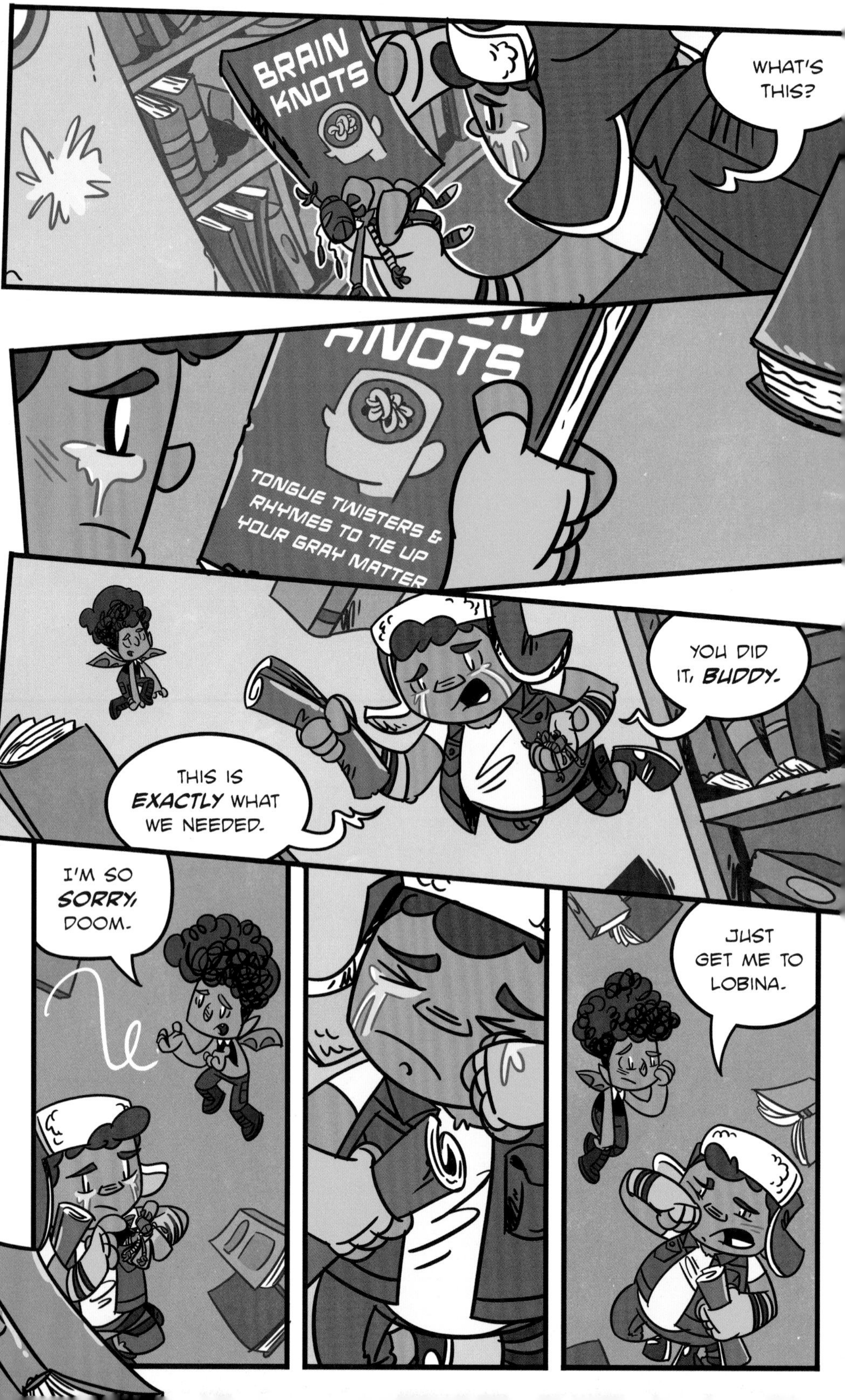
BRAIN KNOTS
WHAT'S THIS?
KNOTS
TONGUE TWISTERS & RHYMES TO TIE UP YOUR GRAY MATTER
YOU DID IT, BUDDY.
THIS IS EXACTLY WHAT WE NEEDED.
I'M SO SORRY, DOOM.
JUST GET ME TO LOBINA.

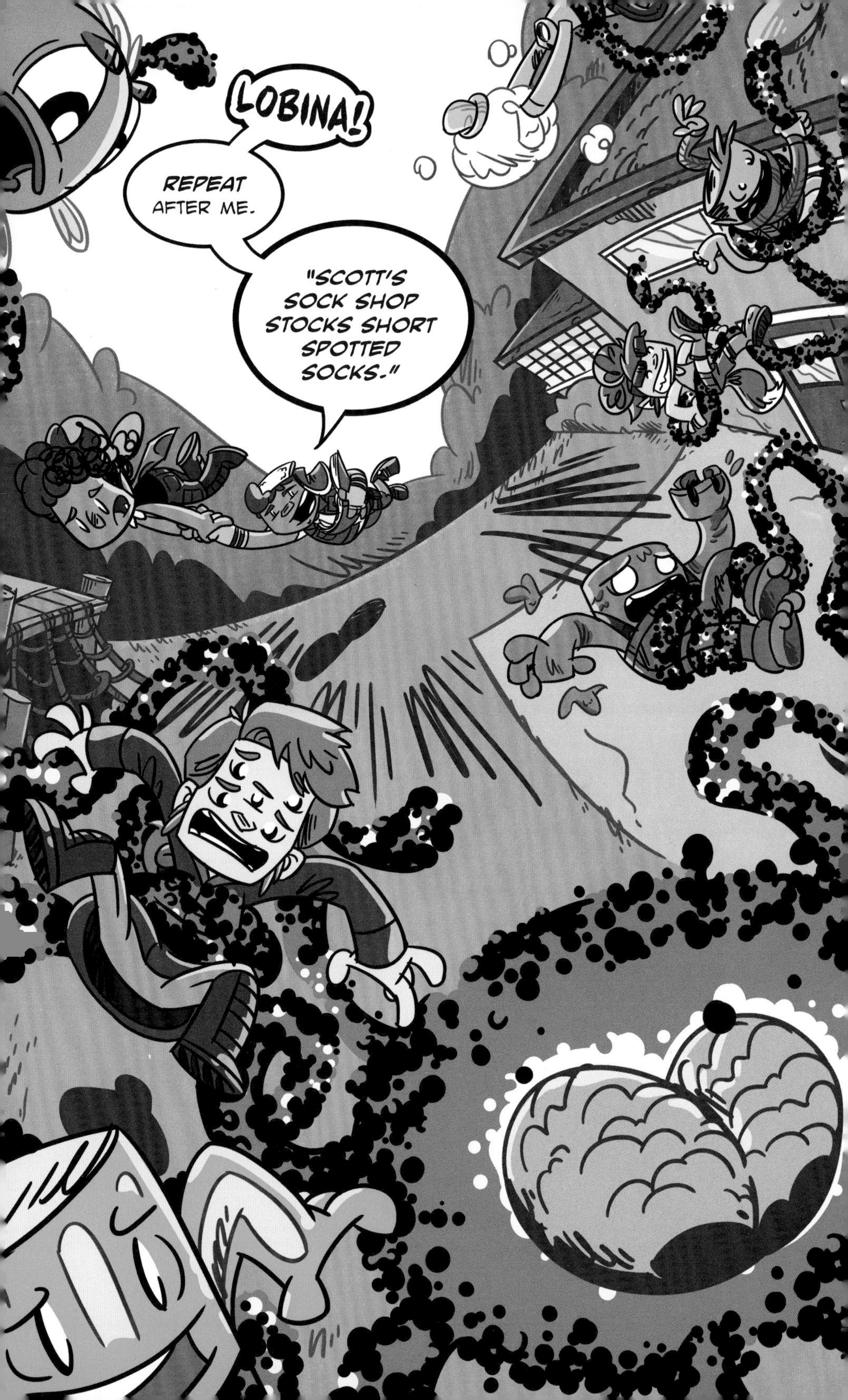
LOBINA!
REPEAT AFTER ME.
"SCOTT'S SOCK SHOP STOCKS SHORT SPOTTED SOCKS."

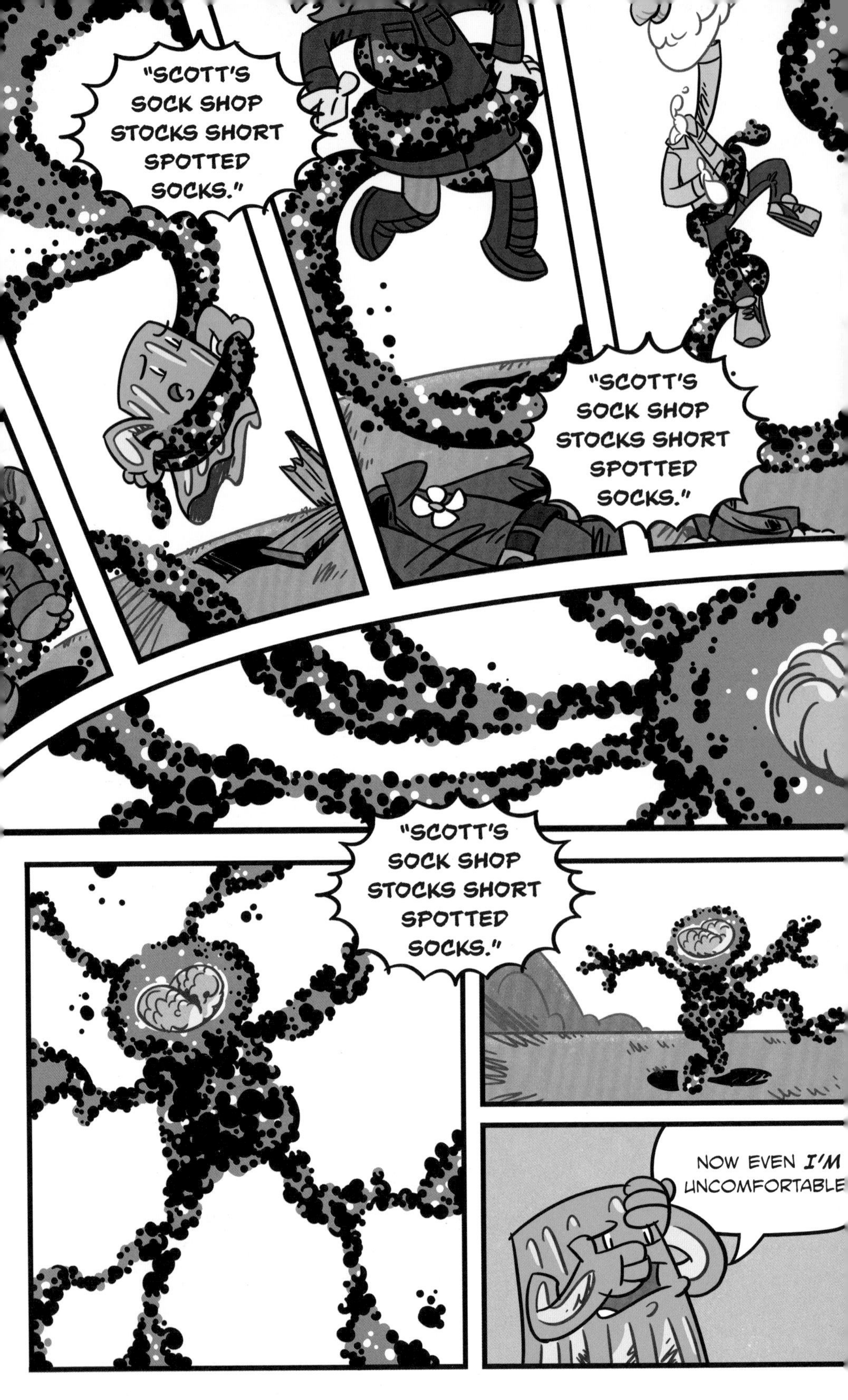
"SCOTT'S SOCK SHOP STOCKS SHORT SPOTTED SOCKS."
"SCOTT'S SOCK SHOP STOCKS SHORT SPOTTED SOCKS."
"SCOTT'S SOCK SHOP STOCKS SHORT SPOTTED SOCKS."
NOW EVEN *I'M* UNCOMFORTABLE

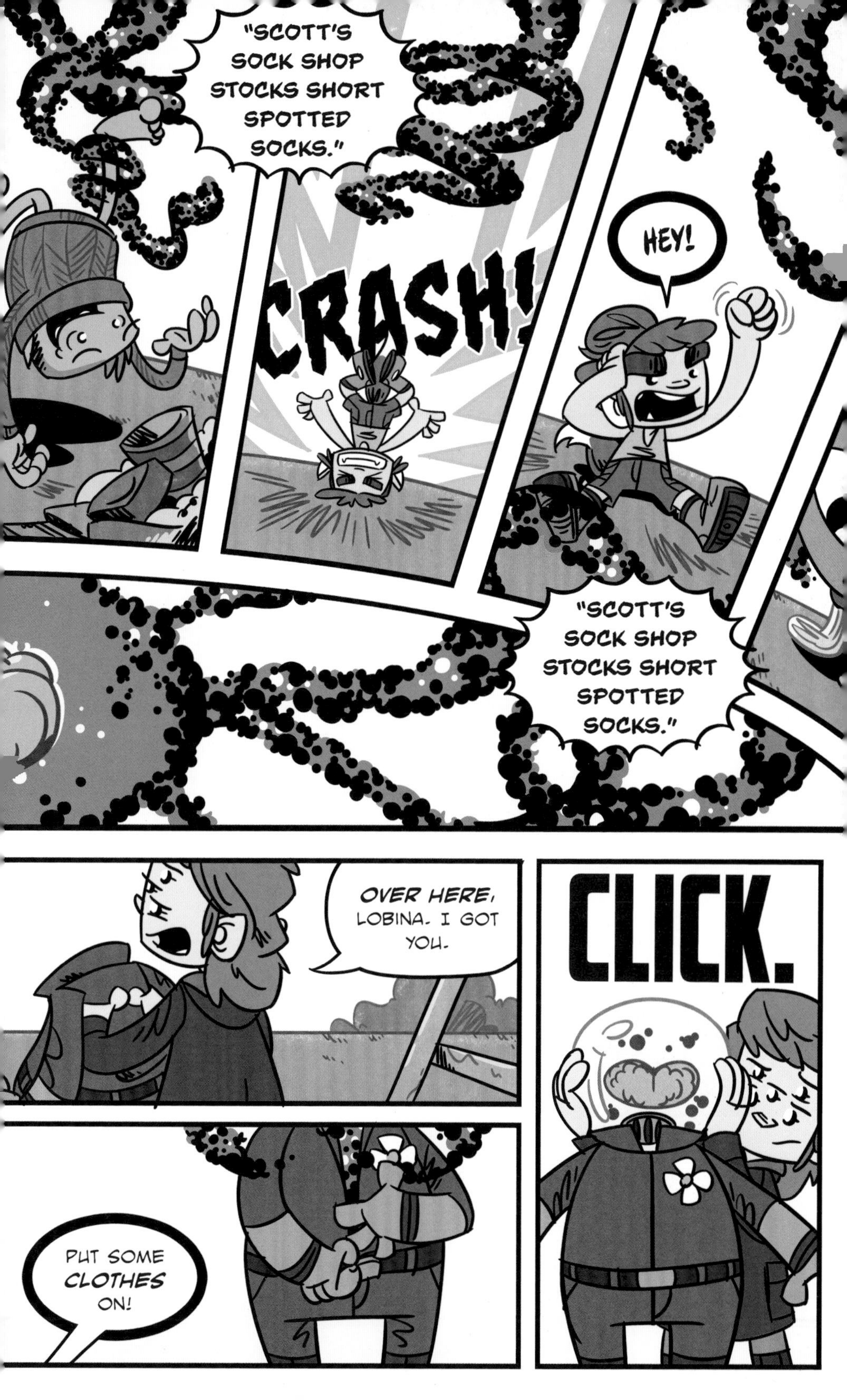
"SCOTT'S SOCK SHOP STOCKS SHORT SPOTTED SOCKS."
CRASH!
HEY!
"SCOTT'S SOCK SHOP STOCKS SHORT SPOTTED SOCKS."
OVER HERE, LOBINA. I GOT YOU.
CLICK.
PUT SOME CLOTHES ON!

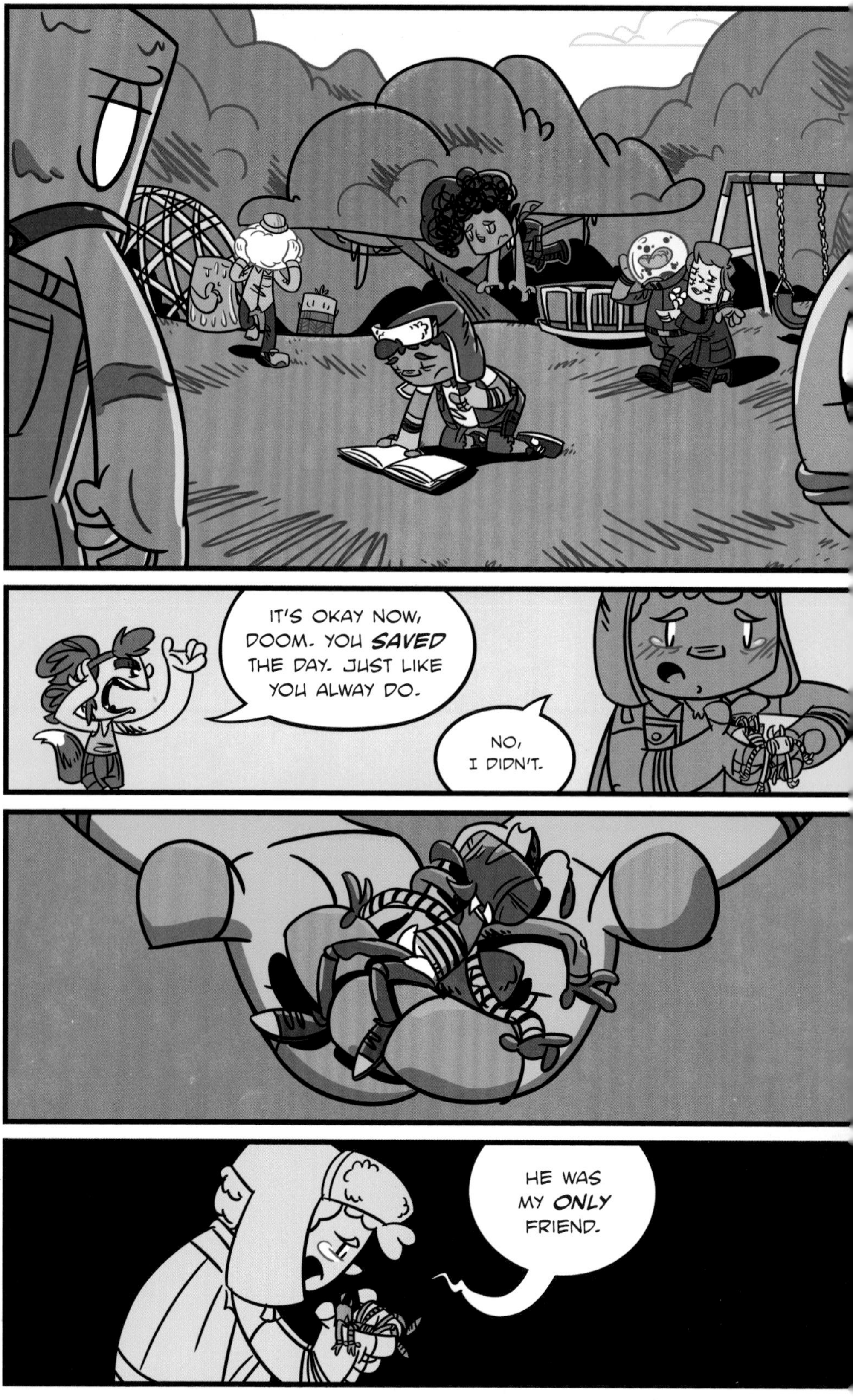
IT'S OKAY NOW, DOOM. YOU SAVED THE DAY. JUST LIKE YOU ALWAY DO.
NO, I DIDN'T.
HE WAS MY ONLY FRIEND.

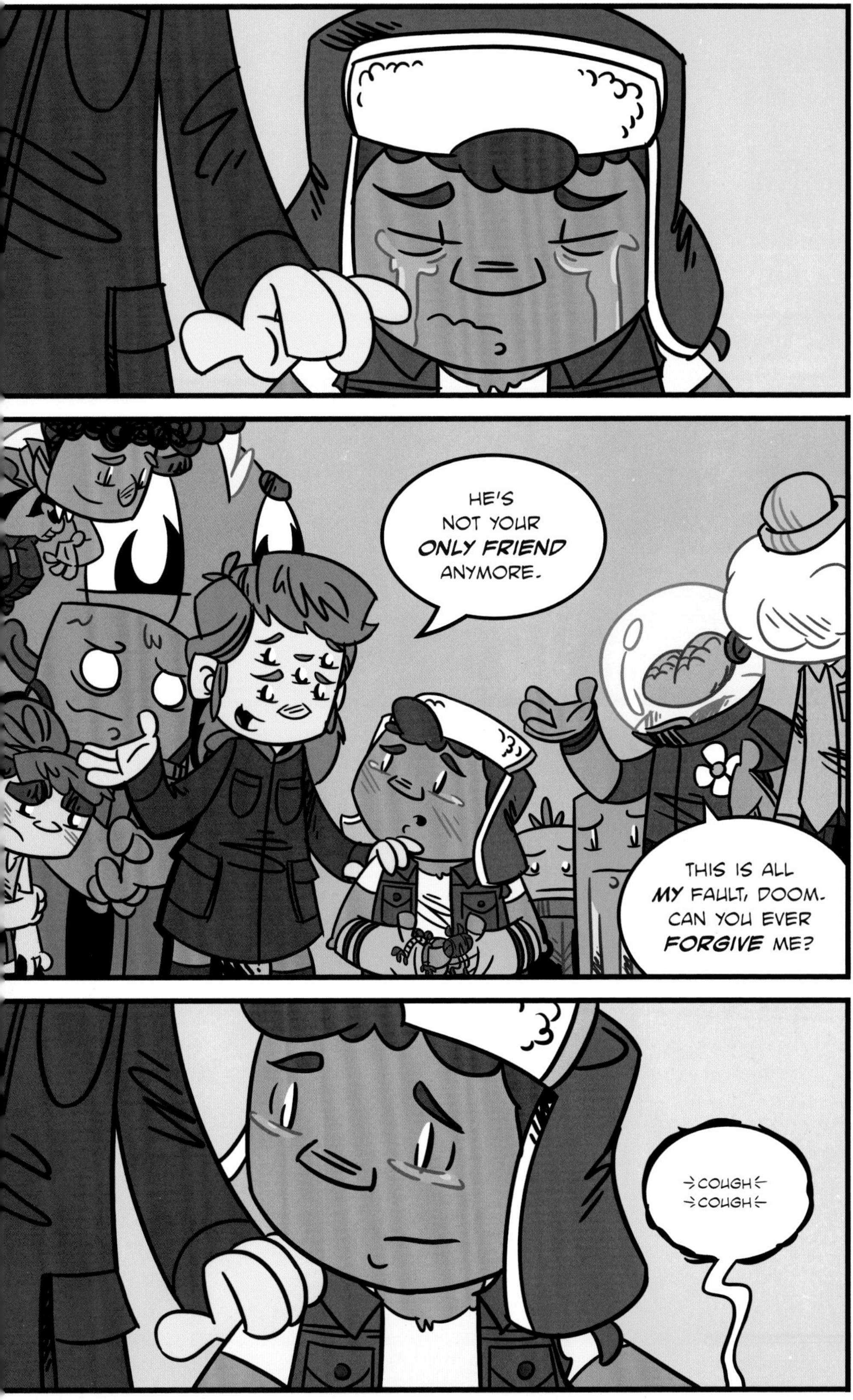
HE'S NOT YOUR ONLY FRIEND ANYMORE.
THIS IS ALL MY FAULT, DOOM. CAN YOU EVER FORGIVE ME?
COUGH COUGH

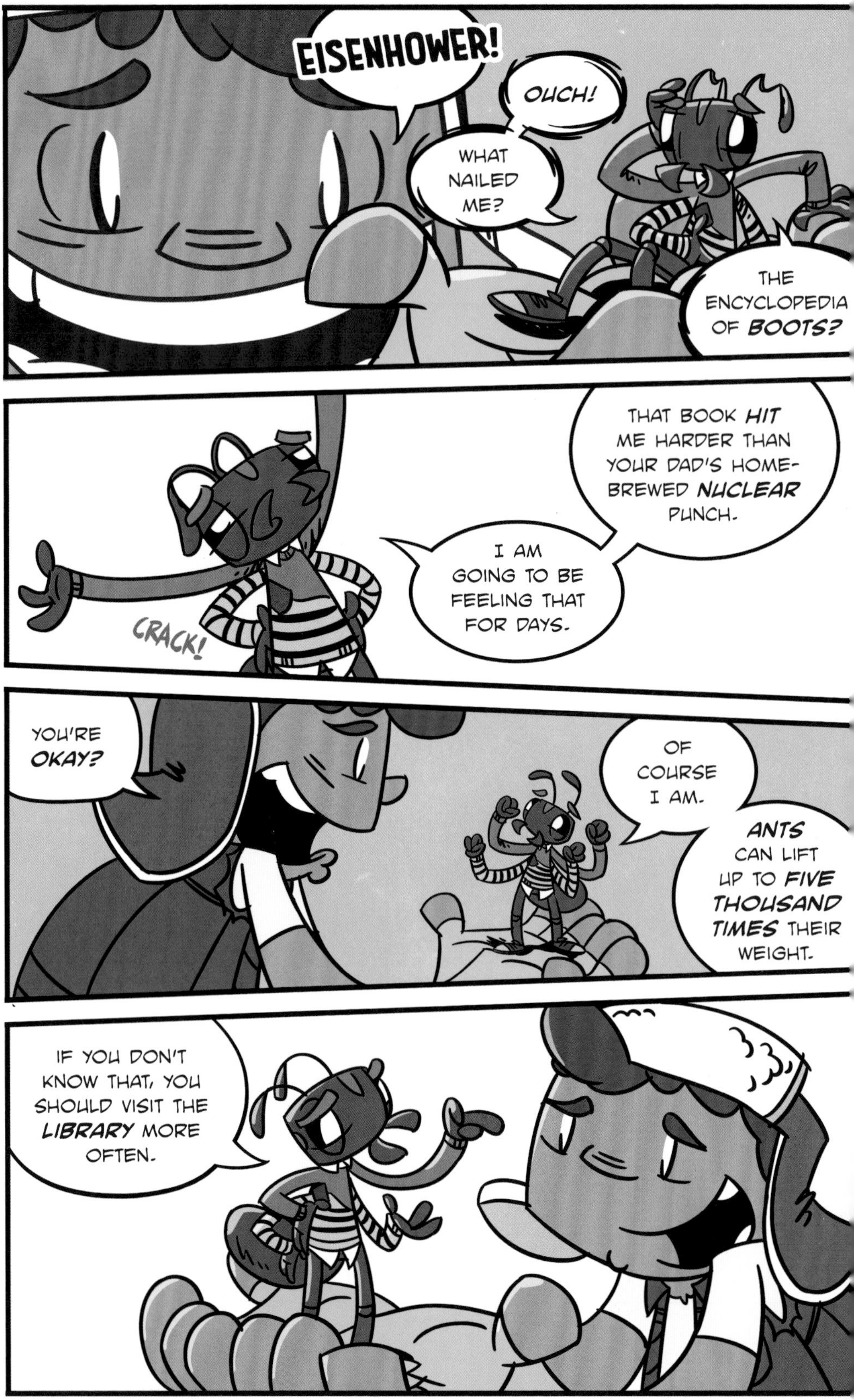
EISENHOWER!
OUCH!
WHAT NAILED ME?
THE ENCYCLOPEDIA OF BOOTS?
THAT BOOK HIT ME HARDER THAN YOUR DAD'S HOME-BREWED NUCLEAR PUNCH.
I AM GOING TO BE FEELING THAT FOR DAYS.
CRACK!
YOU'RE OKAY?
OF COURSE I AM.
ANTS CAN LIFT UP TO FIVE THOUSAND TIMES THEIR WEIGHT.
IF YOU DON'T KNOW THAT, YOU SHOULD VISIT THE LIBRARY MORE OFTEN.

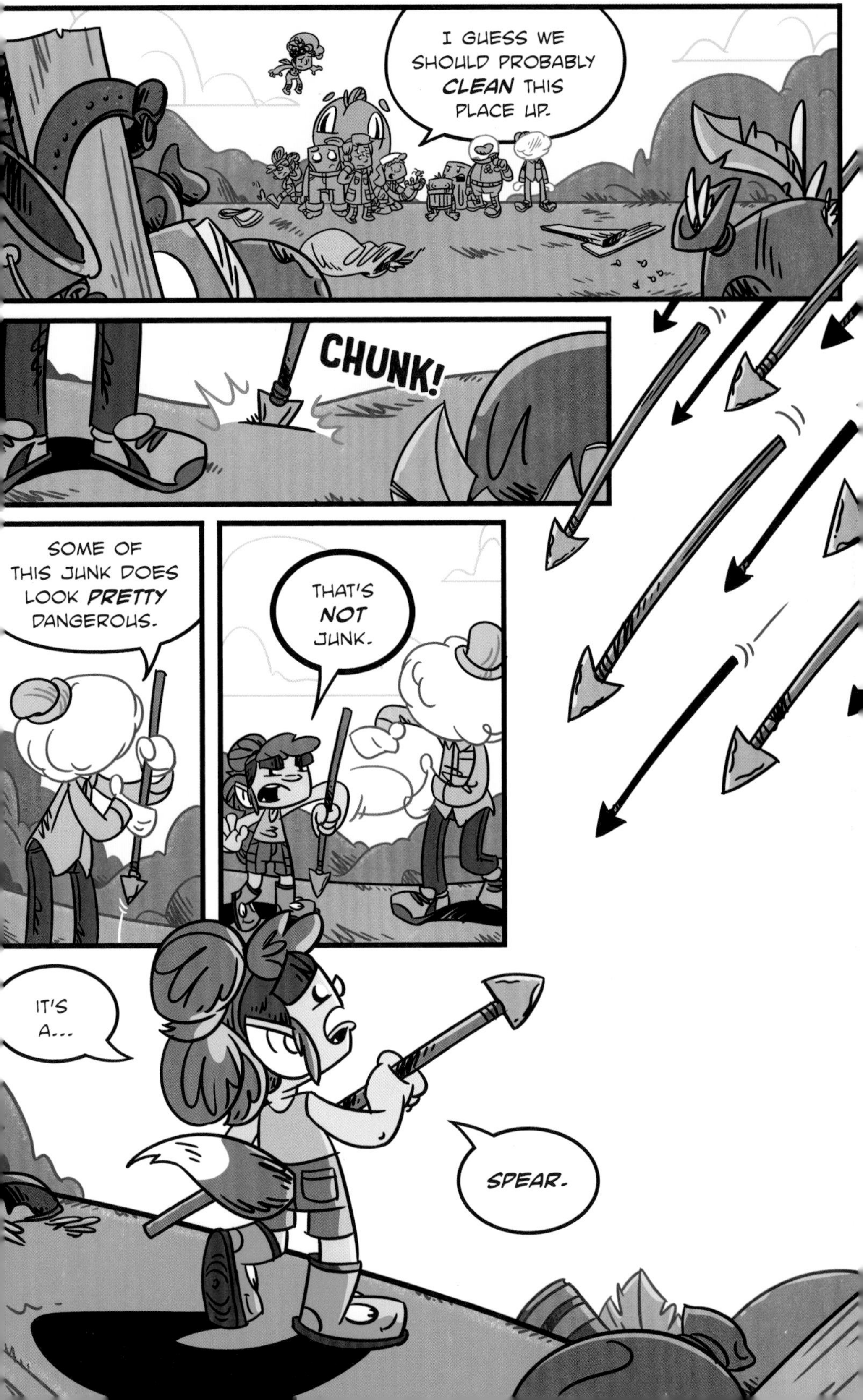
I GUESS WE SHOULD PROBABLY *CLEAN* THIS PLACE UP.
CHUNK!
SOME OF THIS JUNK DOES LOOK *PRETTY* DANGEROUS.
THAT'S *NOT* JUNK.
IT'S A...
SPEAR.

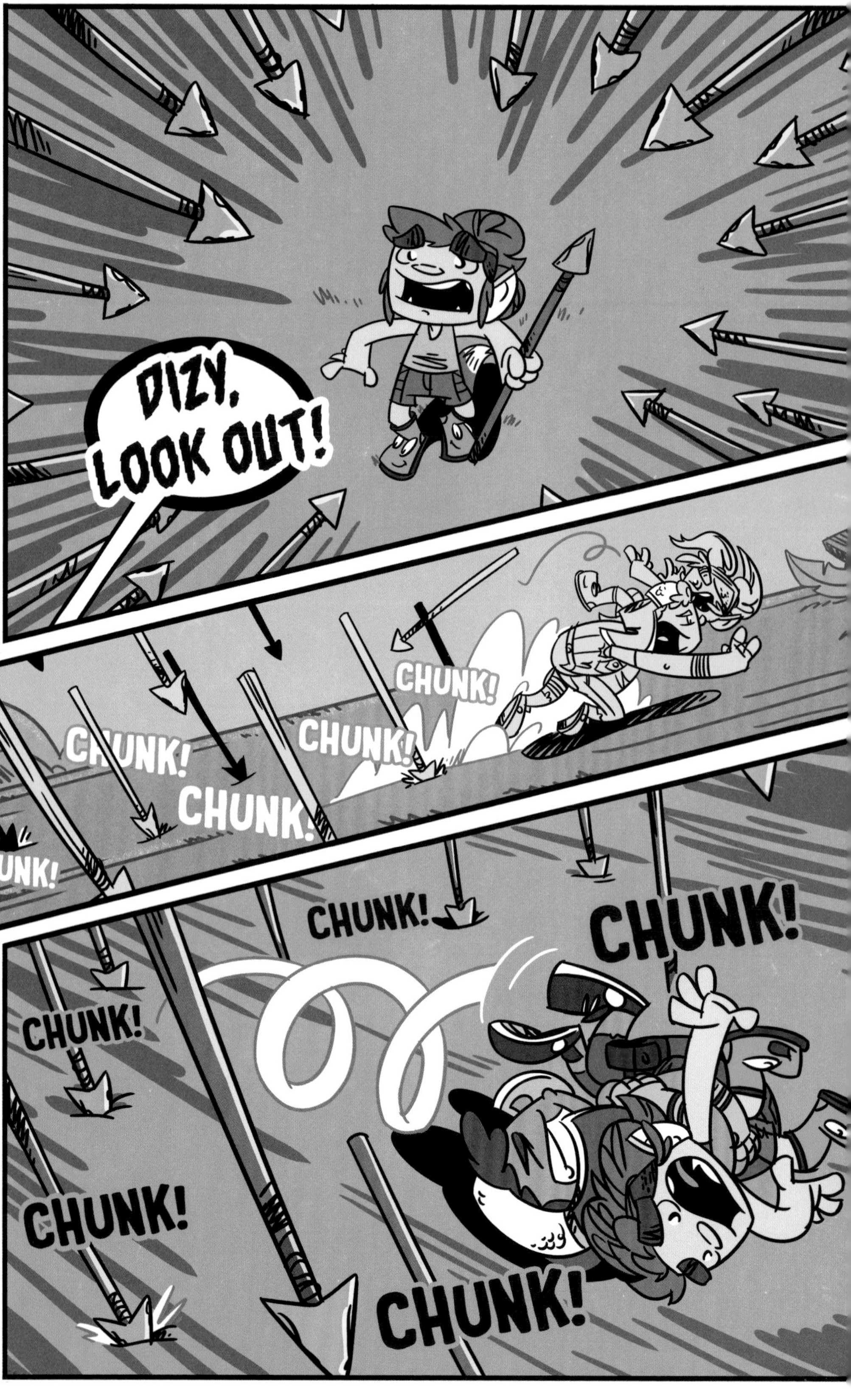
DIZY, LOOK OUT!
CHUNK!
CHUNK!
CHUNK!
CHUNK!
HUNK!
CHUNK!
CHUNK!
CHUNK!
CHUNK!
CHUNK!

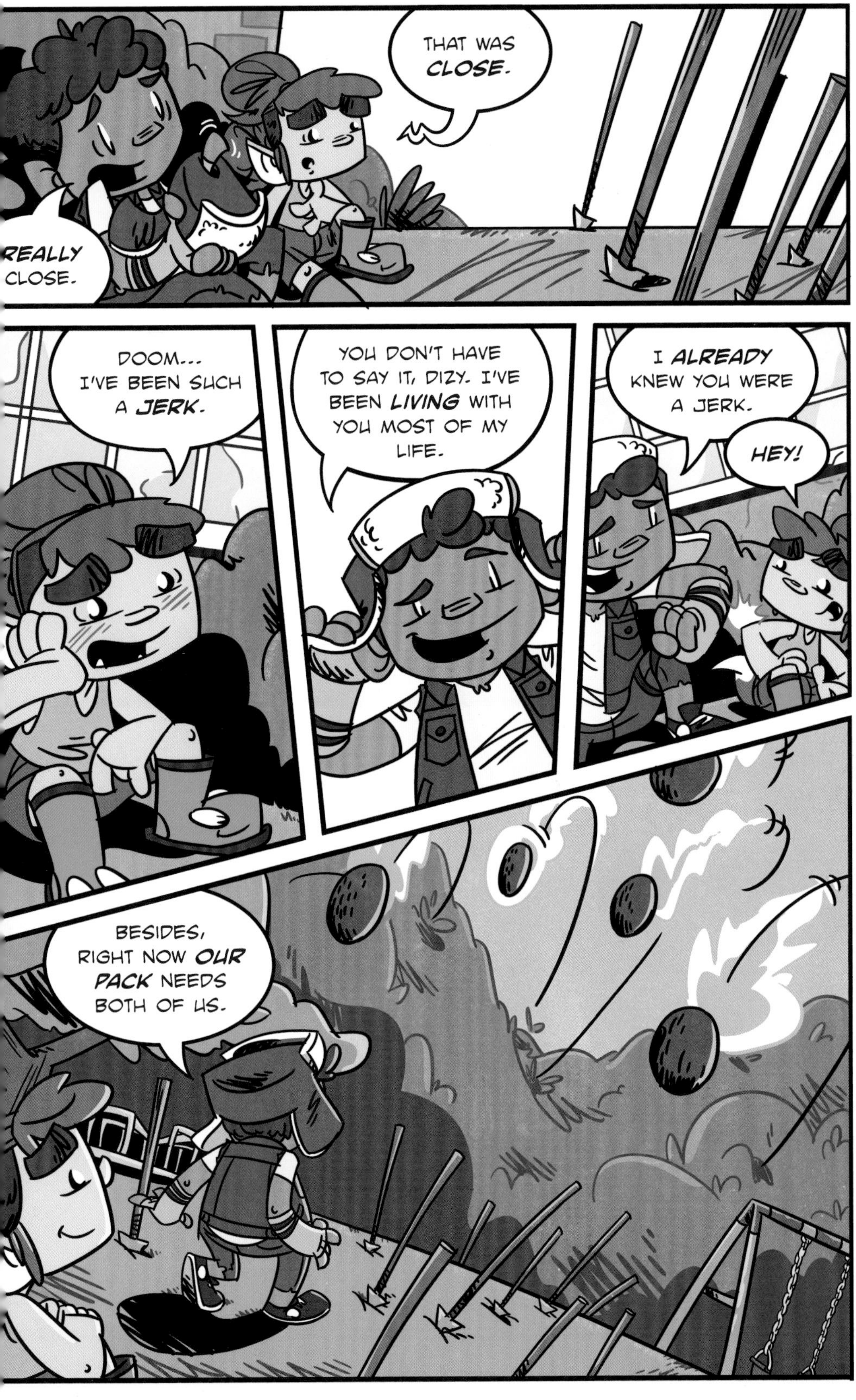
THAT WAS CLOSE.
REALLY CLOSE.
DOOM... I'VE BEEN SUCH A JERK.
YOU DON'T HAVE TO SAY IT, DIZY. I'VE BEEN LIVING WITH YOU MOST OF MY LIFE.
I ALREADY KNEW YOU WERE A JERK.
HEY!
BESIDES, RIGHT NOW OUR PACK NEEDS BOTH OF US.

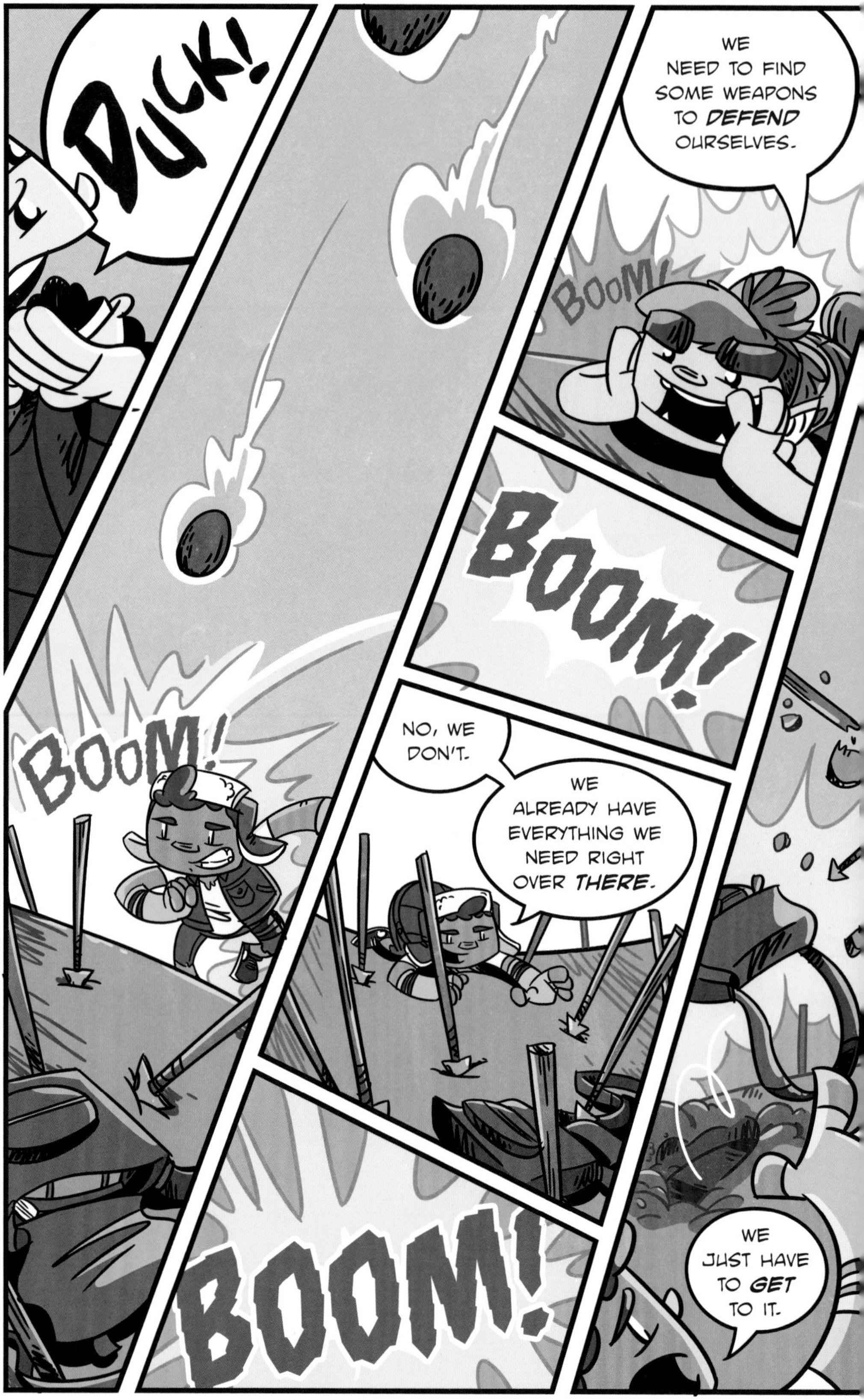
DUCK!
WE NEED TO FIND SOME WEAPONS TO *DEFEND* OURSELVES.
BOOM!
BOOM!
BOOM!
NO, WE DON'T.
WE ALREADY HAVE EVERYTHING WE NEED RIGHT OVER *THERE*.
BOOM!
WE JUST HAVE TO *GET* TO IT.

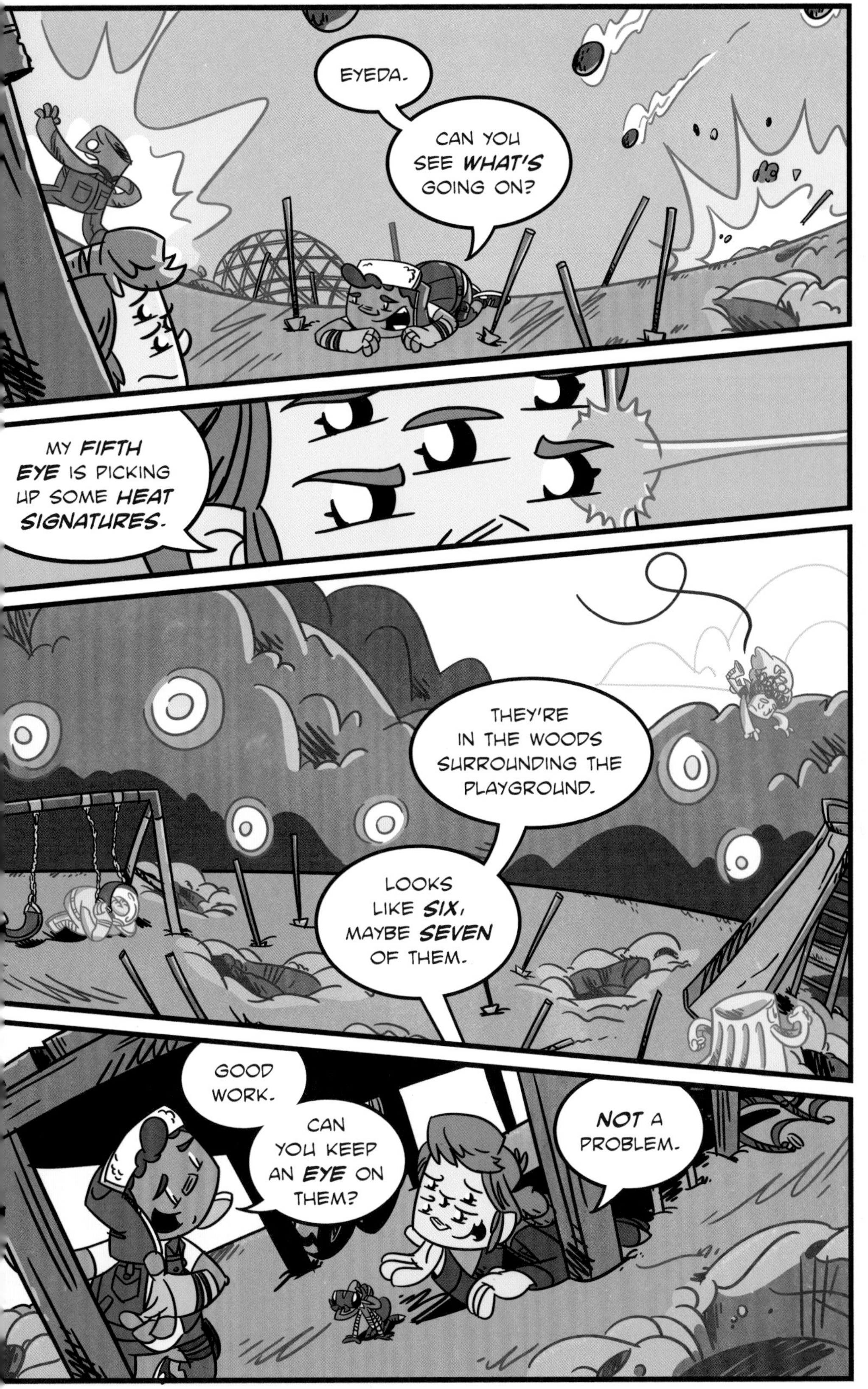
EYEDA.
CAN YOU SEE WHAT'S GOING ON?
MY FIFTH EYE IS PICKING UP SOME HEAT SIGNATURES.
THEY'RE IN THE WOODS SURROUNDING THE PLAYGROUND.
LOOKS LIKE SIX, MAYBE SEVEN OF THEM.
GOOD WORK.
CAN YOU KEEP AN EYE ON THEM?
NOT A PROBLEM.

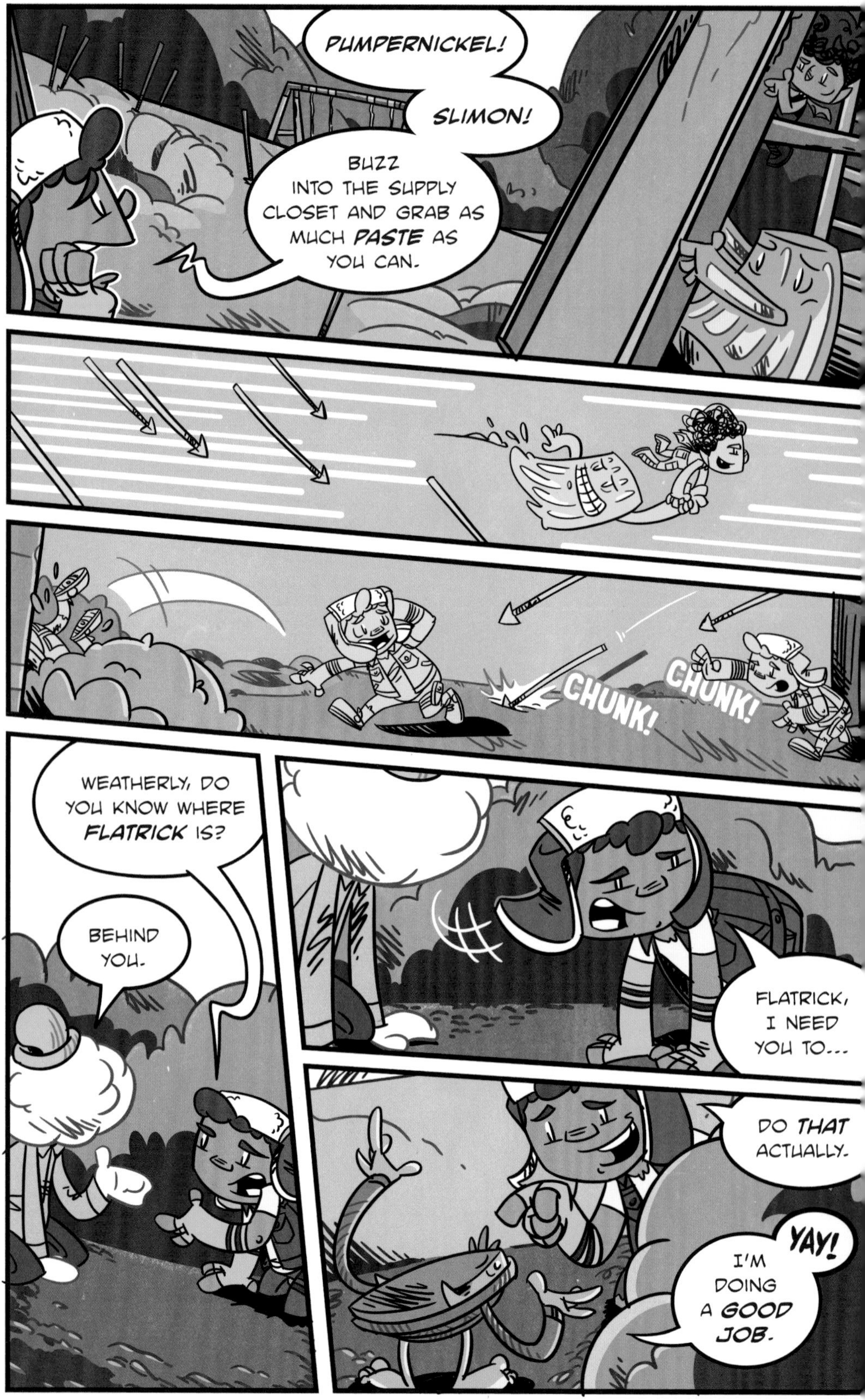
PUMPERNICKEL!
SLIMON!
BUZZ INTO THE SUPPLY CLOSET AND GRAB AS MUCH PASTE AS YOU CAN.
CHUNK!
CHUNK!
WEATHERLY, DO YOU KNOW WHERE FLATRICK IS?
BEHIND YOU.
FLATRICK, I NEED YOU TO...
DO THAT ACTUALLY.
YAY!
I'M DOING A GOOD JOB.

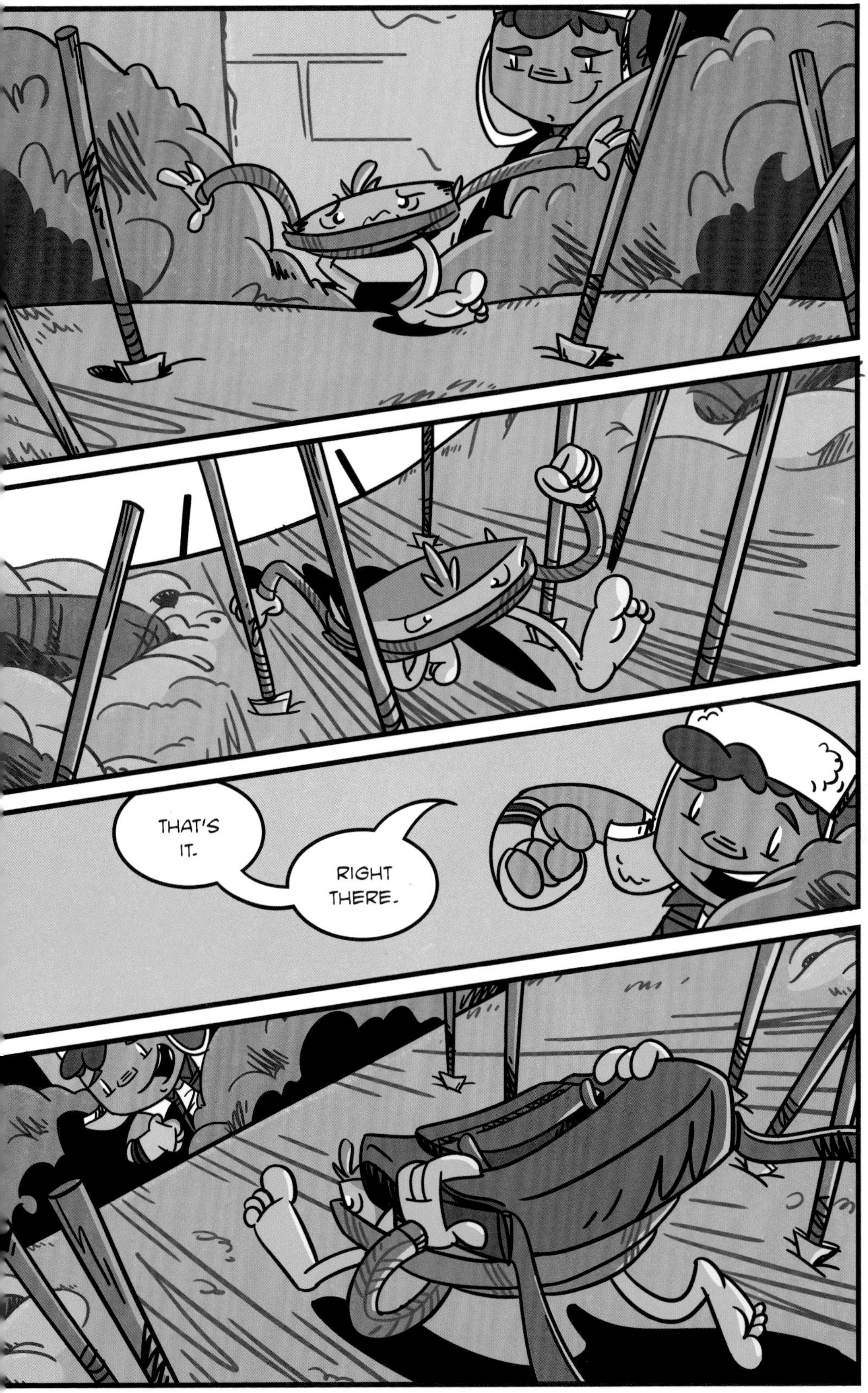
THAT'S IT.
RIGHT THERE.

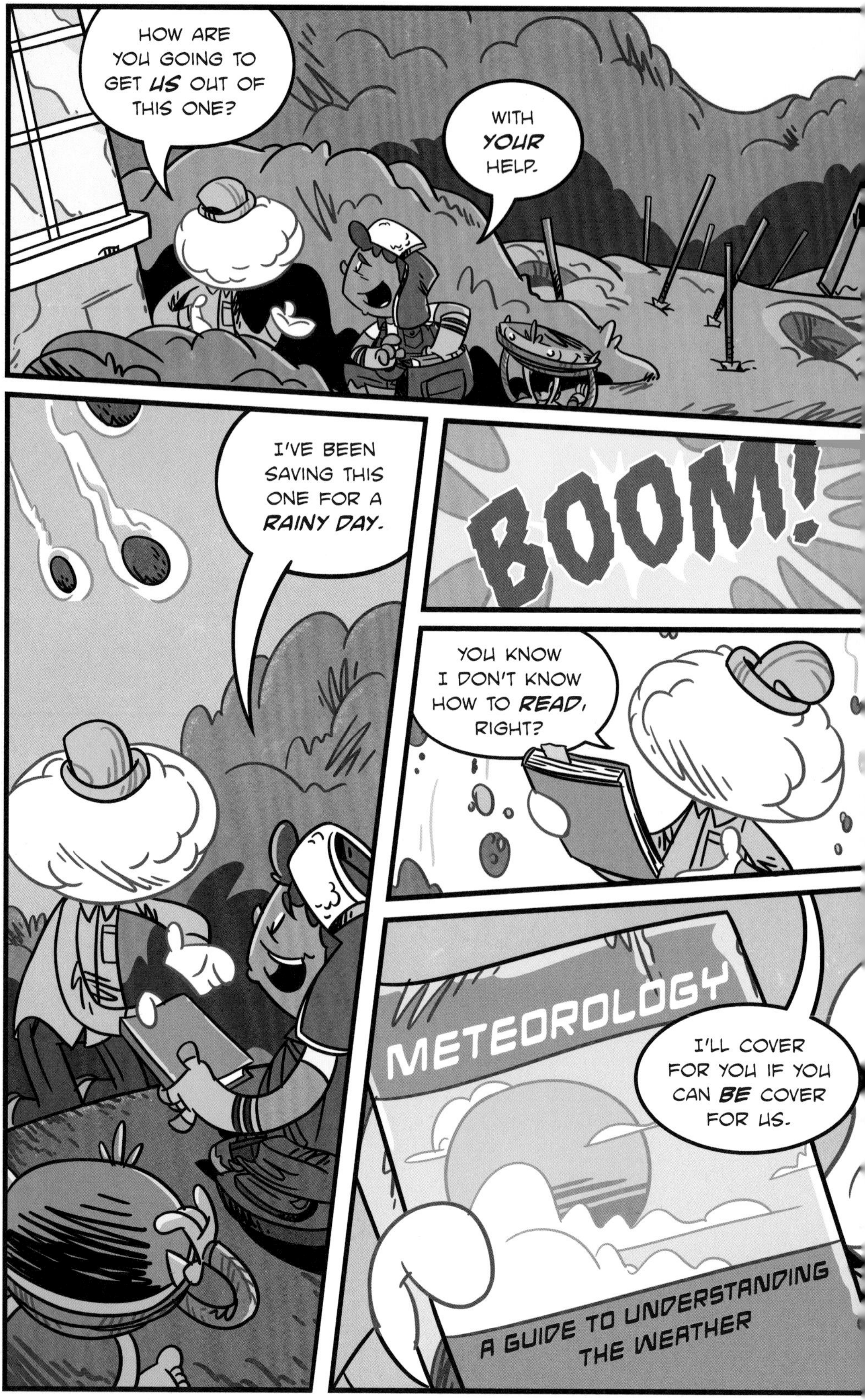
HOW ARE YOU GOING TO GET US OUT OF THIS ONE?
WITH YOUR HELP.
I'VE BEEN SAVING THIS ONE FOR A RAINY DAY.
BOOM!
YOU KNOW I DON'T KNOW HOW TO READ, RIGHT?
METEOROLOGY
A GUIDE TO UNDERSTANDING THE WEATHER
I'LL COVER FOR YOU IF YOU CAN BE COVER FOR US.

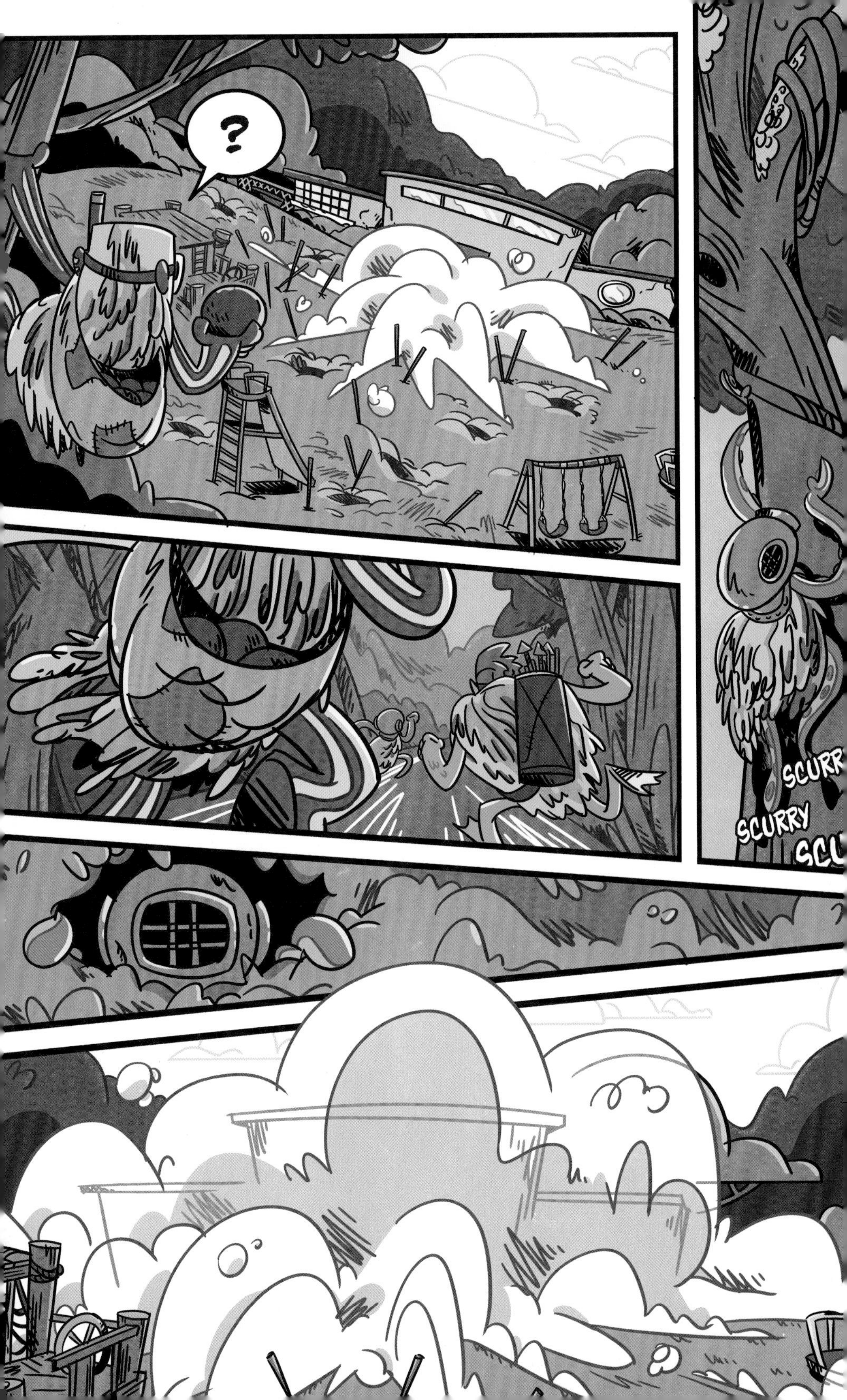
?
SCURR
SCURRY
SCU

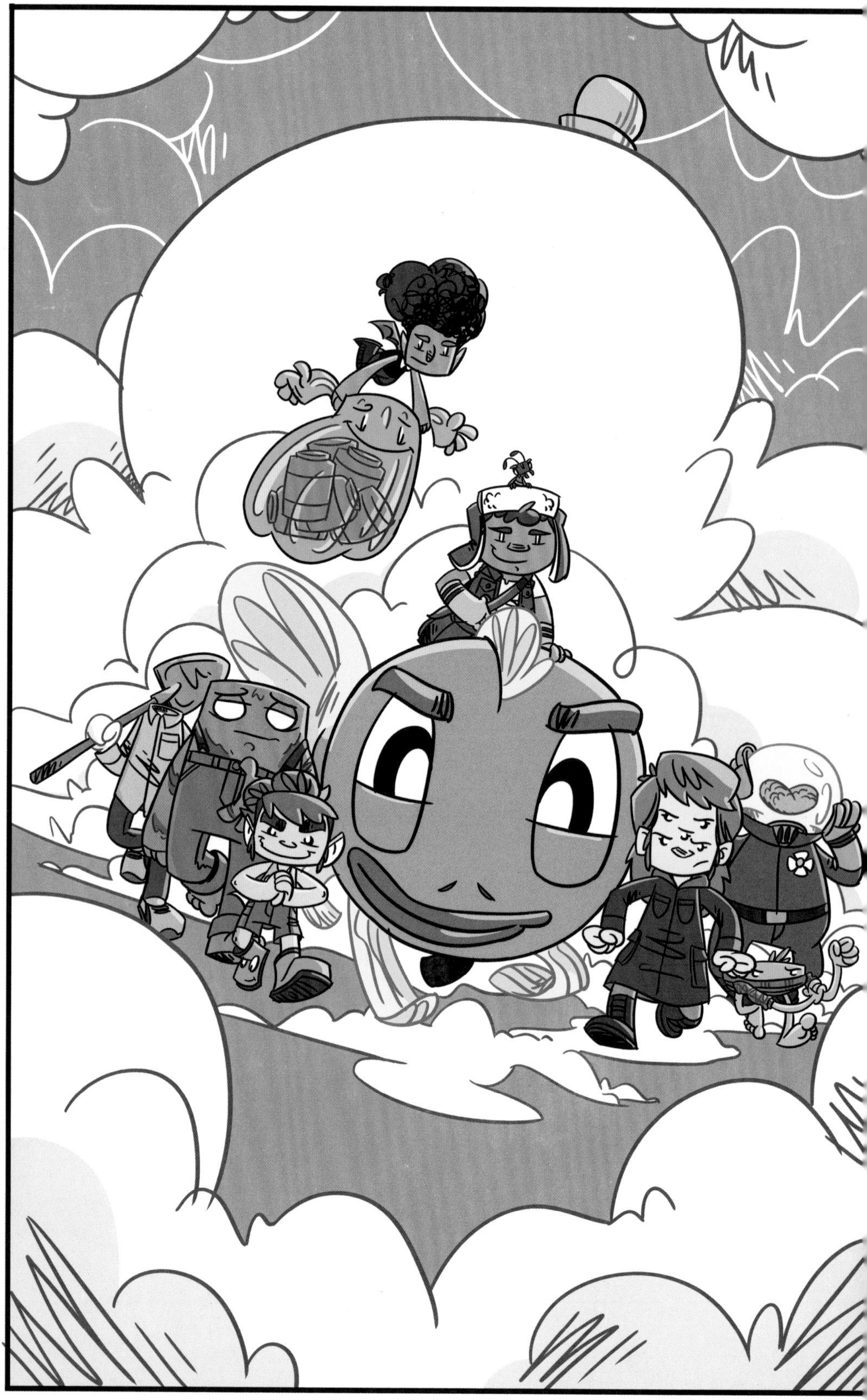

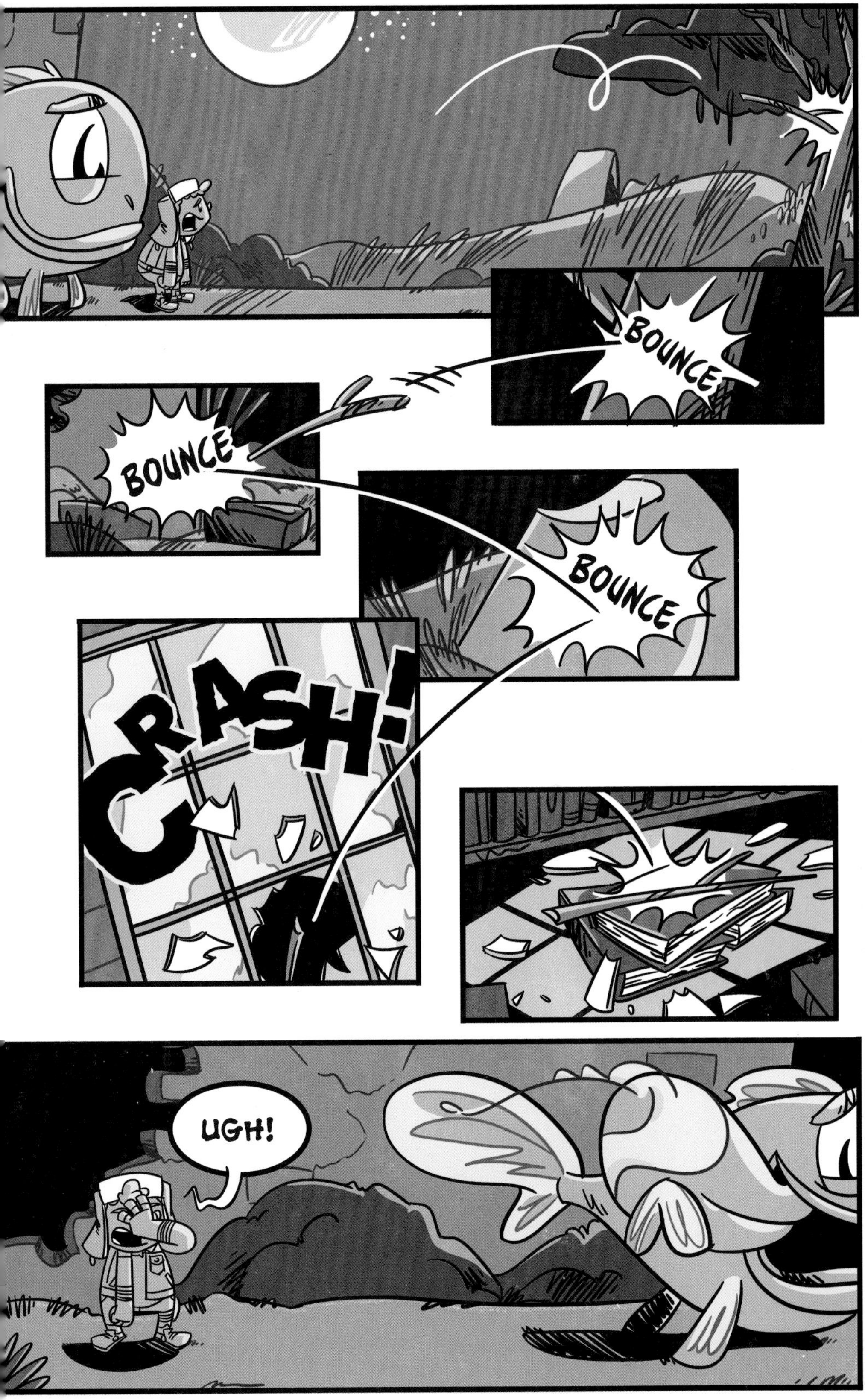
BOUNCE
BOUNCE
BOUNCE
CRASH!
UGH!

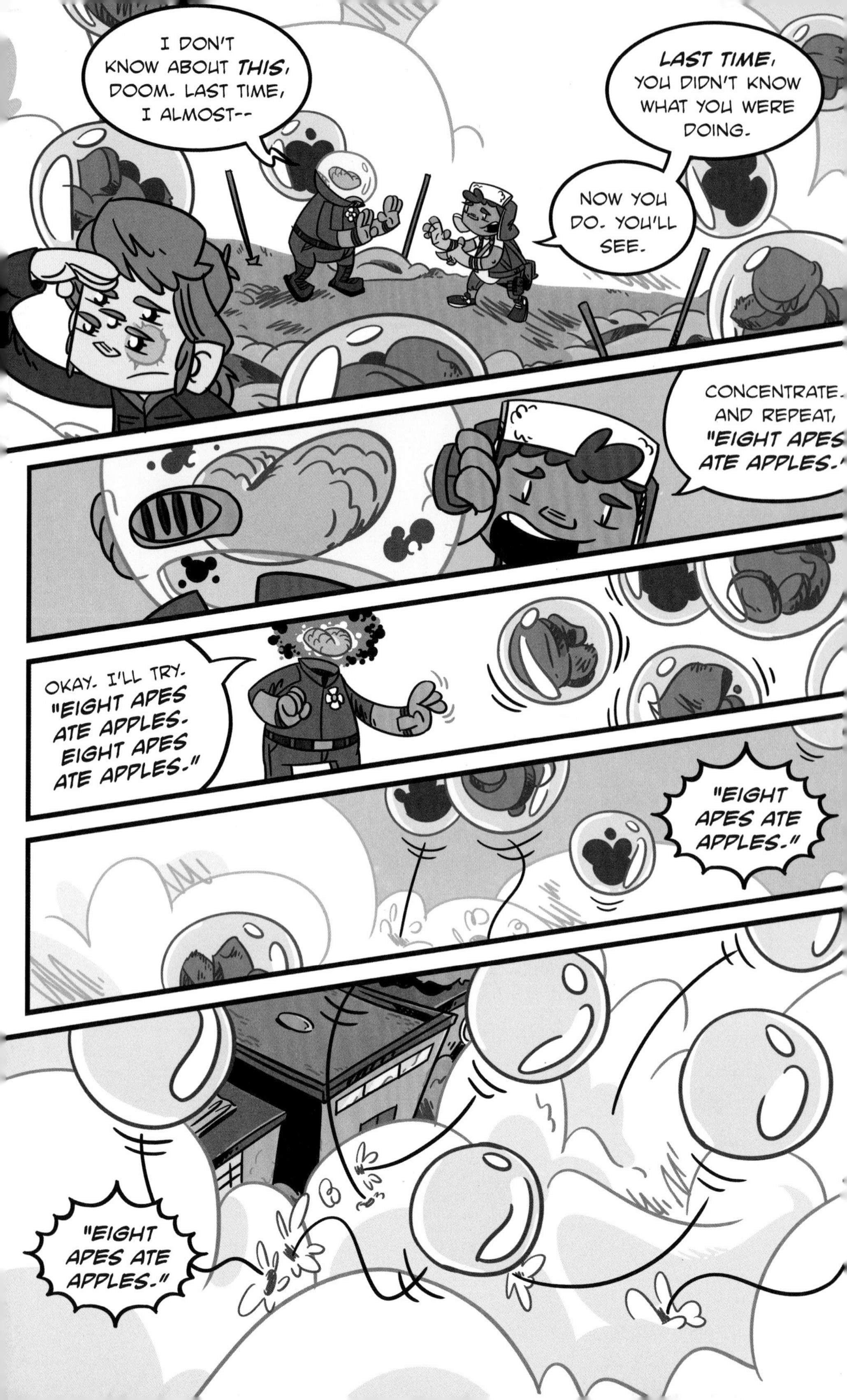
I DON'T KNOW ABOUT THIS, DOOM. LAST TIME, I ALMOST--
LAST TIME, YOU DIDN'T KNOW WHAT YOU WERE DOING.
NOW YOU DO. YOU'LL SEE.
CONCENTRATE. AND REPEAT, "EIGHT APES ATE APPLES."
OKAY. I'LL TRY. "EIGHT APES ATE APPLES. EIGHT APES ATE APPLES."
"EIGHT APES ATE APPLES."
"EIGHT APES ATE APPLES."

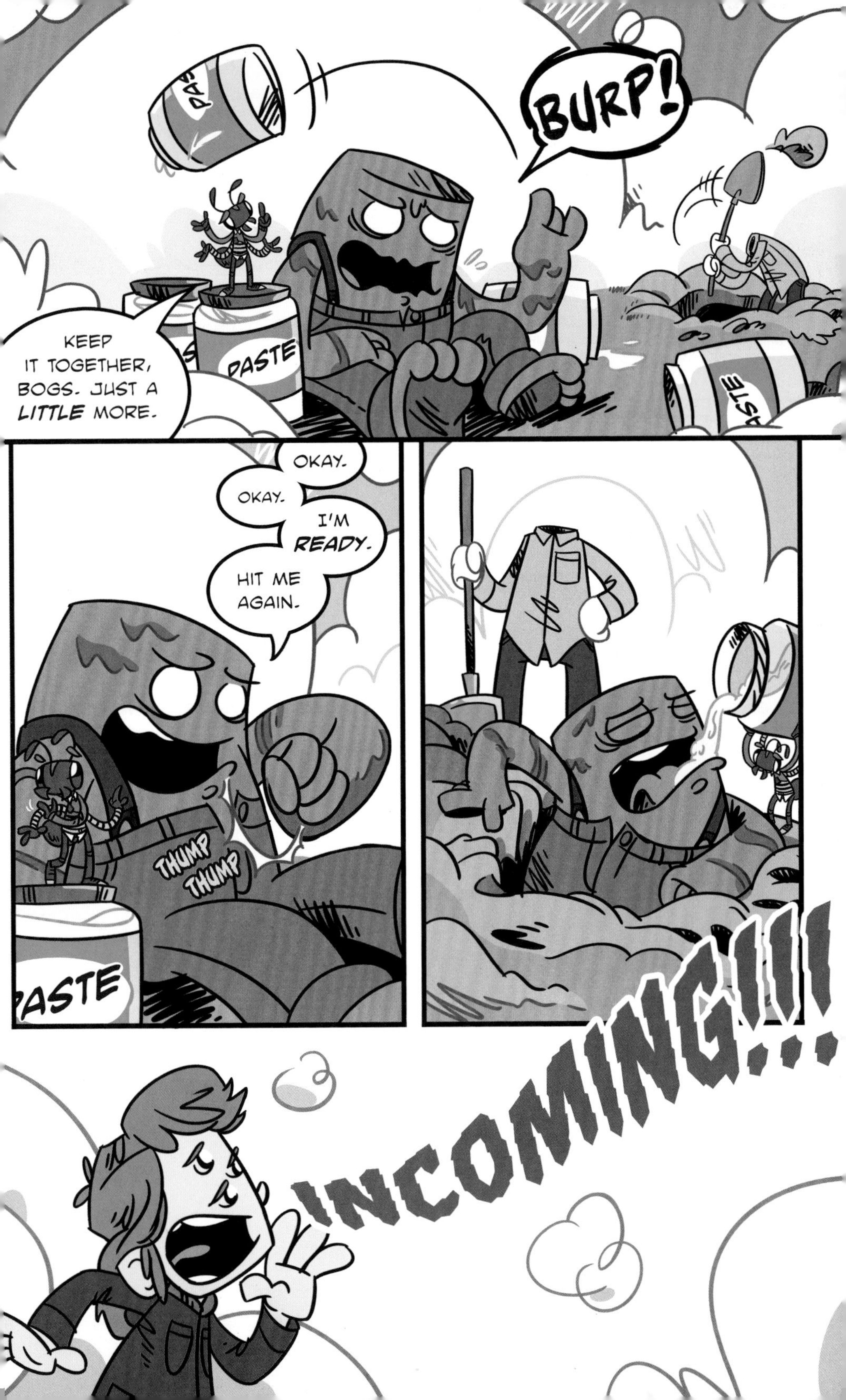
BURP!
KEEP IT TOGETHER, BOGS. JUST A *LITTLE* MORE.
PASTE
PASTE
OKAY.
OKAY.
I'M *READY*.
HIT ME AGAIN.
THUMP THUMP
PASTE
INCOMING!!!

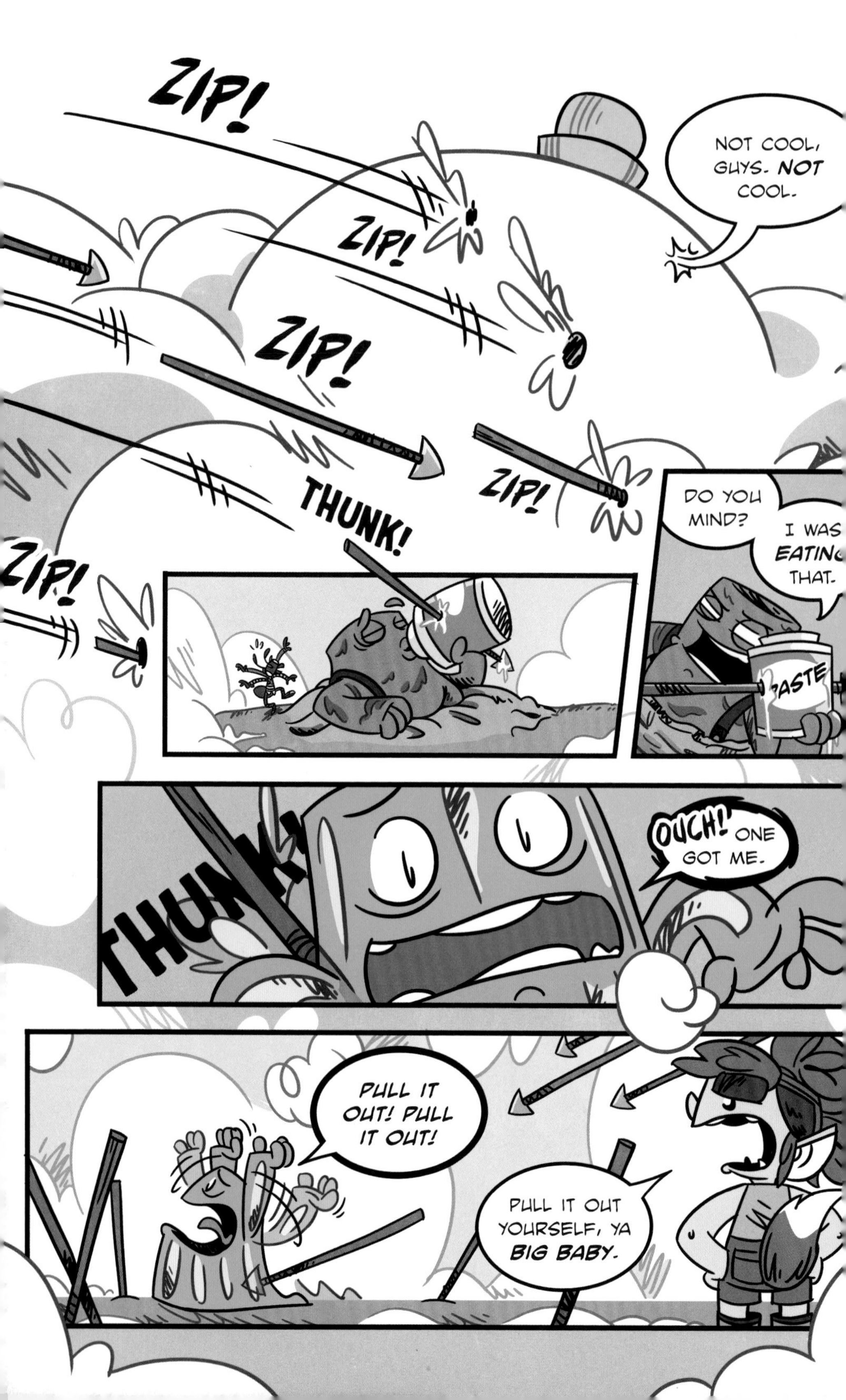
ZIP!
NOT COOL, GUYS. NOT COOL.
ZIP!
ZIP!
ZIP!
THUNK!
ZIP!
DO YOU MIND?
I WAS EATING THAT.
THUNK!
OUCH! ONE GOT ME.
PULL IT OUT! PULL IT OUT!
PULL IT OUT YOURSELF, YA BIG BABY.

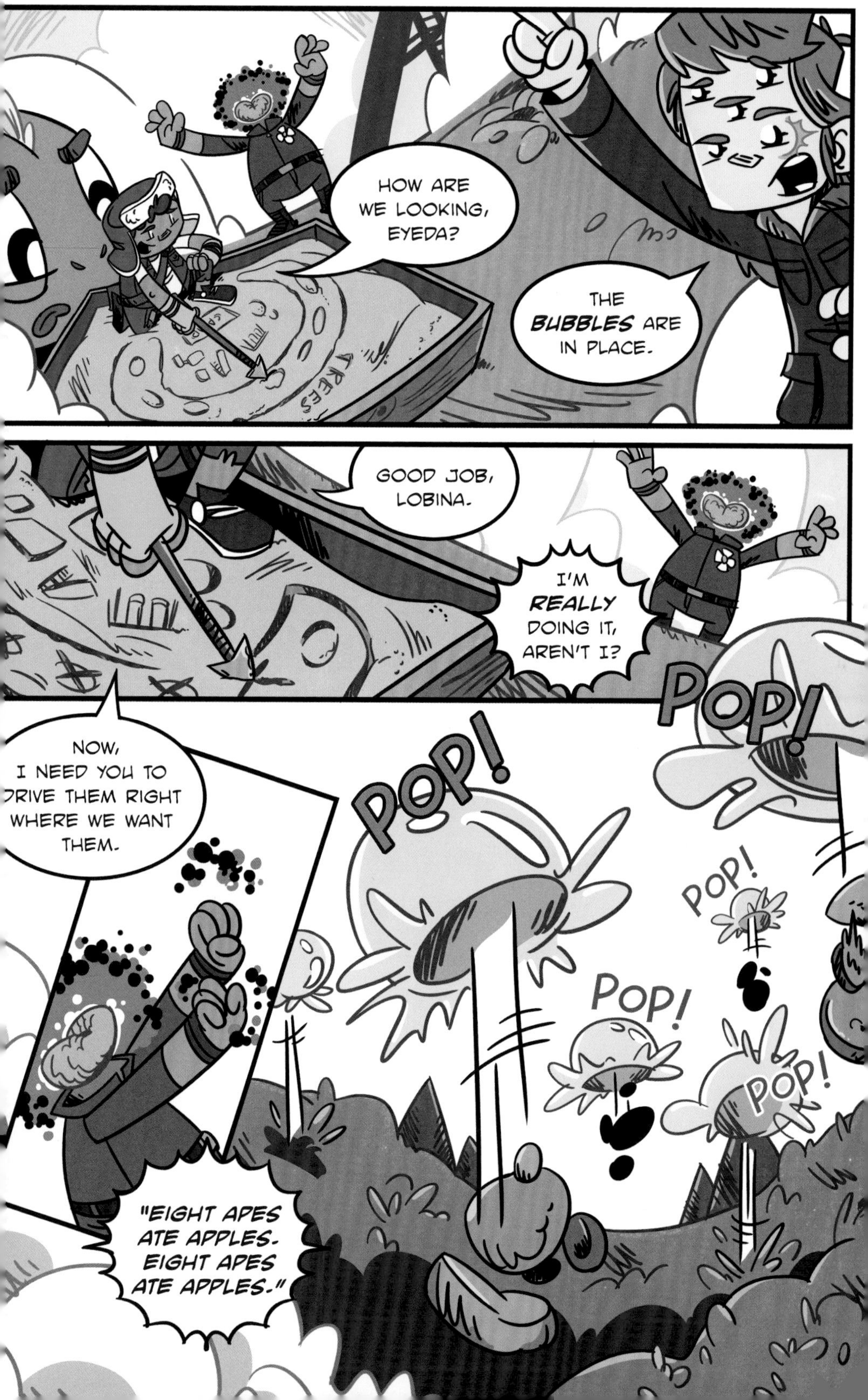
HOW ARE WE LOOKING, EYEDA?
THE BUBBLES ARE IN PLACE.
TREES
GOOD JOB, LOBINA.
I'M REALLY DOING IT, AREN'T I?
NOW, I NEED YOU TO DRIVE THEM RIGHT WHERE WE WANT THEM.
POP!
POP!
POP!
POP!
POP!
"EIGHT APES ATE APPLES. EIGHT APES ATE APPLES."

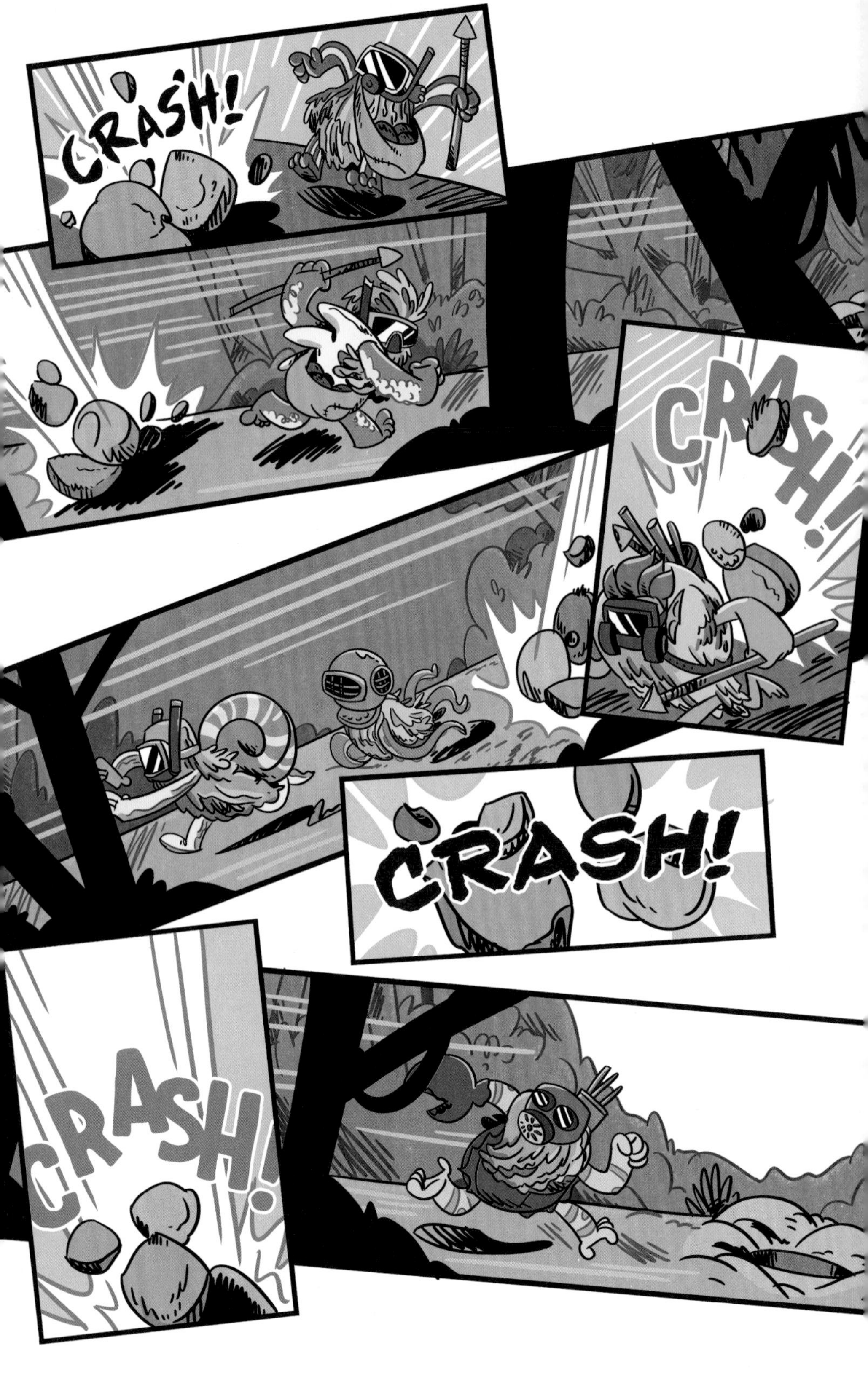

CRASH!
CRASH!
CRASH!
CRASH!

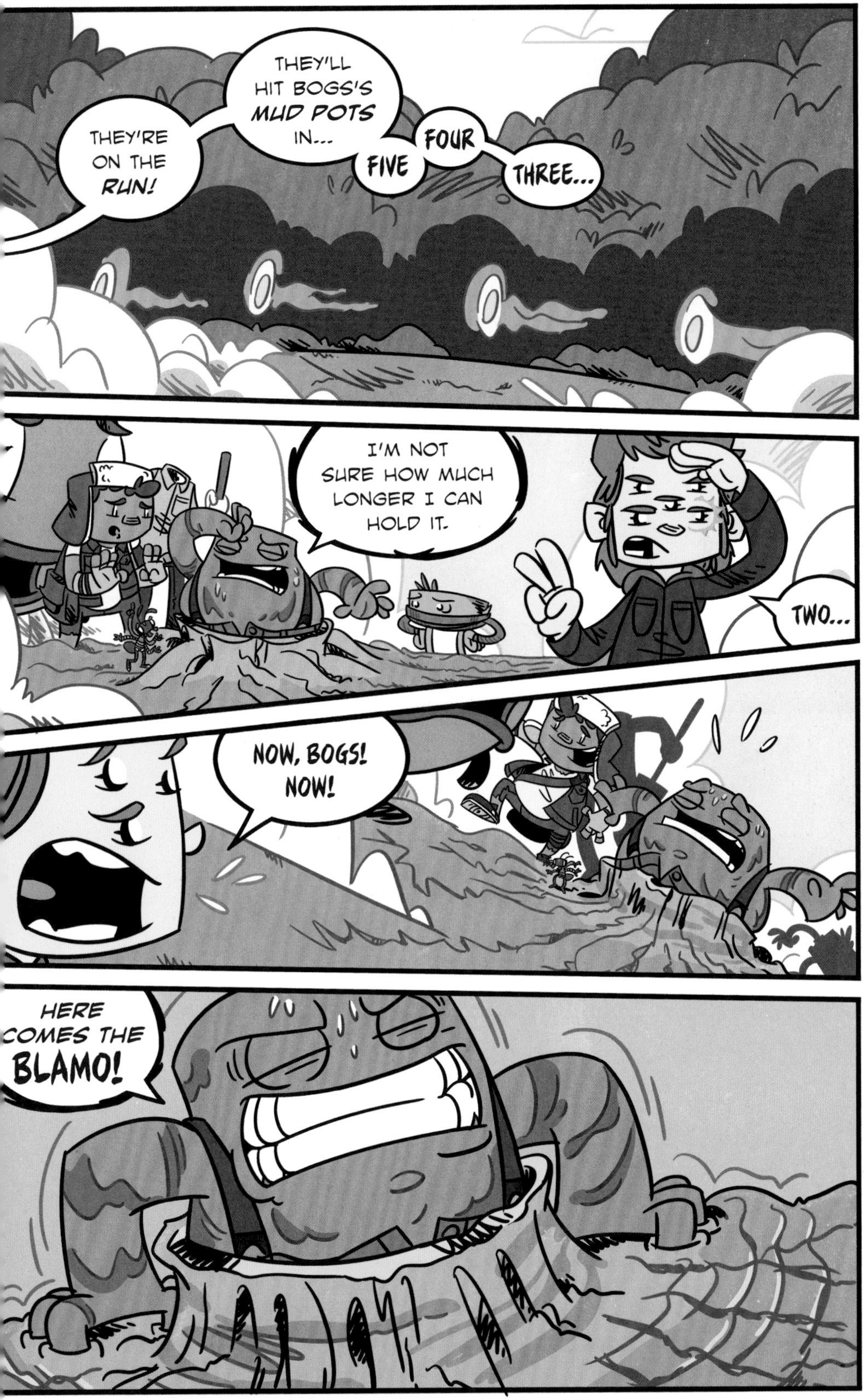
THEY'RE ON THE RUN!
THEY'LL HIT BOGS'S MUD POTS IN...
FIVE
FOUR
THREE...
I'M NOT SURE HOW MUCH LONGER I CAN HOLD IT.
TWO...
NOW, BOGS! NOW!
HERE COMES THE BLAMO!

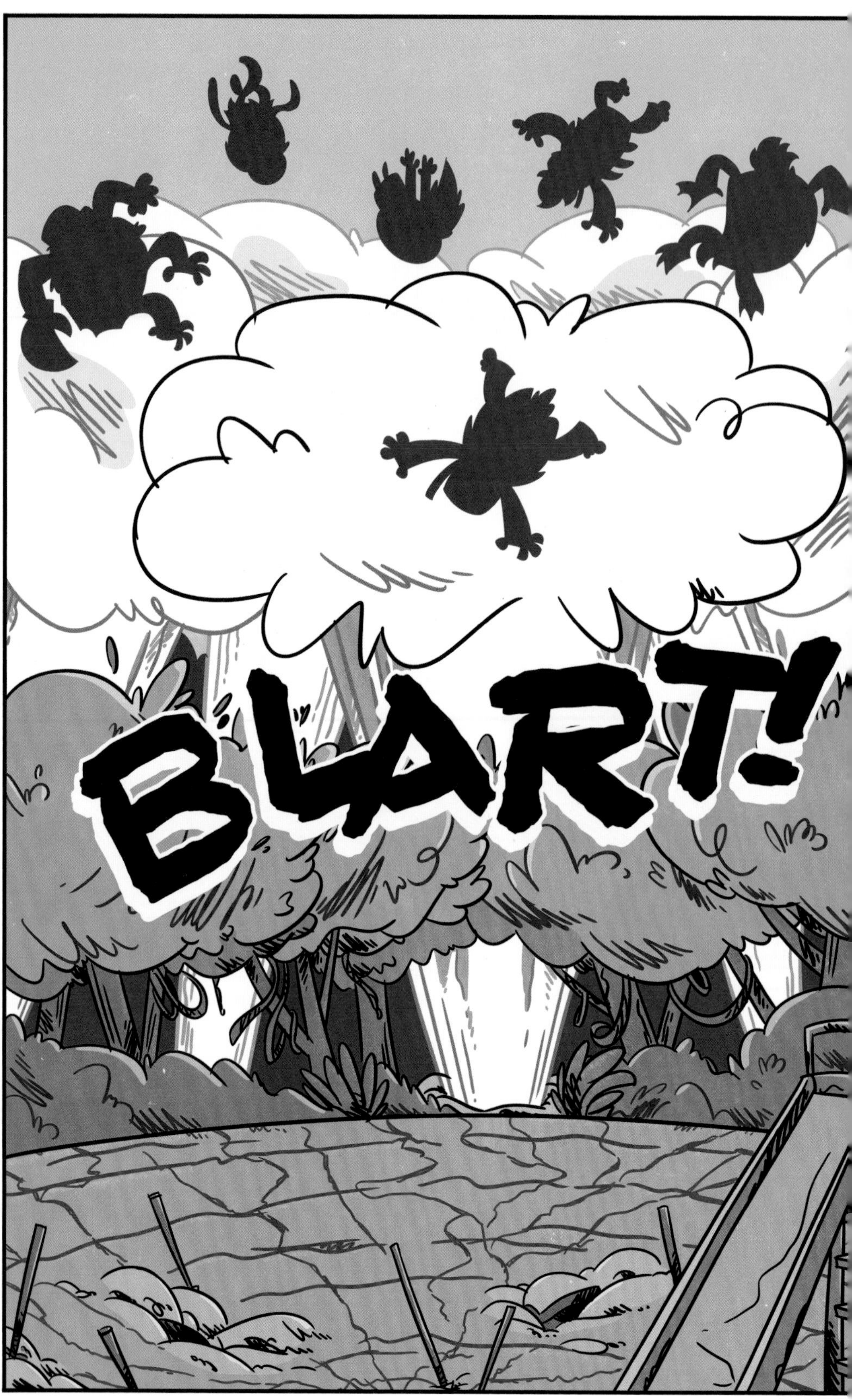
BLART!

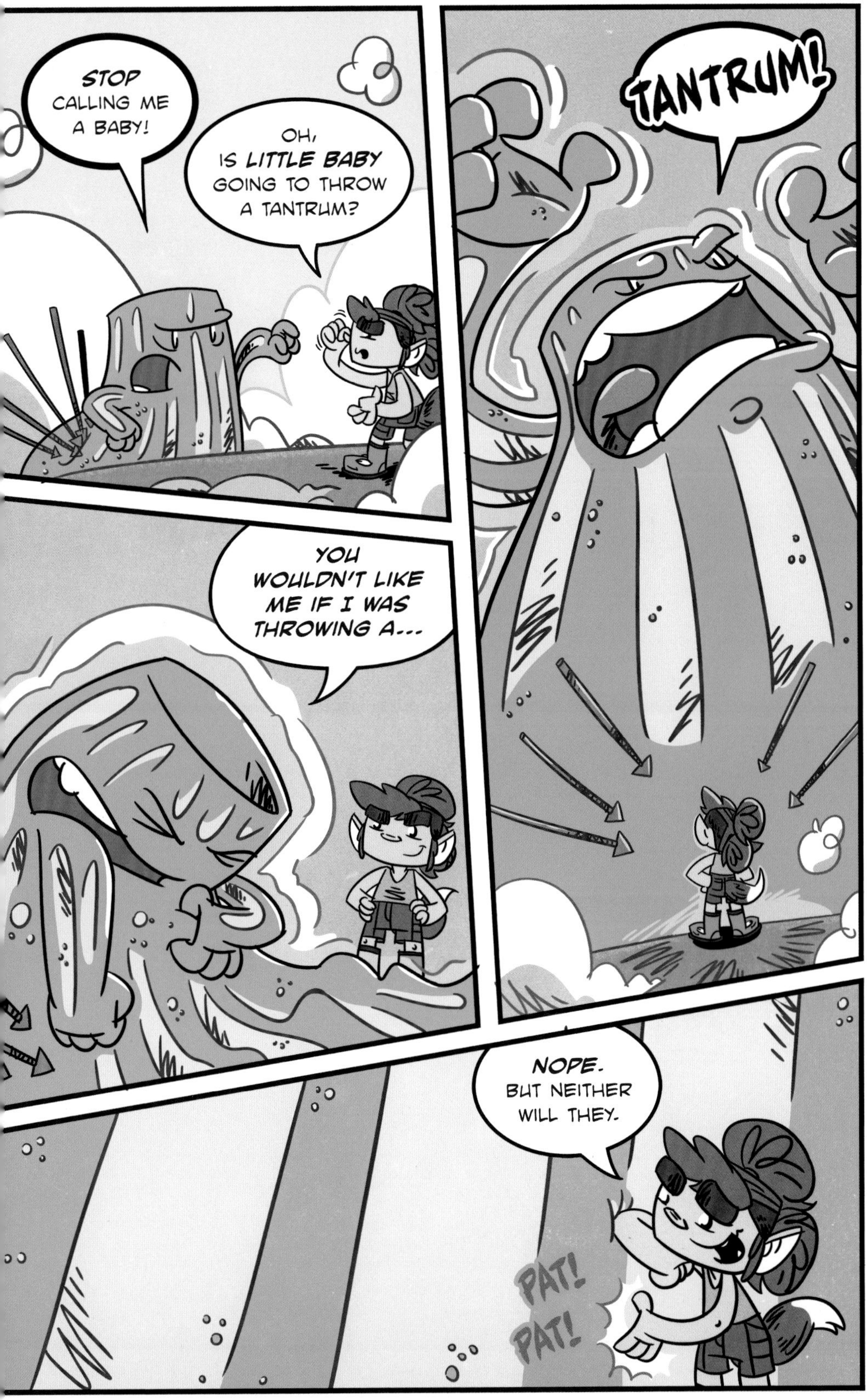
STOP CALLING ME A BABY!
OH, IS LITTLE BABY GOING TO THROW A TANTRUM?
YOU WOULDN'T LIKE ME IF I WAS THROWING A...
TANTRUM!
NOPE. BUT NEITHER WILL THEY.
PAT! PAT!

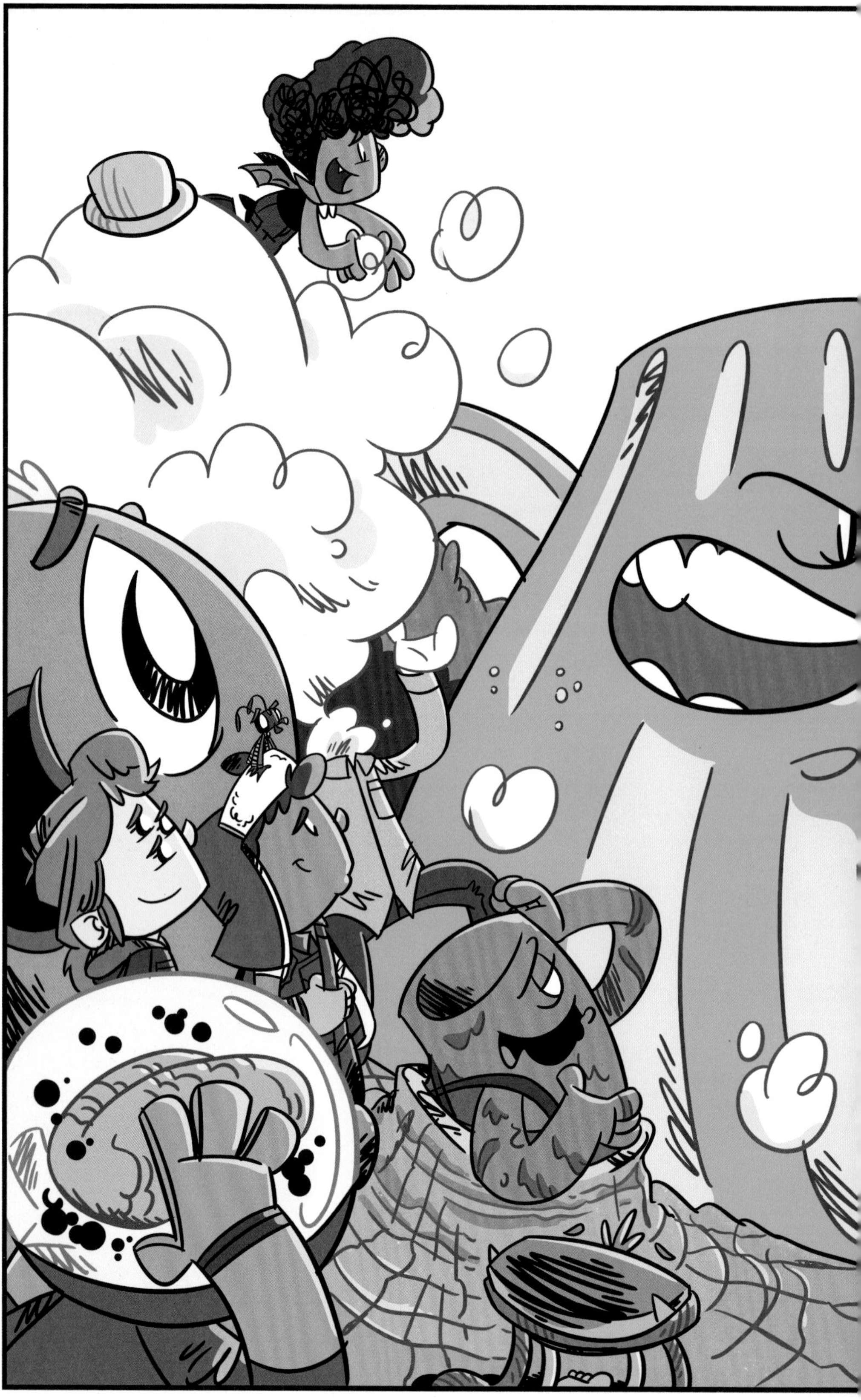

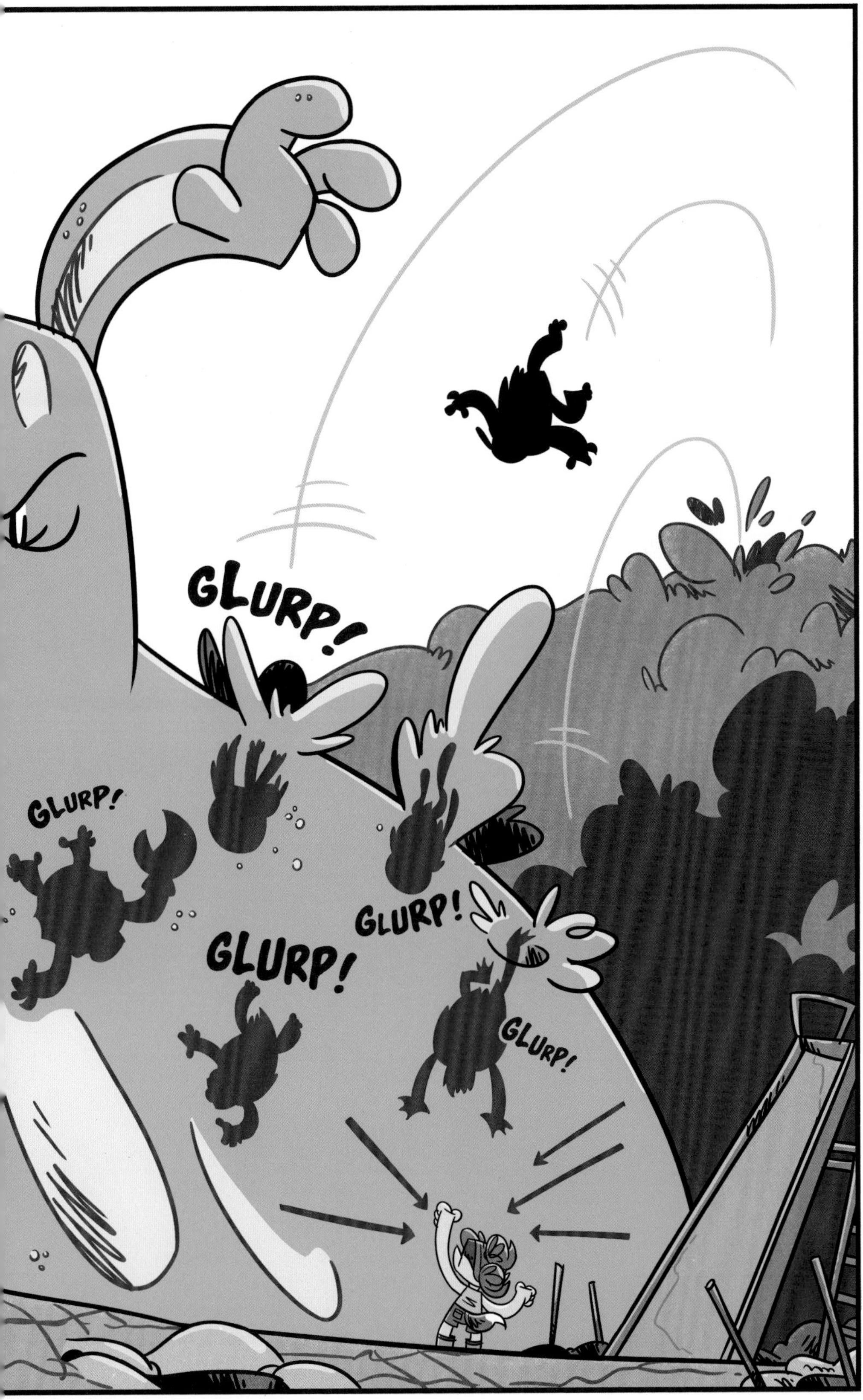
GLURP!
GLURP!
GLURP!
GLURP!
GLURP!

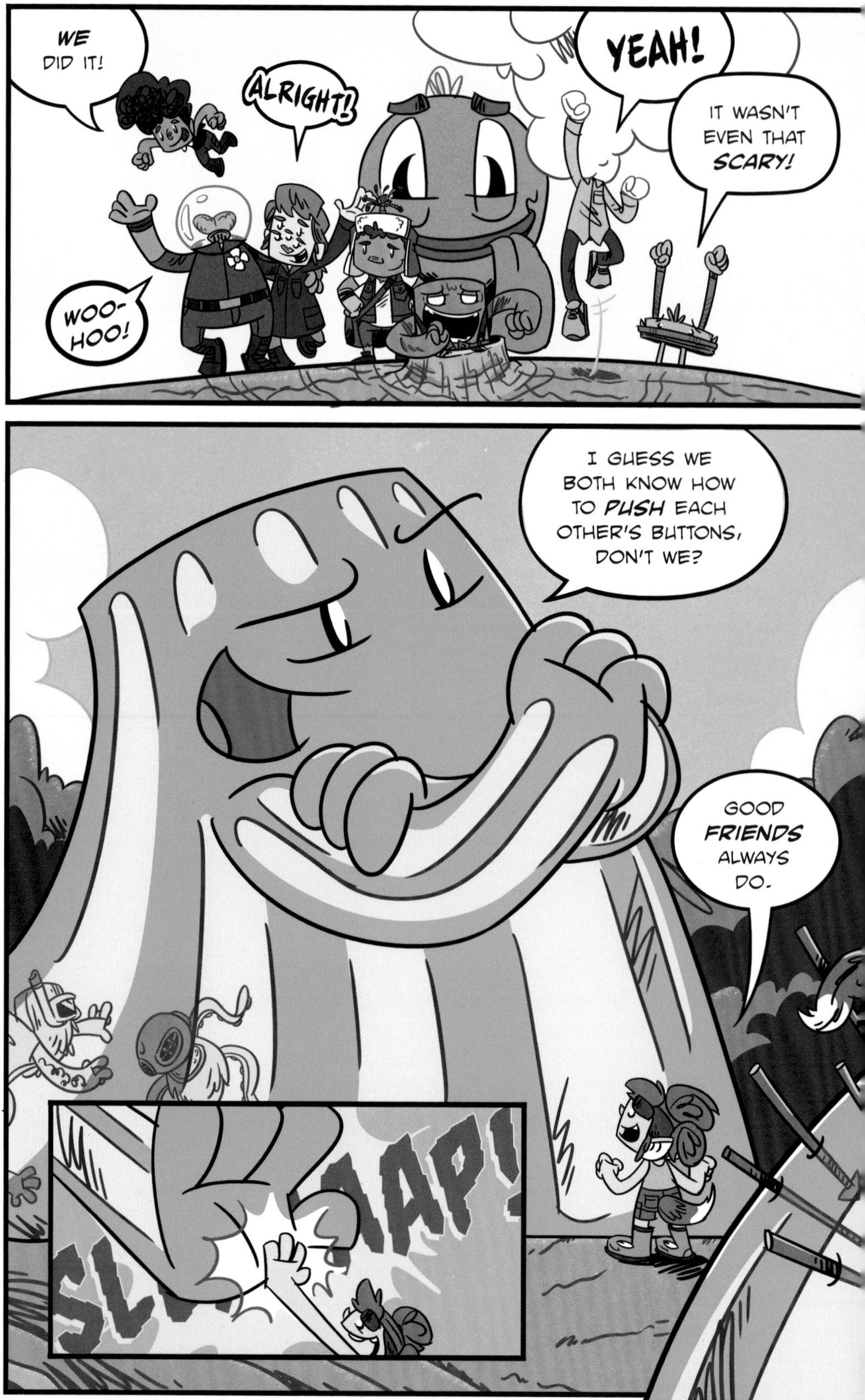
WE DID IT!
ALRIGHT!
YEAH!
IT WASN'T EVEN THAT SCARY!
WOO-HOO!
I GUESS WE BOTH KNOW HOW TO PUSH EACH OTHER'S BUTTONS, DON'T WE?
GOOD FRIENDS ALWAYS DO.

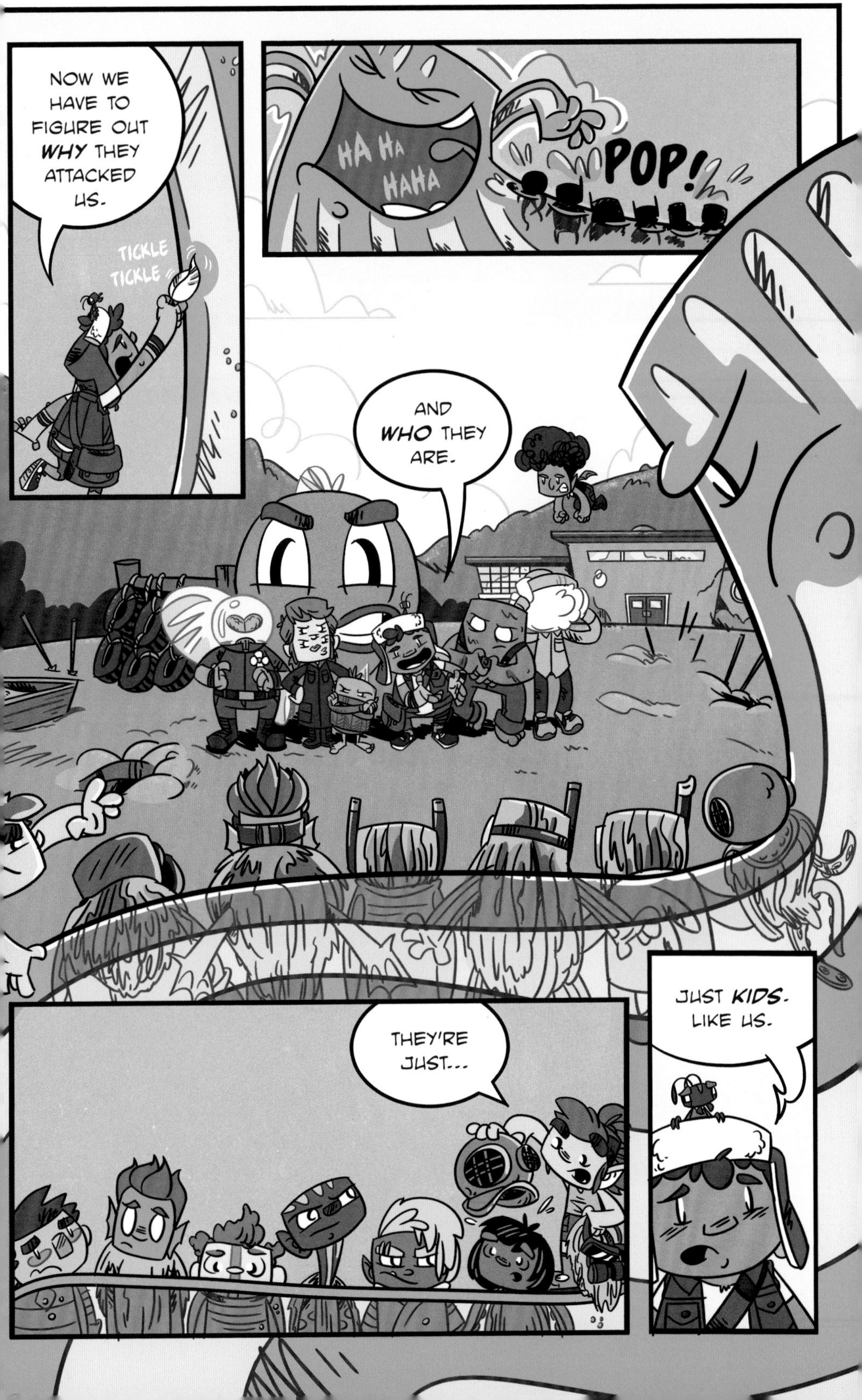
NOW WE HAVE TO FIGURE OUT WHY THEY ATTACKED US.
TICKLE TICKLE
HA HA HAHA
POP!
AND WHO THEY ARE.
THEY'RE JUST...
JUST KIDS. LIKE US.

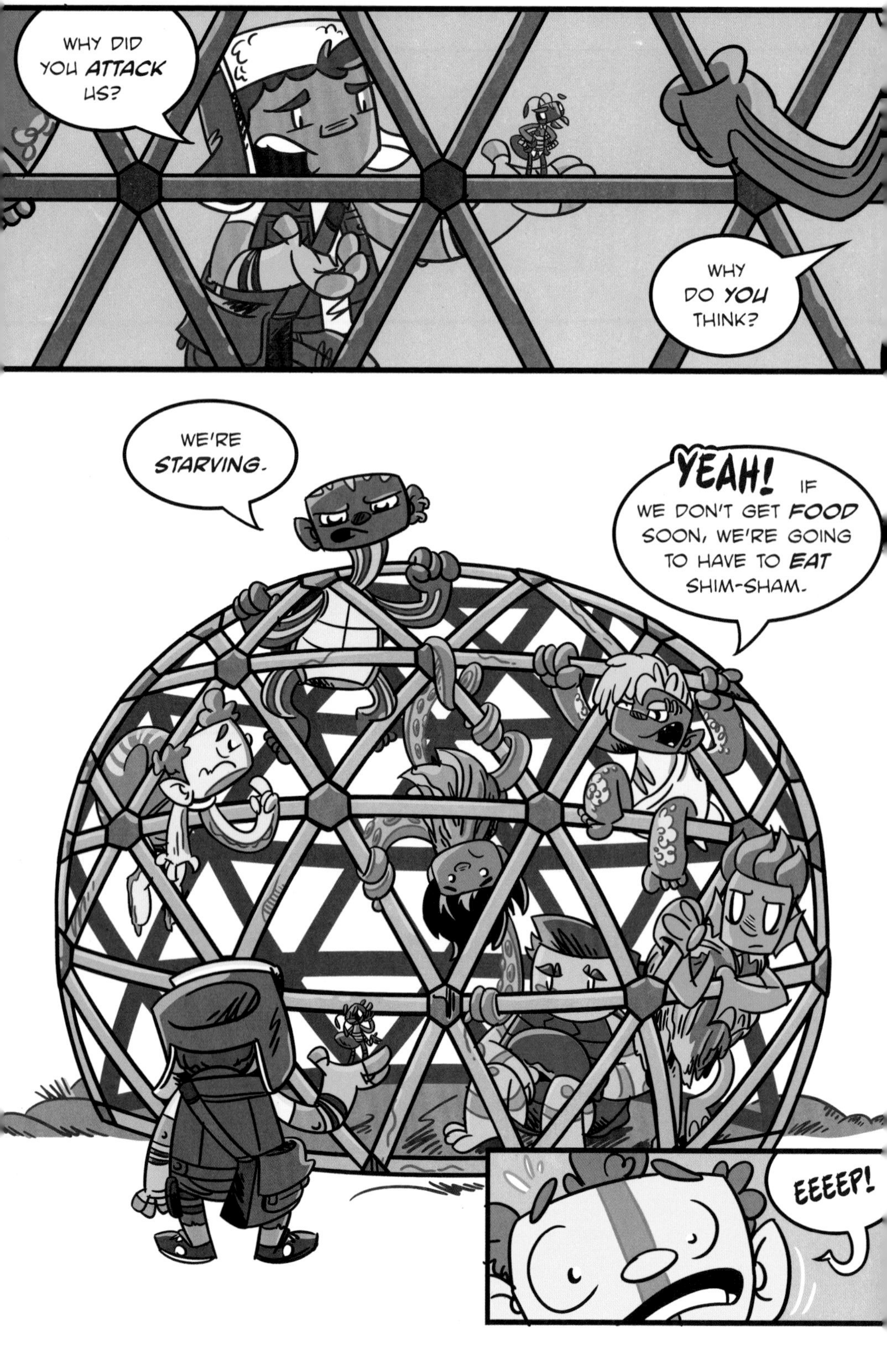
WHY DID YOU ATTACK US?
WHY DO YOU THINK?
WE'RE STARVING.
YEAH! IF WE DON'T GET FOOD SOON, WE'RE GOING TO HAVE TO EAT SHIM-SHAM.
EEEEP!

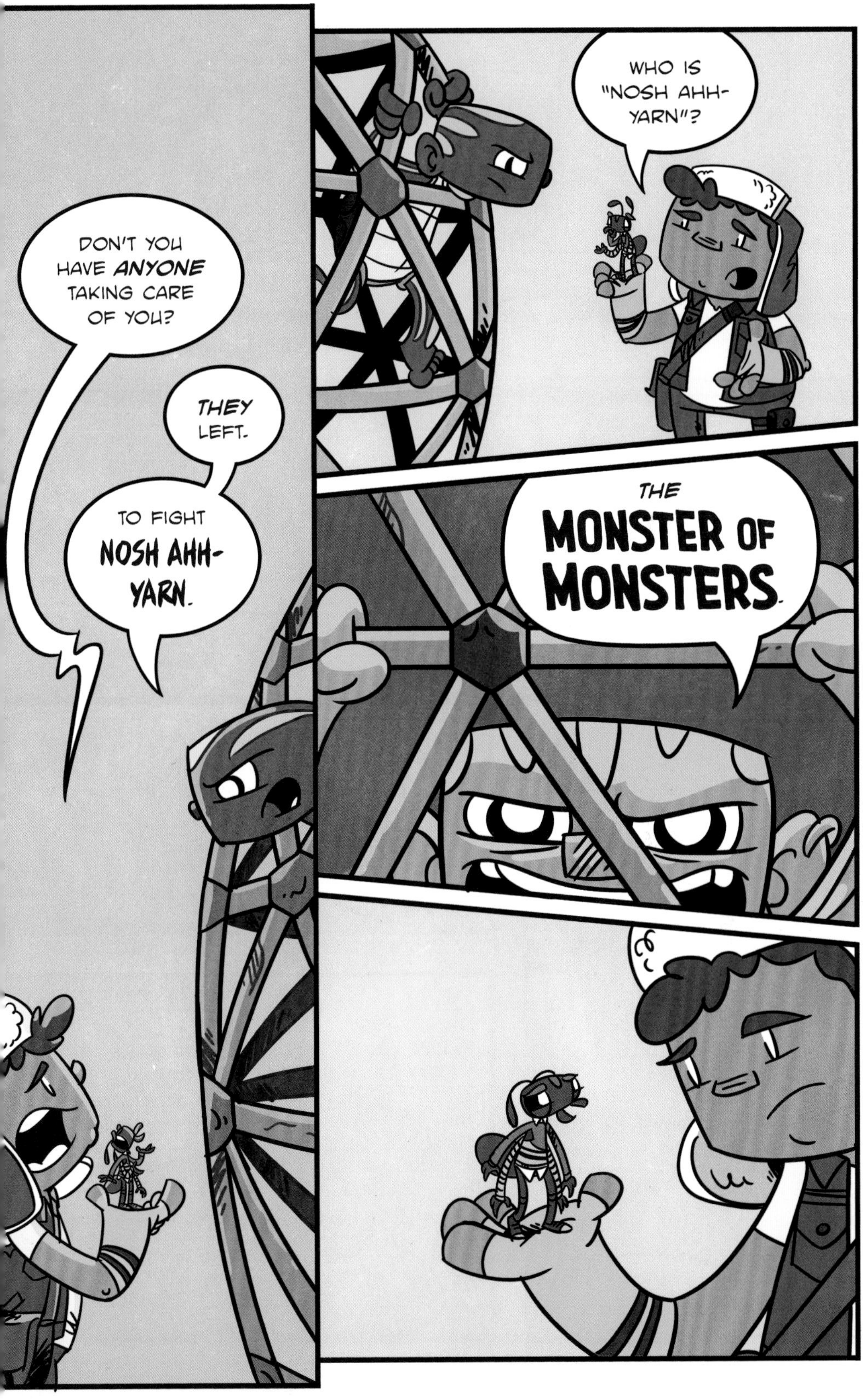
WHO IS "NOSH AHH-YARN"?
DON'T YOU HAVE ANYONE TAKING CARE OF YOU?
THEY LEFT.
TO FIGHT NOSH AHH-YARN.
THE MONSTER OF MONSTERS.

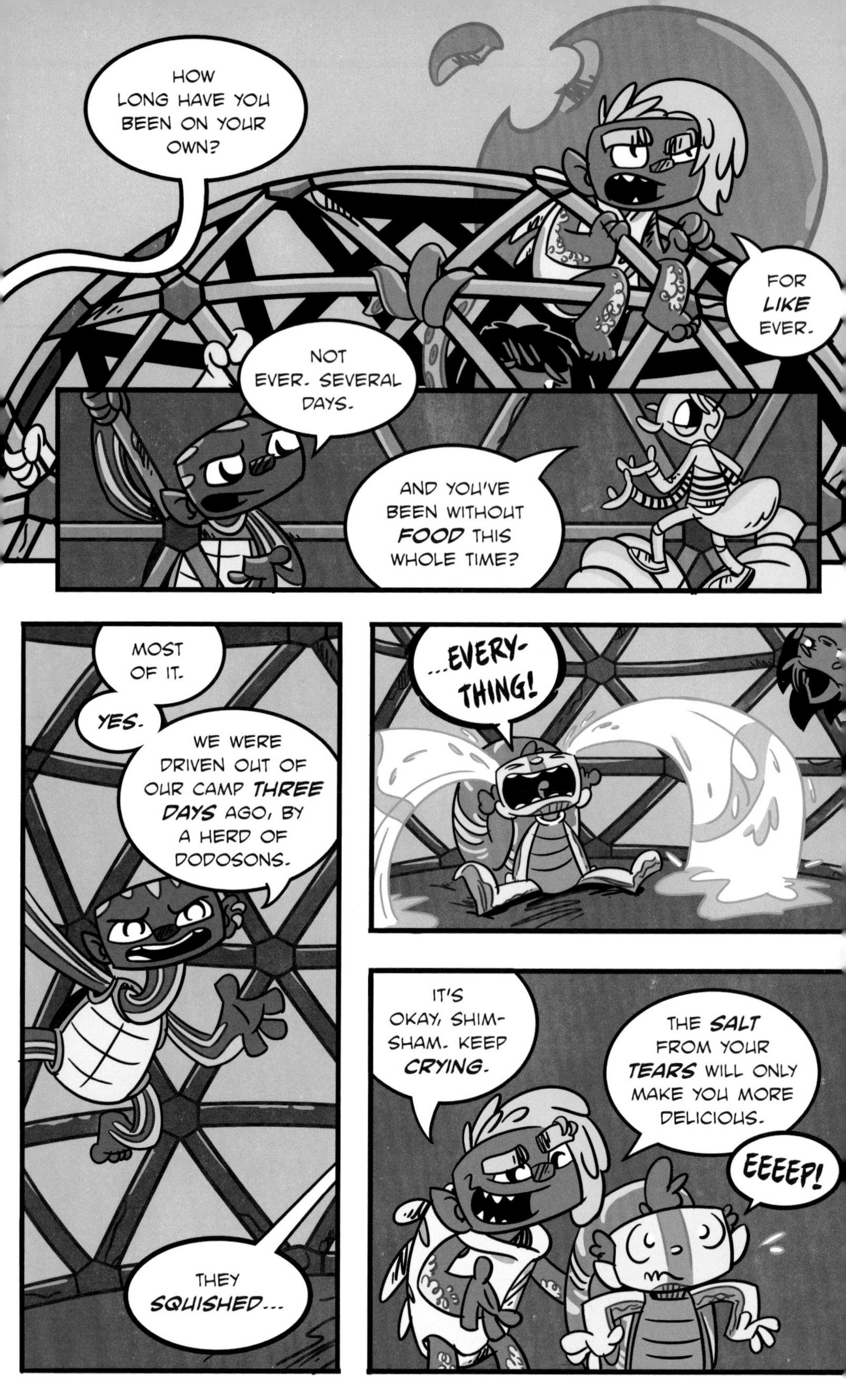
HOW LONG HAVE YOU BEEN ON YOUR OWN?
FOR LIKE EVER.
NOT EVER. SEVERAL DAYS.
AND YOU'VE BEEN WITHOUT FOOD THIS WHOLE TIME?
MOST OF IT.
YES.
WE WERE DRIVEN OUT OF OUR CAMP THREE DAYS AGO, BY A HERD OF DODOSONS.
THEY SQUISHED...
...EVERY-THING!
IT'S OKAY, SHIM-SHAM. KEEP CRYING.
THE SALT FROM YOUR TEARS WILL ONLY MAKE YOU MORE DELICIOUS.
EEEEP!

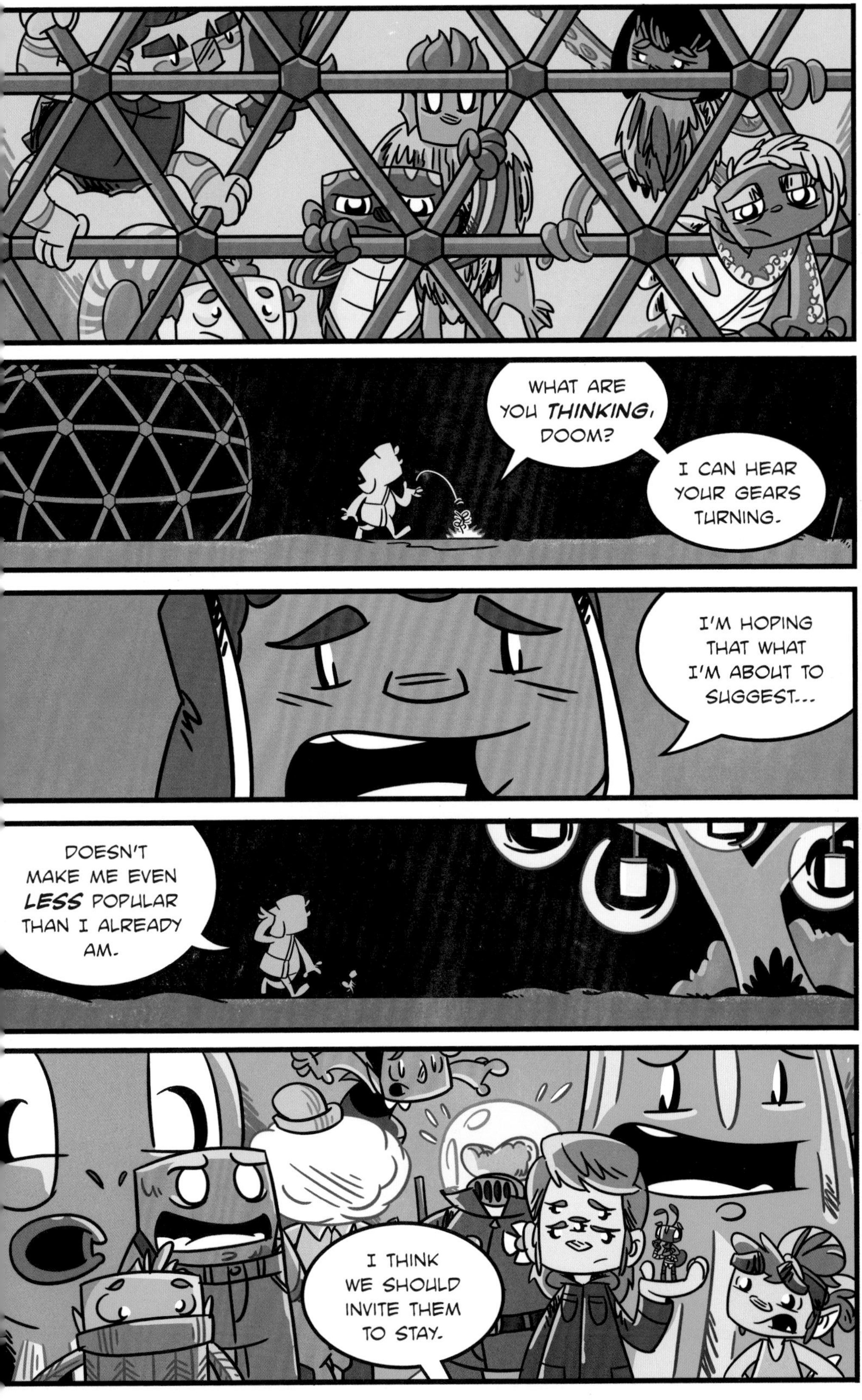
WHAT ARE YOU *THINKING*, DOOM?
I CAN HEAR YOUR GEARS TURNING.
I'M HOPING THAT WHAT I'M ABOUT TO SUGGEST...
DOESN'T MAKE ME EVEN *LESS* POPULAR THAN I ALREADY AM.
I THINK WE SHOULD INVITE THEM TO STAY.

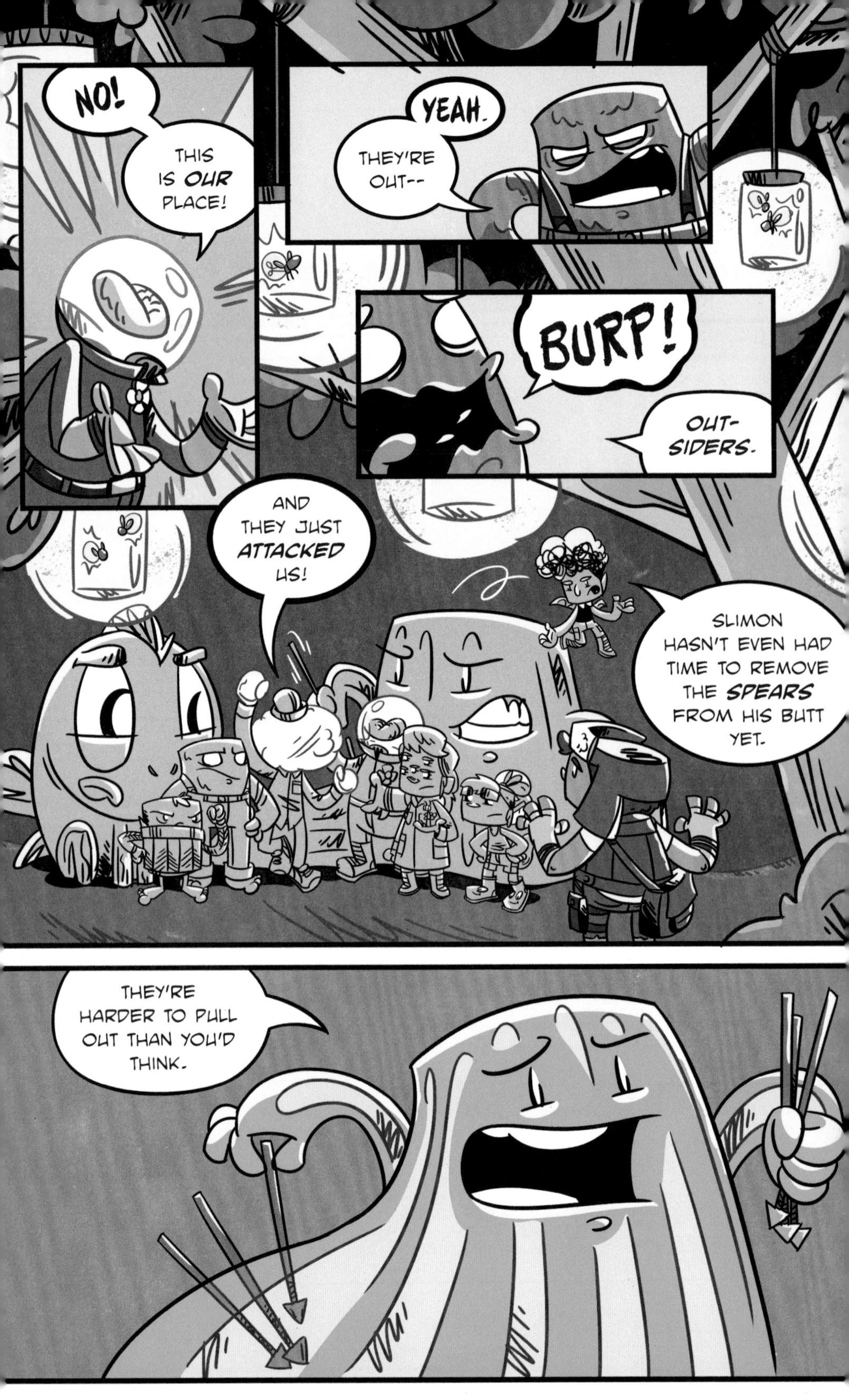
NO!
THIS IS **OUR** PLACE!
YEAH.
THEY'RE OUT--
BURP!
OUT-SIDERS.
AND THEY JUST **ATTACKED** US!
SLIMON HASN'T EVEN HAD TIME TO REMOVE THE **SPEARS** FROM HIS BUTT YET.
THEY'RE HARDER TO PULL OUT THAN YOU'D THINK.

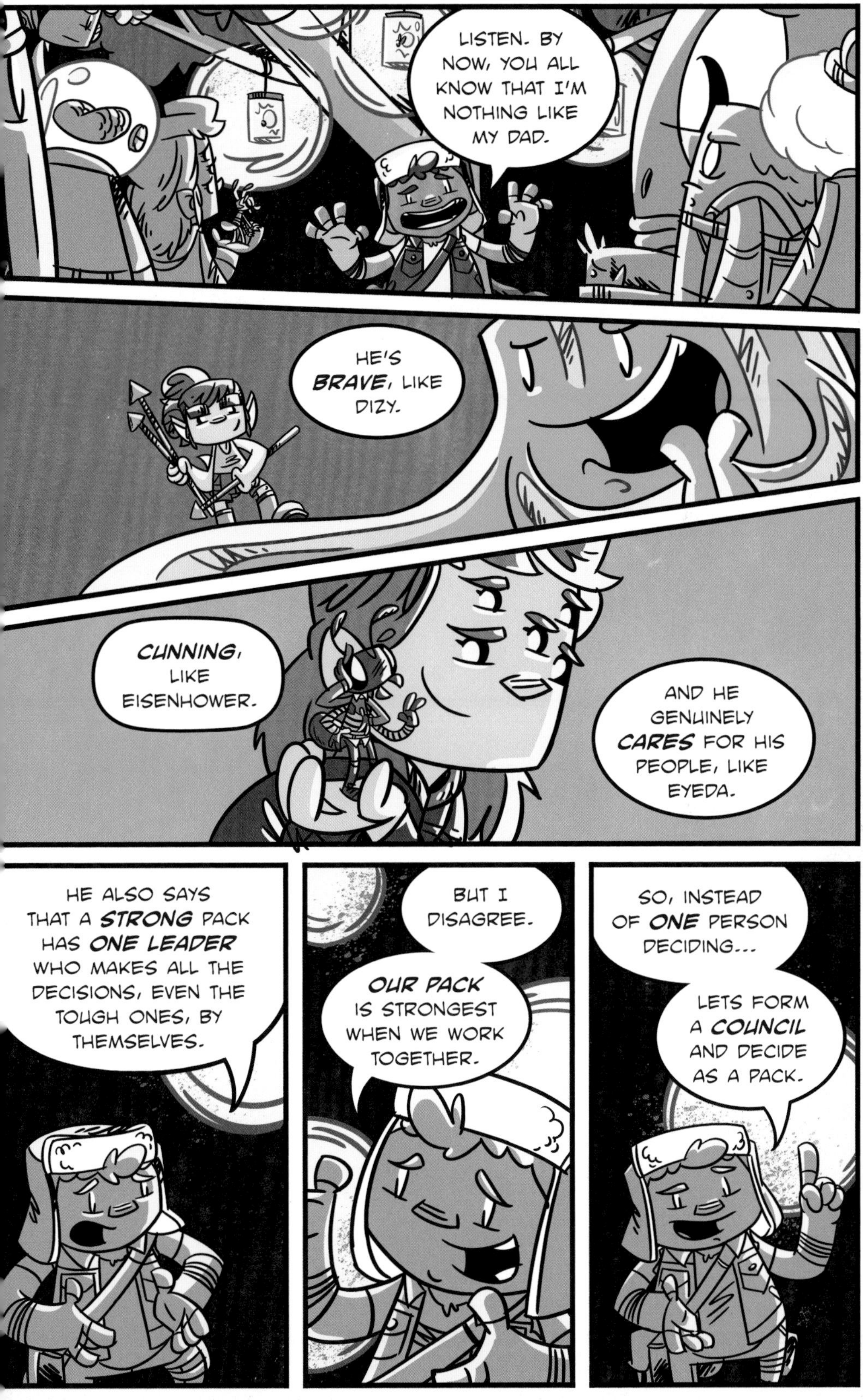
LISTEN. BY NOW, YOU ALL KNOW THAT I'M NOTHING LIKE MY DAD.
HE'S **BRAVE**, LIKE DIZY.
CUNNING, LIKE EISENHOWER.
AND HE GENUINELY **CARES** FOR HIS PEOPLE, LIKE EYEDA.
HE ALSO SAYS THAT A **STRONG** PACK HAS **ONE LEADER** WHO MAKES ALL THE DECISIONS, EVEN THE TOUGH ONES, BY THEMSELVES.
BUT I DISAGREE.
OUR PACK IS STRONGEST WHEN WE WORK TOGETHER.
SO, INSTEAD OF **ONE** PERSON DECIDING...
LETS FORM A **COUNCIL** AND DECIDE AS A PACK.

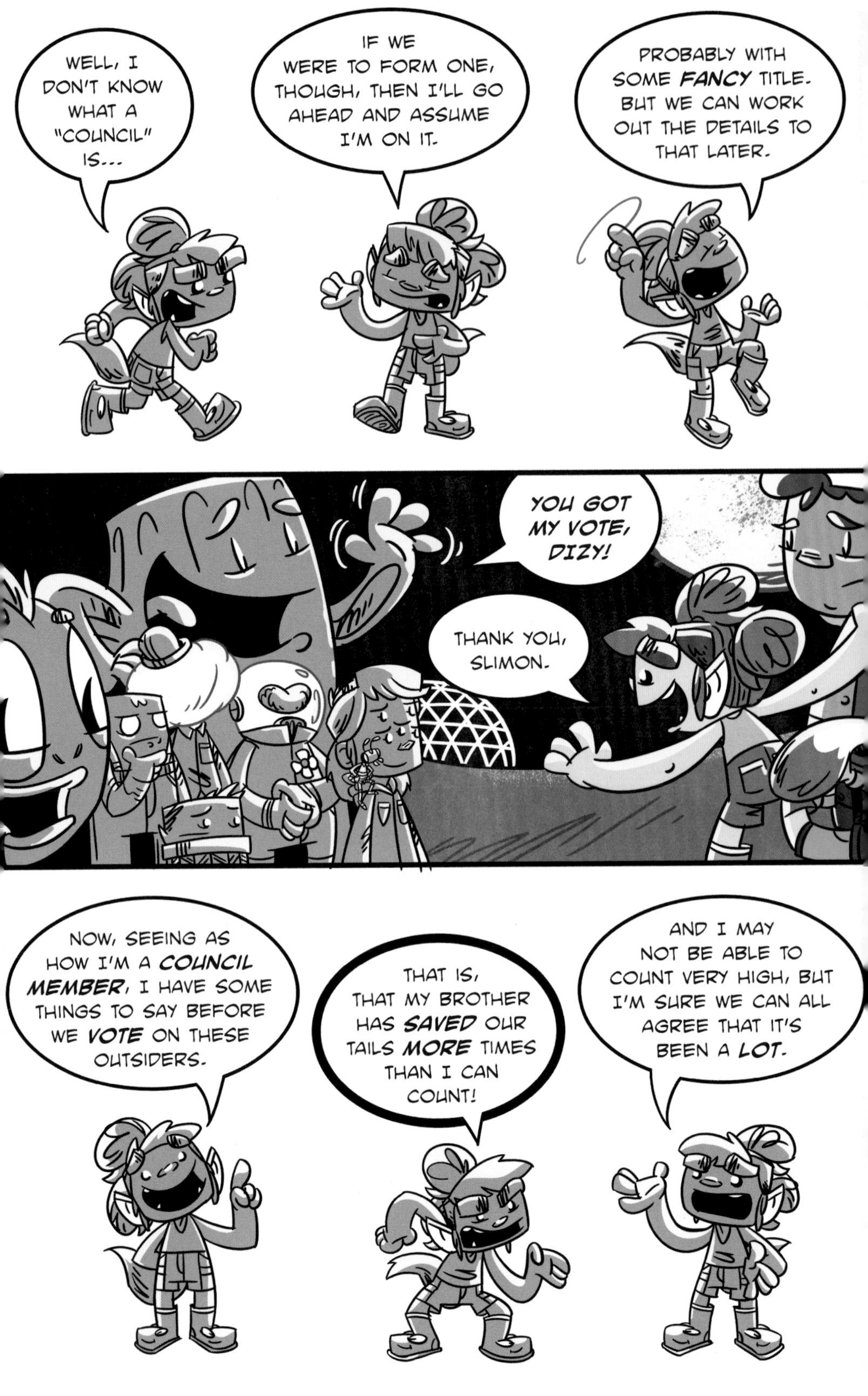
WELL, I DON'T KNOW WHAT A "COUNCIL" IS...
IF WE WERE TO FORM ONE, THOUGH, THEN I'LL GO AHEAD AND ASSUME I'M ON IT.
PROBABLY WITH SOME FANCY TITLE. BUT WE CAN WORK OUT THE DETAILS TO THAT LATER.
YOU GOT MY VOTE, DIZY!
THANK YOU, SLIMON.
NOW, SEEING AS HOW I'M A COUNCIL MEMBER, I HAVE SOME THINGS TO SAY BEFORE WE VOTE ON THESE OUTSIDERS.
THAT IS, THAT MY BROTHER HAS SAVED OUR TAILS MORE TIMES THAN I CAN COUNT!
AND I MAY NOT BE ABLE TO COUNT VERY HIGH, BUT I'M SURE WE CAN ALL AGREE THAT IT'S BEEN A LOT.

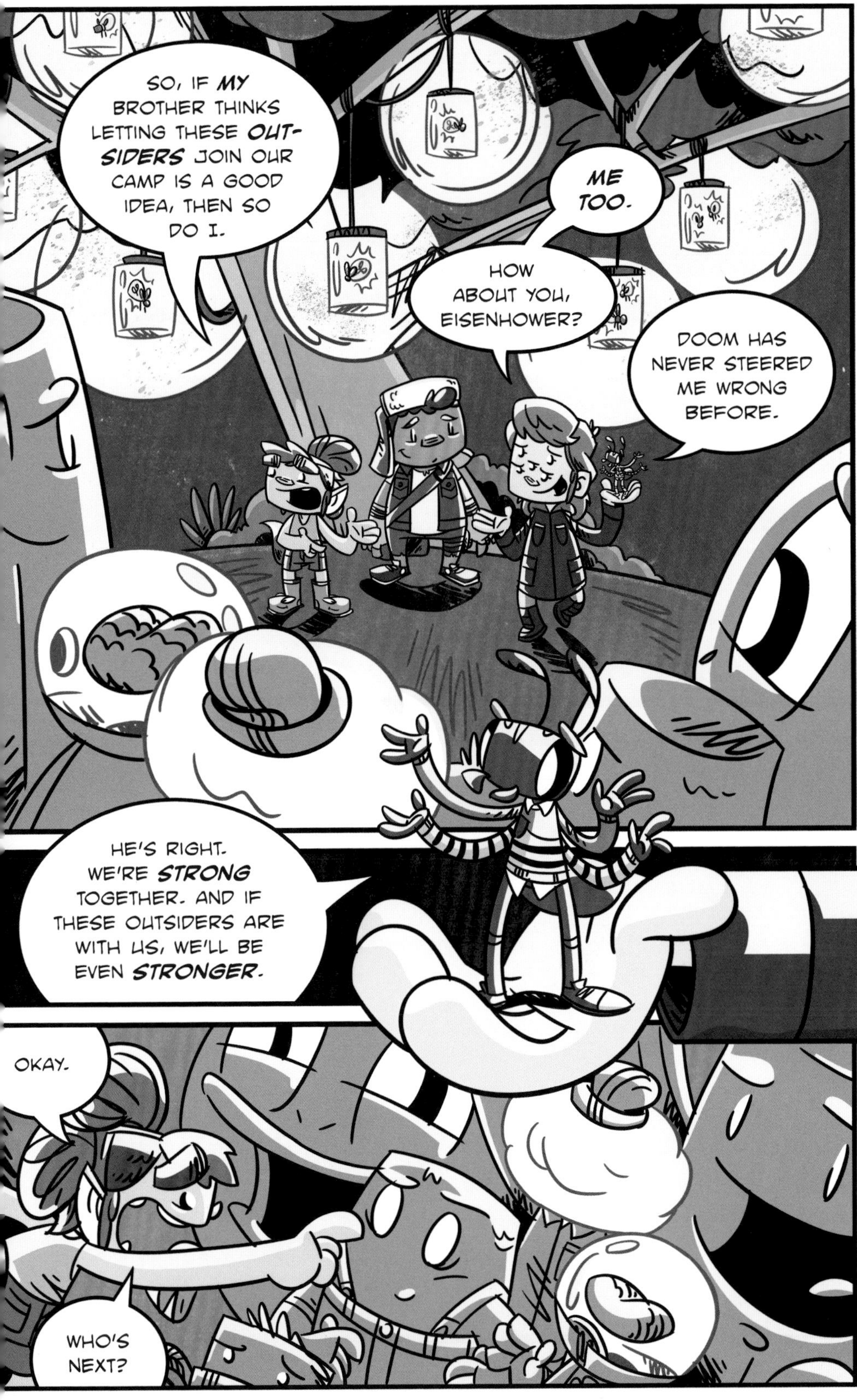
SO, IF MY BROTHER THINKS LETTING THESE OUTSIDERS JOIN OUR CAMP IS A GOOD IDEA, THEN SO DO I.
ME TOO.
HOW ABOUT YOU, EISENHOWER?
DOOM HAS NEVER STEERED ME WRONG BEFORE.
HE'S RIGHT. WE'RE STRONG TOGETHER. AND IF THESE OUTSIDERS ARE WITH US, WE'LL BE EVEN STRONGER.
OKAY.
WHO'S NEXT?

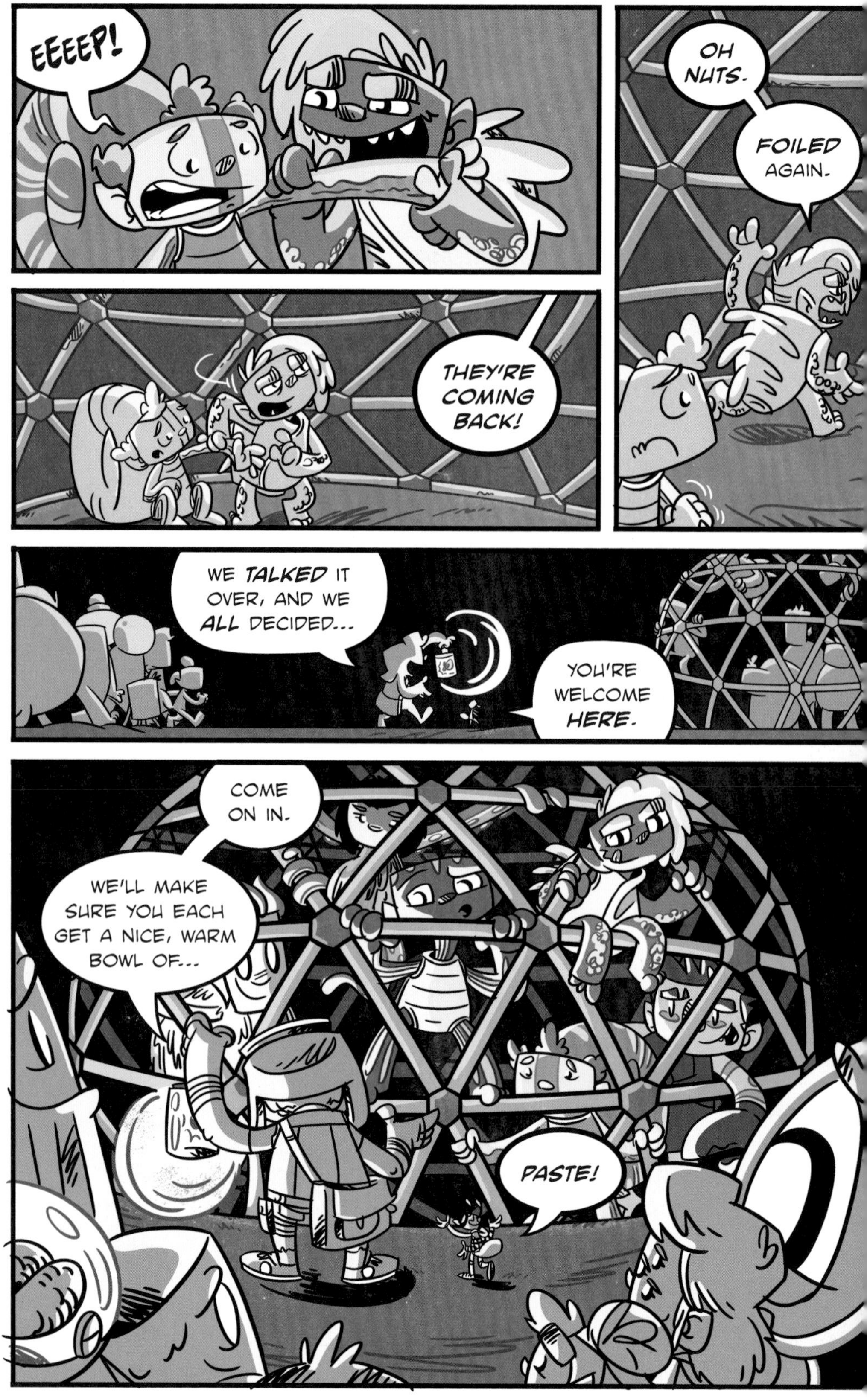
EEEEP!
OH NUTS.
FOILED AGAIN.
THEY'RE COMING BACK!
WE TALKED IT OVER, AND WE ALL DECIDED...
YOU'RE WELCOME HERE.
COME ON IN.
WE'LL MAKE SURE YOU EACH GET A NICE, WARM BOWL OF...
PASTE!

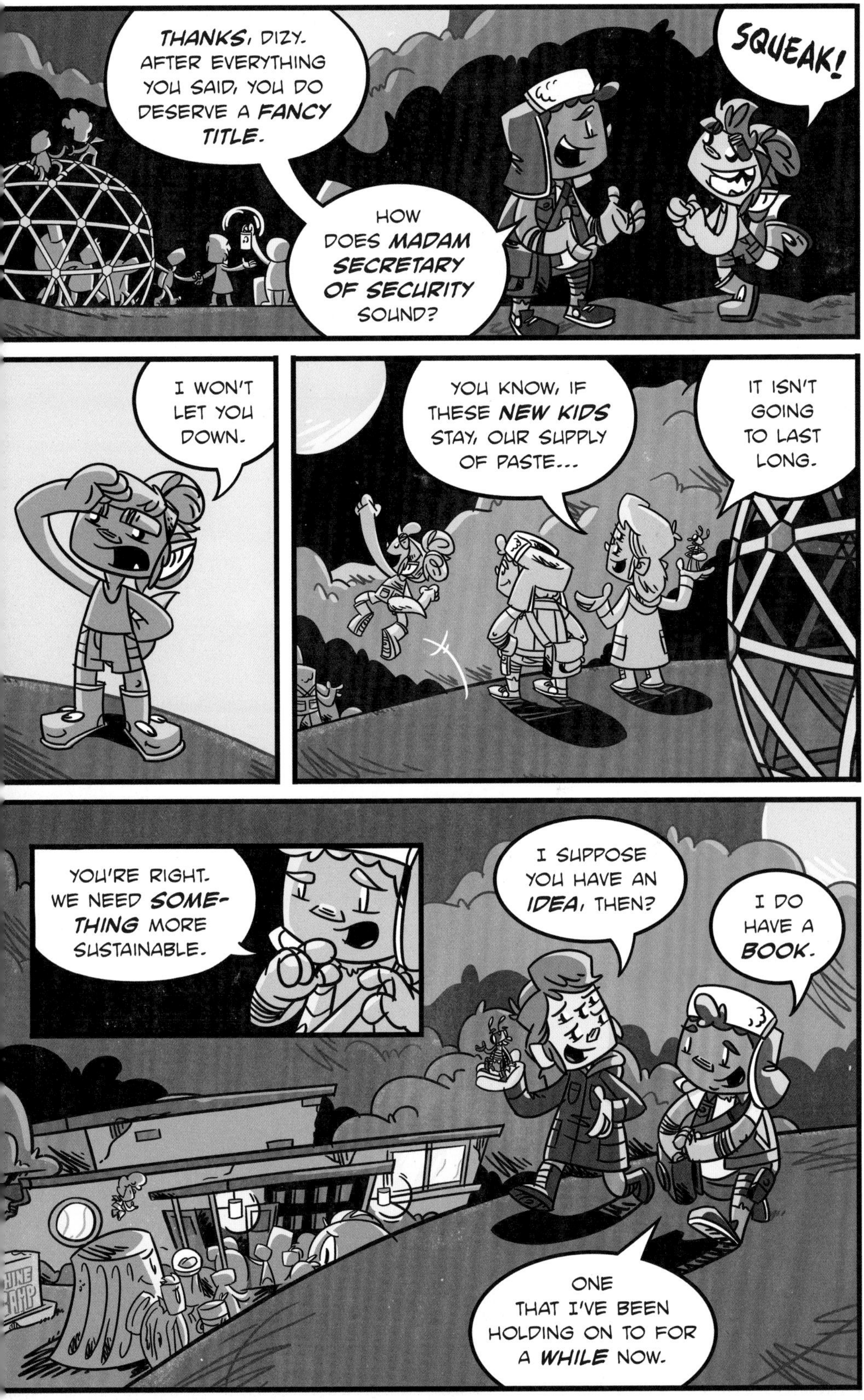
THANKS, DIZY. AFTER EVERYTHING YOU SAID, YOU DO DESERVE A FANCY TITLE.
HOW DOES MADAM SECRETARY OF SECURITY SOUND?
SQUEAK!
I WON'T LET YOU DOWN.
YOU KNOW, IF THESE NEW KIDS STAY, OUR SUPPLY OF PASTE...
IT ISN'T GOING TO LAST LONG.
YOU'RE RIGHT. WE NEED SOME-THING MORE SUSTAINABLE.
I SUPPOSE YOU HAVE AN IDEA, THEN?
I DO HAVE A BOOK.
ONE THAT I'VE BEEN HOLDING ON TO FOR A WHILE NOW.

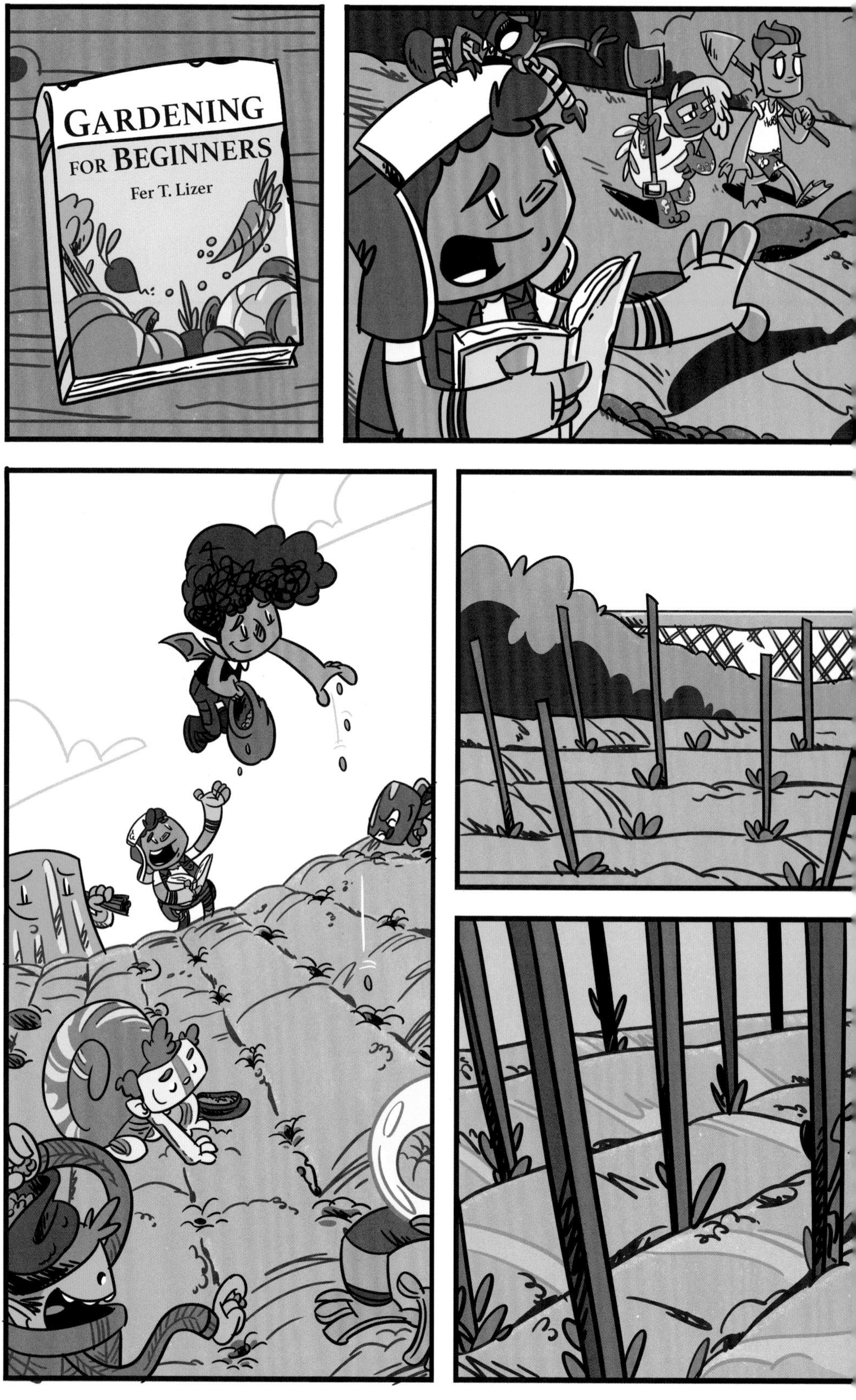
GARDENING
FOR BEGINNERS
Fer T. Lizer

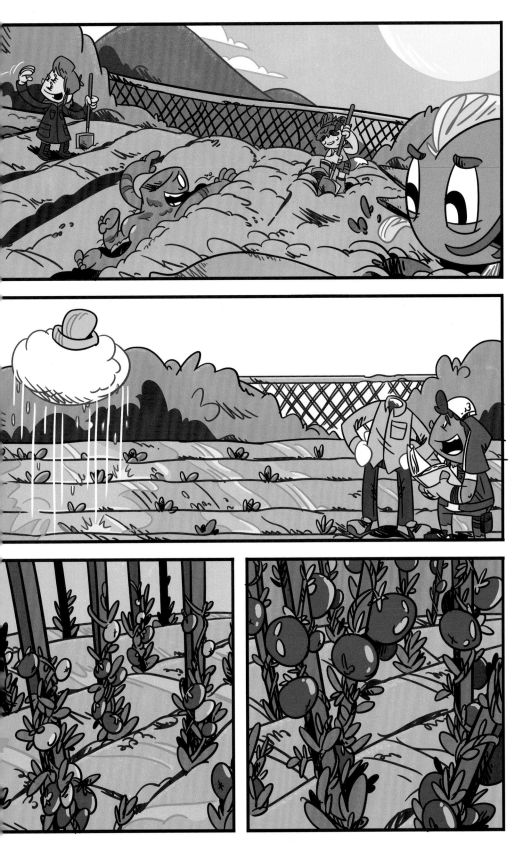

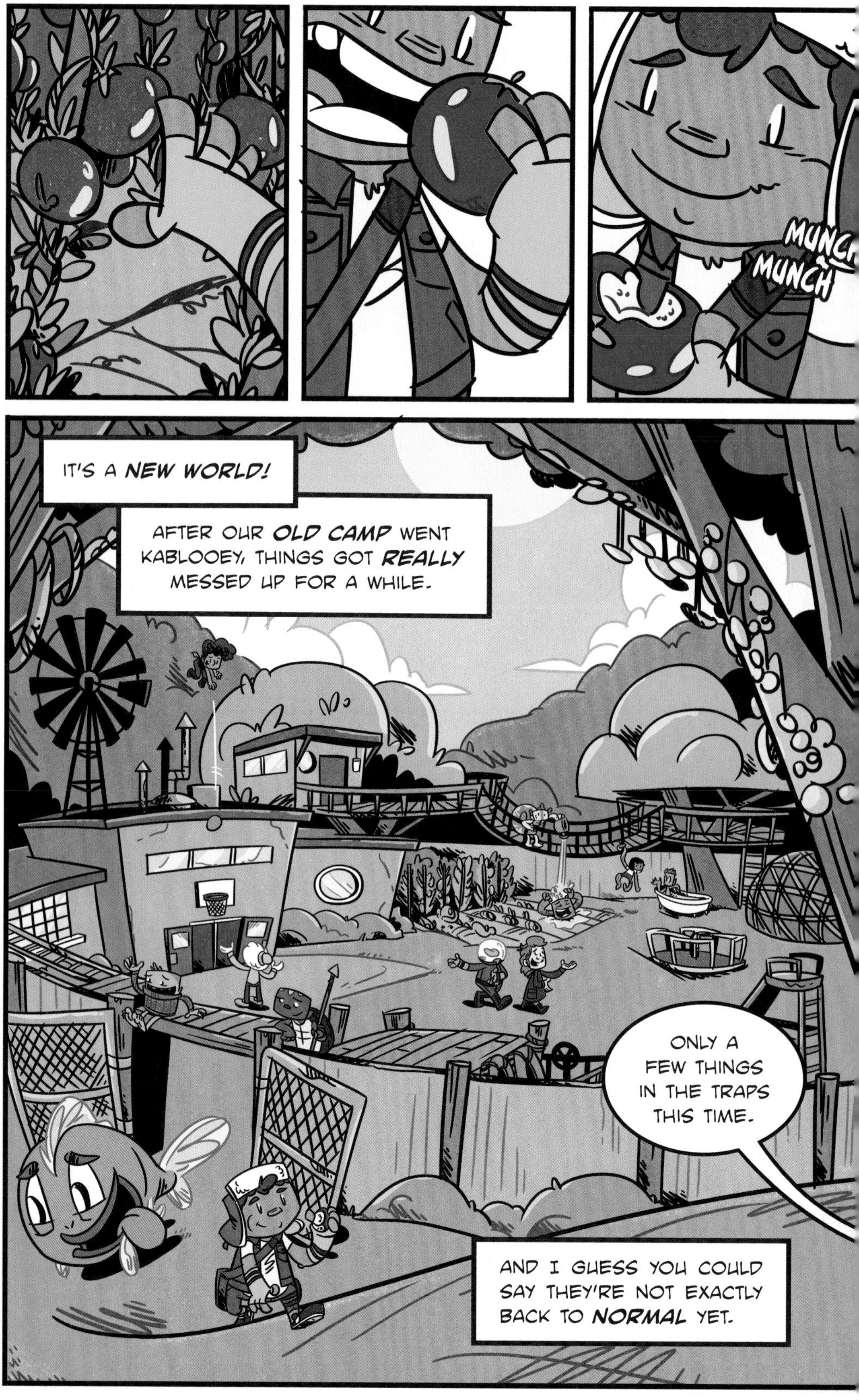
MUNCH
MUNCH
IT'S A NEW WORLD!
AFTER OUR OLD CAMP WENT KABLOOEY, THINGS GOT REALLY MESSED UP FOR A WHILE.
ONLY A FEW THINGS IN THE TRAPS THIS TIME.
AND I GUESS YOU COULD SAY THEY'RE NOT EXACTLY BACK TO NORMAL YET.

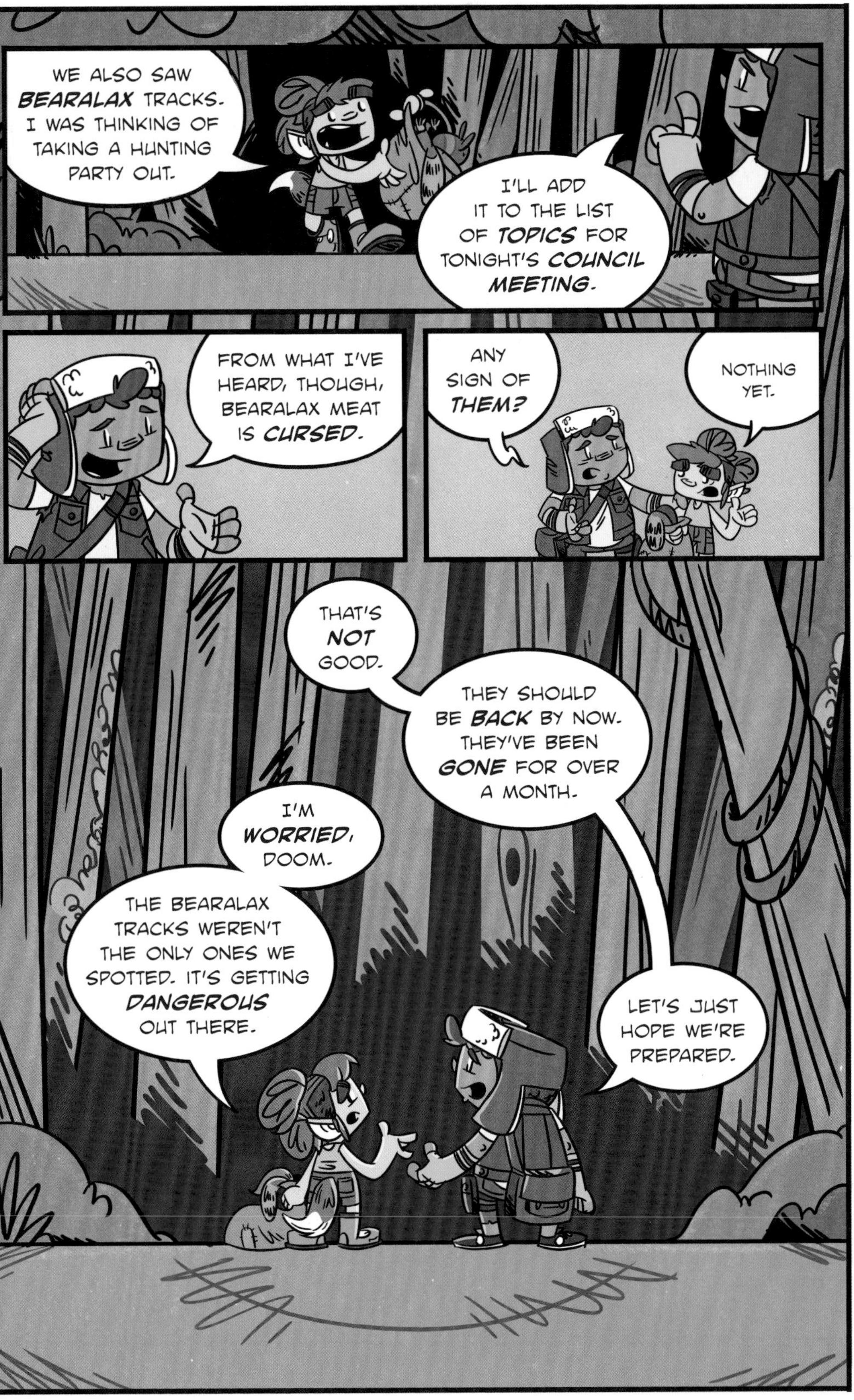
WE ALSO SAW BEARALAX TRACKS. I WAS THINKING OF TAKING A HUNTING PARTY OUT.
I'LL ADD IT TO THE LIST OF TOPICS FOR TONIGHT'S COUNCIL MEETING.
FROM WHAT I'VE HEARD, THOUGH, BEARALAX MEAT IS CURSED.
ANY SIGN OF THEM?
NOTHING YET.
THAT'S NOT GOOD.
THEY SHOULD BE BACK BY NOW. THEY'VE BEEN GONE FOR OVER A MONTH.
I'M WORRIED, DOOM.
THE BEARALAX TRACKS WEREN'T THE ONLY ONES WE SPOTTED. IT'S GETTING DANGEROUS OUT THERE.
LET'S JUST HOPE WE'RE PREPARED.

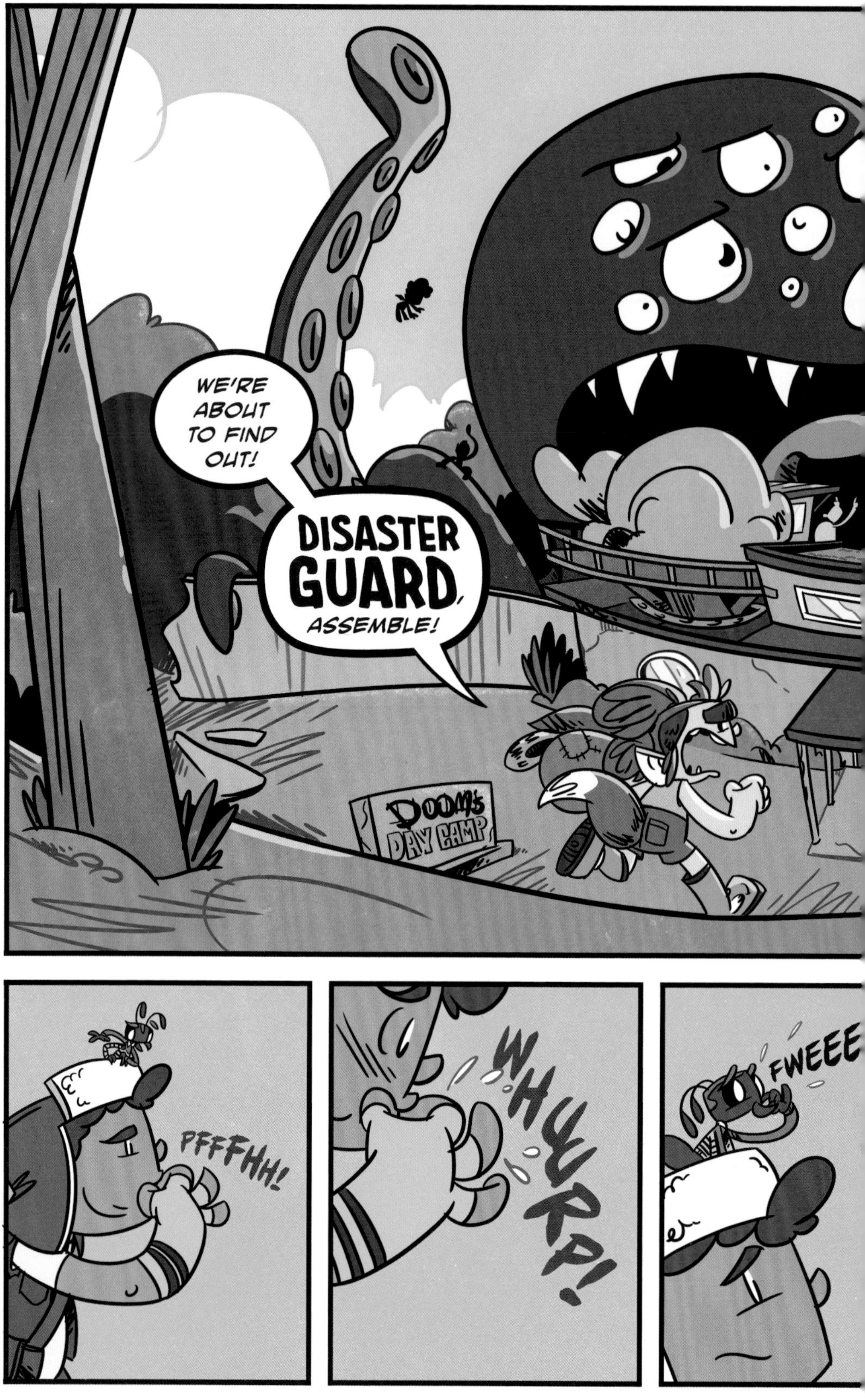
WE'RE ABOUT TO FIND OUT!
DISASTER GUARD, ASSEMBLE!
DOOM'S DAY CAMP
PFFFHH!
WHURP!
FWEEE

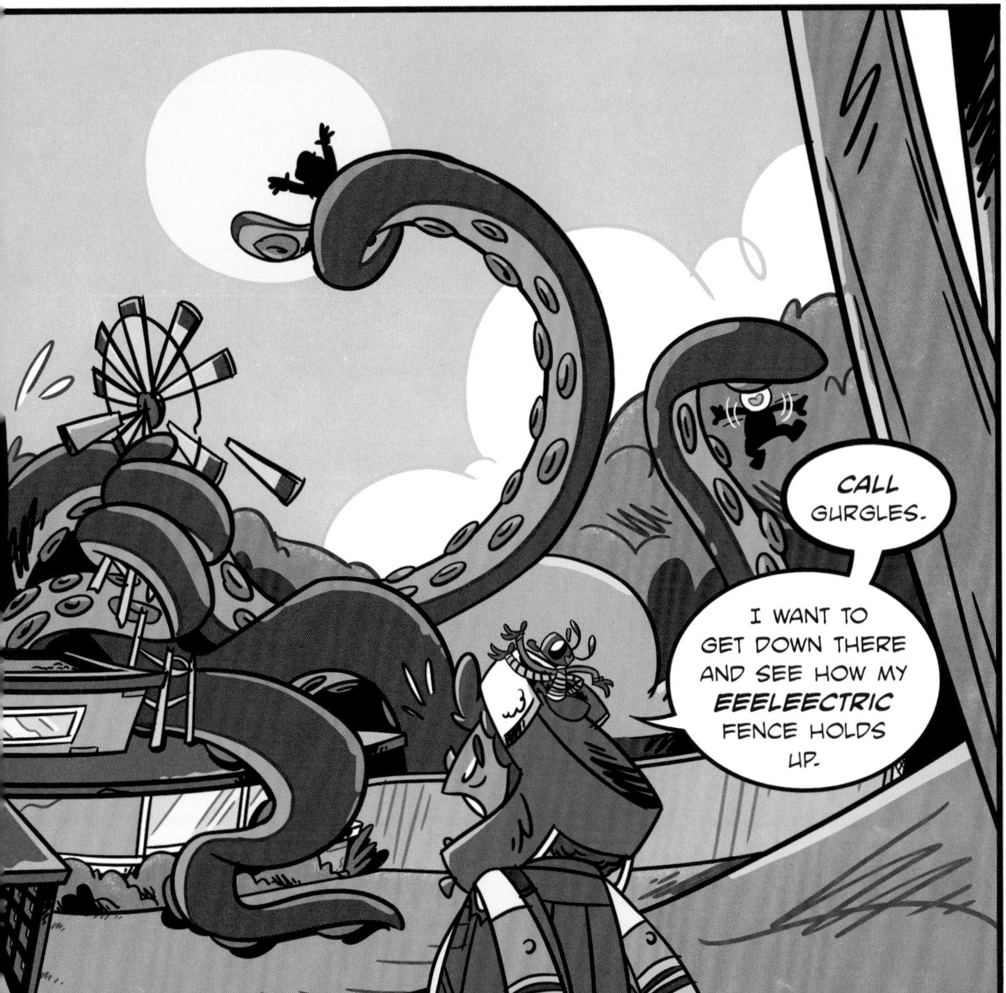
CALL GURGLES.
I WANT TO GET DOWN THERE AND SEE HOW MY EEELEECTRIC FENCE HOLDS UP.

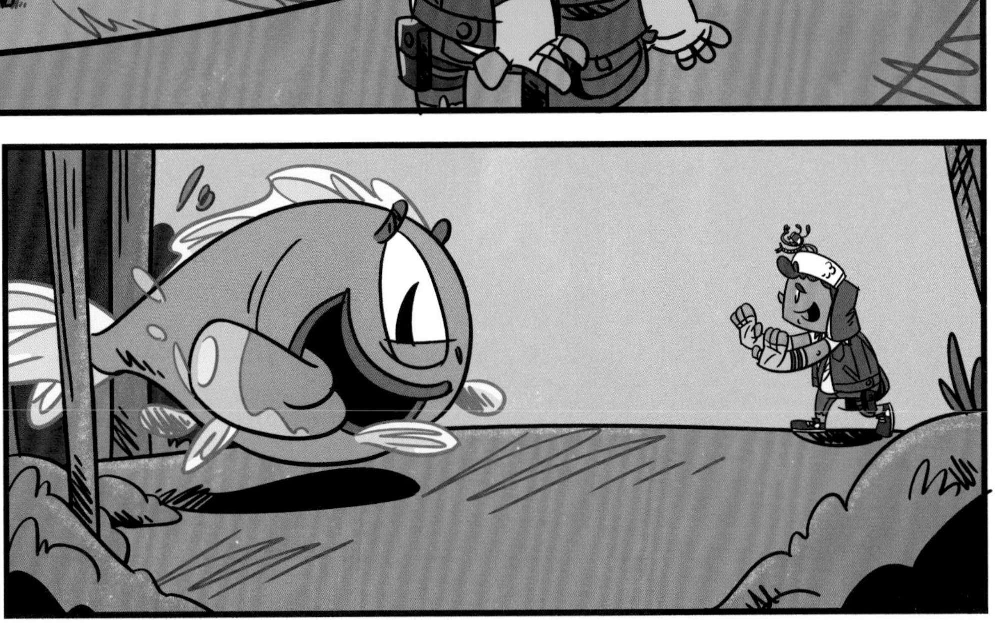

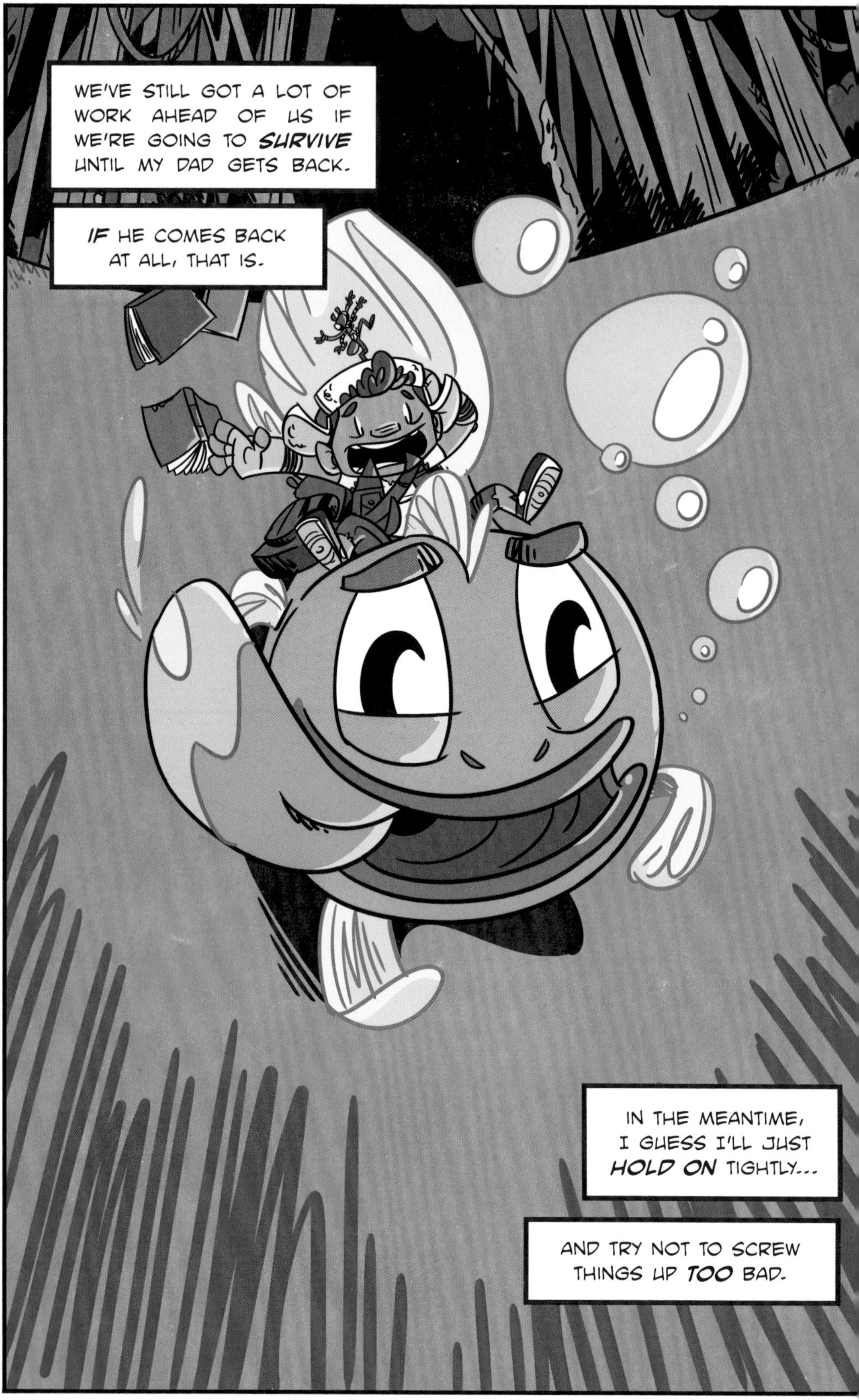
WE'VE STILL GOT A LOT OF WORK AHEAD OF US IF WE'RE GOING TO SURVIVE UNTIL MY DAD GETS BACK.
IF HE COMES BACK AT ALL, THAT IS.
IN THE MEANTIME, I GUESS I'LL JUST HOLD ON TIGHTLY...
AND TRY NOT TO SCREW THINGS UP TOO BAD.

THANKS TO . . .

My main squeeze, the lovely Diana Vu, and to my little squeeze, the legendary Lottie, for always pulling me away from my drawing table. You two are my favorite distraction and my greatest inspiration.

Charlie Cohen and Jeff Cox, for helping to spark this idea in my brain. Matt Herzberg, for constantly coming up with ways to help me improve my strange ideas. Hilary Hattenbach, Kristen Kittscher, Cindy Lin, and Jason White, for helping to develop Doom's world. I couldn't ask for a more talented writers' group.

David Scott Smith, for helping to bring my doodles to life. I'm happy to share a crayon box anytime. Adam T. Newman and Jon Esparza for looking over my endless designs. And to Larry Reha, for his inspiring beard and forearms.

My agent, Caryn Wiseman, for understanding my unique sense of humor and for working overtime to make all this happen . . . sometimes even while on vacation.

Christopher Hernandez and all the fine folks at Razorbill for taking a chance on me and making Doom's world a reality.

My mom and dad, for encouraging my love of comics, saving the Sunday funnies, and stopping at every comic shop we ever spotted along the way. Nathan, Kirsten, Noah, and Sarah, for being an endless source of support . . . and material. Thomas O'Shea, for using his expertise in geology to help me create the world's first land-fart. Kin and Linda Vu, for all the hours spent entertaining the legendary Lottie while I worked. Mike Vu, for being my number one salesperson and con cohort. And to Gus Jorgenson-Hauke, for being my first reader to say, "What happens next?"

Lastly, to all the librarians and teachers out there who get books in front of kids every day that make them feel like they have special abilities too.

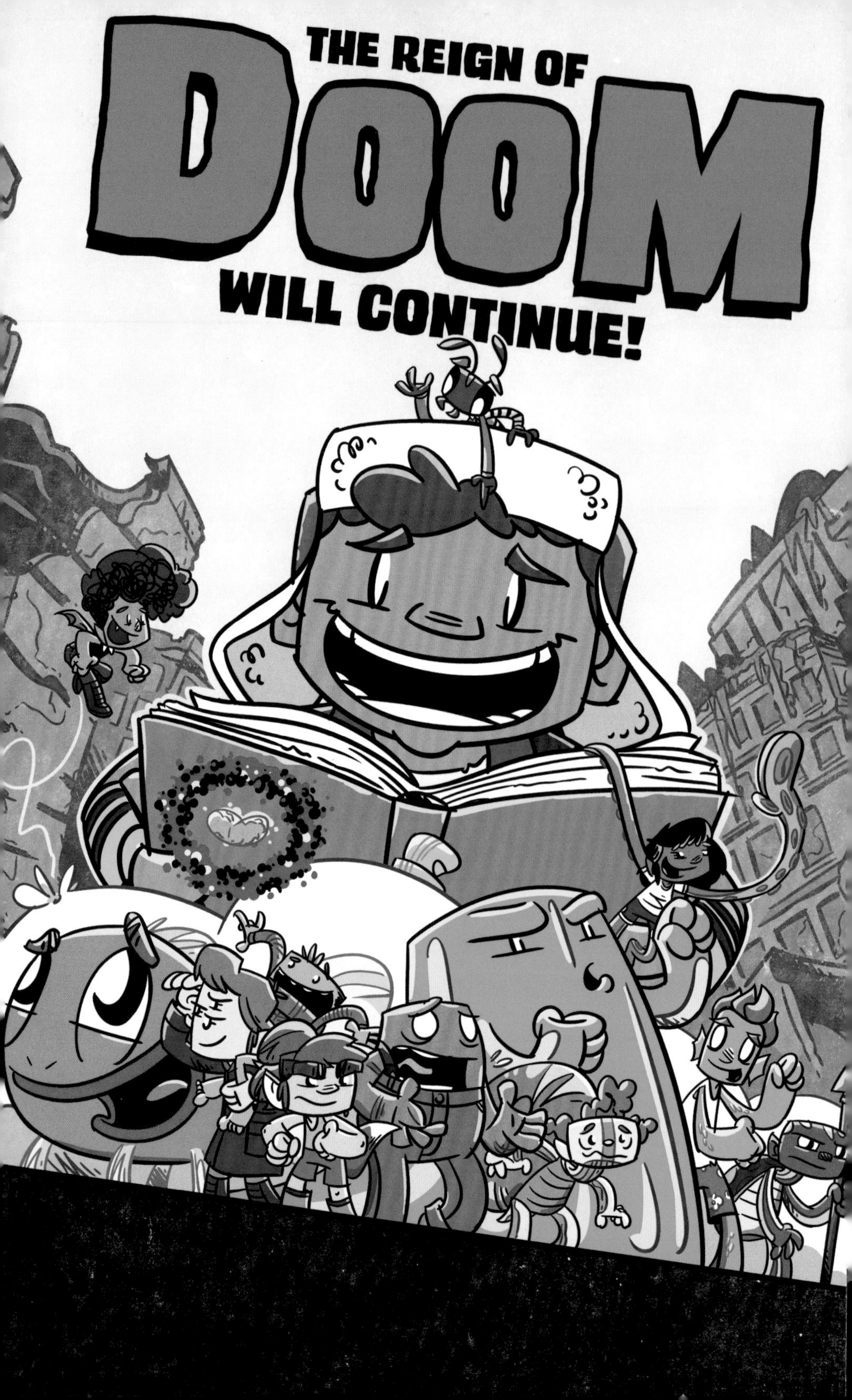
THE REIGN OF
DOOM
WILL CONTINUE!